A Wolf Shifter Mpreg Bundle

Preston Walker & Liam Kingsley

Disclaimer

This is a work of fiction. Names, places, characters and events are all fictitious for

Alpha Reclamation

A Wolf Shifter Mpreg Bundle

Preston Walker & Liam Kingsley

Disclaimer

This is a work of fiction. Names, places, characters and events are all fictitious for the reader's pleasure. Any similarities to

Chapter 1

Those were brighter days. Days when the differences they'd been told about should distinguish them truly didn't matter. When rank and clan loyalty were- not even secondary- but remotely distant to the immediate reality of their friendship, and everything else seemed inconsequential to say the very least. Alpha and Omega, all that Arric and Marcel really knew was their friendship, and such labels only caused them to challenge one another, in what could only be described as the friendliest of rivalries.

"I bet I can race you to the other end of the field," Marcel had said one bright and sunny day, a glint in his mischievous brown eyes.

Marcel smiled - he was always eager to prove himself in this way, hoping to display that his skills as an Omega were just as impressive as those of Arric, an Alpha.

"I bet you're full of crap," he'd said, needing to exert his status. Even so, he knew that there was more than a slim chance that Marcel could beat him- whatever physical edge his familial status should have afforded him, his friend was seldom ever very far behind in terms of strength and speed.

“You're just afraid,” Marcel said with a grin, “because you know I can beat you...”

“Hell no,” said Arric, and Marcel knew that when his friend swore it was a sign he was growing defensive.

“Well prove it to me then,” he challenged.

“An alpha doesn't have to prove anything to an omega,” said Arric, pulling rank on him. “Besides, I wouldn't want to make you cry...”

Marcel began at last to get a little bit pissed at this. Confident as he was that he could beat his friend, he nevertheless took offense at being denigrated by him over his lot in life.

At this, he crouched down on all fours in the tall grass, and Arric tensed up, prepared for an attack. Instead, though, Marcel leapt forward, his small body transforming on the spot into that of a wolf cub, covered in fur and dashing through the meadow at top speed.

It took Arric a moment to fully register what was happening, and when he did his brow immediately furrowed.

"Hey! That doesn't count you dirty cheater! You got a head start!"

Fair or not, though, that didn't stop him from promptly following suit, leaping out into the field and morphing into a miniature alpha wolf, then racing as fast as he could in the direction of his departed friend.

The endorphins coursed through their bodies as they made their way across the rolling expanse of the fields, the air blowing back in their elongated faces, the grass brushing up against them as they made their way along.

It didn't take long for Arric to mostly close the gap between himself and Marcel- he suspected, more than a little irritably, that the punk had slowed down just enough for him to almost catch up. Beyond this point, though, it proved impossible for him to move in any closer, as the omega hovered just feet ahead out of his reach, and absolutely refused to be caught.

Arric bared his fangs and growled at the impudent little runt, then let out a high pitched bark of intimidation. It didn't quite have the intended effect, however, as instead of slowing him down, it only caused Marcel to look back over his shoulder, and give Arric a look that could only be interpreted as the canine equivalent of a smartass grin.

Arric's legs pounded the ground harder than ever, his determination growing tenfold from that singular glance. Marcel, however, was simply too swift and too light on his feet to be caught, and at last Arric was forced to acknowledge that some other means of catching him would be in order.

After several more seconds, during which the sound of Arric's thundering footsteps seemed to have died down, Marcel craned his head back around again to take a look over his shoulder- only to find that Arric had disappeared altogether.

He kept running for a while, jerking his head around to look for any signs as to where he might have gone. When none revealed themselves, however, he forced himself to slow to a halt, stopping in a patch of shallow grass to figure out where his friend had gone. His nostrils flared as he sniffed at the air, his ears piqued, his eyes scanning the immediate horizon for even the slightest sign of movement in the grass.

Alpha or not, he didn't really believe his friend was capable of completely vanishing into thin air...

Only when it was too late did he realize where Arric had gone- he'd veered off to one side, and diverted his path through the tall grass when Marcel wasn't looking. Now, all of the sudden, he came bolting through the stalks like the aspiring predator that he was, crashing down onto the spot with the whole of his weight where Marcel stood, far too flustered to respond in time.

There was a small yelp as one small canine body collided with the other, and soon the two wolves were toppling through the grass, scratching and nibbling at one another, each of them trying to assert their dominance with an equal degree of determination.

Arric, trying to maintain his status as the alpha, and Marcel, doing his absolute damnedest to challenge that standard, to prove that he was every bit as capable as his pack superior.

In spite of these little tussles, however, the issue of who outranked who, was totally secondary to the act of play itself. It never genuinely affected how the two boys felt about one another, and very seldom did it play at all into the way they viewed their very different lives, or the very different paths their futures would hold for them.

But of course, there was no way of knowing that these would be the golden days of their youths. That before long, everything about their friendship would be changed forever, and that things would never be the same. And as they played their little game of alpha and omega, as normal human children might busy themselves playing cops and robbers, they had no way of knowing that these very lines would be the ones that tore the two of them apart, for many years to come...

Chapter 2

Even now, Arric still clung to those long ago memories. So distant in time as they were that they might as easily have been dreams as reality. Marcel himself so far gone from his life, that he mightn't have been blamed for wondering whether the young wolf pup himself had ever actually existed.

He had, of course.

The memories were far too vivid, far too real for Marcel himself not to have been.

Arric now stood in his underground chambers, vast and spacious as they were, a sign of his privileged existence. He almost couldn't help but begrudge his own fate, and the fact of having been born the son of an alpha male.

Survivor's guilt, he told himself, and nothing he should truly have felt bad about.

But he did feel bad about it, regardless of whether or not doing so was in any way rational.

What if I'd been born a lowly omega, like Marcel himself?, he found himself wondering, whenever he let his guard down (and whenever he'd been drinking, which was becoming a far too frequent occurrence these days.) What if, instead of the well guarded chambers in the center of his pack's section of the forest, he'd been living on the outskirts as Marcel had been? What if, when the cursed Pack of the Fang had come calling, slaughtering their people in the night and taking away the children, Arric hadn't been guarded by the protection that he had? What if he'd been exposed as Marcel was on the edge of the forest, had his parents been killed as Marcel's had and been taken away into the ranks of the enemy pack?

At least then the two of them would still have been together, he knew...

But was one life really as interchangeable for another as that, he wondered?

He thought he could eschew the niceties of power and privilege easily enough- he often found himself wishing for a simpler life, after all, away from the burdens and responsibilities of leadership. Able to live and be free, as was the true nature of his kind, yet seemed increasingly elusive for him as time went by.

But was he really willing to leave his pack behind? Was the Pack of the Full Moon, over which he ruled by default, interchangeable with the same Pack of the Fang who might once have stolen him away, as they had his long gone childhood friend?

Of course, every wolf in the pack had been taught since their youth that the Pack of the Fang consisted of nothing more than murderous thieves, as evidenced by the very incident that had once pulled Arric and Marcel apart. And though this was the default belief, Arric knew just as well that the Pack of the Fang likely taught their children the exact same thing. He also knew that, realistically, there was no such thing as good and bad when you got up to a certain scale. It was all about power, no matter what else you tried to make it about. It had been about power back when he and Marcel had run racing through the fields as carefree children, just as it had been about power when the Pack of the Fang came tearing through the forest on a murderous rampage, and forever changed so many lives.

That didn't absolve them of anything of course. But he knew that it was a case of a pack without power trying to tear it forcibly from one with an abundance thereof, and he questioned whether his own Pack of the Full Moon might act any differently had their roles been reversed.

So no, he thought.

Pack of the Full Moon, Pack of the Fang... Alpha, Omega... None of it likely made any real difference when you got right down to it.

But he could only speculate about how very different things might be right now if Marcel had still been beside him. How much better his life might have been, had the distraction of rank and politics not interfered, how much more wonderful and fulfilling.

They'd only been children back then, far too young to fully realize the existence of such feelings, much less acknowledge them.

But whenever he looked back on the time they'd shared together, Arric couldn't help but recall something slightly greater than friendship existing between the two of them. A connection that ran deeper than that, which he allowed himself to believe might have developed more fully with time into something beautiful- had the two of them been granted that time to spend with one another, instead of having it all stolen away.

Whatever you wanted to call that something, it was a force that he'd never felt connecting him with any other wolf in his pack. No friends. No lovers. No associates. Not a soul he'd come across in the ensuing years had ever made him feel the way Marcel had during those long lost days of innocence. And though he knew those times might well have been colored in by the naivete of childhood, he largely suspected that he would nevertheless spend the rest of his life searching, looking high and low for some means of reclaiming that which had been taken from him, so very long ago...

Presently he found himself tilting back his glass, contemplating the wisdom of refilling it once more before bedtime, when came an abrupt, urgent knocking on the door.

“Come in,” he said, setting his glass down, and standing quickly to attention.

The door to his chamber opened, and in stepped Jairus, a beta male, a look of grave seriousness on his face.

“Arric, I have terrible news... The Pack of the Fang has mobilized, after years of apparent dormancy...”

Arric's eyes immediately widened- had he still been drinking, he would have sprayed it out clear across the room at this information.

“What?! Where are they?!”

“They've just arrived on the outskirts of town, and attacked several families while they slept. It's the Midnight Massacre all over again!”

“Speak of the devil, and he will appear...” Arric muttered under his breath, Midnight Massacre being the term his pack used to describe the attack that had taken away Marcel, as well as so many children and their families, so many years ago.

“Sorry?” said Jairus, and Arric shook his head.

“Nothing... How great are their numbers?”

“We aren't sure,” said Jairus, “But there seem to be more of them mobilized since the last time we fought them. It's too dark, and there's too much confusion to figure out what we're up against.”

Arric squeezed his forehead between his thumb and middle finger, trying to think.

He'd never been confronted with a conflict like this before. Since that infamous attack in the middle of the night over a decade and a half ago, during which many of their men were slaughtered in retaliation for their actions, the Pack of the Fang had been scarce in showing themselves, barring the occasional odd scuffle here and there.

“Sir?” Jairus said, when Arric's period of silence became too extended for comfort. “We need to act now, before it's too late...”

“I know, I know,” said Arric. The idea of subjecting his people to any unnecessary bloodshed, didn’t sit well with him, but he knew that in this case there was really no choice but to fight. “Go out and mobilize every male wolf of fighting age in the pack, and any female who's willing to engage in battle. Tell them to meet me out on the battlefield, and not to relent until every last son of a bitch from the Pack of the Fang has been driven a hundred miles from this land, or else six feet under it.”

“Wait- you plan on going out to fight?” asked Jairus, alarmed at this. “But you're the Alpha...”

Arric nodded. "All the more reason I should be out there protecting my people." His father had long ago failed to display such bravery on the night of the original Midnight Massacre, instead electing to stay behind in these very chambers and ensure that his mate and his child remained safe. Perhaps there was some nobility in such a decision, though Arric was inclined to doubt this. In any case, he himself had no such loyalties to consider, and he wasn't about to let his people fight and die while he lingered behind, cloistered in the safety of his underground chamber.

"But if something happens to you-" Jairus began, but Arric was already brushing past him, making his way out of the room.

"Don't worry, nothing's going to," he said gravely. "I plan on making sure of that..."

Chapter 3

He'd seen the fire rising up from the trees the instant he'd set foot outside his chambers, and made the transformation into his canine form. The thick orange smoke rose into the clear night sky and obscured the white disc of the full moon, like some kind of symbolic insult on the part of the enemy pack.

Arric sped along across the forest floor as fast as his four legs would take him, his heart thundering in his chest, his senses piqued for signs of danger- he couldn't help but think of those long lost days of chasing Marcel across the meadows, under such very different circumstances, and this caused him to speed up his pace as he moved along through the night.

Tonight, would be the night, he achieved his long-awaited revenge against the scum who'd taken his friend away from him...

It wasn't long at all before he found himself at the scene of the violence. Trees were burning all around him as wolves tore through the undergrowth, dens were collapsing left and right, and the odd small cottages where some of the more affluent wolves stayed came tumbling to the ground.

Arric knew immediately that his vision would be of very little use to him under the present circumstances- it was far too dark out to even begin to distinguish the members from his own pack from those belonging to the Pack of the Fang.

Thankfully he had his sense of smell to fall back on, and could use this to distinguish with surprising accuracy the scent profiles of the two respective groups.

The first scent that caught his attention was that of an enemy wolf racing past with murder in its eyes. It was headed for a clearing nearby, where a dazed looking wolf pup stood whining in fear, exposed and vulnerable, the absolute perfect target.

This made Arric's blood boil, and he leapt forward to intercept the attack, crashing down on the bastard before he could make it to the helpless youngster. Furious, the wolf instantly began to claw at Arric's pelt and snap his jaws at him, but Arric's fury had merged with his innate strength, and turned him into something like the ultimate killing machine.

He drove the wolf's body back through the air and slammed him against a nearby tree, instantly breaking several bones. The wolf snarled in pain and kicked his legs at Arric, and only succeeded in freeing himself by chomping down hard on the side of Arric's neck. It didn't do any real damage, the beast was far too weak for that, but it did cause Arric to stagger back in pain, and release the enemy wolf from his grip. By the time he'd managed to get back up again his attacker had slunk off into the forest, leaving a trail of blood behind him.

Arric thought briefly about chasing after him, but decided he was likely too injured by this point to remain active in the fight.

Better to focus his energy on the ones who could really do some damage, and let that would-be child killer go die on his own.

He turned back around to the spot where the wolf pup had been, only to find that he'd completely vanished.

A cold, nauseated sensation rose up from the pit of his stomach, and he prayed to the full moon that the child had escaped to safety, rather than have some other morbid fate befall him...

Now, his attention turned to a female nearby, being attacked by two fully grown beta males from the Pack of the Fang. These sons of bitches really knew how to pick their targets, he thought, and with another swell of fire in his body he leapt forward, alive with righteous indignation.

He knocked the larger of the two wolves off of her instantly, clamping his teeth into its side and ripping off an area of flesh so large it actually made him feel a little bit sick as he did it. No sooner had he done this than the wolf's partner came lunging at him, slamming into his right flank like a missile, and knocking the wind clean out of him.

Arric was knocked hard onto his back and landed on the wolf he'd just bitten, who's body was crushed beneath his weight, and had several bones break inside. The injured beast quickly scrambled out from under him and sped off, just as its partner began tearing into Arric, scratching and clawing and digging at him with every ounce of strength he possessed. Arric snarled and fought back, but had to concentrate the wealth of his energy on protecting his face, particularly his eyes, which seemed to be a particularly favorite target. Arric himself was clearly the stronger of the two wolves, able as he was to hit back with twice the force, but he was simply too winded and too wounded to fully escape from beneath the weight of his attacker.

Thankfully, the wolf was just about to bring a claw down and attempt to blind him, perhaps successfully this time given the helpless position of Arric's front legs, when suddenly the female he'd saved came leaping forward, and clamped her jaws into the neck of his attacker.

The wolf rolled off of him and began to struggle with the female eating away at him, and Arric rolled over onto his stomach, panting with exhaustion. He burned to run over and help the wolf who'd saved his life, but for several seconds he remained entirely too weak to even move a muscle to do so.

At last, he managed to turn toward the spot where the fight now ensued, only to see that it was essentially at the point of reaching its conclusion. The female was taking a massive tear out of her attacker's throat, and following a few last spasms of movement, he collapsed to the ground beneath her in a twitching heap.

Arric stared at the two of them for a moment, a bit in shock, and soon the female looked over at him, her face so covered in the other wolf's blood, that it largely resembled war paint. The two of them exchanged quick nods of thanks for the mutual favor of their salvation, and before Arric could blink the female was off, moving on to fight another target.

Arric decided he had best do the same.

The battle raged on in this manner for hours, with Arric and his men taking on the Pack of the Fang as best as they could, but the forces kept coming at them in such unpredictably large numbers that it seemed their ranks might never be exhausted. He looked up at one point to see that the sky was glowing, and thought it was a sign that the battle had drawn on into the morning. However, he then questioned whether this was actually the case, or whether so much of the forest was now on fire that it was bright enough to resemble daylight...

He was forced to shake off this thought quickly due to the sound of a yelp coming from nearby, signaling the presence of some creature in tremendous pain. He sprang into action without even thinking twice about it, leaving the main territory of the battle in order to save the life of whatever poor beast needed it.

He never quite arrived at his destination, however...

He'd no sooner made it a quarter of the way to the spot the sound seemed to be coming from, than an enemy wolf sprang out at him from thin air, it's eyes glowing almost violently in the darkness as he lunged forward.

Arric was too slow to dodge him, and felt the wind being knocked clean out of him for what must have been the third or fourth time that night. The twin bodies toppled around through the undergrowth, skidding through a mixture of blood and dirt and dust, and at last coming to a halt between a closely knit crop of trees.

Arric howled in pain as the wolf's teeth sank into his flesh, and he yanked himself painfully away, kicking at the beast's jaw with his hind legs.

Judging by his size, this couldn't be anything more than omega wolf- an opponent he should be able to handle easily enough- but he was a feisty one at that, and a formidable combatant to say the least.

Arric flung himself forward in a grand display of dominance, dragging his claws across the chest of his attacker and knocking him over onto his back. Then he climbed on top of him, fangs bared, and snapped his jaws in the creature's face, bloodthirsty and furious. The wolf kicked its legs hard at him, yanking its body from beneath him and snarling at him, and Arric had to admit it was a challenge to keep him in place.

It was one thing for a beta male to give him this much of a challenge, but a goddamn omega?

Suddenly, the wolf brought a claw violently through the air and slashed the side of Arric's muzzle, sending streams of blood flying back and splashing into his eyes. Arric yelped as he struggled to see clearly through the red lens of blindness, and by the time his vision had cleared his attacker was lashing back at him, hurdling through the air and striking at him with claw and fang alike.

He got in several vicious bites and tears before Arric managed to subdue him, at last rolling him back over onto his stomach and climbing up onto him from behind. He dug his claws into the omega's back, ripping through flesh and fur in thick, hot streams of blood. The omega managed, with considerable difficulty, to roll over onto his back and return the blows as best he could, swatting away at him and struggling to hold his own, but to very little avail.

To Arric, this felt like a culmination of sorts. Every angst-ridden notion, every pang of injustice he'd felt with regard to all that had been taken from him, was now expressed in the vigorous sweep of his claws and teeth through the air, ripping the creature beneath him to pieces. And nothing, nothing in the world he thought, would be sufficient to slow him down to stop the righteous punishment that was now being rained down upon the head off this bloody and contemptible icon.

Nothing in the world- except for the mysterious force that stopped his paw in mid-air, keeping it from swinging down and finishing the loathsome beast off at the very last second.

He had no clue how to identify this mysterious force. No idea what had given him pause for consideration, what had held him back at the moment of truth from ending the wolf's life, once and for all.

But a moment after that divine force intervened, Arric found himself endlessly grateful that it had the good grace to have done so...

He sat astride the creature, his paw still hovering, and wondered what it was that held him back.

A sense, vague and unfocused, of abstract familiarity...

Then he flared his nostrils, taking in a single whiff of the omega's scent.

And instantly, all of the puzzle pieces fell perfectly into place...

He sat back, reeling at this unbelievable truth, not fully able to believe it.

But beneath him the wolf was now squirming feebly in the dirt, too weak to sustain the energy required to keep him in his canine form. His body slowly shifted and contorted, shedding fur and muscle and giving way to the tan flesh of a man, bruised, tattered, and vulnerable, but instantly recognizable. His muscular physique was topped with a handsome if bloody face, pronounced cheekbones and a nose that looked like it may have been broken at some point long ago, though in a way that came across as oddly attractive, rather than unnerving. Thick dark locks of hair ran in wild tangles along the omega's shoulders, either jet black or chestnut, and it spanned the course of his chin in a rugged scruff of beard. His eyes were only halfway open, as consciousness drained away from him, but Arric instantly recognized the dark brown irises glistening up at him, seeming to glow somehow with some unnatural light, despite the oppressive darkness now surrounding them.

They were eyes he'd once known, long ago, and that he hadn't looked into for so long he might nearly have forgotten them.

Except that there was no real possibility of ever forgetting such eyes as these...

It was unclear whether the man beneath him shared this sense of recognition before the tide of unconsciousness swept over him, pulling him beneath its surface. Once he was out, Arric stood quickly up off of him, and transformed back into his human form, transfixed and horrified. He shot a hand forward and placed it on the side of the man's neck, and breathed a sigh of relief when a faint pulse made itself felt.

"Oh thank God," he said, although he knew there was still a long way to go before anything even remotely resembling full relief would be at all appropriate...

He stepped back again and considered the situation for a moment, though he knew that too much consideration of such, was something of a luxury, that he really couldn't afford. Then, deciding the hell with it, he stooped down and slid his arms beneath the unconscious body of his attacker, and lifted him up to his chest like a mother carrying her child, delivering him from harm with the utmost tenderness.

"Don't worry," he whispered, moving through the forest as quickly as he could without embroiling the two of them in further danger. "I've got you... I've got you... You're finally going home..."

Chapter 4

Pain brought him fully awake at long last. He'd felt surges of unease threatening to tear him from unconsciousness over the course of- well, over however the hell long he'd been lost in the distant chambers of his mind. But he'd only ever come to the furthest periphery of alertness before being swept back down under again, lost indefinitely in the haze of his mind.

Now, though... He felt a burning, hot and intense, against his stomach and it was far too potent to be ignored any longer.

He swore and swiped at the hand that had been responsible for the application of such agony, and it disappeared obediently, not wishing to upset him.

"Oh, fuck," he swore again, his head feeling like it had been smashed beneath a boulder and left as a pile of mush. He gradually became aware that he was naked, his body concealed only by a thin layer of sheets, cool and soft against his bare and tattered skin.

Not the sort of accommodations he was by any means used to.

He brought a hand down to the spot that had been burning, fingers sliding precariously into the open red wound and the clear, liquid salve that had been applied to the spot, and was responsible for the burning.

“Don't poke around at that,” said a low male voice. “I'm trying to keep it from getting infected.”

He took in the scent before he'd even looked up to see who it was, and found that it was instantly familiar to him- so long entangled as it was with so many bittersweet memories as to make it virtually unforgettable.

He hesitated for a moment, unsure he was ready for this so soon after his return from the brink of death. But he knew it would have to happen sooner or later and so, mustering up every ounce of his courage, he looked up.

Staring back at him was the chiseled face of the child he'd once known, morphed almost unnaturally into that of an adult. His short blonde hair had gotten just a little bit darker over the years that had ensued since their separation from one another, but his clear blue eyes were as bright and as piercing as ever. His sculpted chin was lined with a light fuzz of stubble, which seemed all but incongruous with the face of the boy he remembered. But then again, he himself was now hairy enough to resemble the wolf man while still in his human form, and so he supposed he shouldn't be so surprised.

“I... I'm glad you're awake,” the man said, gazing at him with an equal measure of wonder and astonishment.

“Arric...” was all he could think to say, and the alpha nodded his head, unsure of how else to respond.

“It's... been a while,” he said, his voice tense and uncertain.

Marcel sat up in bed, thinking a more alert stance was necessary to even begin to try and comprehend any of this. A wave of pain shot through his gut as he did so.

“Don't exert yourself too much,” Arric cautioned, extending a hand of warning to him. “You've still got a lot of healing to do...”

Marcel gave him an almost astonishingly dark look, as though he seemed to know that Arric himself had been responsible for doing this to him. But then again, he also must have been responsible for saving his life, and so he begrudgingly sat back on his pillow, and gave a curt nod of assent.

“How long have I been out?” he asked, less curious than he was eager for something to say about any of this.

“It's been a few days,” said Arric. “You've still got a way to go before you'll be as good as new, but you're doing a lot better than you were when I brought you here.”

Marcel nodded again, and had a sudden, burning urge to ask about the outcome of the battle. He thought this unwise, of course - after all, the two of them had been fighting on opposite sides of it, and any news he had to report would surely come across very differently from Arric's perspective than it would Marcel's own.

“Thank you,” he said, when nothing else seemed to come to him. “For saving me...”

Arric nodded, and sighed. “I couldn't leave you. I *wouldn't* leave you... And I... I know these aren't the rosiest of circumstances but... Well... It's very good to see you again. I never really thought I would have that opportunity.”

Marcel stared at him. He seemed to think long and hard about how to respond to this. He'd grown up to look so wild and untamed, and appeared more than a little remiss to display such personal emotions. And Arric supposed he really couldn't blame him for this- he'd seen his parents killed in front of him, after all. Taken away from the only home he'd known at such a young and vulnerable age. God knew what they'd done after that, evidently built him up to become a heartless warrior, indoctrinated him with lies about the pack he'd grown up in, and convincing him they were really his enemy.

You couldn't really fault a person for putting up internal barriers when such had been the circumstances of his life up until now...

Nevertheless, though, Arric thought he could see a distant glint of longing in his eyes. A look of wanting to reclaim those long lost days of innocence, to feel as glad about this long-awaited reunion as Arric seemed to feel.

But the internal barriers, it seemed, still remained far too great for that, and Arric knew it was better not to push things any further.

“Well,” he said at last, forcing his way through the oppressive silence that had ensued, “I better go and let you get some rest... I just came in to treat some of your bigger wounds. We'll have to catch up when you're feeling a little bit better.”

“Yeah,” said Marcel, “We'll have to do that.” He didn't even know what sort of tone he was trying to strike in saying this. Part of him thought it was meant to sound gracious, but there was a callousness that he couldn't deny- and that he couldn't really guarantee to have been fully unintentional.

Arric just nodded at him, and made his way toward the door.

“Well, I won't be too far away if you need anything. Just let me know.”

And with a final nod from his old friend, Arric exited swiftly from the room, shaken by the first exchange the two of them had shared in upwards of fifteen years.

Marcel settled back onto his pillow with a shudder of pain, then closed his eyes and tried to let sleep find him again. He was still dog tired, after all.

But against the black of his eyelids, all he could seem to see were the glowing blue irises of the man who'd saved his life, and the wolf he'd once spent endless days racing against in the tall grasses of the meadow.

He also noticed that his heart had been beating quite a bit faster than normal up to that point, and he sincerely doubted whether it had anything remotely to do with the extent of his injuries...

Chapter 5

Things progressed slowly.

Arric came in every day to treat his many wounds, dabbing them with a variety of medicines and salves that hurt like a son of a bitch, and usually lingering around for a while afterward , trying to ease the two of them into talking without pushing Marcel away.

At first, he found himself moderately successful on this front- as long as he kept the conversation personal, and not in any way political.

"This reminds me of the time I had the flu for like a month," he said one day as he was treating Marcel's injuries. "I was pretty much stuck in bed the whole time, and you would come by almost every day to tell me what was going on with you and the other kids. Who was doing what, rumors about which pups had crushes on one another."

This had been his first victory in getting Marcel to crack a smile at him.

“Yeah... And then you ended up giving me the flu in return. That's what I get for trying to be a good friend...”

Arric had laughed, savoring the fact of something at least remotely casual had made its way into their interactions.

“No good deed goes unpunished, I guess,” he'd said, and a kind of tenderness had passed its way unspoken between them.

This happened quite a lot lately.

Little moments, tense but not unwelcome, during which a kind of intimacy welled up between them, made them forget about their respective allegiances and the differences that divided them.

They didn't always last long, and could come in any form, a brush of skin against one another, a stolen glance. A long silence after the sharing of a particularly happy memory, a silence during which, under much different circumstances, the two of them might have seen fit to lean in and kiss one another. Giving an outlet to the pressure that was building between them, and had been since the moment Marcel had first opened his eyes again.

Things didn't always pass so smoothly between them, however.

One night, for instance, the conversation fell to the subject of Marcel's abduction, and his enslavement by the Pack of the Fang at such a young age.

“I was heartbroken for months when they took you away,” Arric had told him, gambling on sincerity. “I didn't even really know whether you were still alive. That attack was so... So vicious... So brutal...” he trailed off here, wary of the tightening of muscles in Marcel's face, indicating that he didn't actually see eye to eye with him on this.

“It was hard at first,” he allowed with a curt nod. “Change always is. But sometimes you end up better for it. And I like to think that was the case in this instance.”

It was odd, Arric thought, not once had he heard Marcel explicitly condemn the actions of his abductors, or the indiscriminate slaughter that had immediately preceded it, including that of his own family.

Whatever the hell they'd been doing in the way of indoctrination, it must have worked on Marcel like a charm-to a degree that was more than a little bit frightening, in fact.

As far as Arric could tell, Marcel seemed to think that the Pack of the Full Moon was too corrupt, too powerful, and that he owed the Pack of the Fang a debt of gratitude for showing him that fact. It was a shame, of course, that his parents and so many others had to die for the stolen generation of the Midnight Massacre to escape their unjust bias and discover the truth, but perhaps to some degree it had been necessary.

Arric alternated between engaging him and trying to change the subject whenever he began to talk this way. The truth was that the Pack of the Full Moon and the Pack of the Fang were enemies as old as time itself, or at least practically so. One of them was always on top, and the other always clawing away at them for dominance. The main difference now was that modernity had caused the amount of available territory for both packs to shrink, reducing the number of locations they could occupy and remain safe from the notice of normal human beings, who didn't take at all kindly to beings who were in any way different from themselves. And so competition between the two packs for space grew fiercer and fiercer, as had the disparity between them. The Pack of the Fang was left largely in the dust, whilst the Pack of the Full Moon claimed a great deal of the remaining resources for itself.

Arric honestly didn't know whether he believed his pack was any more deserving of its status than the Pack of the Fang. His main priority as alpha was minding his own people's business, and preserving the society his pack had worked so very hard to build for itself. But he didn't understand how Marcel could justify the killing of innocents for political gain, or how he seemed to think the bloodshed of the Fangers was in any way acceptable.

And so the conversation between the two old friends alternated between three areas— fond and fuzzy memories of their childhood together, moments of sexual tension in which long harbored feelings threatened to overtake them both, and heated exchanges of political rhetoric, which always left their blood heated to the point of boiling over.

Until finally one night, about a week and half into Marcel's stay, all of these disparate areas of conversation and emotion managed to converge, sweeping them both up in a tide they hadn't been at all prepared for...

Arric had just been applying medicine to one of Marcel's remaining wounds, he was healing up quite well, and would likely be able to depart soon if he so chose (they really hadn't discussed this very much up to the present point in time.)

They were both laughing, remembering their races across fields that always culminated in wrestling across the ground like the animals they were. It was funny, they agreed, that this should basically be the same way in which the two of them had reunited. After so long, locked in mortal combat, biting and tearing at one another as they had when they were puppies.

But then, a long silence ensued, during which they could both feel the tension of the situation growing, beyond the point where either of them could hope to escape.

It was Marcel, at last, who gave a voice to it, as Arric might just as soon have guessed.

“It has always kind of bothered me, you know...” he said.

Arric raised an eyebrow at him. “What has?”

“That alpha and omega bullshit... You shouldn't teach a kid that...”

Arric sighed. “I guess I always felt kind of weird about that too...” This was true- he really had- but he wished Marcel would let it go.

“I mean, I know it's not your fault. But I always hated feeling second best to you. Like I always had to prove myself all the time, and work just as hard, just to compensate for something I had no control over."

Arric nodded sympathetically at first, but then shrugged his shoulders.

"I know but... That's just the way of things. There'll always be the strong and the weak... The powerful and the feeble..."

"The feeble?" said Marcel, clearly offended.

"Relatively speaking, I mean. I'm not saying you are. I'm just saying..."

"You're saying we need ranks to survive?"

"Well... *Yeah,"* said Arric matter-of-factly. "Doesn't your pack have ranks?"

"We have ranks," he said tensely. "But they aren't decided by something as stupid as the family you're born into, and you aren't treated better or worse based on whether you're an alpha or omega, or anywhere in between..."

“I never treated you badly,” Arric said defensively, though he tried to wrack his brain to remember whether this was genuinely true.

Marcel recognized his defensiveness, and grinned as though this proved his point. “I never said you did. Or that you didn't... but never mind that. Think of it this way, who were left on the outskirts of the forest to be vulnerable to attack whenever enemies struck? *The Omegas*... And who was shut up in a hidey hole with his mommy and daddy when danger struck?”

Arric grew indignant at this. “I had no control over-!”

But Marcel continued, “The Pack of the Fang sees to it that every wolf's need is met. And the system we use to determine rank is based on merit, not arbitrary family connections. We have more than just one alpha, for example. The strongest and wisest among us lead, but we're smart enough to know that that doesn't come down to just a single alpha male in control of the whole pack. And as far as betas and omegas go, ability and experience have a lot more to do with what rank you hold than inherent genetic qualities. I mean, if I'd stayed here all my life I never would have risen past the rank of an omega. But as a Fanger I've managed to rise to the rank of a beta male, because they actually know enough to recognize my power and strength..."

Of all he'd been told up until now, this seemed to get under Arric's skin the very most. He'd spent so much of his childhood, after all, trying to make sure that his best friend and competition never managed to catch up with him. And now it seemed like he was closing in on him, taking away from the pride of his rank which, up until now, he'd only ever begrudgingly tried to defend.

"That's ridiculous!" Arric erupted, standing up to loom over Marcel, who's relaxed expression only made him angrier. "That's not how ranking works!"

"Why is that ridiculous?" spat Marcel. "I've seen natural born omegas that could run circles around betas, and betas that could nearly overpower alphas. Hell, I kicked your ass half the time when we were kids... stop acting like you or this idiotic system you worship are anything special!"

Arric lost himself at this. He simply couldn't help it any longer.

He surged up over Marcel on the bed, fire burning in his eyes, his expression and gestures threatening.

"You might have kicked my ass when we were kids, but your life was hanging on by a thread by the time I was finished with you out in the forest the other day. Your weak ass pack can slap whatever the hell label on you they feel like, but you're nothing but an omega, and that's all you'll ever be! Understand?!"

His animosity, deep down, was not toward Marcel. It was a result of his attempts to dismiss Arric's way of living, the entire system that he'd dedicated his life to as the pack alpha. The veins in his forehead were bulging, his teeth were bared, and he felt the sweat pouring along his skin, his appearance fierce and intimidating. Marcel's teeth were gritted in response, his eyes glowing with defiance. He seemed to be contemplating a response, trying to think of an appropriate reaction to this denigration.

At last, all he said was, in a low voice, "Why don't you prove it then? Put me in my place, if you're such a big strong alpha..."

Arric was caught slightly off guard by this, but realized by the growth in his trousers that he was very much of the same mindset in this regard.

He looked at Marcel, lying there in his nudity, that solid, muscular physique covered below the waist by nothing but the bunched up sheets, and his own erection pressing visibly through the cotton threads.

It was far too tempting a challenge for him to think about resisting...

Marcel almost didn't think he would be man enough, but suddenly he felt his long hair being clumped up painfully in Arric's clenched fist, causing his scalp to ring with pain. He tilted his head back with a gasp of agony, trying to relieve the tension, but then Arric pushed him forward, forcing his mouth toward him.

Marcel didn't resist, but fell into submission as Arric tasted the lips of his oldest friend, drinking him back greedily, letting the flesh of their mouths slide all over one another. He straddled him on the bed, sitting directly on Marcel's vertical erection through the sheets, forcing it down hard between his legs. Marcel gasped, and found himself dangerously short of breath as Arric pressed his tongue forward, sliding it into his mouth, making him choke on it. Marcel pressed his own tongue back against him, twisting and lapping in tandem with his movements, and Arric tightened his grip on his flowing locks, as though to punish him for enjoying this all too much.

He could tell that he was suffering, that he was struggling to breathe, but Arric wanted to make him endure it. Wanted him to suffer through the depths of their kisses until the message began to sink in.

He was in control... He called the shots... And this consummation of lust that had been years in the making would be his to direct as alpha, while his omega was forced into subserviency, made to suffer against Arric's every last whim.

He pulled away at last, delivering Marcel from the brink of his destruction, leaving him gasping for breath with his hair hanging mussed and tangled from his head.

“Are you starting to understand now?” Arric asked, his blue eyes glowing with a furious lust. “Are you starting to see your place, and how very far beneath me it truly is?”

Marcel was breathing through clenched teeth, with a crazed look on his face that straddled the line between depraved want and pure, unadulterated vitriol.

“Fuck you,” he wheezed, as much a challenge as it was an insult.

Arric glowered at him, and tore out of his clothes. Marcel's eyes fell over the terrain of his perfect musculature- the endless expanse of his heaving chest; the statuesque hills of his abs and the mouth-watering trenches of his Adonis muscles; that tight white ass as he strode over to the bed, and of course the vigorously bouncing shaft of his cock as he moved in on his prey, at least eight inches long and seeping with an abundance of jizz.

Before he could pull himself from his preoccupation with this visual wonderland, Arric had yanked the covers back off of his naked body, revealing his own fully tumescent member. He then actually leapt up onto the bed and tackled him naked, pinning his limbs down and knocking the wind straight out of him.

An intense, prickly heat washed over Marcel's body as he struggled to regain control of his strength. He felt Arric rubbing his cock between the cheeks of his ass and up along his spine, and was marked by a clear, wet trail of pre-ejaculate, claiming him as Arric's own. He loved the oppressive weight of the alpha bearing down on him, and the way no possible exertion of his muscles seemed adequate to free himself from the force of Arric's body straddling him in this way. At the same time, though, he knew he couldn't let him win so easily- knew he couldn't surrender without putting up a show of resistance- lest he totally abandon his point of worthiness as a lowly omega.

He let out a low growl and thrashed beneath Arric's weight, managing after several attempts to topple him backward, and climb back onto him in a feat of herculean strength.

Arric wasn't about to stand for this, and no sooner had Marcel gotten him pinned down than he was wrestling his way free, pulling himself out from beneath his weight with as much force as he could muster. They twisted and writhed over the surface of the bed, limbs entwined, flesh and muscle smacking together, genitals colliding and stiffening with every movement they made. Each sought to top and overpower the other, Arric with full sincerity, Marcel in it for the sake of the challenge, burning to prove himself, but almost wishing far more to end up on the bottom, and bear the full force of what Arric had to offer him.

It went on for several minutes, the men's sweaty bodies toppling through the sheets seemingly without end, until finally Arric emerged victorious, pinning his legs hard around Marcel's back and digging his heels into the base of his spine. He had Marcel's wrists in his hand, pinned down to the bed on either side of him, Arric's face hovering just above his lap, warm breath blowing from between his open lips onto the burning shaft of Marcel's cock.

"Open your mouth," Arric commanded, determined to teach him his lesson.

Marcel could already taste the delectable fullness of swallowing that massive thing, but knew above all else that he needed to keep resisting, needed to keep refusing Arric what he wanted in order to force him to take it from him.

"Make me," he snarled, and was met seconds later by that vice-like grip on the back of his head, pulling his hair from its roots, and forcing his skull downward.

Arric's thick tip pressed up against his lips, pouring its fluid all over him, but Marcel kept his jaws wired shut- he wanted to feel it forced in, to experience it shoved down his throat so hard and so deep that he couldn't stand it.

Arric grinned at this, well aware of what he was doing, and more than willing to oblige his little kinks. He loved how powerful it made him feel, how dominant, to the point of near excess.

He pulled harder on Marcel's hair, squeezing it so tight in his hand that his knuckles started turning white. He pushed his skull forward and forced his cock up as hard as he could against his puckered mouth, until finally he managed to slide it in through his lips and push it toward the very back of his throat. Marcel started choking as his tip hit the back of his throat, and Arric held it there for several seconds, making him suffer through it. He decided to relent after several seconds of such torture, pulling it back and rolling it around his cheeks, savoring the hot flesh of his inner mouth, and even more the complacency with which Marcel lay in his lap and took it, unwilling as he was to resist any longer.

“You like that don't you?” whispered Arric, as he grabbed the back of Marcel's skull and started pushing it back and forth along the expanse of his cock, sliding himself repeatedly along his tongue and savoring the tight suction of his lips with every pass he made.

Marcel didn't answer, tears were welling up in his eyes, and he was too focused on the task at hand to even begin to think about offering a response.

“I asked you a question,” Arric said. “Answer me...”

Marcel managed to nod at him, looking at him with wide innocent eyes that turned Arric on more than he thought possible.

He tilted back his head and sighed, as a shudder of immense pleasure rippled through his entire body.

He craved Marcel's submission, and the way his tongue wrapped around him, and the way his saliva welled up around him as he sucked him off, spilling into his beard and degrading him even further with every pass he made.

Never in his life had sex felt this amazing, and the height of his current bliss strongly tempted him to let go and release himself inside Marcel's tight, perfect mouth. But then, as he was still sucking on him, he happened to glance casually down along the course of that firm, muscular anatomy of his- the planes and ripples, the solid flesh and of course the tight, clenched ass- and he thought he would prefer to wait and save his essence for just a little bit longer.

He ran his hands slowly over the flesh of Marcel's back, causing him to erupt in goosebumps as he did so. Then with a last, hard yank he pulled his face forward, holding it against his crotch, and savoring the heat of his mouth for another half a minute or so.

Then at last he pulled himself out and released Marcel's head from his grip, sliding his penis back out and instantly grabbing it to make sure it stayed ready for him.

Marcel pulled away, gasping and coughing, and was just about to move back when Arric grabbed him around the waist, straightening him out onto his hands and knees.

Marcel's shoulders tightened as he climbed up onto him from behind, enveloping him in his masculine perfection, and sliding his wet cock up and down between the cheeks of his ass. Marcel shuddered, feeling weak and insubstantial, starving for every touch, every second of it at this point, and not sure how the hell he'd gone so very long in his life without it.

Then, to make matters even harder for him, he felt the warm slide of Arric's hand between his legs, fingers wrapping around him, stroking the solidity of his hard-on in slow, silky motions. He sucked in air through his teeth and closed his eyes with pleasure, surrendering himself fully to it. Arric loved the way the grown, hulking man beneath him seemed to wilt like a flower at his touch. He loved the way his scrotum tightened and his testicles seemed to rise up into his body as he stroked them. He savored the fantasy of what he would feel like inside, a fantasy he would have the luxury of realizing in a matter of mere seconds.

But first, he had another matter to attend to, of the utmost urgency...

He brought his body forward, all the way up overtop of Marcel's own, and the omega thought he might just collapse from the heat now enveloping him. Arric's lips melted along the flesh of his neck and pulled softly on it, as all the while he continued to fondle him down below. It was the perfect counterpoint of tenderness, to contrast the pure domination that had ensued between them, up until now.

After a while of this, Marcel suddenly felt the press of Arric's tip against the opening of his body, not pushing its way in just yet, but strongly hinting at the possibility, and already making Marcel feel utterly and completely full to capacity.

"Before I enter you, I need you to tell me something..."

He brought his lips forward imperceptibly close to Marcel's own, then pulled away again just as Marcel tried to lean in and kiss them.

"Anything," he gasped, almost pleadingly.

Arric kissed him again on the neck, and felt his penis spasm and leap in his hand as he did so.

"Tell me," he said, moving back to his ear, *"who your alpha is..."*

Marcel knew what he wanted to hear, but he also knew what he *really* wanted to hear...

"Alder is my alpha," he said, giving him the name of the senior most alpha among the Pack of the Fang.

"No..." Arric said, shaking his head slowly, and rubbing his stubble against the back of his neck as he did so. "Tell me who your *real* alpha is..."

Suddenly his fingers closed in around Marcel's scrotum, sending a jolt of pain through his body, and causing him to gasp, wide-eyed with pleasure.

"Alder... Is my alpha..." he stammered, needing to be pushed to his limits.

Arric was happy to oblige, pressing tighter and tighter, until it felt so damn wonderful that Marcel didn't think he could stand it.

"Tell the truth... You and I both know that's not it... You and I both know who your real alpha is..."

Marcel's body trembled beneath him, seeming as though it might collapse on the spot, yet the weaker he became, the harder and harder Arric squeezed on him for answers.

At last, he knew he couldn't take it anymore. He wished that he could hold out longer. Wished that he could keep delaying until Arric had him seeing stars.

Nevertheless, he felt the words seeping through his lips like a gas leak, almost independently of his control.

"You... Are my... True alpha..." he seethed, and Arric at last nodded with satisfaction.

"That's right..." he said, running his fingers through Marcel's hair. *"You're mine..."*

He eased his grip away from around his scrotum, only to have it replaced an instant later by the hard thrust of his erection up between Marcel's open buttocks, driving into the channel of his body, and striking his prostate so vigorously with his tip that the omega's penis leapt out from between his fingers and slapped up against the surface of his washboard stomach.

Marcel moaned at the top of his lungs, and Arric savored the warmth of him, the perfection of his body now enveloping him. He held himself like that for several seconds, easing himself slightly back and forth, sometimes applying pressure to watch Marcel jolt beneath him, sometimes pulling back to let the burning heat of pleasure sink in. All the while he continued to stroke and to fondle him, making sure his omega stayed hard for every last second of what he had in store for him.

At last, once he thought he'd built up the tension long enough, he slid his way back out again, extricating himself up to his tip, and slammed into his body with double the intensity.

Again, a cry of pleasure as Marcel took it up the ass, his breaths deep and heavy as Arric proceeded to assert his dominance over him, beyond any reasonable shadow of a doubt. His thrusts were hard, fast, and deep, the movements of a true alpha, striking him repeatedly and vigorously, making absolutely sure that he drained every ounce of pleasure out of him that he could from that hulking omega body of his. The unmanly groans of pleasure that spilled from that bearded mouth of his only emboldened the ferocity of his lovemaking, causing him to strike harder and harder, to nail Marcel to his deepest, most sensitive core, to make sure he suffered proportionately to the level that Arric himself was enjoying this.

Marcel meanwhile, felt like he'd died and gone to heaven. Not in years had he felt this safe, so secure in someone's arms as he did now, as his one true alpha hurled himself repeatedly into him, and drove him to the brink of his own destruction. He may have brutalized and demeaned him, but there was a strange comfort in knowing that the man on top of him, inside him, knew exactly how much he could take. And though he may push him ever so slightly beyond that point, he knew without a doubt that no real harm could come to him whenever he was wrapped up like this, secure in his embrace, savoring every blow of Arric's tough love and wanting more with every violent collision that ensued.

Suddenly, Marcel felt the force of Arric's palm shoving his head down into the bed spread, angling his ass up just a few degree highers and then repositioning his legs around him. This allowed for even deeper penetration, and made Marcel feel even more like an animal, as did the light placing of a foot on the side of his head, pinning it in place, and making him feel so submissive, so servile that he now considered himself Arric's exclusive property.

At last, with a final, vicious burst of energy, Arric drove himself all the way up inside Marcel, striking his prostate with a vicious force, and causing him to howl out with orgasmic agony. He pulled back on his omega's erection as his own reached its apex inside him, the slow burning pleasure giving way to a fireworks display of ejaculation, pulsing deep and thick into his body, spilling back out onto his scrotum and the bed beneath in the process. He felt Marcel spasming repeatedly in his hand with a climax of his own, his ringing prostate finally erupting in pure carnal bliss, and pouring his love all over Arric's tightened fist, and all across the surface of his washboard stomach.

The two men held and held like this for minutes on end, waves of orgasm that seemed unnaturally long coursing through their bodies in a circuit, each shiver and spasm of pleasure by one man evoking an empathetic match in the other, until finally every last drop of sensation had been exacted from inside them.

Arric pulled his body out of him with a mighty gasp of satisfaction, and Marcel fell immediately to the surface of the bed, soaked in sweat, feeling light and ephemeral in the brilliant, consuming haze of the afterglow.

He felt absolutely humiliated, completely demeaned, and as alive as he could ever remember feeling in his entire short life up to this present point in time.

No sooner had his body hit the mattress than he felt Arric's hands on him again, rolling him over onto his stomach.

“Hey,” said Arric, his voice laced with feigned seriousness. “Who did you say your alpha was?”

Marcel hesitated for a moment, as though he really had to think about the question.

“You are,” he said, his eyes half open, but the brown irises awash with light.

Arric smiled at this, and placed his hands on Marcel's stomach.

“You're goddamn right I am,” he said, moving up over him, and beginning to kiss him softly, tenderly on the lips. Marcel closed his eyes, and wrapped his legs around his naked body as they made out in the afterglow, never again wanting to let his friend depart after this long awaited reunion.

Chapter 6

Things continued on largely as they'd done up until the present point in time, with

Marcel gradually healing, and Arric tending to his wounds.

Fond recollection of childhood memories, and catching up on what had been going on in their lives since they'd been pulled apart from one another.

The same old political discussions, always heated and never seeming to lead to any kind of resolution.

Only now there was another regular activity the two of them found themselves adding to the rotation. Their bouts of mind-blowing, vigorous sex, usually the culmination of some heated argument about alphas and omegas, or some other concept they couldn't quite seemed to come to an agreement upon. Arric sometimes wondered whether Marcel intentionally provoked him in this regard, just so that he could end up crushed underneath him and subjected to the humiliation of being forced to take him in his entirety. Not that Arric was complaining...

He craved their sub/dom play, and the degree to which their lovemaking made him feel in total control, totally powerful over himself and over Marcel.

He had to wonder, though, just how long this dynamic could be sustained.

He kept thinking that, maybe, there was still a chance that the two of them could learn to get along with one another outside the confines of the bedroom- after all, so much rubbing up against one another seemed like it should lead to rubbing off on one another sooner or later, at least to a degree anyway.

But the depth of Marcel's indoctrination seemed far too great for him to penetrate, although perhaps that was more his own indoctrination, he wasn't really sure. And though he had all the patience in the world to try and reason with him, and wear him down over time, he wasn't sure the same could be said for Marcel himself...

He noticed after another week or so that Marcel's gaze kept becoming more and more distant. He was all but healed at this point, his injuries little more than scars across that perfectly chiseled body of his. There was no practical reason for him to stay with Arric any longe,- only a romantic one, and Arric continuously wondered whether that was enough for Marcel. Whether that could possibly be a sufficient trade-off for the only life he'd ever come to know, for leaving behind the Pack of the Fang as he'd left behind the Pack of the Full Moon so long ago.

And then one day he received his answer, in the form of a note that caused a sickening lurch in the pit of his stomach.

He'd been out that afternoon, discussing possibilities for resolving the war with the Fangers with several of the pack beta males. There had been no follow up attacks on the scale of the attempted repeat of the Midnight Massacre, but the skirmishes between the packs had grown increasingly violent lately, and there were fears of an all-out war if the situation didn't resolve itself soon.

It had been a long and stressful day, and finding this final trace of Marcel's presence, instead of the man himself, filled Arric with a sense of sheer, dismal hopelessness.

The note read:

"Arric,

I can't thank you enough for all that you have done for me. Both for sparing my life, then for saving it, and in more ways than one. Thank you, most of all, for the love that you gave me, which I will never forget, and which I can never forget. I've thought about you every day since we were so abruptly torn from one another, and I have to imagine I'll continue to do so even more from now on. But as much as I care about you, we both know that there's no denying the differences that separate us. The truth is, I can't sit by for another day while my people are struggling. I can't pretend that I belong by your side, when so much of what we both stand for is in direct conflict with one another.

I'm sorry that things can't be different. I hope that one day

they can, and that our packs can work through the differences

that divide us. But until that day, I'm afraid I must take my leave,

and fight for what I believe is right.

Goodbye my old friend, my dearest love, and my one true alpha".

Yours always,

Marcel.

Arric, alpha strongman and indomitable wolf shifter, found that he couldn't quite prevent the tears from welling up in his eyes while reading this, or from streaming down his face in hot, wet rivulets.

Chapter 7

Something wasn't right.

That much, Marcel had known shortly upon his return from the territory of Arric and his people, possibly before that, if he was honest with himself. He'd never felt this way before, and so had no realistic means of identifying the sensation.

Yet somehow he knew, without much doubt, exactly what had happened.

Even if he remained in denial about it for the first several weeks of his return home...

Alder and the fellow pack alphas had welcomed the fallen hero's homecoming with open arms. He'd been presumed dead after so long away, and was treated as nothing short of a hero for his service, and for his valiant return to them.

"If only more of those among us could show the strength and determination that you have in the midst of such tremendous hardship," Alder had said, placing an affectionate hand on Marcel's shoulder. Something about this felt strangely hollow- perhaps, he thought, some of what Arric had been trying to tell him had sank in after all, and he'd been forced to question the truth about the Pack of the Fang in spite of himself. “You're the sort of young man who should be considered a hero to us all.”

“I don't know about that,” Marcel said with a shrug. “All I did was survive...”

“Even so... You've fought bravely for your people, and were trapped for weeks behind enemy lines. In many ways, survival is a victory in itself, and you should be proud of that.”

Of course, Marcel couldn't really go into detail about the fact that he'd survived behind enemy lines thanks solely to one of the enemies in question, or that he and that enemy had been having wild, raucous sex with one another for the past week and a half.

All he did was shrug, deepening Alder's impression of his hero's modesty.

He smiled, and nodded. “I trust you'll be back on the battlefield as soon as possible to show our other boys how it's done? We're making great headway against the enemy I believe. As long as we stay persistent...”

“Actually,” Marcel broke in, “I think I might need to take a break for a while. I know times are tough, but I was a little bit shaken up by my experience... I'm not sure how useful I'll be in combat...”

The truth was, he no longer felt up to fighting and killing an enemy he could no longer hate with the passion he'd previously borne. At least not until he sorted through his true feelings about all of this. Or until he figured out just what this strange feeling in the pit of his stomach proved to be...

Alder seemed disappointed by this news, clearly having put a bit too much faith in this valiant young hero of his.

“Oh... I see,” he said, nodding with clear reluctance.

"But I would be more than happy to serve in some other way," Marcel quickly added. "If you need men to work in the medical tent performing basic services..."

Underwhelmed, but appreciative, Alder nodded again.

"That would be fine... a very... admirable means of serving your people, to be sure..."

Marcel breathed a sigh of relief, grateful not to have to go back out on the battlefield and contribute to the cause of so much carnage.

Maybe this way, he thought, he could at least begin to repay in kind the favor Arric had done for him in saving his life.

And so he made his way through the weeks, bandaging up tattered men and women, witnessing the horrors of war as they passed through the Fangers' medical tents, and feeling less and less certain with every sad body that came through that any of this could possibly be worth whatever differences existed between the packs.

Growing in proportion to this doubt, meanwhile, was the sensation of complete alienness rising up inside him. Coupled with this were any number of strange feelings- including a number of intense food cravings, as well as the frequent recurrence of nausea upon waking up in the mornings.

He continued for as long as he could to pretend he didn't know exactly what had happened to him, and who was responsible, until at last he noticed the abrupt bulge in what was usually a flat, chiseled stomach.

It was at that point that the reality of the situation became a certainty, and he found that he could no longer deny the truth...

He decided to take his leave of the pack late one night, sneaking off beneath the cover of darkness to a high spot in the mountains. Far enough away so as to remain undetected, but near enough to the territory of both packs that he could monitor the growing war being waged between them, as it continued to consume more and more of the sacred forest over which they were sparring.

During the day he would sit in a cave, rubbing a hand over his pregnant belly, contemplating the path that had led him to this point. He remembered with fondness the feeling of being dominated by his true alpha, forced to submit to him fully and completely, and pushed to his utmost limits by the irresistible force of his love. It aroused him to consider it, and more than once he had to touch himself to release in order to escape the oppression of his lust.

It was a poor substitute for the real thing, of course, and more often than not it only left him wanting more...

It wasn't unheard of for male shifters to become pregnant, but it was uncommon enough that he hadn't really considered it a risk whenever the two of them were in bed together. Alphas were often endowed with especially potent seed for impregnation, and their partners were among the most common candidates for male on male fertilization. That was especially true when the intimacy between partners ran particularly deep- the receiving partner's body released a special hormone that facilitated the union of sex cells, and increased the likelihood of pregnancy.

And so here he was. Pregnant with the child of his best and oldest friend, who also happened to be his sworn enemy. Caught between two different worlds, neither of which he could genuinely call home, and feeling as though there was no real future to look forward to for either him or his child.

Naturally, he sometimes allowed himself to fantasize.

Maybe the differences between their packs really weren't so insurmountable.

Maybe they could overcome the many obstacles they faced, and learn to coexist based on their commonalities.

But then at night he would look down from his cave, and see the fire rising from the battle presently raging below. He would imagine all the senseless bloodshed, all the loss of innocent life, and it began to seem all but an impossibility that things could ever really be any different. That the individuals responsible for such chaos could ever really change, or be stewards to a world fit for a newborn child to enter into.

He felt lost. Confused. Alone.

And more than anything he missed the feeling of Arric's arms wrapped around him. Missed the comfort and reassurance he'd had simply knowing he was near, and regretted that that feeling had been so fleeting, so short-lived, after the two of them had spent so very long split apart.

But then again, whose fault was that?

The question to whether or not the two men would ever see one another again was answered quite unexpectedly, by the sudden, intense jab of something against the wall of Marcel's stomach.

Marcel bolted abruptly from sleep, his eyes wide, his head spinning in confusion. He wondered what the hell had happened, and was reminded of the sharp pains of Arric treating his injuries, when first the two men had been reunited.

He looked down in confusion, and only slowly did he realize that the pain he'd felt had been coming from inside him- *the baby had been kicking...*

Marcel's expression lit up, and he quickly sat up from his spot, placing a hand on his womb, and waiting patiently.

There it was again.

And again...

God, it was an incredible feeling!

He found he was grinning from ear to ear as the little thumps continued inside him, and tears were streaming gently down along the lines of his face, and into his tangled black beard. Gradually the kicks settled down, then stopped altogether, and Marcel held his hands in place for several more seconds after they'd stopped.

Then, with the smile still on his face, he made the mistake of tilting his head just a few degrees upward, and his eyes lighted on the sight of the forest burning down below.

The smile quickly fell.

He watched for a long time, and heard the distant cries of battle roars and woofs and howls of pain.

It didn't sadden him like it normally did.

It angered him...

He rose up onto his feet, cradling his stomach as he did so, and took a deep breath.

“Fuck this,” he said. “I don't give a damn about this war, or any of the excuses the packs are making for killing one another. Arric's child is growing inside me, and there's no way in hell I'm letting it come into the world without his father knowing about it...”

For the first time in almost a month, Marcel made his way down out of the cave, descending in cavalier fashion for the place where the battle now raged. He knew it would be a challenge getting into Full Moon territory, but reasoned that it was safer to travel under the cover of darkness at least, than to wait until it was daylight out.

Really, though, he was driven on by his enthusiasm alone, and a need to make the truth known to his alpha, as soon as was physically possible.

And so, perhaps unwisely, he found himself bounding across the forest on all fours, his stomach not quite large enough to drag cross the undergrowth, in the direction of his one true love.

He did his best to block out the sounds and sights of the ongoing battle as he skirted his way around its perimeter, hoping that if he stayed far back enough, he might make it over to Full Moon territory with a minimum of hardship.

It seemed to go alright for at least a short time, anyway.

He kept his ears piqued and his other senses on full alert, trying to spot any signs of trouble coming at him from all possible directions. He caught a sudden flash of movement from the corner of his eyes, and turned abruptly to prepare himself for it.

Unfortunately he wasn't quite fast enough to escape the oncoming collision, due mostly to the fact that he was distracted as it happened.

This couldn't be right, he thought, as the wolf plummeted toward him- the scent profile... It seemed to belong to a member of his own pack- he was almost certain of it.

So why the hell were they attacking him?

Before he could discern an answer to this, the wolf's body came slamming into him, knocking him up against the trunk of a tree. Marcel felt a surge of panic for his unborn child, and lunged to sink his teeth into the wolf's neck before he had a chance to do him any damage.

Did this count as treason?, he wondered as he felt the wolf beginning to twitch, and he decided to relent before the creature went totally limp in his jaws. He spat the beast back out and stared at him for a moment, badly injured but not dead. He couldn't figure out any possible motive for him having attacked a member of his own pack, no matter how hard he tried.

He decided after a while that he'd best be continuing on his way, and without another second's delay he left the beast behind, hoping he would survive his injuries.

He kept on moving, the distance to Full Moon territory seeming insurmountable, but his legs thundering against the ground as fast as he could possibly make them go. He'd scarcely gotten further from the spot of the first attack when suddenly he spotted a second wolf rocketing toward him from the periphery of his vision.

He wheeled around to face it, and realized with growing disorientation that it was, yet again, a fellow Fanger- a member of his own pack turning on him for some totally inexplicable reason.

In the nanoseconds that ensued, Marcel tried to sift through the possible explanations in his mind...

Could the Fangers have found out about him having fucked the rival alpha, and assumed that he now qualified as an enemy? Could they have discovered the pregnancy, and decided it was better to prevent the half-breed baby from entering the world while it was still in the womb?

That was closer to the right track, but it still wasn't quite the correct answer.

That answer, instead, came when Marcel decided to try and run, and saw a second shifter running toward him from the opposite direction. This one, he recognized immediately, a member of Arric's pack.

And that was when the facts clicked into place in his mind, a horrific realization suddenly dawned over him.

The beasts' respective paths collided before they made it up to Marcel, and they settled on ripping one another to pieces instead of the awestruck father-to-be. Marcel had no intention of staying around to watch the bloodbath that ensued, and continued on his way at a frenzied pace, trying to figure out what the hell he should do with the unfortunate nugget of information he'd just acquired.

He realized, now that there was a reason both his and Arric's men were attacking him. That was because, with Arric's child developing inside him, he now carried very strong scent profiles of both sides in the skirmish. Strong enough, in fact, to make him a very strong and indistinguishable target for anyone he came into even remote contact with, and to set them instantly on his trail.

Damn it! Damn it! Damn it! he thought, and after a few more paces he spotted a whole slew of wolves coming toward him from both sides, cascading over a nearby embankment, and colliding with one another in a massive display of violence, distracted as they became from their would-be prey.

This was not good... This was not good at all...

Marcel should never have come here. Never should have subjected himself to this madness, and put his child in danger.

But there was no turning back now...

He had to find a path away from these monsters. Some way he could make it to Full Moon territory, into the protecting arms of the man he loved, and his one true alpha.

And then his eyes lighted on the glowing orange rose of fire, rising up in a nearby section of forest.

It suddenly seemed to him the only way...

Thinking it the only place he might be able to traverse the woods and avoid being trailed by his frenzied attackers, he headed in the direction of the wildfire, hoping against all hope that the gamble he was about to make would pay off for him.

Several of the trailing wolves immediately veered off after him as he made his way toward the flames, unwilling to relent until they tasted his blood on their tongues.

Marcel almost cursed the failure of his plan, but then leapt into the raging inferno and thought perhaps it was smarter than he'd suspected. The other wolves took pause when they saw him disappear- none of them seemed quite as brave, or as foolish as this, and considering he might well be killed of his own bravado before they even got to him, they didn't really know whether it was worth the risk of following him.

Marcel didn't look back to see who'd followed and who had lingered behind, but kept on going as fast as he could, running for his life, trying his best to see through the smoke and the heavy flow of tears now obscuring his vision.

He hurdled through the fire at top speeds, feeling like he'd stepped directly into an oven, and quickly grew uncertain as to whether his present circumstances were really all that better than they had been moments earlier.

But he had to at least try to make it through this...

Had to try to get himself and his unborn son to safety, no matter what the cost.

After several disorienting minutes of running, he at last managed to leap out into a clearing, gasping for breath, and hoping against hope that he'd lost the abundance of shifters on his tail.

For a moment, it appeared very much as though he had.

But then he heard the growl of the beasts approaching from all sides, causing his blood to run cold.

Evidently, they'd found another path to the spot where he stood, and had arrived there moments after he'd done so himself.

There were dozens of them, all Fangers, circling around him everywhere he looked. He thought for certain there must be an opening- some way, *any* way, that he might escape.

But no...

He turned hopelessly back to the raging flames from which he'd just escaped, and suddenly his eyes widened at the appearance of a humanoid figure, striding through the fire with the utmost calmness and composure.

Alder...

On the approach of his pack alpha, Marcel rose onto his haunches and shifted back into his human form, hoping to plead his case with the man and save his own life.

It quickly became apparent, however, that this was not about to happen.

“Traitor!” he spat, brows furrows, fists clenched.

“Alder... Please, I-” Marcel began, but was promptly interrupted.

“You were never a hero... Never the martyr I believed you to be. You were just a filthy traitor. Sleeping with the enemy. Getting pregnant with his child...”

“Alder, no-” he began, but he knew it was no use.

How else to explain the massive swell of his belly, which he now clutched protectively in his hands?...

“There's no point in denying it,” he spat. “I can smell it on you. All of us can. We have since the moment you came down from the mountains with your tail between your legs, like the coward that you are...”

Marcel tensed up, and did some hopeless calculations in his mind. In a more normal condition, he might just be able to hold his own against Alder in a fight. *Maybe.*

But not while he was swollen like a balloon with his pregnancy, or while so many other wolves stood by waiting to finish the job of tearing him to pieces if their leader should fail...

But then came a sudden call-

“Enough!”

And the dim hope to which Marcel so desperately clung suddenly flashed back to life inside him.

Everyone turned, as Arric strode confidently forward from the opposite direction, his eyes alight and his brow furrowed. Alder snarled at him, his hands curling into fists.

“I am Arric. Alpha of the Pack of the Full Moon, sire of the child being carried by the man who stands before you. This man is no traitor to his pack- neither to yours, or to the one he was torn away from so very long ago.”

The Fangers around him began to growl at this, but Arric remained as determined as ever.

“Power hungry swine!” roared Alder, and Arric held up a hand to silence him.

“Please...” he said. “...Marcel and I were separated from one another as children, and our love for one another has persisted, true and undying, over the course of the ensuing years. Upon our reunion that love was consummated, in spite of the great differences between our people, and a child was produced from the resulting union. Throughout the course of our affair, however, Marcel never wavered in his conviction that he owed his life to the Pack of the Fang- to the point that in the end, as you know, he made his return to you, in order to support the advancement of your cause. And while my loyalties lie with the brave and noble wolves of my own pack, as they always will, Marcel, as your people's representative, has revealed to me many of the errors of our ways.”

This seemed to catch some of the Fangers' attention. They stood with their ears piqued, and their muscles relaxed somewhat- whatever they'd been expecting, it wasn't the extending of an olive branch by any stretch of the imagination.

Alder, however, continued to look at him grimly, unwavering in his fury.

Arric continued, “How much longer must this bloodshed ensue between our packs? Shall we drive ourselves to the point of extinction, when the differences that separate us are truly so minimal, as evidenced by the offspring produced by our union? Alpha and omega, Full Moon and Fang... All are nothing but labels, dividing us and keeping us at one another's throats. I realize now, as the forest burns around us, that we are very much in the same boat, and that there is more than enough space on it to share. I am willing to compromise with you and your pack, if you are willing to agree to peace. I am willing to accept you into our fold, share with you that which we have, I no longer consider it just our own. I am willing to expand the definition of rank and promote the equal treatment of all, regardless of class or tribe of origin. It will be a long road, full of work and compromise on both sides, but I believe it is a road that must be taken. Please. Will you take the first step, in creating that new world which my mate and I might inhabit together?"

He held his hand outstretched in a gesture of goodwill, and Alder stared at it for a very long time.

And when he did at last respond, it was with a low, wicked bout of laughter...

The wolves around him looked up, curious- they'd seemed engrossed by Arric's offering, willing to listen to what he had to say. It was unclear exactly why their leader's reaction seemed to differ so strongly.

"You call yourself an alpha?" Alder said at last, still grinning. "You believe yourself to be in any way worthy of such a rank, and yet you really think that I care about any of those things? About equality among alphas and omegas, or peace among the packs? How great are the depths of your illusions... How naive are your ideas about leadership!?"

Marcel's brow furrowed at this- he'd always believed Alder a wise and generous leader, with the best interests of the pack in mind. But now, at this critical junction, the walls of his facade seemed to be crumbling down, and the man behind the curtain at last rearing his true and terrible head.

"There can be no mercy..." he continued. "There can be no compromise... There is only power, and the courage to acquire the resources necessary to maintain it- human or otherwise... Do you think I had dozens of innocent children kidnapped, and their parents slaughtered, in the hopes of one day offering them a better life? Do you think I promised them equality, and made them believe in a future that could never be, for any reason other than to keep them in line, so that I might bend them to my will? And now, do you think I plan to let all of that go to waste, only to have my power consolidated away from me by some two-bit alpha and his pregnant little fuck boy of an omega? *No goddamn way...*"

Before Arric could even think to respond to this, Alder was leaping through the air, his human body vanishing, and a massive alpha wolf taking over in his place. Arric hurried to shove Marcel out of the way to safety, then swung back around and shifted in turn. Alder's momentum was already too great for him to hold his own against it, however, and no sooner had he transformed than he felt himself being flung through the air, wheezing for breath, the alpha's head digging hard into his stomach.

He toppled to the ground and writhed on his back as Alder bit at his exposed belly, and with considerable effort, managed at last, to land a powerful blow to his enemy's chin. Alder growled furiously in response, and Arric slid out from under him, scrambling to his feet and quickly trying to calculate the best places on his opponent's body to try and target.

He opened his jaws wide and rocketed for Alder's neck, biting at it repeatedly, his teeth sinking like nails into his grizzled silver pelt. Alder roared with equal parts fury and agony, and managed to pry himself free with considerable effort. He paced back several feet, and the two wolves circled one another cautiously, eyeing one another like hawks as they did so, and both ready to strike the instant the other's guard was down.

It was Alder who moved first, lunging forward and swatting a powerful claw through the air. Arric jerked his head up to avoid a blow to the face, but felt a surge of pain across his chin as the skin was pierced in a long red trail. He leapt forward and bit Alder's side in return, and soon the two of them were brawling like mad, twisting and toppling across the undergrowth, each bound and determined to put an end to the other.

Claws tore through fur, teeth sank into flesh, blood spilled across the the cold dark ground in alarming quantities.

All the while- Marcel and the Fangers stood by on pins and needles- Marcel burned to intervene, but feared for his child's safety if he made even the meagerest attempt at doing so. The Fangers, meanwhile, seemed totally at a loss as to how to respond to this. With that one speech, made in the passion of the moment, Alder had challenged years of his own indoctrination, revealing that they'd only ever been pawns in his relentless quest for power.

Did they really want to risk their lives for the man who'd taken them away from their families and treated them as commodities, as he fought against the man who now seemed to be extending a genuine offer of peace, wealth, and equality?

In any case, the time for deciding their loyalties was rapidly drawing to a close. The violence of the ensuing battle was now at an apex, the two alpha wolves roaring and snarling like crazy in the crackling firelight taking the battle to new extremes.

Alder bit down hard into Arric's throat and jerked his head back and forth, filling him with a terrible pain. Arric struggled to free himself as hard as he could, but seemed unable to find any leverage with which to do so. Then, as a last ditch effort, he flung a claw through the air and felt it sink into something soft and vulnerable. He heard Alder yelp with pain, and instantly his teeth were pulled out of his neck. Arric sank back, panting, and looked up eagerly to see what sort of damage he'd done.

And that was when he saw that Alder now had only one eye...

The shock hadn't even had time to register in his mind, when suddenly the half-blind alpha was thundering toward him, mad as hell, his fangs bared and ravenous for vengeance. Arric tried to turn and flee, but wasn't fast enough to escape. He felt Alder's teeth sinking into his flesh, ripping and tearing, penetrating his body several times over, so fast and in such wild succession that he was helpless to stop it. Then, just as he was at his weakest, he felt himself being lifted up off the ground in the cradle of Alder's teeth. He reared back, then rushed forward, dragging him wildly across the undergrowth.

WHAM!

He felt his bones breaking, and the air being knocked out of him as his limp form was slammed against the trunk of a tree, with every ounce of strength Alder appeared to possess.

He realized upon hitting the ground that his drained anatomy had transformed, reverting to its human form, too weak to sustain his wolf form or even think about moving.

Alder waited for a moment to make sure he was down for the count, then transformed back as well, his face painted with shadow, and twisted into a dark, malevolent grin.

He stepped slowly forward, and placed the sole of his foot on Arric's windpipe, applying a slight but suffocating pressure.

"And so," he said, his voice low and crazed, his one good eye like a black hole staring down at him in the night, "may it be remembered that tonight, in a blaze of embers, the Pack of the Full Moon met its inevitable demise, with the death of their esteemed and foolish leader..."

He pushed his foot down harder, making it even more difficult for Arric to breathe. Tears streamed down his face, and he swiveled his eyes over to the spot where Marcel stood nearby, clutching his womb and helpless to intervene.

"Arric!" he yelled, and the only response Arric could muster came in the form of a whisper, visible but inaudible past the foot on his throat:

"I... Love... You..."

And, *WHAM!*

Arric gasped for breath, beyond surprised that the next flash of movement turned out not to be the one that ended his life forever.

Instead, Alder had been knocked clean off of him across the clearing, and was writhing in pain against the force of the wolf now straddling his chest.

"What the hell are you doing?! Get off me you ungrateful son of a bitch!"

He transformed with the wolf's teeth still lodged into his arm, and somehow managed to pry himself free from its grip and toss him across the ground. No sooner had he done so, however, than a second wolf had come thundering toward him, followed by a third...

Evidently, Alder's confession had at last set his former subservients over the edge, and now they sought their revenge for his long ago killing of their parents, as well his abduction and years of indoctrination designed to keep him in power indefinitely.

Alder toppled across the ground, trying his damnedest to ward them off, but not even an alpha male could resist the force of the dozens of betas and omegas now coming at him from all directions, burying him alive beneath their weight.

Arric was still coughing and struggling for breath as he watched Alder being torn to pieces- the sounds he made as he died were gruesome and harrowing, but not totally unsatisfying, he had to admit.

Moments later, he felt a pair of arms wrapped around him, and felt the heat of Marcel's body as he was pulled up into him.

“Arric! Oh my God! Are you alright?”

Arric coughed a while longer, then cleared his throat at last.

“Yeah... I'm alright... In fact I'm a whole lot better now...”

He placed the palm of his hand on Marcel's swollen womb, and Marcel felt a radiant warmth spread across his entire body. He looked up at him, smiling wide, and tears fell from the corners of both men's eyes.

They leaned in and kissed one another for a long, long moment, holding each other fiercely in one another's arms, needing to feel the mutual warmth and solidity of their embrace, in order to fully convince themselves that this could possibly be real.

“God I love you,” said Arric, when at last the two of them pulled away from one another, “And I've missed you so, so much...”

“I've missed you too,” said Marcel, almost laughing with joy, then added, after a moment's thought, “Did you really mean that? What you said, about finding peace between our people?”

“I did,” said Arric, nodding. “Every word of it. I haven't stopped thinking about the things you told me ever since you left, and I realize now that you were right. It's time that our people worked together, and learned to set aside our differences. I want us to create a better world together. For you. For me. For our unborn child. For all the generations of our people still to come, who deserve to live a peaceful and prosperous life.”

“Oh, Arric,” said Marcel and, unable to think of anything else worthwhile to add to this, he fell back into the arms of his one true alpha, and allowed himself to be dissolved by the mesmerizing warmth of his lips.

Once again, and in spite of seemingly insurmountable odds, the two men had found one another.

Woodworking Alpha

A Wolf Shifter Mpreg Bundle

Preston Walker & Liam Kingsley

Disclaimer

This is a work of fiction. Names, places, characters and events are all fictitious for the reader's pleasure. Any similarities to

“And one more thing before you all fuck off for the weekend,” Knox said, glancing up from his clipboard full of notes taking in the small group of employees gathered around him. “We’re coming up to the deadline on the Walsh order, and we’re a little behind.”

“Only ‘cause Probie nearly lost a finger!” The shouted answer came from the back of the group, and Knox saw Bill Stanford ruffling their apprentice’s dark, shaggy hair, letting it fall back into place as it always seemed to, covering just enough of Jamie’s face to make his crooked smile seem a little brighter.

At nineteen, Jamie Peters was the youngest in the shop, doing an apprenticeship before he decided if he wanted to go on to college or join the shop full time. Knox had been distracted by him since he first showed up—a tall, slender Beta, only just growing out of his awkward, gangly phase. His eyes were astonishingly blue under his mane of dark hair, and he never took it amiss when the guys teased him or called him Probie.

“All right, all right,” Knox said, holding his hands up for quiet to calm the laughter still murmuring around the workshop. “Nobody’s to blame. But it means overtime for anyone who wants it. Hopefully just tonight, but if we don’t finish, there will be hours available tomorrow too. Any volunteers?”

Knox never forced anyone to work overtime, and he’d never had to. His crew were pretty good at taking a couple extra hours if needed. This time, though, the only hand that went up was Jamie’s.

“Sorry,” Bill said with a shrug. “It’s my anniversary.”

Similar reasons were muttered throughout the group, and Knox nodded, making a quick note on his clipboard. “No worries. Peters and I will make up for the rest of you slackers.”

There was another wave of laughter, and Knox waved it off. “Okay, that’s all. Go home and enjoy your weekends.”

He watched the men filing out, nodding goodbye to anyone who looked to him before leaving. It had been a good week. They’d done good work, despite the delay on the Walsh order, and every man in the place deserved a weekend after this one. *Every woman too,* he amended in his head, giving Gina a quick wave as his office assistant ducked out, jogging to catch up with Kyle, the rangy Beta she’d been trying to pretend she wasn’t sleeping with. Knox had scented her on Kyle weeks ago. He didn’t mind, though. So long as they didn’t bring any drama to his shop, he was okay with his crew working out their stress on their own time, in their own way.

“Want me to finish the desk first or work on the chair legs?” Knox was drawn out of his thoughts by Jamie’s voice. It always sounded just a little hesitant, like he was apologizing for bothering Knox. It was sort of sweet, really, and Knox had more than once imagined what Jamie’s voice would sound like in other situations. Other situations like bent over Knox’s desk with Knox’s cock buried inside him.

“Um...boss?” Jamie was waving his hand, and Knox shook his head to clear it.

"Right, sorry. Finish the desk. The legs will be easy. I've got some paperwork to deal with, but I'll be in to help you with it later."

"Sure thing, boss," Jamie said, that crooked smile twisting his face before he turned to head to his station.

"Peters!" Knox called after him.

"Yeah?"

"Don't call me boss. I've asked you a million times."

Jamie grinned, tossing back his head, blue eyes sparkling. "Sure thing, boss."

Knox laughed, shaking his head, and settled himself at his desk, glad he could see Jamie's station through the empty door frame that led to his office. He'd had a door once upon a time, but an angry shifter could pull a door from its hinges without a thought, and Knox had had his fair share of angry shifters in his office. After the third replacement, he'd decided just to leave it open.

It meant that he caught every glimpse of Jamie as he worked, the bench light illuminating his long, athletic form as he bent over his work, t-shirt riding up enough to show a sliver of tanned skin, back arched just right to show off that perky ass of his.

Knox felt more than heard the rumble in his chest, his wolf a little too excited about the curve of that ass. It brought him back to the present and his mind back to his paperwork.

"Paperwork" lately seemed to mean "bills." Unpaid bills mostly. Knox had been working out of savings for a month now, and the Walsh order was his last big client with an order on the books. Ever since the fish had started dying in the lake, business was down. Not just for Knox Woodworking, but for most of the town.

Granite Springs counted on hunting and fishing tourism to keep itself running, and ever since the trout had started dying off, the steady stream of tourists through the town had slowed to a trickle. No tourists meant nobody was needing to replace the rustic, hand-carved furniture Knox Woodworking specialized in. And that meant, Knox's bank account just kept getting slimmer and slimmer. If business didn't pick up soon, he was going to have to start laying people off.

The thought made him glance up at Jamie again. He'd be the first to go, of course. Last in, first out. He'd probably take it pretty easy too. With what he'd learned here, he could easily get picked up by another shop, and Jamie had an artistic eye and a steady hand that made his work distinct. If he had the chance, Knox was sure Jamie could make art of his work.

Not that he'd ever say as much. Knox had been trying to keep his distance from the Beta, knowing that his wolf was far too interested in him. Knox was an Alpha and more than that, he was next in line to take over the Granite Springs Pack when his dad retired. It was his duty to find an Omega from a suitably well-bred line and sire pups to carry on the Knox name. He had no business looking at a Beta the way he looked at Jamie.

Muttering under his breath, Knox deliberately turned his chair away from the door and opened his laptop to work some magic with his remaining funds. He didn't need the distracting Beta getting in his way right now.

***

"Thanks for staying late tonight."

Jamie glanced up from the bench seat he was carving detailing into, to see his boss, Aaron Knox, leaning against the door frame that led to his office. Tall and broad-shouldered, Knox took up nearly the entire frame, silhouetted by the light from his desk lamp. As he stepped into the workshop's better lighting, Knox's smile became clear, and Jamie could feel his cheeks heating. Knox's smile always had that effect on him.

He cleared his throat and turned his attention back to the chisel in his hand. "Sure thing, boss," he finally answered, turning his own smile toward Knox. *I'd do anything you asked,* he thought but didn't say. Knox didn't need to know about his stupid Beta crush. He probably had a dozen Omegas sniffing around him that he could have his pick of.

"Yeah, but you're barely getting paid for this. Even with overtime." As Knox stepped closer, Jamie inhaled instinctively. There had always been something about Knox's scent that Jamie found appealing. He knew he could scent Alphas better than most of the other Betas he'd grown up with, but Knox's scent always seemed to come through particularly strong, and something about it tonight was...different. Jamie couldn't put a finger on it, but it made him almost light-headed.

“It’s nothing. And I get to learn from the best.” Jamie shifted in his seat a little, uncomfortably aware of how Knox’s shoulders stretched the seams of his blue Henley when he shrugged. Everything Knox wore always seemed to struggle to contain him.

“Still. It’s more than you owe me as an apprentice.” Knox ran a hand through thick, auburn hair, shaking it out with a careless ease that Jamie had always sort of envied. Everything about Knox was enviable. He was the essence of what an Alpha should be: strong and fearless, able to put Betas and Omegas alike at their ease. Not to mention he was six foot something and made of solid muscle.

Jamie made a deliberate choice to turn his attention back to his work, never an easy thing with Knox around. “Yeah, but Bill was right. We wouldn’t be this far behind if I wasn’t so slow on the lathe.”

Jamie could hear Knox stepping closer, but he still nearly jumped when he felt the Alpha’s hand on his shoulder. “You’re doing just fine. No one expects you to be a master yet.”

Heat seemed to radiate out from Knox’s palm on his shoulder, and Jamie felt that heat in his cheeks again, and knew he was blushing like an Omega. When he’d started his apprenticeship at Knox Woodworking, he’d told himself he could handle working with someone he was attracted to, even knowing Knox wouldn’t, *couldn’t* be interested in him. Even if he weren’t a Beta, Jamie was only nineteen. Just getting out of school. There was no way a successful Alpha like Knox was going to want someone like him.

“I wanna make sure it’s not late because of me.”

Knox squeezed his shoulder, and Jamie swore he felt that touch go straight to his dick. “If we’re late, it’s because I didn’t plan out the schedule right. Take a break. I ordered dinner.”

A moment later, Jamie heard the tapping at the workshop’s door, signaling dinner had arrived. “Good timing,” he said to Knox, who dipped his head and laughed.

“I heard him coming. Didn’t you?”

“I guess not.” Of course he hadn’t. All his senses had been tuned to Knox’s movements, hearing him rustling about in the office, scenting that worry over whatever it was Knox was dealing with. Jamie had had a weird compulsion to go and make sure Knox was all right. He’d shaken it off, but his focus had definitely been with the Alpha and not on whoever might be driving up to the shop.

Knox squeezed his shoulder again, and just like that, all his focus was back on Knox. “Grab some plates in the breakroom?” the Alpha said as he strode to the door to answer it.

This time, Jamie did catch the appealing whiff of Chinese food—chow mein and sweet & sour—from Granite Springs’ only Chinese restaurant. His stomach rumbled, and he heard Knox laughing as he stepped into the breakroom. “I knew you needed a break,” Knox said, setting the take-out bags on the broad, oak table that dominated the small break area. He gave Jamie a wink that almost made him drop the plates. Dammit. What was his problem tonight? It wasn’t like Knox hadn't winked at him before. Jamie was pretty sure Knox didn't even realize how often he got flirty.

"That's what makes you a good Alpha," Jamie answered, without considering, as he set out the plates. "I mean, boss," he quickly amended. "It makes you a good boss."

Jamie hadn't realized how close Knox was until he reached around Jamie to pull chopsticks from the bag on the table. That intoxicating scent was stronger so close, and Knox's broad shoulders made Jamie feel suddenly small. They were nearly the same height, but everything about Knox was *bigger*.

"It makes me a good Alpha too." Knox's lips were almost touching Jamie's ear, and he could feel Knox's warm breath like it was sliding through his entire body, leaving trails of goosebumps.

Instinctively, Jamie tilted his head to the side, baring his throat in submission. It was something he never would have done outside of a pack ritual, but Knox's words made the action involuntary. A shiver ran through Jamie's frame as Knox dipped his head, scenting along Jamie's throat, and when he felt the faint brush of Knox's lips on his skin, he had to reach down to brace himself against the table before his legs gave out.

The movement tilted his hips as well, pushing them back toward Knox, settling Jamie's ass right against the unmistakable heat of Knox's erection.

A low growl from Knox had Jamie's wolf tripping over itself to present for mating, but before Jamie could even process that, he felt the sudden cold at his back where Knox had been a moment before.

Knox mumbled something about still having work to do, and then he snatched a container from the bag and disappeared. Jamie heard him stomping his way across the workshop

This was not good. So not good. What had possessed him to submit like that?

That was a stupid question. Jamie knew exactly what had possessed him. It was that Alpha scent that had gotten into his brain and shot straight to his dick. What the hell was that about? Betas could barely scent an Alpha normally. Even Jamie, with his Omega-like affinity for it, had never smelled one so strongly before.

It was weird. He was going to have to talk to Cole about it. It was the sort of thing his best friend had probably already researched, and if he hadn't, he'd be more than happy to.

In the meantime, there was nothing he could do but eat his dinner and finish his shift and hope Knox didn't fire him for behaving like that.

***

There was a continuing litany of: *Shit. Fuck. Shit.* rolling through Knox's head as he sat at his desk, wishing he'd replaced that damn door for once. What the hell was wrong with him, rubbing himself all over the kid like that. Jamie was a *Beta* and his *apprentice* and still a *teenager*. There were so many reasons why Knox should not be touching him, that Knox had lost count.

Knox could give no excuse for his behavior. But Jamie had smelled *so good.*

He must have been hanging out with an Omega on the edge of heat. It was faint, but Knox was almost certain that was what he'd scented. Nothing else could account for the way his wolf had practically mounted Jamie right there. A second later, and he'd have been biting hard into Jamie's shoulder, marking him.

Even thinking about it now had him rubbing a hand over the front of his jeans, providing some much needed friction to his still hard cock.

He could still hear Jamie in the breakroom, or he'd have been tempted to take care of himself right there. His wolf was definitely interested in the idea, even more so knowing that Jamie would be able to hear him, smell him, know that Knox was in this state because of him.

Glancing at the past due notice taunting him from the top of his desk, Knox growled. Much as he needed the Walsh order finished by Monday, he was not going to get anything done with his wolf so focused on Jamie.

Not certain he could even trust his wolf around Jamie long enough to tell him to go home, Knox pulled out his phone and fired off a quick text.

Calling it for tonight. Come in tomorrow? We can finish then.

He heard Jamie's phone dinging across the workshop, and a few moments later he had a response.

Sure thing boss

It was a good reminder. He just needed to give his wolf a chance to run, get some energy out. Hunt. Tomorrow he'd come back with a clear head, and they'd finish what they'd started.

***

Almost as soon as he'd gotten Knox's text, Jamie had sent one to Cole, asking for a ride. Going home by himself after having been so completely rejected sounded like the worst possible way to spend his Friday night.

Luckily Cole only lived a couple miles from the workshop, so by the time Jamie had cleaned his station and gathered his things, he heard Cole's Tesla rolling quietly into the parking lot. He glanced through the door frame into Knox's office to see his boss bent intently over a seemingly endless stack of paperwork, and he felt again that weird compulsion to go check on him, make sure he wasn't working too hard. Make sure he'd eaten.

Instead, he called out, "Night, boss. See you tomorrow," and got only a grunted response and a distracted wave in response. It didn't feel right, leaving without a smile from Knox, but Jamie shouldered his backpack and headed out into the night anyway.

Cole was drumming his fingers on his steering wheel to the rhythm of something indeterminately country playing from his stereo system. He turned it down as soon as Jamie slid into the passenger seat, settling his bag at his feet.

"Overtime?" he asked, peeling out of the parking lot at a speed that was due more to distraction than recklessness.

"Yeah, sort of," Jamie answered.

"At least you got time with the hot boss?"

"Don't remind me." Jamie glanced to the side view mirror, watching as Knox Woodworking disappeared slowly from view.

"Okay, spill," Cole said, glancing over at Jamie before pushing his horn-rimmed glasses up his nose.

The glasses were just for show. Cole's eyesight was as perfect as the rest of him. Cole would be a perfect Alpha too if not for the way he deliberately tried to pass himself off as a Beta. Not that anyone who knew him for more than five minutes would be fooled. Cole rivaled Knox in both height and build, but where Knox's hazel eyes were warm and dark, Cole's green eyes sparkled with mischief. He had a smile to match, and it all worked together with his blond hair, cut short on the sides with a wavy, golden top, to make him easily one of the most attractive people Jamie had ever met.

He was also Jamie's oldest friend, and they knew each other better than anyone else. Jamie had been there for Cole when he was dealing with all the hormones that came with an Alpha puberty, and Cole had listened when Jamie explained his fears of being a Beta and never finding a mate because of it.

With anyone else, Jamie would have brushed off the concern, but since this was Cole, he said, "I…kind of came on to him tonight."

"You what!?" Cole overturned into a curve in the road that led out to the lake, where Cole's family had their enormous home.

"Jesus, watch the road, Cole!"

"Sorry," Cole said as he corrected the car. "You know better than to surprise me when I'm driving."

"Maybe we should wait til we get to your place…"

There was another squealing turn into Cole's driveway. "We're here! Spill."

"Can we at least go inside?"

Cole rolled his eyes, but he didn't argue. Cole's mom was a terrible snoop, and she'd more than once listened in to their conversations in the driveway. When Cole had turned eighteen, he'd moved into the guest house. It was just far enough from the main house for them to have privacy, so long as they kept their voices low.

Just before Cole closed the door, Jamie scented something in the wind. Something familiar. Some*one* familiar, but the door cut him off from the scent before he could place it.

"Okay, we're in," Cole said, tossing his keys in a ceramic bowl on a stand by the door. It was a bowl Jamie had made in pottery class in high school. It was misshapen and rough, but Cole said it was a thing of beauty, and he'd insisted on keeping it, mostly because Tessa Frank had laughed when Jamie had shown it to the class. "Talk."

"It was...really weird," Jamie began, dropping his bag by the door and flopping himself onto Cole's couch. He recounted the entire incident to Cole, right up to his embarrassing inability to stay standing.

When he finished, Cole said, "Huh."

"Huh?" Jamie scoffed. "That's all you've got for me?"

"Well...it's not *that* weird," he said, avoiding Jamie's gaze.

"It's weird for me!"

"Okay, but...that's... I mean that's how it goes. With Alphas. And...Omegas."

"I'm a Beta," Jamie reminded him, sitting up a little. Cole still wasn't meeting his eye.

"Yeah, that part's a little weird. But the rest of it is...how it sort of goes. Maybe you got some Omega scent on you."

"You think?" Jamie held out his arm, practically shoving it under Cole's nose. If that was it, if he'd just rubbed against an Omega without noticing, especially an Omega close to heat, that would explain a lot. He could just shower really well tonight and again tomorrow morning, and then things would be fine again with Knox.

Cole sniffed his wrist. "You do smell a little Omega-y."

"Omega-y?"

"Yeah. I mean, you still smell like you? So you're Beta, but with a side order of Omega. Omega sauce, maybe."

"Gross, man." Jamie tossed a pillow at him and Cole laughed as he caught it.

"Whatever. You're the one who got a little Omega on you before spending the night with your stupid hot Alpha boss."

"I didn't mean to!"

Cole shrugged. "So shower tonight. You'll be good to go in the morning. You wanna use the steam shower here? You can spend the night."

"Yeah, sure." The Omega scent definitely explained Knox's actions, but not his own. Why had Knox's scent hit him so hard?

Cole pulled himself to his feet then yanked Jamie up onto his own to pull him into a hug. Jamie was aware of the Alpha scent of Cole, but mostly he just smelled like *Cole*, and that was comforting at least. "Come on. Shower. I'll look into Betas picking up Alpha scents tomorrow and text you what I find, okay?"

Jamie took a deep breath, letting the familiar scent of Cole calm him a little, leaning into the embrace. "Yeah," he said again. "Okay."

Cole pressed a quick kiss to his temple and slung an arm over Jamie's shoulders to pull him toward the bathroom. Lowering his voice into an almost comical exaggeration of the Alphas in porn films, he said, "Now come on, you filthy little Beta. Let's get you all cleaned up before you get into my bed."

Jamie laughed. It was hard to stay worried about anything around Cole.

***

When Knox pulled his truck into the workshop lot the next morning, he was still restless, his wolf pacing and grumbling. He'd tried to run last night, but all the wolf wanted was to follow Jamie. They'd followed him to that Alpha's place. Jamie's scent was all over it. Clearly he spent a lot of time there. Knox's wolf had not at all appreciated how the other Alpha touched Jamie, held him, made him laugh. Even after they'd left the living room for the bathroom, the wolf had paced outside for another hour. By the time Knox had finally gotten the run he wanted and made it to bed, he got about an hour's sleep before his alarm went off and he had to get up and come back in.

He was determined, though, not to take this out on Jamie. Whatever issues he was having were his own, no need to punish the Beta for them. With that in mind, he'd stopped by the local diner on the way in for coffee and donuts. A peace offering.

A sorry for almost mounting you offering, more like.

His wolf might not be sorry, but Knox was.

Jamie was already there when he arrived, leaning against the workshop door, his phone out. Probably texting Cole Gunnersen. Knox's wolf growled in his chest at the thought, and Knox struggled to keep the sound inside. He may not have been entirely successful because Jamie glanced up just at that moment, crooked, sheepish smile on his lips.

"Morning, boss," he said.

Knox struggled a little to return the smile, but he held up the coffee and donuts in greeting. "I brought incentives," he said, keeping the coffee close to his nose so he wouldn't be distracted by Jamie's scent.

"Ooh, donuts!" Jamie answered, taking the box from him. "You're the best boss, boss."

Knox laughed. He could do this. Jamie was easy. He was sweet and funny, and Knox just had to remember that he was the boss here.

"You're easy to please, Peters," he said, sliding the key in the lock to open the door, holding it as Jamie slid past him into the workshop. Even the scent of coffee in his nose couldn't mask that sweet, spicy smell coming off Jamie. It was even stronger than it had been last night.

I am so fucked, Knox thought, unable to stop his gaze from settling on Jamie's tight, round ass as he made his way to his station.

"Coffee first?" Jamie asked, dropping his bag at his station before detouring for the breakroom to deposit the donuts.

"Yeah, coffee," Knox mumbled. Coffee would help. He was just tired. Tired and frustrated.

Jamie was already pulling two mugs from a cupboard when Knox came in with the coffee.

"Sugar, right? No cream?" Jamie asked, looking up from where he was adding copious amounts of sugar to his own mug.

"Yeah, but maybe not that much."

"I'm a growing boy," Jamie protested, turning his smile on Knox, as Knox set the pot of coffee down on the counter.

"Don't remind me," Knox said, suddenly aware of how close Jamie was, how that scent from last night hadn't dissipated at all. If anything, it was stronger this morning. Knox took a step closer, needing to find the source of that scent, figure out why it had his wolf howling and his dick hard as steel. He leaned in to scent Jamie, and Jamie bared his throat.

It was just as much an invitation now as it had been last night, and Knox couldn't possibly turn it down. He buried his nose in Jamie's throat and inhaled deeply. There was no mistaking that scent, or the whimper from Jamie that accompanied it.

"Peters," Knox growled softly, holding back the instinct to bite, to mark, to leave no doubt in anyone's mind that Jamie was *his*. "Jamie...are you...in *heat*?"

Jamie whimpered again and *fuck* that noise went straight to Knox's cock. He pressed forward, pinning Jamie against the counter, bringing their hips together sharply. Even if he couldn't smell arousal coming off Jamie in waves, Knox would have no doubt after feeling the hard heat of Jamie's erection against his thigh.

"I...I'm a Beta," Jamie protested, but the way he pressed himself against Knox's thigh was definitely not a protest.

Knox gave in to the temptation he'd been resisting for months now and grabbed onto Jamie's hips, bringing them tighter against his own, one hand sliding back to cup that beautiful ass. "Are you in heat, little Beta?" he asked, all too aware of how his words echoed the ones he'd heard from Cole Gunnersen the night before.

"Fuck," Jamie gasped, clinging to Knox's shirt. "I...fuck, I think I am?"

Knox's head came up sharply. There was fear in Jamie's voice, and no wonder. Nineteen and getting his first heat? The kid was probably terrified. Knox could see that terror in his eyes, and he bent his head to Jamie's neck again, teeth closing around the enticing beat of Jamie's pulse, holding firmly. A moment later, Jamie's breathing evened out, and Knox gave a rumbling growl into Jamie's throat before pulling back again.

"I've got you, Jamie," he said, cupping Jamie's cheek in one hand, forcing Jamie to keep his gaze on Knox's face. "I've got you. I'm gonna take care of you. You're gonna be just fine."

He wanted to reassure Jamie, but being this close, feeling Jamie's pulse against his leg, Knox couldn't resist any longer. He brought their lips together, meaning the kiss to be tender, reassuring, but it wasn't long before it became something altogether different. Rough and claiming, his teeth catching on Jamie's lip, not quite drawing blood but close.

Jamie gave back as well as he got. After a moment's hesitation, the Beta—*no, Omega*, Knox corrected himself, *my Omega*—threw himself into the kiss, arms wrapping tightly around Knox's shoulders, hands burying in his hair.

Another time, Knox would have taken his time with this, undressed Jamie slowly, licked over every inch of him, memorized his taste, his scent, the noises he made under Knox's hands....

But the scent of Jamie's heat pushed him past all that. His wolf was restless, pushing him to *claim, take, fuck*. He took just enough time to yank Jamie's shirt over his head and toss it to the side, unconcerned over the faint sound of fabric ripping. He cared much more about getting Jamie's jeans undone and shoved down his slim hips. Jamie's hands shoved Knox's shirt up his stomach, heated fingers scratching down his abs, drawing a deep growl from Knox's that was echoed by a howl from his wolf. In moments like these, he and his wolf were nearly one, focused on the same goal.

Just as Knox was about to spin Jamie around, bend him over the table, Jamie surprised him by giving Knox's chest a firm shove and turning to the table. He finished the job of shedding jeans and underwear, bracing his hands on the table, presenting himself perfectly to Knox, just as he had last night.

Only now...Knox couldn't help responding to it. He stepped up behind Jamie, sliding one hand slowly up the Omega's spine, resting on the base of his neck, pushing him down, forcing his shoulders to the smooth surface of the table.

"Tell me you want this," Knox said, the only concession his wolf was willing to allow to asking for consent.

"I want this," Jamie whispered, and any doubts Knox had were driven out by the hunger in his voice. Knox had always avoided mounting an Omega in heat, but he'd heard that tone before, that desire, that *need* to be filled.

He teased them both only a moment longer, just as long as it took for him to yank his own jeans open, freeing his aching cock. Jamie was whimpering again, and Knox brought two fingers to his hole, feeling the slick Omega heat inviting him in.

"Fuck," he growled, bending over Jamie, nosing at his throat until Jamie bared it again. "You're so tight."

"Please," Jamie responded, hips arching back, pushing to take Knox's fingers deeper. "Please...fuck. Fuck me."

"Don't you worry, sweetheart," Knox growled. "I got you."

And then he pulled his fingers back, lining himself up, the tip of his cock teasing at Jamie's entrance. "Just one thing first."

“What?” Jamie gasped, pushing back so desperately Knox had to grip his hip to keep him from forcing Knox into him. “Anything!”

“I want to hear you say my name,” Knox growled.

As soon as Jamie opened his mouth, Knox was pushing in, forcing the grunted, “Knox!” from the Omega’s throat.

He couldn’t hold back any longer. All he wanted was to lose himself in the tight, willing heat of this boy he’d been fantasizing about for months now. This sweet *Omega* who was his now. His wolf echoed each thrust with *Mine, mine, mine,* and Knox’s focus narrowed to the tight grip around his cock as he buried himself again and again to the chorus of Jamie’s groans and gasped encouragements.

Another time, he’d go slower, learn Jamie’s body, his touch, his needs. This was just a rush, a race to completion, a deep need to find satisfaction.

“Please, please, please, please,” Jamie groaned under him, and Knox would have done anything for Jamie when he begged like that.

“Please what?” he asked, almost too far gone to hear an answer, let alone comply.

“Please,” Jamie said again, reaching his slender, toned arms across the table to grip the other side. “Knot me.”

If Knox had had any chance of stopping himself, Jamie’s plea shattered it. His wolf took over, and he pounded himself into

Jamie, his balls drawing up tight, feeling his own pulse in his dick to the rhythm of Jamie's repeated, "Yes, yes, yes, yes."

He pushed into Jamie as though, by sheer force of will, he could bury himself completely, and then he felt it, the swelling at the base of his cock. Another thrust, then one more, and he pushed Jamie to the table, feeling the Omega's body tightening around him, knot pressed deep, Jamie's body squeezing him as he came.

Knox held tight to Jamie's hips, his cock still pulsing, spilling into Jamie as Knox panted against his shoulder.

"Fuck," he breathed.

"Yeah," Jamie returned, his words slightly slurred. "Yeah, fuck."

***

Maybe it was because he'd been raised as a Beta, and they didn't exactly cover the post-mating protocol of Omegas in his sex ed class, but no one had ever told Jamie that an Omega should really give some thought to *where* he presents for an Alpha, because Alphas are heavy, and after coming as hard as he'd just done, Jamie wasn't sure he could move himself, let alone Knox's weight on top of him.

Not that he wanted to move Knox right now. He could feel Knox's heart beating through the thin layer of t-shirt separating Knox's chest from Jamie's back, and the thick scent of a sated Alpha seemed to create a blanket of warmth around them both that Jamie was in no rush to disturb.

Knox shifted slightly, as if reading Jamie's thoughts. He slid one arm firmly around Jamie's waist and, with surprising skill, eased them both to the floor so smoothly that Jamie only once sucked in a sharp breath when Knox's still-swollen knot tugged at his newly sore hole. Knox responded by carefully settling them onto their sides, his hips comfortably cradling Jamie's ass. The cool linoleum of the break room floor was a relief against Jamie's too-hot skin.

Knox nosed along the curve of Jamie's shoulder, and Jamie tilted his head again, the motion now as instinctive as breathing. For a brief moment, he wished that Knox had actually bitten him, claimed him properly, but he knew that expecting Knox to give him the bonding mark just because he happened to get stuck with Jamie at his first heat wasn't fair to either of them.

But especially Knox.

"Stop thinking so much," Knox breathed, a hot puff of air ghosting over the glistening sweat on Jamie's shoulder. "Thinking isn't allowed during heat."

Jamie shifted, a smile tugging his lips upward. "Not even thinking about how fucking amazing that was?"

Knox rolled his hips deliberately, reminding Jamie that they were still knotted, Knox was *still inside him*. More than that, Knox's come was still inside him. He should be worried about that. The pack was full of Omegas who'd gotten pregnant on their first heat, caught off guard and saddled with pups before they were ready. He should be worried about trapping Knox into something permanent just because

Jamie was too careless to go to a doctor when he noticed something weird going on.

He should be worried, but with Knox's teeth grazing the column of Jamie's throat, Jamie couldn't manage to worry about anything other than how soon he could get Knox to fuck him again.

"You can think about *that* all you want, Jamie." Something about the way Knox said his name sent shivers all through Jamie. Knox must have felt them because he groaned, his face buried in Jamie's shoulder, and nipped lightly at Jamie's skin. "Fuck, sweetheart.... Warn me if you're gonna do that."

"Warn me if you're gonna make me," Jamie countered, laughing and twisting as well as he could in Knox's arms without moving his hips. He brought a hand up to touch Knox's jaw, fingertips tracing along the strong line of it, stubble rough against his fingers. He frowned. Knox hadn't asked for this. And if last night was any indication, he didn't even want it.

Knox caught one of Jamie's fingers between his teeth, tongue swirling around the tip, suckling gently. Jamie gasped, his breath catching in his throat. His dick twitched a little, interested but not yet hard again. Knox gave him a wicked smile and pulled Jamie's hand away.

"Already, little Beta?" he murmured, his hips giving an experimental roll forward. His knot had only just started to release, but Jamie could feel the Alpha getting hard again inside him. "You're gonna wear me out before we even get to do anything fun."

"This...*fuck*...this isn't fun?" Jamie breathed, his head falling back, resting on Knox's shoulder as he shuddered with each roll of Knox's hips.

"Oh, sure," Knox whispered, his teeth just teasing over Jamie's shoulder. Jamie could practically feel his skin pulsing with the need to feel Knox's teeth biting him properly, breaking the skin and sealing the mating bond. "This is all kinds of fun. But I want a chance to watch your face while I fuck you."

"Ah, Jesus," Jamie breathed, groaning, reaching back to grip Knox's hair as he settled into a rhythm with the Alpha, slower this time, pushing in so deep Jamie thought there was no way Knox could be more a part of him than he was right then. "What...what else?"

"Hmmm." Knox's response rumbled against Jamie's shoulder, and his cock throbbed in answer. "I want to taste you. Taste the sweet nectar you make just for me." He rolled smoothly into Jamie again and again, and Jamie let his hand slide from Knox's hair to his thigh, holding on like it was the only thing keeping him from floating away.

"What...what else?" Jamie asked again, just to keep Knox talking, loving the way it rumbled straight through him.

"Wanna taste this too," Knox continued, his hand running up from Jamie's hip to his chest, fingers finding one tight nipple and giving it a sharp tug, drawing a whimper from Jamie's throat. "And this," Knox went on, his hand teasing lower, tracing the faint definition in Jamie's abs. "But especially..."

Knox's hand paused, fingertips just barely reaching the hair at the base of Jamie's now-aching cock. Jamie's breath caught, and it took him too long to find it again, so that when Knox's strong fingers finally curled around his cock, Jamie's breath came out all in a rush.

"Mmm, especially this," Knox said, gripping firmly, his hand working over Jamie's hard flesh in rhythm with his slow-rolling hips.

"Yes, fuck," Jamie gasped when he finally managed to inhale again. His fingers dug into Knox's thigh, and Knox's teeth found his throat again, holding him without breaking skin the way Jamie wished he would.

Gradually, Knox quickened his pace. His hips and hand moved faster and faster, and Jamie let himself ride each thrust, pushing closer and closer to his finish. He braced himself, thinking of how Knox's knot had felt in him the first time, how feeling his Alpha knot him felt like finally finding the missing piece to a puzzle he'd been stuck on for years.

He felt it again now, the base of Knox's dick swelling gradually until Knox could no longer pull back, until his thrusts became shallow and *hard* and Jamie felt the unrelenting pressure of that knot against his prostate. He stretched his neck, baring as much of his throat to Knox as he could manage, the invitation to bite as clear as he knew how to make it.

Knox thrust hard into him, once, twice, and then he was spilling into Jamie, growling as he came, and Jamie felt the overwhelming rush of pleasure that came with his own release, spilling over Knox's hand.

Knox held onto him tightly, his arm firmly curled around Jamie's waist like he was worried Jamie would disappear on him. The same compulsion Jamie had felt the night before—to take care of Knox, to make sure he didn't worry—hit him again, and he curled his own arm around Knox's.

"I'm not going anywhere," he mumbled, wrapping his fingers around Knox's wrist. "Might pass out on you, though."

Knox laughed, a deep, reverberating laugh and nipped again at the spot he never quite bit hard enough. "You go right ahead, sweetheart," he said. "You earned it."

***

When Jamie woke again, he was not entirely surprised to find he'd been moved to the breakroom couch, a blanket tucked in around him, and a glass of water close enough to reach. His first instinct—after downing the water—when he didn't immediately see Knox, was to panic. His wolf yipped restlessly inside him.

He could still catch Knox's scent in the air, though, and a moment later, he'd calmed down enough to hear the sound of the wood lathe in the workshop. Of course. The Walsh order. Not only had Jamie's heat forced Knox into this mess, he'd screwed up the order *again*. They couldn't afford to lose a whole day to Jamie's heat. Two days, more likely, given that it was Jamie's first heat, likely to last longer.

Before he could think too much about that, though, the sound of the lathe stopped, and he heard Knox say, "Stop worrying so much. Never knew an Omega could worry so much while they were in heat."

Jamie couldn't help smiling at that. He gingerly pulled himself to his feet, sore and tired, but already feeling himself grow slick at the sound of Knox's voice. He wrapped the blanket around his shoulders and went to the doorframe of the breakroom so he could see Knox.

The Alpha looked like pure sex. Next to his frame, the lathe looked like a child's toy. The scent of sawdust somehow mixed with Knox's natural scent to make something undeniably masculine.

Knox glanced up and saw Jamie in the door. A low growl echoed through the open workshop, and Knox crossed the space between them in long, quick strides. Jamie backed himself against the doorframe when Knox approached, unsure what he'd done wrong, eager to make it right.

When Knox reached him, he tugged the blanket out of Jamie's grip, letting it fall to the ground. "Don't you dare cover up," he said, his fingers curling around Jamie's wrists, pulling them back, pinning them against the walls to either side of the doorframe. When Knox pushed forward, the rough drag of denim against Jamie's over-sensitized skin served as a sharp reminder that Jamie had yet to see Knox naked.

Even the buttons of Knox's Henley were almost painfully hard as they pressed into Jamie's chest. "I want you ready for me all the time," Knox said, his lips brushing Jamie's ear before he caught the lobe between his teeth, tugging sharply.

Jamie whimpered like a pup, pushing toward Knox's heat, into the strength of his frame. "Look who's talking," he answered, breathless. Knox laughed, a dark chuckle just behind Jamie's ear, and pulled back, a hand on Jamie's chest to keep him pressed against the doorframe still. His forehead rested against Jamie's, and Jamie felt each exhale, hot against his lips.

"You wanna see me, sweetheart?" he asked, and Jamie could only nod, arching forward, suddenly aware that Knox hadn't kissed him. Not since last night. Knox barely brushed his lips against Jamie's, more a tease than a kiss, and stepped back, growling softly, "Stay."

Jamie wasn't sure he was even capable of disobeying that order, no matter how much he wanted to touch, to get his hands all over Knox.

Knox took another step back, into the breakroom. His eyes never left Jamie's as he slowly peeled off the shirt that clung to his torso. Jamie's mouth went dry when he finally managed to drag his gaze down to Knox's chest. It was broader than he would have thought possible, a dusting of auburn curls scattered across it, freckles sprinkled over his wide shoulders.

As Jamie watched, Knox slid a hand slowly down his chest, over his abs, coming to rest at his belt, fingers curling enticingly over the bulge at his crotch. "Like what you see, little Beta?" he asked, slowly, slowly working his belt open.

Jamie nodded, swallowing, not trusting his voice right now.

"Say it," Knox said, firm and sure.

"I like it," Jamie managed, voice cracking a bit. He cleared his throat. "I like what I see. I...fuck, Knox. You're...you're so hot."

"You wanna see more, don't you?" Knox's hand paused, just after undoing the first button on his button-fly jeans.

"Yeah," Jamie breathed, licking his lips, glancing back up at Knox's face to see pure hunger in Knox's eyes. Hunger for *him*. "Yeah, I wanna see more."

"Say it," Knox said again, undoing another button. "Tell me what you want to see."

"You," Jamie said, feeling his pulse throbbing from his throat to his dick. "I want to see you. All of you. I...I want to see your cock." He felt the heat in his cheeks, straight up to his ears, burning through him as he admitted it.

"Good boy," Knox murmured, and Jamie's wolf preened, howling in delight. Knox made quick work of the last few buttons and shoved his jeans down, toeing his boots off as he did so he could chuck them aside, leaving him clad only in boxer briefs, his erection peeking through the slit.

Jamie took a step forward, but Knox held up a hand to stop him. "Not yet, sweetheart. I want to play."

He strode to Jamie, pushing him back against the wall again, and sliding to his knees. Jamie felt his heart stutter, and he couldn't take his eyes off Knox as the Alpha leaned in, at first just scenting along the curve of Jamie's hip before wrapping his lips around Jamie's straining erection.

He was good at this too, and Jamie knew he shouldn't be surprised, but he was. How could Knox be this good at everything necessary to turn Jamie into a whimpering Omega?

The heat of Knox's mouth, the pressure of his sucking, the way his fingers teased over Jamie's balls before sliding back, pressing into him, talented fingers easily finding Jamie's sweet spot and pressing undeniably against it, it was all too much, and Jamie could barely tug at Knox's hair in warning before he was coming hard, his head falling back against the frame as he groaned Knox's name, hips jerking.

Knox held him through it, fingers still rubbing, gentling, his free hand steadying Jamie's hip. By the time he pulled his mouth off, Jamie could no longer stand, and Knox helped him to the floor, curling protectively around him.

"Fuck," Jamie whispered. "I think you might have broken me."

Knox chuckled, his fingers teasing back toward Jamie's eager opening. "We're just getting started, sweetheart," he said, and then finally, *finally*, his lips were on Jamie's and Jamie threw himself into the kiss, opening up to Knox's claiming tongue, his nipping teeth. He clung to his Alpha as Knox pressed them back further, settling between Jamie's legs. "I'm gonna make you mine," Knox growled, catching Jamie's lip between his teeth.

"Yes," was all Jamie could answer. "Yes, all yours."

***

Every time Knox thought Jamie's heat was waning, he inhaled another wave of that sweet, tantalizing scent, and he was on the Omega again. When Jamie slept, Knox worked on the Walsh order. When he was awake, if they weren't fucking, Knox was feeding him, making sure he had enough water. Bathing him as well as they could manage in the workshop shower.

Knox wished he had the chance to do this properly, in his home, in his bed, where they could leave the scent of their mating heavy in the air for days, soaked into sheets and pillows. As much as Knox tried to only take Jamie on the floor or a table or a counter, they'd fucked on the couch enough that Knox was going to have to replace it. Not an Alpha in the shop would be able to concentrate on their work with Jamie's scent lingering like that. The whole shop would have to be hosed down and aired out.

But that could wait until he was sure Jamie's heat was finally over. Late Saturday night, Knox made Jamie text his parents so they wouldn't worry. He tried not to hover as Jamie pulled out his phone, worried Jamie would be texting Cole too. Knox's wolf was being stubborn on that one, and eventually Knox settled for turning and taking a step back, so he wasn't hovering so obviously.

When Jamie laughed, though, reading a text, Knox stepped closer again. "What?" he asked, wrapping his arms around Jamie's waist, chin resting on Jamie's shoulder.

"Nothing, just... I asked my friend Cole to look into Betas being sensitive to Alpha's scent. He just texted me that it could be I was a late blooming Omega."

"You think?" Knox laughed as well, nosing behind Jamie's ear and along his shoulder. Not for the first time, he felt his wolf rousing, eager to bite, to claim Jamie as his, once and for all, but Knox held back. It wasn't fair to Jamie to claim him on a first heat. Besides, he probably wanted to be bonding with Cole. At least Knox had gotten the chance to be with Jamie once, before he and Cole mated, before Knox lost out on any opportunity he'd ever have.

"Hmm, maybe," Jamie answered, turning in Knox's embrace, blue eyes sparkling when they met Knox's. Knox felt a tightening in his chest. He wanted to be the one to put that look on Jamie's face. He wanted to have the right to claim that.

But he'd settle for this, for having one heat with Jamie.

"We should test the theory, don't you think?" he asked, fighting against the temptation to kiss Jamie again. It was too easy to go from kissing to biting, too difficult to tamp down the instinct to mark Jamie as his, even if it wasn't a bonding mark.

"We really should," Jamie answered, and when he pressed his lips to Knox's, Knox knew it was a losing battle. He might never get to claim Jamie, but Jamie, for all intents and purposes, had already claimed him.

***

By the time Jamie woke, late Sunday morning, to the soft sound of Knox snoring behind him, he knew that his heat was ending. Everything around him still smelled of sex and

Knox and his own pheromones, but they weren't having the same effect anymore. He still wanted Knox, would gladly take him again, but the driving *need* to mate was gone. It was more like a pointed suggestion than an imperative now.

Knox stirred, and Jamie shifted to look at him. This would be his last chance. The last time he got to be close to Knox, to pretend he didn't know this was nothing but a chemical reaction to his heat. Burrowing into the warmth of Knox's body, Jamie pressed his face to the Alpha's shoulder, inhaling deeply, wanting to remember this scent for as long as he could.

Slowly, Knox blinked his eyes open, looking sleepy and rumpled and more like a giant puppy than the hulking Alpha he usually came off as.

"Morning," he rumbled into Jamie's ear before nosing along his throat. "Mmm, you smell...."

Jamie stilled, wishing he could postpone this, let the moment before Knox realized Jamie was no longer in heat stretch just a bit longer.

"Fucking amazing," Knox finished, nipping at a bruise he'd left at the base of Jamie's throat.

"I...still?" Jamie asked, twisting to look at Knox. He didn't *feel* like he was in heat anymore. Maybe he was just getting used to it?

"Mm, yeah." Knox's hips were rolling against him, and Jamie felt the now-familiar heat of Knox's erection settled in the cleft of his ass. "It's different, but it's...really fucking good."

"Oh," was all Jamie could manage. Even without the bright, physical *need* of his heat, Knox's touch was intoxicating. When Knox's teeth nipped sharply at Jamie's earlobe, Jamie sucked in a breath, letting his head fall back against Knox's shoulder, throat bared.

He felt the hot drag of Knox's mouth down his throat, settling at the spot in his shoulder where he could feel his pulse throbbing. "You don't have to," Knox told him, as though Jamie would ever have said no.

Jamie reached back a hand to fist in Knox's thick auburn hair, keeping him right where he was. "I know," he breathed. "I want to."

Knox growled against his skin, and Jamie could feel it running through him, making his skin vibrate. "You should know," he said, something dangerous in his voice, "I don't share well."

Jamie huffed out a laugh, rocking back to Knox, feeling the tip of Knox's cock settle at his entrance. "Who would you have to share me with?"

"Gunnerson," Knox growled, nipping hard at Jamie's shoulder, right where he most wanted Knox to bite.

"Cole?" As Jamie spoke, Knox pushed forward, stretching Jamie's hole and then pulling back again, making Jamie stutter his response. "He's...he's my best friend. He's not...he could never be my Alpha."

"Swear it," Knox growled again, and Jamie twisted until he could look Knox in the eye.

"I swear," he said quietly. "You're the only Alpha I've ever wanted."

Knox's lips met his at the same time as he pushed forward, sliding deep into Jamie in one smooth thrust. There was a hunger in Knox's kiss that was different than it had been during Jamie's heat. Knox moved in him in a sure, solid rhythm, but his kiss was rough, uneven, teeth catching on Jamie's lips and tongue until they both gave up and Jamie dropped his head to the side again, baring his throat for Knox once again.

That was different too. In his heat it had been all instinct. Omegas were supposed to submit to their Alphas. It was in their nature, in their DNA. This time, though, it was a conscious decision, and though Jamie didn't point that out, Knox seemed to pick up on it.

A low growl reverberated through Knox's chest, and he wrapped an arm tightly around Jamie's waist, lifting him smoothly up to his knees on the pile of blankets and cushions they'd turned into a sort of nest over the past twenty-four hours. Jamie shifted his weight to his knees, lifting his hips for Knox.

"Fuck," Knox muttered. "You look perfect."

Jamie grinned back at him, hardly able to believe that Knox was really here, that the Alpha really wanted him.

But Knox was here, and he was already, nudging Jamie's knees further apart, lining himself up and pushing into Jamie without any further comment. Jamie dropped his head with a groan, reaching for his aching dick.

Knox stopped him with a hand around his wrist. "No," he said sharply, pressing Jamie's hand to the floor and reaching for the Omega's cock himself. "Mine."

"Ah, fuck." Jamie's breath caught and he pushed into Knox's grip, stuttering for a moment before he found a good rhythm between Knox's hand and his cock. "Yes, fuck...."

Knox drove into him. Jamie thought he must be pushing deeper with each thrust but that had to be impossible.

"Mine," Knox muttered as he bent low, his body draped over Jamie's back. "All mine."

"Yeah," Jamie gasped. "All yours, Knox. All yours, always."

"Fuck yeah." Knox's teeth grazed his shoulder. "Gonna fucking put my pups in you, sweetheart."

"Ah, Jesus yes!" Jamie's hips bucked hard into Knox's grip, and he had to bite down hard on his lip to keep from coming right there. He could have Knox's pups. Knox could breed him. He'd never wanted anything more. "Breed me, Knox...please!"

"That makes you mine," Knox rumbled, his hips slowing maddeningly. "You wanna be mine, Jamie? You wanna be my Omega?" He was back at that spot, that throbbing spot in

Jamie's shoulder, and Jamie knew what Knox was asking, what he was offering, and he didn't hesitate.

"Yes. Yes, make me yours."

Knox thrust into him again, hard, picking up his pace, until Jamie was crying out with each thrust. Just when he thought he couldn't take anymore, couldn't hold on any longer, Knox breathed, "Now," into his ear, and then bit down hard on Jamie's shoulder, and Jamie shattered into his orgasm. It seemed to radiate out from the fiery heat in his shoulder, the bonding mark already blooming on his skin, until it reached his balls and shot straight back again. His eyes closed, and sparks seemed to shoot behind his eyelids.

When he could see straight again, Knox was lapping gently at his shoulder, at the faint traces of blood left by the skin-breaking bonding bite. Jamie felt his entire body relax at the touch.

"Mine," Knox said again.

"Yours," Jamie murmured. "All yours."

***

Once they'd gotten the workshop cleaned up well enough that Knox didn't think he could smell Jamie's heat anymore, Knox had insisted on taking Jamie to the doctor.

"You had your first heat at nineteen, sweetheart. You haven't had any of the regular Omega checkups. You should go. I'll go with you."

So here Knox sat, in the waiting room of the town's Omega physician. They'd been lucky enough to catch him on his once a month Sunday shift, and Knox was grateful for that.

He was not grateful for the way he'd been relegated to the waiting room. His wolf was restless. Their mate was in a room, alone, with another shifter. Granted, Dr. Weber was a Beta, but that didn't make Knox or his wolf feel any better.

Picking up an old copy of Reader's Digest, Knox flipped through it, hoping it would distract him some.

After this there would be a million other things they'd need to do. They'd have to tell Jamie's parents, which Knox knew would not be easy. Not when Jamie had always assumed he was a Beta.

They'd have to tell Knox's dad as well, and that could be tricky. Knox knew his dad had a few suitable mates picked out for him already, and Jamie Peters, with a dad who worked as an assistant manager at the hardware store and a mom who taught art at the elementary school, was definitely not on that list.

Knox would have a hell of a fight ahead of him. They both would.

"Aaron Knox?"

He glanced up sharply to see the nurse who'd brought Jamie back standing in the doorway leading to the examination rooms.

"That's me."

"Dr. Weber wanted me to escort you back."

"Finally." Between the two of them, he and his wolf practically shoved past the poor woman into the hallway. "Where is he?" Over the stringent, clean scent of antiseptic, Knox could pick out that distinctly Jamie smell. He knew that if something were really wrong, he would feel it through their bond, even new as it was, but that didn't stop him worrying entirely.

He wasn't satisfied until the nurse pointed him toward a room at the end of the hall, and he opened the door to see Jamie sitting up on the exam table. It was all he could do not to wrap himself around his Omega, check every inch of him, make sure no one else had touched Jamie.

Dr. Weber seemed amused by his reaction. "Your mate is just fine, Mr. Knox," he said with a chuckle. "More than fine, actually. That's why I called you back."

Knox was working on settling himself onto an exam table far too small to accommodate both him and Jamie, but he sort of half-managed, leaning a hip against the table and pulling Jamie firmly against his chest.

"What do you mean, more than fine?" he asked

"Well, it seems congratulations are in store. You're going to be fathers."

There was silence in the room for a full minute. Jamie was the one who finally broke it.

"Bullshit."

"I'm afraid not, Jamie," Dr. Weber said.

"But it was...it was my first heat."

"That's not at all uncommon, especially not in late-blooming Omegas."

Knox felt his throat tightening, making it difficult to breathe for a moment. Fathers. They were going to be fathers. Any worries he'd had about Jamie's family or his own dad seemed to slip away in the face of that news. When his throat loosened again, he swallowed and saw that both Dr. Weber and Jamie were staring at him, clearly waiting for him to say something.

He took a deep breath, smelling Jamie's scent, soothing and sweet. "Well, fuck me," he said. "I'm gonna be a dad."

***

It wasn't all that late, but Jamie was exhausted. Dr. Weber had said he was still recovering from his heat but also that the pregnancy might sap his energy, especially in the first weeks.

Still, Jamie suspected he would not feel so worn out if he and Knox hadn't been interrogated by both their parents for over an hour each. When Knox had finally taken them home, Jamie had wanted nothing more than to collapse straight into bed. Knox, however, wouldn't let him sleep before eating something and taking a bath.

He was so exhausted by the time he made it to bed that he thought for certain he'd be asleep as soon as his head hit the pillow. Instead, he found himself restless. Knox was curled around him from behind, and Jamie could feel the Alpha's heart beating against his shoulder, just below the bonding mark.

Knox's hand lay protectively over Jamie's belly, where Knox's pups were growing. Twins, Dr. Weber had told them. Too early to tell more than that. In just a few months, Jamie would be a dad. He'd have two tiny people to look after. And on top of that, he'd be learning how to be an Omega, figuring out how he and Knox worked together, and deciding what he even wanted to do with his life now that something so basic as his biology seemed to have changed overnight.

"Everything okay?" Knox asked, nosing over Jamie's mark. His hand rubbed slowly over Jamie's belly. "With all of you?"

"Yeah," Jamie murmured. It wasn't a deliberate lie. He just didn't know how to say all the things he was thinking. "It's fine."

Jamie yipped when Knox's teeth caught around the base of his throat. Knox growled, and a shiver ran through Jamie. He whimpered softly and Knox let him go.

"Don't lie to me," Knox said. "You're upset. You think I can't feel that?"

Right. The bonding.

So often today, he and Knox had been feeling so close to the same thing that Jamie forgot they were connected like that.

When something happened to remind him, he was always a little startled.

Knox's voice was a little softer now. "Talk to me, sweetheart. Tell me what you're thinking."

Jamie swallowed, nodding. He still wasn't sure he had the words, but he *wanted* to talk to Knox about this. Knox deserved that from him.

He turned to face Knox, letting his hand rest over Knox's steady heartbeat, hoping it would help ground him.

"Aren't you," he began, searching for the right word. "Aren't you scared?"

Knox smiled, a crooked smile that tilted up just one side of his mouth. He lowered his head until his forehead pressed against Jamie's. "Of being a dad? I'm terrified."

"Then why are you smiling?"

"Because you'll be there with me," Knox said, holding Jamie closer as he caught Jamie's lips in a slow, sweet kiss. It was something different than the heated kisses they'd shared so far. It was comfortable, soothing.

Even so, it took Jamie's breath away, and all he could do when Knox finally pulled back was to blink slowly, lips parted.

"Look," Knox said, his voice a low, calm rumble. "Neither of us planned this. I get that. And it's gonna be even harder for you than usual because...well, because you weren't planning for this *ever*." His broad hand rubbed wide circles over Jamie's back, easing some of the tension in his shoulders. "But I know that I don't want anybody but you in my life. I wanted you before I knew you were an Omega."

Jamie opened his mouth to speak, taken aback by the suggestion that Knox had wanted him as a Beta. Knox laid a finger over his lips that turned to a slow stroke of his thumb over Jamie's lip.

"I wanted you before I knew you were an Omega," Knox said again. "So I figure whatever we have to deal with because you turned out to be in heat, and I couldn't keep my hands off you...it's worth it. If it means we get to be together, if it means I get to call you mine? It's all worth it."

Jamie felt a tightness in his chest that twisted once, then released. He laughed, shaking his head. "Well, shit, Knox. If I try to argue that, I'll sound like an asshole."

Knox leaned in for a warning nip at the corner of Jamie's jaw, and Jamie grinned, his head leaned back, arms wrapped around Knox's shoulders. "Better not argue, then," Knox said, the scratch of his stubble spreading goosebumps across Jamie's skin.

Jamie's grin widened. "Whatever you say, boss."

***

Knox paced back and forth, striding purposefully from one end of the hallway to the other, pivoting sharply on his heel at each end. The nurses were starting to point and whisper. It was incredibly difficult not to snarl at them as he passed.

"You know," one of them said, on his sixth pass, "the waiting room is really cozy. There's coffee. Probably even donuts still."

Knox ignored her, and he heard her whispering to her friend a moment later, "That right there is why Alphas aren't allowed in delivery rooms."

Just after his next pass, a door opened down the hallway. Knox all but sprinted down to it. Dr. Weber stood in the doorway, his expression mild and unreadable.

"Is it...?" Knox began, not at all sure what he was going to ask.

"Everything's just fine, Mr. Knox," Dr. Weber assured him. "You can go on in."

From the way Dr. Weber quickly dodged out of Knox's way, it was clear he was a veteran in dealing with post-delivery Alphas.

The room smelled like blood and antibacterial soap, but Knox's senses immediately locked in on Jamie's scent, and something else, a scent that had been getting stronger and stronger over the past few months.

He pulled back the curtain to see Jamie, looking completely exhausted and holding two tightly wrapped bundles, one pink and one blue.

For half a second, Knox couldn't even *breathe*, let alone take the few steps necessary to be at Jamie's bedside.

"Well?" Jamie finally asked. "Aren't you going to say something?"

Knox was at his side in three steps, and Jamie offered him the pink bundle. Knox's hands trembled as he took it, looking down into the most perfect face he'd ever seen. Tentatively, he settled into the chair next to Jamie's bed, and Jamie offered him the other bundle.

One tiny package of blanket-wrapped perfection in each arm, Knox felt like his heart might actually burst from how much love suddenly seemed to have flooded into his life. He looked from his son to his daughter and then up to Jamie, *his* Omega.

"Yeah," he said, leaning his head against the bed at Jamie's side. "Absolutely worth it."

Three's A Crowd

A Wolf Shifter Mpreg Bundle

Preston Walker & Liam Kingsley

Disclaimer

This is a work of fiction. Names, places, characters and events are all fictitious for the reader's pleasure. Any similarities to

ANNIVERSARY

Michael eyed the dregs of vodka and coke in his glass as the bar swayed around him. He'd probably had a bit too much. But hey, he was entitled to that after the day he'd had. He could sense the stares of the other people around him on his skin, the scents of curious alphas who were no doubt wondering if he'd come here on his own. He was sure they'd be thrilled to know that he had, although he wasn't exactly planning on going home with anyone new tonight. His gaze shifted to the tan line on the ring finger of his left hand. He missed the weight of the stone that had rested there. He wished he hadn't thrown it in Joseph's face like that. Even if they were ... taking a break, he still felt like he should be wearing it. Joseph might not have had the best priorities or been the most tactful, but their relationship had been comfortable. Michael downed the rest of his drink with a shudder and signaled for another.

Across the bar, a tall, rough-looking alpha had his gaze locked on Michael, trying his best to intimidate the omega, who was solidly ignoring him. Michael had no interest in alphas. In his experience they were all too full of themselves, and tended to treat his kind like trash. He'd had an alpha boyfriend in high school, and it hadn't ended well. He had no intention of going down that road again. Instead, Michael turned to the man on his left, an older omega with subtle silver streaks at his temples.

"God, this place is packed, huh?" The man glanced at him briefly, before returning his attention to his phone. Michael felt briefly annoyed, but tried again. "My name's Michael. Do you come here often?" This time the man looked at him directly, distaste evident in his gaze.

"Sorry, I'm not interested in omega pups. Go get knotted." Michael bristled at his comment.

“For your information, I wasn’t coming onto you. I was trying to be friendly. And another thing, I don’t need to *get knotted*. The day I let an alpha touch me is the day hell freezes over.” He was aware he was talking too loudly, but at this point he didn’t really care. The man gave him a disgusted look.

“Jesus, you’re drunk. And you’re making a fool of yourself. Go home, runt.” Michael stood in anger, feeling the world shift abruptly around him. The older man remained seated, towering over the 5’6” omega with one brow cocked in disdain.

“Maybe I don’t want to go home. You’re not the boss of me. And if you’re sitting around here instead of with an alpha at your age, maybe *you’re* the one who needs to go get knotted.” The other omega’s expression darkened and Michael could sense people gathering around the two of them, expecting a fight. He felt a strange sense of satisfaction as his nemesis stood, proving much steadier on his feet than Michael was. The man bared his teeth as he spoke.

“It’s not really any of your business whether I have an alpha or not, pup. Maybe you need to be taught to respect your elders.” He took a step forward, causing Michael to waver, and for a moment the floor was much too close. Suddenly he felt a hand catch him by the back of his shirt, and strong arms pulled him to his feet again. The omega’s expression had changed to one of nervous apprehension, and people were subtly moving away from them. “Officer Burr,” he said nervously, “I hope you don’t think I was going to cause any trouble?” The faceless alpha behind Michael tightened his grip on the young man’s collar. When he spoke, it was in a low Southern drawl.

“I’m sure you weren’t, Trent. I’m sure you would’ve been no trouble at all. But I think someone needs to get this kid home, and the only place you looked like you were gonna send him was the hospital. I'm not dealing with this crap on my night off." Trent nodded sheepishly, watching as the alpha maneuvered Michael out of the bar and into the cool outside air. Once they were alone, the officer released him with a sigh. He was tempted to run, but even turning was proving difficult without falling over, and the alpha's strong scent seemed even more intoxicating than the alcohol. He examined his unexpected savior with suspicion, noting his dark eyes and lean physique. The alpha seemed to be watching him with equal wariness, no doubt wondering if he would try and get into another fight. "Do you have anyone to come pick you up?" Michael shook his head.

"I'm twenty-three, I don't need a babysitter. I can get home on my own just fine." The other man frowned.

"Didn't sound like you wanted to go home. I need to make sure you're safe. Don't want you getting into any more trouble tonight." The drink was making Michael hot and irritated, and it made it hard to think straight. The alpha seemed to notice his discomfort. "You feeling alright? You gonna be sick?" The omega shook his head and fought to regain stability.

"I'm okay, thanks. And now, I'm leaving." He didn't need this jerk calling Joe now, of all things. If he got hauled into the station and they checked his tags, the beta was his emergency contact. If there was one thing to convince his ex-partner that he wasn't suited to being a father, it would be a drunk and disorderly charge. He stumbled at the corner and immediately the alpha was behind him again, the musky scent of concern making Michael dizzy and flushed.

"I'm walking you home. You're in no state to be on your own." He cringed, but didn't argue. Honestly, he wasn't even sure how to get home from here. He had reached the bar by walking aimlessly from the restaurant where he and Joseph had dinner. Or tried to, at least, before ... *that* happened. He felt a faint twinge of pain at the memory, dulled by alcohol and alpha pheromones. *At least this guy is a police officer,* he thought. *He'll keep me safe.* And then: *Keep me safe?* Michael stopped walking, a quiet bloom of panic erupting in his chest. Next to him, the officer grumbled at their sudden halt, but the omega ignored him. When was his last heat? Surely it was only two weeks ago? Two and a half at the most. He'd been off suppressants for a while, and so far he'd been regular as clockwork. There was no way he could be starting early. "What's up?" asked Burr, finally noticing the distress Michael was in. The omega blushed uncomfortably.

"I just ... really need to get home." His companion looked confused.

"But I thought you said –"

"It doesn't matter what I said, okay? I just really, *really* need to get home. Which direction is Fifth Street in?" The alpha sighed.

"This way. Can you walk alright?" Michael took a few steps and nodded, noting that he seemed to be sobering up pretty quickly. From the alcohol, at least. The distracting warmth that was spreading through his body was another matter entirely. He took a deep breath and followed the officer. He was looking back with every few steps, concern etched into his expression. Michael avoided eye contact. As much as he resented alphas, he couldn't trust himself in his current state. He already felt like the man's cinnamon-tinged scent had wormed its way through his defenses. He needed his guard up if he was going to hold off his heat until he got home.

They made their way through the streets, and Michael finally began to recognize where they were. Luckily he hadn't traveled far in his earlier wandering. Everything was fine until about two blocks from his apartment, when it finally happened. One moment he was perfectly in control, and the next, there was a positive river of slick coating his underwear and soaking through to his favorite jeans. He groaned and doubled over as the cramps hit him, biting the inside of his cheek in an effort to maintain his composure. Next to him the officer stooped to help him, only to step back, reeling as the scent of omega in heat hit his sensitive nose and threatened to overwhelm his senses. He took several deep breaths, struggling to center himself as the smaller man whimpered beside him. With great effort, Michael managed to straighten his back and take another step, only for another wave of dizziness and pain to crash over him. His vision went blurry for a moment, before he felt Burr grip him once more and hoist him up so he was being carried like a baby in the alpha's arms. Under normal circumstances he would have been humiliated, but now the only thing he felt was relief. He buried his face in the man's shirt, breathing him in and feeling the rush of emotion his scent brought. Whether he intended it to or not, Burr's scent had changed to soothe the troubled omega, making Michael feel loved and protected. He groaned internally. He really didn't need this right now. Another rush of slick left him, and he felt a momentary prickle of guilt at probably ruining the alpha's clothing, before it was again eclipsed by the sensations of his heat.

After some prompting, he managed to mumble his address to the alpha, and before he knew what was quite happening, they had arrived. He was carefully placed on the ground in the doorway, and managed to unlock his door with shaky hands.

"I guess this is my stop," he managed to say, fighting to stay upright on legs that trembled like Bambi on ice. He couldn't help but to cling onto the alpha, who seemed a little worse for wear himself. His large hands still held onto the omega's arms, supporting him when he threatened to collapse. Michael held back a moan as the officer's thumbs gently rubbed the tense muscles in his biceps comfortingly, the automatic reaction from Burr doing nothing to calm his growing libido. "I think," he murmured, giving up the fight and sinking back against the alpha's warm body, "I might be having a problem."

"No shit," growled Burr huskily against his forehead, fighting the urge to take control of the omega and screw him right there in the doorway. He hadn't had a rut in years. He was supposed to be on blockers, so why the hell was this guy having such an effect on him? He breathed in the omega's musk, chocolate and cherries and pinewood, and the honey-scented slick that called to him, telling him that *his* omega was ready for him, that he was wanted. He could feel the smaller man burrowing into him and tried to ignore his growing arousal. He was better than this. They were both kind of drunk, and biology was getting in the way, and ... Michael moaned into his shoulder, feeling the heat growing stronger, and looked up at the officer with pleading eyes. His shaky fingers clung to the larger man's waistband and brushed against the hot skin beneath his shirt. Growling low in his throat, the alpha pressed Michael against the doorframe, his lips finding the nape of the omega's neck and pressing hungry kisses onto its velvet surface.

"Please, Alpha," whimpered Michael, melting under the pressure of his attentions. Somewhere in his fuzzy mind he realized that they were still outside his apartment, that anyone could see them, and he wanted to be the only one to see his alpha. Whining, he tugged on the man's collar, trying his best to pull them both inside, and it must have worked, because the next thing he knew, the door had slammed behind them and they were in a heap on the hallway mat, with his back pressed against its woven surface and every other part of him against this stranger. He panted as the alpha's hands found their way under his shirt, tugging and teasing at his sensitive skin and making his heartbeat spike with every movement. Their mouths collided at last and he felt swept away by the passion with which the other man kissed him, their teeth and tongues fighting for dominance. He gave up all restraint, pawing at his alpha's belt impatiently. Burr had also given up on keeping a level head, mainly due to the sudden release of rutting hormones that the scent of the omega's heat had triggered. Through a haze of lust, he felt Michael's back arch beneath him, acting purely on instinct as he explored the man's body. He could already feel his knot beginning to swell as Michael finally got his belt and jeans undone, brazenly rubbing the alpha's cock through the fabric of his underwear. Michael's own boxers were soaked through with slick, making them stick to his skin when the officer lifted the omega's legs up and tugged down his jeans. He yelped as Burr buried his face in Michael's ass, lapping up the excess and making his body jerk involuntarily as every pass over his tender hole sent waves of stimulation through him.

"Such a good little omega, so ready for me," panted the Alpha, nuzzling Michael's skin and sucking marks into it that would be visible in the morning. "Gonna make you my mate, knot you and breed you and –" The next words were drowned out as he inserted two fingers into Michael's ass, seeking out the omega's sensitive prostate and causing him to let out an extended whine.

"Knot me, Alpha, please, it hurts, God, it hurts." The cramps in his stomach were becoming unbearable, nearly eclipsing the lust he felt. Burr growled at the thought of his omega being in pain, releasing him for a moment to flip him onto his front, before gripping his hips and pulling the smaller man toward him, grinding his painfully swollen cock against Michael's ass and placing more hickeys on his neck and back. When the omega huffed impatiently, he gave in, stretching out the man's slick ass with his cock until he was buried to the hilt, gasping at the omega's hot muscles clenching around him. There was a moment of stillness as they both adjusted to the sensation, before Michael started wriggling against him, craving the friction they both needed for release. Gripping the omega to him tightly, he pressed a kiss behind his ear and nipped lightly at the skin of his neck.

"*Mine,*" he growled quietly into the omega's ear, tugging at the man's nipple with one hand and using the other to stroke his cock, "this is all mine." Beneath him, Michael whimpered.

"Yes, Alpha," he whined, before Burr began pounding into him, driving any kind of logical thought from his mind. He moaned wantonly as his chest was pressed into the rug by the weight of his alpha, as every nerve was set on fire when his alpha's cock hit *that part* inside him that made him arch his back and beg, his words jumbling into streams of filth that didn't make any sense. In the back of his mind, he was vaguely aware that he might need to apologize to the neighbors later, but the thought passed so quickly it might as well have never been there. He reached his arm around to grab his Alpha's shoulder, desperately trying to pull them as close as possible. Burr willingly obliged, bringing his mouth down against his omega's neck, sucking and nipping at the tempting space where it joined his narrow shoulders; the spot where he so badly wanted to sink in his teeth and permanently mark Michael as *his property*. The smaller man mewled in response, rolling his hips and tensing his ass around the alpha's shaft.

"Oh *shit,* baby, I'm gonna – a" Burr choked the words into Michael's back as he held his hips hard enough that they would probably bruise. He felt the omega tense beneath him, panting as his own climax hit, and held off just long enough for the man to ride it out fully before he let go, emptying himself into the omega with a groan and a few choice curses. They lay panting together on the rug, locked together by the alpha's knot, and after a moment or two, the omega started grumbling. Realizing how heavy he must be on top of the slight man, Burr shuffled until they were spooning on their sides. Within a minute, he sensed that the omega had fallen asleep, the post-coital haze and remaining alcohol acting as the most effective sleeping draught. He could feel himself also getting close to sleep, but fought to remain conscious as long as he could, enjoying the feeling of holding the mystery omega in his arms. He resolved to move him to the bed as soon as the knot went down, since the rug (as nice a rug as it was) probably wasn't the most comfortable place for the man to wake up. With a slight smile, Burr eyed the marks he had left behind. There was no doubt about it. He was screwed. But for now, at least, he felt happy.

DAY ONE

Michael woke in an empty bed, sticky, but serene. He'd forgotten to close the blinds last night, and the sunlight streaming in through the window made the room seem somehow more welcoming, even without Joseph by his side. There was a sense of peace in him, his muscles ached pleasantly, and the whole place smelled of warm cinnamon. He relaxed, a smile on his face, before the last thought stopped him. Cinnamon? There was no reason for him to be smelling cinnamon. He couldn't smell himself, and Joseph had a beta scent, a calming, neutral musk that he'd sometimes compared to fresh laundry, or lavender. This smelled earthier; cinnamon, coffee and petrichor. It was so comforting, and yet just that thought alone was enough to make him uneasy. He levered himself out of bed, feeling his overworked muscles stretch and pop with the effort. He made his way over the window, checking that he wasn't flashing anyone in the courtyard below before drawing the blinds. He padded barefoot over to the dresser, still puzzling over what had happened last night. True, he had gotten a bit too drunk. He and Joseph had argued ... he remembered that now. He winced as he remembered what they had said to each other. The insults they had thrown into each other's faces, making a scene that no doubt would be all over their social circle already. Grabbing fresh underwear and jeans from the drawers, he frowned. He had given back his engagement ring. He looked at the space where it should be and another rush of memories hit him. There had been another bar ... he felt a hot flush of embarrassment at his treatment of the other omega. The guy was right, he'd been disrespectful. Michael would never have reacted like that on a normal day. Getting into fights, insulting his elders? That just wasn't him. He wasn't quite sure how he'd avoided being put in the hospital after saying things like that.

Passing by the mirror, Michael caught his reflection out of the corner of his eye and did a double-take. He turned to face the glass fully and froze as the final memories from the night before came rushing to the surface. The alpha from the bar, who'd been watching him. Whose name he hadn't even thought to ask before he threw himself on the man like some knot-hungry teenager. He turned a deep red, his cheeks and ears matching the shade of his many, many hickies perfectly. Michael took a few steadying breaths. God, he'd been so stupid. They hadn't even used protection. What if the guy had some horrific, incurable STD? Where was his self-control? It wasn't his first heat, he should have known better by now. Admittedly, it had come out of nowhere, but still. He was an adult, dammit. He grimaced as he examined himself again in the mirror. The damn things were everywhere, and although he was mortified, he felt a slight hint of pride at the thought that apparently Mr. Officer had been as into it as Michael was. He pressed the ones on his neck with morbid interest. There was a perfect cluster over the spot where his mating bite might one day go. Luckily none had broken the skin, but he was surprised that the alpha had even ventured into that territory. It seemed a little risky, to say the least. He sighed. There was no way he could show up to work at the hospital like this. Maybe if he had been mated, but by now he was sure everyone on the ward knew he was single. That's what he got for dating his boss, he supposed. Time to call in sick.

Around 3 p.m., he got the dreaded call. Michael eyed the name flashing up on his display warily. Joseph was probably the last person he wanted to talk to now – okay, maybe second to last, after the guy from last night (who thankfully appeared to have left before Michael woke up). But if he was going to be a mature adult about this – getting drunk and having risky sex notwithstanding – then he couldn't avoid his ex forever. He picked up the phone.

"Joseph," he responded casually, "I wasn't expecting you to call after last night." That was a lie. The beta had always been a fan of the "talking-it-out" approach. Plus, skipping work probably hadn't been the best idea.

"You weren't at the hospital today. I was worried." Michael had to fight back a laugh. The only thing Joseph would be worried about was his reputation if his (now ex) boyfriend became known for being an unreliable worker.

"I wasn't feeling too well. I think I ate something bad at the restaurant." The lie slipped off his tongue almost like his alpha's – he had to stop himself. He couldn't think about *that*. Not ever. And definitely not while he was on the phone to his boss. He could hear Joseph's sigh echo through the speakers.

"Can I come and see you?" Michael blinked. He hadn't been expecting that. If Joseph came over, he would see the marks on his skin, and smell the apartment, and know everything. But if he said no ... was it over? Did Joseph maybe want to apologize for last night? Michael toyed with the hem of his T-shirt nervously. It was probably over either way, but at least if the beta came over he might get some answers.

"Sure. In an hour or so?" He could hear the other man's relief when he answered.

"Yeah sure, I'll swing by after work. Love you." There was an awkward pause before the other man hung up, as Michael wondered whether he should say the same, and Joseph probably regretted opening his mouth at all. Placing his phone back on the counter, the Omega sighed. As doubtful as it was that it would make a difference, he would try and clear the evidence of last night's encounter. At least his random heat seemed to have passed. He would see a doctor about going back on suppressants tomorrow. At least he hadn't been out of commission for a whole week this time. He remembered his younger heats with a prickle of embarrassment. He never wanted to go through that again. Grimacing, he threw open some windows and began stripping the bed.

When Joseph arrived, Michael was ready. He'd spent the last two hours preparing for this conversation and was almost relieved at the sound of the intercom buzzing. He took a deep breath and let the beta in.

His apartment was practically gleaming, with no trace of last night's encounter left. It had been strangely difficult to do, as Michael had found himself enjoying the alpha's scent more as time passed. But he had been thorough, and now the only reminders of what had happened were on his skin, hidden under the thick winter layers his casual clothes provided. It seemed unlikely that he and Joseph would be getting up to any ... *other* business while he was here, so he figured his secret would stay safe. He answered the door in silence, deciding that he would let Joseph do the talking. It had been his words that did the real damage last night, after all, so if he wanted Michael back, he could damn well work for it. The beta seemed appropriately subdued as he entered, and Michael even felt the slightest twinge of guilt as he took his shoes off at the door and placed his bare feet on the rug that they had *defiled* the night before. Once again, there was a rush of heat at the memory, but Michael managed to keep his expression neutral while he was being observed. Once he was sure he had the omega's attention, Joseph launched into his speech.

"Michael, I know we're not exactly on the best of terms right now, and I know that's partially my fault. I said some things last night that were unkind -"

"You called me *barren*." The beta winced, but continued.

"They were unkind, but I didn't mean them to be. I was attempting to address a situation we've been avoiding for a while, and while I may not have stated it in the best way, I still feel like my concerns are relevant and justified, and if we're going to continue along this road, we should maybe seek some advice from –"

Michael cut in, speaking incredulously. "*Continue along this road?* Joseph, I ended things last night. Was throwing the ring back at you not clear enough? Do I need to draw you a goddamn diagram? It's over." The beta paled a little, but did his best to plow on.

"Well, I think that was a mistake, and perhaps we should rethink that a little. We work well together, you know that. Our families have been close for a long time. It would be insane to break things off this late in the game. Together, maybe, we could..." He trailed off as Michael shook his head slowly, almost feeling sorry for the beta. He sighed.

"I can't believe you seriously think that I'm going to be with someone who would humiliate me like that, just to make our families happy. I care about you a lot, Joseph, but -"

"I love you, Michael. You know that. I might not always express it in the best way, but I do. I don't want us to end like this." Michael groaned, realizing there was only one way to do this. He looked his ex-boyfriend straight in the eyes.

"Joe, I slept with someone else last night." There was a dead silence as the beta fought to process what he had said. Finally, he spoke.

"What?" He sounded genuinely like he didn't believe what Michael had said. Hating himself, the omega pulled up the hem of his sweater to expose the mess of hickeys on his hips.

"My heat came on unexpectedly, I was upset because of what had happened, and I'd been drinking all night, and ..." He stumbled, not wanting to continue, but knowing he had to. "It just happened. It was a dumb mistake, but as far as I was concerned, our relationship was over." Joseph looked dumbstruck.

"Who was he?" he asked, in the quietest voice ever. Michael grimaced.

"Just some alpha I met at a bar." Now the other man looked like Michael had slapped him.

"An alpha," he stated in an incredulous tone, "you slept with an alpha? What happened to "all alphas are dumb knot-heads" and not being able to trust them?" The omega flushed.

"I told you, I was drunk! It's not like I'm dating the guy. It was a one-night stand; I'm never going to see him again." The beta still looked upset, his eyes glued to the hickeys on Michael's skin, and the omega shuffled uncomfortably under his gaze.

"Possessive, was he?" he eventually muttered, seemingly disgusted. Michael held his tongue, though he wanted to tell Joseph the truth, that he'd liked it, liked the feeling of being wanted by someone else that much that he would want to mark him as his own. The beta had never minded when other men and women had eyed him up or even blatantly flirted with him. He'd always been so sure that Michael would never stray, never want anyone else. He could still hear the husky growl of last night's alpha in his ear, claiming him. *Mine.* Just the thought of the word sent a shiver down his spine. "I still ..." Joseph sighed, a pained expression on his face. "I still want to try. You made a mistake. We all make mistakes. Every couple has problems, and maybe I said the wrong thing, and maybe you got drunk and slept with someone else because you thought we were over. I can understand that." Michael raised an eyebrow in disbelief.

“Just like that? I slept with someone else and you’re not even angry?” The beta grit his teeth and fought to keep his voice steady.

“Of *course* I’m angry, Michael. I am ... fuming. But not at you. This alpha took advantage of you while you were drunk, and I fully intend to find out who he is and ... That’s not important.” He took a deep breath. “But I value our relationship and I think we’re better than this.” He pulled a ring box out of his pocket and tossed it to the omega, who caught it with an automatic movement. “Anyway, in case you’d forgotten, we’re going to dinner with my parents tonight, and you’re going to need that. They *cannot* find out about this.” Michael felt slightly queasy as he opened the box and looked at the ring inside, but he took it out and slipped it back onto his finger as he was told. Joseph was giving him a second chance. It was more than he had expected. And this marriage was about more than them, after all. The Adams and Robinson clans had been close for generations. There was a strong chance that either or both of them could be cast out if they broke off the union based on just one night of drunken stupidity. The beta turned to leave, but stopped at the door. “I do love you, Michael. You just make things so damn hard sometimes.” The omega grimaced, before going to Joseph and hugging him gently.

“I’m sorry. It won’t happen again. And for the record, I love you too.” His fiancé sighed.

“I know you do.” He sniffed the air with a frown. “And next time you bake something, save some for me. You better fit into your suit for our wedding.” Michael’s stomach turned to ice, but Joseph was gone before he could notice anything else was amiss.

Dinner that night was exhausting, as interactions with the Robinson clan always were. Michael was used to it at big social events, but he usually avoided one-on-one encounters like the plague. Joseph's parents were nice enough, but they were also very intense, and proud. Like Joseph himself, Michael thought. He shut the front door to his apartment and threw his dress shoes into a corner, wincing as his cramped toes finally got the chance to move from their curled-up position. Normally, his fiancé would have come home with him on nights like this, to work off the steam from having to stay quiet and polite all evening, but after the revelations of the morning, they had decided it might be best to avoid sex for a while - at least until the alpha's bruises had faded from Michael's skin. He still felt wound up from the night, though, so what better way to unwind than with some solo fun? He made his way to the bedroom, leaving a trail of clothes as he went. These were the kinds of things he wouldn't be able to do once he was married and living with Joseph. The beta was always so damn tidy. Plus, he thought using toys in the bedroom was tacky, so the next part would definitely be frowned on. Grinning at the thought of his fiancé's disapproval, he reached under the bed and pulled out his toy box, feeling himself leaking slick in anticipation. He selected a heavy butt plug and got to work opening himself up, gasping at the contact between the cold metal and his skin. Breathing deeply, he eased the toy in until it finally popped into place, the thick neck keeping him just wide enough to be uncomfortable.

Lying back against the cushion, he set to work, stroking his already semi-hard dick and amusing himself with thoughts of how scandalized the Robinsons would be if they knew he did this sort of thing. He'd fought so hard to live away from his family, the overly respectable and ultimately *boring* Adams clan, but still carried the same veneer of respectability they all had. No one ever thought about how the quiet, refined omega was behind closed doors. No one except ... His eyes were drawn to the deep red marks on his thighs, the bruises on his hips and the lines across his chest from where the alpha had raked his fingernails across tender skin.

He took a shaky breath and wiped a bead of pre-cum from the head of his cock. It was okay, he figured, to relive it in his mind, just this once. It wasn't like he was cheating. The alpha wasn't actually here, fucking him right now. He and Joseph had been on a break, so there was nothing bad about the memories. He shuffled further backwards into the pillows and the plug tugged at his rim, making his hand falter for a moment. God, that felt good ... almost as good as the alpha's tongue. Michael could feel himself getting heated as he remembered that tongue, how dirty it had made him feel. Why did Joseph never do things like that? He had to beg the beta to go down on him at all, and rimming was out of the question. But last night he'd had to practically beg the alpha to stop rimming and just *fuck him*. He moaned, pulling on the plug a little so a rush of slick was set free. He let it coat his hand before resuming his jerking, closing his eyes and imagining his alpha was there. *Mine.*

It didn't take long for him to reach climax, spilling over his fist with a groan, as in his head, his alpha soothed him and told him what a good omega he was, how perfect he was and how much he was wanted. There were tears in his eyes that he hastily wiped away, frowning at the instant guilt that followed his fantasy. He didn't belong to anyone, especially not some knot-head he'd hooked up with once, and who hadn't even stuck around until morning.

Sighing, he sat up from the bed and grabbed his phone from the nightstand. He scrolled through until he found Dr. Rennis and fired off a quick message. Hopefully he could get this crap sorted out and get back to his normal life as soon as possible.

DAY TWO

Dr. Rennis frowned as he re-read his notes, twirling his ballpoint in his hand while Michael sat on the examination bench impatiently.

"I've gotta say, Michael, I really don't have much experience with omega-specific medicine. I'm a general practitioner, not a gynecologist. I've never heard of someone having such a short heat. But you aren't experiencing any adverse effects?" The omega shook his head and cast a despairing look at his colleague. The doctor sighed. "Well, I don't think there's much I can do then, in that case. You're clean for all the STDs we can test for at this point, so I wouldn't worry about that too much. I'm not going to prescribe you suppressants, just in case you're pregnant, but we won't be able to tell that for another month yet - unless you get another heat, in which case, call me."

"Wait, pregnant?" Michael did a double-take. "Me and Joseph have been trying for months, and it wasn't even a proper heat. Surely I can't be?" Rennis shrugged, placing his clipboard back on the desk.

"Honestly, I don't know. But a heat is a heat, so I'd keep the possibility in mind. And alphas tend to be more fertile than betas, so..." He gave Michael a knowing look. "I just wouldn't rule it out. I'm signing you up for an appointment with Dr. Mitchell in a month's time. Even if you've had a heat by then, he'll still have a better idea about this blip that you've had. He's a gynecologist, works at the Brooke Street clinic, you know it?" Michael nodded, still feeling slightly numb. Pregnant? That couldn't happen. "Well, good. Anyway, I have an official patient in like, three minutes, so get your ass out of here." He waved a hand towards the door and started redressing the examination table.

"Thanks, Dr. Rennis," the omega mumbled.

“No problem,” the doctor answered. “And start calling me Luke, we’ve worked together for four years,” he called over his shoulder as Michael left the room.

He made his way down the corridor of the hospital, idly playing with his phone in his pocket. Should he tell Joseph? True, they’d been trying for a while now, but ... His stomach churned slightly at the prospect of the beta’s reaction. He’d be angry, that was for sure. Maybe it would be the final straw, the ultimate insult. Not only had Michael slept with someone else when they’d only been broken up a few hours, but he’d gotten pregnant with another man’s child. If his parents found out ... Michael felt a deep chill settle into him. No, Joseph didn’t have to know. Not yet, anyway. If it turned out that he was actually pregnant, he would have to deal with this. But right now, he would keep his mouth shut and act like everything was fine.

ONE MONTH

Michael sat in the waiting room of the Brooke Street Omega clinic, nervously tapping his phone on his thigh. Around him, happy omegas chatted with their partners and family members, oblivious to his discomfort. He could see a heavily pregnant female omega in the corner of the room, reading a novel while twin toddler pups played with dolls at her feet. The scene gave him a heavy, icy feeling in his stomach, like he'd swallowed a rock. He focused on taking deep breaths and paid attention to his heartbeat in an effort to calm himself, trying to block out the cheery atmosphere. He had just managed to successfully take himself into his happy place (a quiet, sandy beach where just he and Joseph were walking hand in hand) when a smiling beta nurse came and tapped him on the shoulder, bringing him abruptly out of his reverie.

"Michael Adams?" He nodded, feeling nauseous. "Great. If you'll just follow me, I'll take you to see Doctor Mitchell. Is it your first time visiting the clinic?" He walked behind her, trying to make himself look as small as possible.

"Um, yes, I work at the hospital, so usually I just get a checkup from one of my colleagues." Her scent was soft and soothing, and reminded him of lilies. She glanced back at him and smiled.

"Well, it's always nice to meet a fellow medical professional. Are you a doctor?" He shook his head.

"No, a nurse, I work in the recovery wards." She chuckled.

"Well I'm glad you didn't let them do this checkup. We're the leading provider of ante- and postnatal care in the country. I hope you get good news," she replied. He nodded, although her definition of good probably wasn't the same as his. They arrived outside the door to Dr. Mitchell's office and she gestured for him to enter. “Have a nice day,” she remarked cheerily, before leaving him for the waiting room again.

Dr. Mitchell greeted him with a nod and waved at him to sit down. He was another beta, friendly and middle-aged, with a slightly harried expression and frameless glasses. He stayed silent for a short while, reading what Michael assumed was his file on the computer, before finally turning to the omega with a smile.

“Mr. Adams, you’re new to my clinic, yes? Can I call you Michael?” The younger man nodded, feeling simultaneously soothed by his demeanor and nervous about where his questions were going to lead. “And you’re unmated, were on suppressants until a few months ago, and have been trying for a pup with your partner ... A beta, correct?” Another nod. “So, then, Michael, could you tell me why you’re here?” The omega took a deep breath.

“Well, doctor...” He struggled to find the right words to describe his current situation. “Me and Joseph – that’s my partner – had been trying for quite a while, and we didn’t have much success. Honestly, we kind of thought it might be a problem with me ... I used to have very bad heats, I was put on suppressants at a young age to try and control them, and my old doctor said that might be an issue. Then about a month ago, we had a – a blip, in our relationship.” Dr Mitchell raised an eyebrow and Michael flushed. “We had a serious argument, and temporarily split up. I wasn’t on suppressants anymore, but my heats had been pretty regular since I stopped taking them, and I wasn’t due one for another week at least. But I was out at a bar and got drunk and –” he paused, feeling like he might be going into too much detail. “Anyway, I had, like, a mini heat? And ended up, uh, sleeping with an alpha.” The doctor frowned.

“A mini heat?” Michael nodded.

“Yeah, it came on really suddenly, within about half an hour, and was gone by the next morning. And it was really intense, like I didn’t even ...” He felt a shudder of guilt, “I didn’t even use protection or anything. I was so stupid.” Dr. Mitchell looked concerned, glancing at Michael’s notes again before resuming his questioning.

“You say it came on very quickly – did it start before or after you made contact with this alpha?” Michael thought for a moment.

“After, I think. I’d seen him at the bar, but it wasn’t until after we went outside that I started feeling it coming on.”

“Had you made physical contact?” Michael nodded.

“Yeah, I was going to get into a fight and nearly fell, but he caught me.” He could almost feel the ghost of those hands on him as he spoke, and shivered. The doctor wrote something down on the pad on his desk, then turned back to Michael.

“So your heat came on, you had unprotected sex with this alpha, and then it passed. And you haven’t had your scheduled heat since then?” The omega shook his head. “Did your previous doctor give you a pregnancy test?” His heart dropped. Please no.

“No, he said it was too early to tell. But that was only two days after it happened. I know I should have done one in the meantime but ... Honestly, I was kind of hoping it couldn’t be that. I mean it wasn’t even a proper heat.” His tone had become pleading by the end of his sentence, and the look the doctor gave him was sympathetic.

“I understand how you feel, Michael. But it sounds like what you experienced was a true heat. They’re rare, but not entirely unheard of. When two individuals who are both unmated and genetically compatible with each other meet, and there is an initial physical attraction, this can trigger simultaneous mating readiness in both individuals. So when you and this alpha met, and were attracted to each other, your heat would have been triggered, and this in turn would have sent him into a rut. The timing was unfortunate, but medically, nothing was awry. In fact, I'm impressed that your body was capable of producing the reaction; not many are. However, this does mean you're almost certainly pregnant. Copulation during a true heat has been proven to have a 78 percent positive pregnancy rate. I'll get you some tests, and then we can discuss your options."

Joseph sat on the edge of the bed, staring at his shoes.

"I, just ... I don't get it, Michael. We tried, for so long. And now you slept with this ..." He struggled, trying to find the words for a moment. "This stranger, one time, and bam, you're pregnant? How could you even ...?" Michael felt his temper flare.

"It's not like I chose to get knocked up, Joseph. I didn't look at him and think, oh yeah, that's an idea, I just broke up with my boyfriend, so why not make this guy my baby daddy?" He spat the words out, feeling his anger rise with every syllable. Joe flashed him a look full of hurt before exploding.

"Well, then, what the hell were you thinking, Michael? How could you be so stupid?" Michael felt like he'd been slapped across the face. Stupid. Of course that would be the word Joseph used to describe him. It would always be the same. Perfect beta Joseph, with his seven years in med school and his reputation to uphold, would always think less of Michael. And why? Because he had to work hard for his grades? Because he *only* wanted to be a nurse? Yeah. Clearly he was *stupid*. Deserving of less, worth less. But not enough to continue taking Joseph's shit.

"I'm sorry, Joseph. I'm sorry I couldn't magically choose to become pregnant when we were together. I'm sorry I was upset, because you ended our relationship and some *stranger* had to come to my rescue. And I'm sorry my heat came on early, when I was around an alpha, because *you* wanted us to have a pup together before we got married, instead of waiting like everyone else, and told me to stop taking suppressants. But I am having this pup, whether or not you think that's the right thing to do." He fought to regain his composure, feeling sick as he thought of how his family would take the news of him and Joseph breaking up. Of how Joseph's parents would take the news. He looked at the beta, feeling his pain. Joe had been so desperate to be a father, to do better than his own had. And Michael would be lying if he said he hadn't felt that drive too. "I'm not asking you to help me, but if you still want a relationship with me, I'm leaving that door open. Make your own decisions, Joseph. But don't think that I'm just going to stand by and agree with you anymore. I have someone else to worry about now." By the time he finished his tirade, he was breathing heavily. Joseph stared at him, seemingly stunned, and Michael could feel himself becoming embarrassed. This wasn't like him. He didn't do these kinds of things.

"What about the alpha?" Joseph's question took him by surprise.

"W-what? What do you mean?" Michael looked at him, confused.

"The pup's dad. The guy you ... the guy you slept with."

Michael flushed, thoughts of that night flitting through his mind like a guilty secret. "What about him? I haven't seen him."

Joseph frowned. "But don't you think he should know? I mean there's going to be a pup out there with half his DNA, that's kind of a big thing."

"You think I should ... hunt him down?" Joseph shrugged.

“Probably, he deserves to know. I know I’d want to.” There was silence for a moment. Michael had been so caught up in thinking about what this meant for him and Joseph that he hadn’t even considered the father. Eventually he spoke.

“I don’t know where I would start. I don’t even know the guy’s name.” Joseph wrinkled his nose in distaste.

“Seriously? You’re having the guy’s kid and you don’t even know his name?” Michael glared at his partner.

“Joseph? Back off.” The beta swallowed and nodded. Michael sighed. “But yeah, you’re right. I should have known more about him. Honestly, I should never have gotten myself into this at all. But I do have to find out who he is.” He paused. “And I have an idea. I could go back to bar see if he’s there often. Or at least ask the bartender if he remembers.” Joseph looked doubtful, but shrugged.

“It’s worth a try, I guess.” He sighed. “Do you want me to come with you?” The omega looked at him sternly.

“No, I don’t think that would be a good idea.” He paused. “Are we going to try and make this work, though?” Joseph stood up and crossed the room to where Michael was standing.

“I guess so, yeah,” he sighed, pulling the omega into a hug. “What other choice do we have?” Michael could feel his spirits sinking as he hugged his fiancé back. He had a point; they were boxed into a corner, no doubt about it. All they could do now was try to salvage the relationship and give this pup all the love they had. And if the mystery alpha wanted to be a part of that, maybe it would be for the better.

FIVE WEEKS

Michael stood in front of the police station, a look of determination set on his face. He was doing this. He'd found his adversary from the other night at the bar. Drake Burr, the omega had told him, was the name of the mystery alpha. God knows it had taken enough to get it out of him. A police officer, apparently a damn good one, was the father of Michael's pup. His own father would probably tear him to pieces if he knew. Better to keep the man's identity a secret than to let daddy dearest know that his precious son had gotten knocked up by a blue-collar worker. Joseph was only considered acceptable because one day he would inherit the family fortune; a lowly vice detective would never make the cut.

Taking in the brownstone facade of the building, Michael knew that he had to do this. No matter what his own feelings about alphas were, this pup deserved to know both its biological parents, and to get all the love and support it could. He entered the building with butterflies in his stomach, and approached the front reception with as much false confidence as he could muster. The receptionist, a pretty male omega with short blonde hair and a surfer's tan, gave him a bored glance and then went back to his paperwork.

"Um ... Hi," Michael started, hoping that he wasn't speaking too quietly, "I'm looking for someone." The receptionist didn't even look up as he pushed a form towards him.

"Missing persons is on the third floor, room 108, fill in this paperwork before you go in and they'll be able to help you." Michael flushed.

"N-no, that's not what I meant. I'm looking for a police officer. He works in the vice department, I think." The receptionist (his name tag said Dale) had a pained expression as he gave Michael a once-over.

"Right ... visitor center is down the corridor and to the right, you can get a nametag there, and then vice is on the second floor, you can follow the signs once you're through security." Michael felt a rush of relief as he nodded his thanks to the omega and left the queue.

The station was bigger than he'd expected, and reminded him a little bit of a rabbit warren. He had followed the signs, but was now stuck in a corridor full of closed doors, none of which appeared to be marked. He could feel his anxiety rising as he debated knocking on one of the doors, before deciding that he didn't want to get kicked out.

He made his way further down the hallway, only to be greeted with a dead end. Evidently this was the extent of the vice department. He'd just turned to leave when a door clicked open and the sound of laughing could be heard. Michael spun on his heels and came face to face with a short, female alpha, dressed in a smart office shirt and with gold earrings so large he was surprised her earlobes didn't stretch to her elbows. She was also the very last person he wanted to see.

"Aunt Maria! What ... what are you doing here?" He fought to keep his voice cheery as possible, but inside he was panicking. His father's sister worked here, in this station? His father could not know he was here. Maria raised her eyebrow at him.

"I work here, Michael. I think the bigger question is what are *you* doing here, and..." she paused, scenting the air, before her face broke into a wide smile. "You're pregnant! Congratulations, honey! When's it due?" He felt his stomach twist into uncomfortable knots at her obvious excitement.

"Eight months, but ... We haven't told the family yet. Could you possibly keep it a secret? Just for now?" His aunt pouted for a moment, but then gave a slightly gentler smile.

“Of course, sweetheart. But your parents will be thrilled, so don’t wait too long to tell them, okay?” Her expression shifted back to confusion. “But really, why are you here? Your father wouldn’t be too happy if he knew you were hanging around the station. God knows he goes on enough about it at me.” She seemed amused, and in that moment Michael decided that he liked her. Not enough to tell her the truth, however.

“I’m looking for one of your officers. Drake Burr? He helped me out a while back when I was in some trouble on a night out. I was hoping I could speak to him and thank him properly. I was a bit too wound up at the time to process things, you know?” Maria seemed to consider for a moment.

“That sounds like Burr, alright. Well, I don’t see why not. He should take a break anyway, the man’s going to work himself to death.” Michael smiled, relief washing over him like a wave. Now all that was left was ... to tell the guy he was pregnant. Instantly, the anxiety was back. “Do you mind waiting in one of the interrogation rooms? It’s not pretty, but we’re not really meant to take civilians into the operations office. Breach of security, you understand?” Michael nodded and she ushered him into a room off the corridor that smelled of cleaning fluid and stress. The combination made him a little nauseous, but he made himself focus. Maria waved. “I’ll just be a moment,” she called as the door closed behind her, and Michael was alone. He sighed, taking in the metal desk and bare walls, save for the large two-way mirror on one side. He had to pray that no one was in the room beyond when he actually spoke to Drake. If Maria was anything like his father, he wouldn’t put it past her. She seemed nice enough, though. Smart, undoubtedly, but kind too. It was strange to think that someone like that existed in the Adams clan. While wits were one of their strongest characteristics, the majority of the family weren’t exactly gentle.

He picked at a hangnail absently as thoughts of his family went through his head. Even with all the plans he and Joseph were making, there was no guarantee that this pup would be accepted into the fold. There were just too many uncertainties. If the pup looked like him, maybe it would be okay. But Drake and Joseph looked nothing alike. Drake had dark eyes, freckles and sandy brownish blonde hair, while Joseph was blue-eyed, pale and porcelain in everything except his auburn locks. And if the pup presented as an alpha ... Michael could feel despair settling heavily on his shoulders. They had no chance.

His self-flagellation was interrupted when Burr himself walked into the interview room. Maria obviously hadn't given him any warning, as he froze upon seeing Michael seated at the desk. For a moment, the omega thought he would bolt, but he quickly recovered his composure, making his way over and seating himself on the opposite side.

"So ... I'm guessing you're not in here with information for a pending investigation." His tone was questioning, and Michael couldn't help but be slightly amused.

"Is that what my aunt told you?" Drake stared for a moment, not quite registering the statement, before the penny dropped.

"Lieutenant Adams? Maria Adams? Is your aunt?" The color seemed to drain from his face when Michael nodded.

"Yep, my father's sister. I'm Michael, by the way. Michael Adams." He held out a hand for the alpha to shake, which was silently accepted. "I don't really know her that well, though. And she doesn't know why I'm here, either." Drake's brow furrowed.

"Well, that makes two of us. I might have thought you would come by a bit sooner, but... Why now?"

Michael took a deep breath. Time to take the plunge. "Officer Burr, I'm pregnant." The silence in the interview room was palpable. Drake blinked at him for a few seconds, trying to make sense of what he'd said.

"You're ... pregnant?" The omega nodded, looking nervous. "And it's definitely mine?" That earned him a glare. Michael and Joseph still hadn't had sex since the breakup, and it was starting to wear a little on his nerves.

"Put it this way," he bit out, "If it's not yours, it's pretty damn miraculous." Drake flushed, and Michael had to admit that he couldn't really blame the guy. After all, they'd had sex without even knowing each other's names; was it really such a stretch to imagine he slept around a lot? Which reminded him. "Oh, and I did a few tests as well, and I'm clean, so either you are too, or I'm very lucky." The alpha shook his head, his expression returning to one of concern.

"I'm sorry. This is on me. I should have –" Michael cut him off.

"Let's not do the whole blaming thing. Me and my boyfriend have been doing that a lot recently, and to be honest, I'm sick of it." Drake's frown deepened.

"Boyfriend?" Now it was Michael's turn to feel embarrassed.

"We were on a break."

"Right." He bristled at the slightly derisive tone in the alpha's voice.

"I'm sorry, I don't think our relationship is really any of your business. The important thing is that we're together again now. So if you don't want to be in this pup's life, it will still have two loving parents." Drake was quiet for a moment before answering, and his expression was impossible to read.

“You don’t want me to be in their life? Your boyfriend doesn’t mind that it’s not his?” Michael grimaced.

“That’s not what I meant,” he sighed. “No, Joseph – that’s my boyfriend – is not *okay* with this pup not being his. But he loves me,” *I think,* he added in his head, “and he wants to support me through this, which includes supporting my pup.” He paused. “*Our* pup, I guess.” The phrase sounded awkward, but it still sent a strange thrill through him. He chose to ignore it for now. “That being said, I get that this wasn’t a planned pregnancy, and you and I don’t know each other. And if you decided that you wanted to be there for us too, then I would like that. I can’t promise that Joseph will like you very much to begin with, but he won’t stop you being around your own blood.” The alpha stared at him for a few more moments, making Michael’s stomach flutter. Somehow just being around Drake again, just inhaling his scent and seeing him so close by, was making it very hard to concentrate. He remembered Dr. Mitchell’s words, “an initial physical attraction,” and instantly felt guilty. He needed to make this relationship with Joseph work. He couldn’t let biology get the better of him again and threaten his future, and his pup’s future too. Finally, Drake stood and nodded, his expression complacent.

“I suppose that’s all I can ask. Will he be going with you to your scans and stuff?” Michael started slightly.

“I…I haven’t asked him,” he admitted, “But I’ll ask.” Drake shrugged.

“I guess as your boyfriend he’ll want to. But if he’s busy, I’d be happy to accompany you. I want to be there for my pup. And …” he trailed off slightly and seemed unable to quite look Michael in the eye, “For you, too, if you need me.” Michael had to fight back the wave of affection that threatened to overwhelm him for a moment. His inner omega was straining at the leash, wanting nothing more than to go to the security of *his* alpha. But he knew better than that. Michael offered the man a brief smile. Best to keep this businesslike.

"Thank you, I'll be sure to do that. Do you want to give me your phone number, so I can contact you?" The alpha's face brightened for a moment, and he fumbled with his phone for a moment before giving the required information. Once it was done, they faced each other slightly awkwardly, from opposite sides of the interview table. "I guess I should go, then ..." Michael mumbled, unsure of how to end the visit. Drake nodded.

"My break finishes soon anyway, and then I've got a mountain of paperwork, and three witness statements to process ..." He grimaced and carded a hand through his dark hair, and Michael smiled slightly at another glimpse of the real human personality behind the strong, silent cop persona. The alpha caught him looking and smiled back, before holding out a hand to shake. "Call me if you need me; as long as I'm not in a meeting or at a crime scene, I'll answer. My shifts are all over the place right now because of a changeover in HR, so ... don't worry if it's at night or anything. And, for the record," he sighed, glancing momentarily at Michael's lips before looking away again, "I'm sorry about this whole thing. I didn't intend for this to happen and hope this doesn't cause you to be hurt or," he frowned slightly, "create any issues between you or your boyfriend." Michael let out a dry chuckle.

"Don't worry, I don't think you're going to be the one starting anything there." Drake raised an eyebrow slightly, but didn't ask any questions, instead directing the omega out of the building in silence. Outside when he was about to leave, Michael suddenly found himself being drawn into a hug. Without thinking, he relaxed into Drake's arms, pulling himself tighter against the alpha's chest and surrounding himself with his now-familiar musk.

“Thank you for finding me,” Drake mumbled into his hair, “thank you for letting me be a father to our pup.” All too soon it was over, and Michael almost protested as he was released from the warm embrace. He managed to keep a hold of himself long enough to watch Drake disappear back into the station, before sinking down onto the building steps. It was just the hormones, he told himself as he struggled to draw breath. Every nerve in his body was shouting at him to run back in there, to find his alpha and cling to him until they were mated. But that wasn’t right, for anyone. Ignoring the concerned look from passersby, Michael managed to get to his feet and start off towards the tram that would take him home. It was going to be okay, he told himself, and for the sake of the pup in his stomach, he prayed he was right.

EIGHT WEEKS

Michael tugged at his collar as they waited in the hotel reception. He hated big family dinners, although at least some of his parents' focus would be on the Robinsons instead of just him. Next to him, Joseph stood poker straight, with the only indicator of any nervousness on his part being the slight tapping of his foot to the music in the lobby. As always, both sets of parents were late. These days, the couples seemed to be competing at who could keep everyone waiting the longest. He heard a sigh of relief from his fiancé and switched his attention to the front entrance, where both sets of parents were entering together, chatting leisurely. Michael fought the urge to flip them all off , but instead, followed Joseph over.

"...and of course, then the damn thing wouldn't start! That's the problem with not employing a skipper anymore, I just don't have anyone to keep her going while I'm not around." Joseph plastered a smile on his face and Michael followed suit.

"Father, what a pleasure, it's been too long." The beta gripped his father's offered hand, both standing slightly awkwardly and inclining their heads towards each other. "And Mother, you're looking radiant." He stooped to give an awkward side-hug to his mother, who was significantly shorter than he. "Mr. and Mrs. Adams, charmed as always." He shook hands with both of Michael's parents.

"Please, Joseph, as we've said before, you can call us Samuel and Michelle," his mother replied graciously. Michael and his parents exchanged brief nods, Samuel giving him a once-over before speaking.

"Your hair's getting too long, don't they make you keep it short at that damn hospital? You're a health hazard. You look like a hippie." Michael kept his eyes on his father's collar, making it clear he was listening without appearing to challenge his judgment. “And that shirt’s getting tight on you; can’t you get new clothes? This is a nice hotel, for God’s sake.” Michael’s jaw tensed, but otherwise he didn’t react except for a brief, “Yes, Dad.” His mother said nothing until Samuel had walked ahead of them to join the Robinsons. She wasted no time in getting to the point.

“You smell different; are you well?” He was once again reminded of the perceptive skills of female alphas.

“I’m pregnant, mom.” She narrowed her eyes slightly, the cogs clearly turning in her head.

“You don’t seem too pleased about it; I thought you two had been trying for a while?” Michael fought back the nerves as he added yet another lie to the list.

“It’s just early days, that’s all. It took a while to actually get pregnant, I don’t want to get everyone’s hopes up only to lose the pup a few months in.” She nodded, seeming to buy his excuse.

“I understand. You were a difficult pregnancy; God knows we nearly lost you a few times.” She frowned as she remembered. “But hopefully you should have an easier time, being ...” She paused, not wanting to say the word “omega,” “... as you are. Take your vitamins, go to your scans.” She sighed as they rejoined the group, who were now seated. “And for God’s sake, get a haircut.”

By the end of the evening, Michael was exhausted. The constant small talk and pleasantries had done nothing to soothe his anxiety, and to make things worse, he hadn’t even been able to drink. Of course, after about ten minutes at the table, his mom had told everyone he was “with child,” so he had to cope with the gushing from Joseph’s mother and the stern educational talks from their fathers on how to properly raise the pup –none of which either he or Joseph had any intention of following. The experience was made worse with the knowledge that in fact this pup would not be carrying on the Robinson family genes, and unless he and Joseph managed to procreate in the future – which, right now, was looking exceedingly unlikely – there would be no heir to the Robinson business, fortune or name. He watched his fiancé struggling more and more with the atmosphere until he finally came to his rescue, feigning tiredness and nausea, at which point both mothers insisted he be escorted home.

They stood outside Michael's apartment, Joseph leaning against the omega as he unlocked the door.

"Do you ... want to come in?" Michael felt weirdly uncomfortable just saying the words, and the beta seemed indecisive as they stood in front of the open doorway.

"I mean ... it's kind of late, and I have an early shift tomorrow. It's not really a good idea –"

"No, it's cool, I get it, don't worry." They stood in silence facing each other for a moment before they both laughed, shedding some of the tension. Joseph sighed.

"This is weird, huh? It's like when we were first dating, right at the beginning." Michael rolled his eyes, remembering the occasion his fiancé was talking about vividly.

"Right, when I invited you in for coffee and you freaked out and told me you were a virgin, right out? I think my neighbors still remember that, to be honest." The beta's pale cheeks colored slightly.

"I didn't want you to have any false assumptions, or expectations of me –"

"We'd been friends since third grade, Joe, I knew you were a virgin. God, I don't think I knew anyone more of an awkward nerd than you." Joseph scoffed slightly.

"You mean apart from you?" Michael shrugged.

"At least my mom wasn't my prom date."

"At least Jack Meers wasn't mine." Michael winced at the reminder of his poor taste in men. Meers had been your standard alpha knot-head jock, and their relationship, while passionate, had been exceedingly brief.

"Low blow, dude. Low blow." The beta smiled softly at him, before leaning over and kissing him gently. It only lasted a few seconds, but it was progress.

"I've missed you, Michael." The omega smiled slightly and fidgeted with his jacket sleeve. Joseph looked into the apartment wistfully, and then back at his fiancé. "I really do have to be in early tomorrow; otherwise I would stay over. Do you have the afternoon shift?" Michael nodded. "Ah, well. I'll drop into the ward in the afternoon, maybe, but otherwise I'll call when you finish." He gestured for Michael to go inside. "Go inside, you'll catch a cold or something. You've got to stay healthy." The omega sighed.

"Text me when you get home. Goodnight, Joseph." He got a smile in return.

"I will. Goodnight, Michael."

TWELVE WEEKS

They met outside the clinic, about twenty minutes before the appointment. Michael took a moment to appreciate the alpha's lean figure and thoughtful expression before greeting him.

"Sorry, the trams are running late. Were you waiting long?" Drake's eyes seemed to light up when he saw the omega had arrived, and he shook his head.

"Only about ten minutes or so. No biggie. Are you nervous?" Now he was. Michael had forgotten about the alpha's accent, the way his eyes seemed to fill with concern whenever he saw the slightest bit of worry. He'd also forgotten how damn hot his scent was. He did his best to take shallow breaths when he answered.

"Only slightly. It's just an ultrasound, nothing painful or difficult, right?" Drake nodded and they walked in together. Last time Michael was at the clinic, it had been almost painful to see all the pregnant and nursing omegas; now it felt strangely calming. He wasn't sure if it was because he was more comfortable with being a dad now, or just because he was with someone. Or because of who that someone was. Despite his best efforts, he had to admit that he was developing a certain affection for the handsome officer who currently sat next to him with a protective arm thrown around the top of his chair. It just felt right. Michael settled back against the seat and tugged the arm around his shoulders. Drake glanced down at him briefly, but didn't say anything, instead just giving a soft smile before returning his attention to the other occupants of the room. And there it was; that alpha scent, the loving pheromones that just made him want to curl up with this guy – who was most definitely not his fiancé – and never leave. He was distracted by the arrival of the nurse, a different one from last time. The girl looked barely old enough to have gotten her nursing degree, and kept glancing at Drake with clear nervousness.

"Mr. Adams? I'm here to take you to the scan room. Will your mate be coming with you?" They both started slightly, and Drake laughed uncomfortably.

"We're not, um..." The look of confusion was clear on the poor girl's face, and Michael stood, aware that he probably stank of alpha. "Shall we go?" he asked Drake, who looked, if possible, even more embarrassed than he did. They followed the nurse down the hallway to the scan room, where Dr. Mitchell was waiting.

"Doctor, I didn't realize you were doing my scans as well." The beta smiled.

"I've been assigned to you, I'm afraid, orders from the top. So, you're two months in now, how have you been feeling?" Michael lay down on the examination table and pulled up his shirt as the doctor gestured.

"I've been okay, I guess. A bit nauseous when I wake up some days, but nothing severe enough to be late to work or anything." He winced a little as the cold gel was applied to his stomach. Dr. Mitchell nodded, handing Drake a form.

"I presume you're the father?" The alpha nodded, looking surprisingly docile under the spectacled gaze of medical authority. "Good. I'll need you to fill out this paperwork on your family's medical history, just so we can check if we need to screen for anything in particular." He turned back to Michael. "Shall we get started?"

Michael couldn't hide his nerves as Mitchell ran the sounding wand over his slightly distended stomach, watching the screen in tense anticipation as the grainy image shifted. Drake came over and silently took his hand, rubbing a thumb over his knuckles in a comforting motion. Suddenly the alpha gasped and leaned forward, his eyes practically lighting up. The doctor laughed. "Yeah, that's your pup. No limb deformities that I can see, and a strong heartbeat. You're definitely about twelve weeks along, so if all goes well, I'd say you'll have a November due date." Michael was too distracted by the picture on the screen. The pup was barely recognizable, but he could see its tiny heart beating. Drake looked down at him, beaming.

"That's our pup," he whispered, just loud enough for Michael to hear, "I'm gonna be a dad." The awe in his voice made the omega's heart skip a beat. It was almost painful to hear his happiness, under the circumstances. Dr. Mitchell flashed him a sympathetic look, and Michael was thankful for the beta's presence. If only Joseph was as excited about this pup, maybe he wouldn't feel as guilty. They had barely been speaking lately. He watched the doctor and Drake chat for the rest of the appointment, knowing the alpha would fill him in on what was needed afterwards. Right now, he felt disconnected from it all.

Drake waited at the tram stop with the omega, still smiling. Every few moments, his hand went to the front pocket of his jacket, where his copy of the ultrasound was. Michael watched him, amused. Drake was going to be a great dad, he had no doubts about that. And it would be good to have someone around the pup who'd had a better childhood than him or his fiancé. Although to be fair, he didn't really know that much about the alpha.

"Drake, what are your parents like?" The officer glanced at him, looking surprised.

"They're great, wish I could see them more. They live down south, so I can't visit as often as I'd like." He gazed fondly into the distance. "My family are from Georgia, I only moved up here for work. It was meant to be only a few months' placement, but..." He laughed. "I've got five brothers, and every time I call, they ask if I'm tired of the city yet. Don't know how Ma and Pa put up with us all." Michael smiled. The way the alpha spoke about his family gave him a warm feeling in his chest. Maybe they could visit Georgia sometime once the pup was born ... he shook himself slightly, remembering that Drake's parents were unlikely to take kindly to him being married to someone other than their son. He sighed and watched as the tram approached their stop, and the alpha turned to him. "I'll see you at the next scan, then?" Michael smiled.

"Yep, 20 weeks. I'll text you." He paused, then stood on his tiptoes and pressed a kiss to Drake's cheek. "Take care of yourself, officer." The man's eyes softened and he gazed down at the omega wistfully.

"You too. Don't work yourself to death at that hospital." Michael gave him a mock salute before boarding the tram, and waved as it pulled away. Drake waited until it had turned the corner before leaving. He was going to be late for his shift, but right now, he didn't care.

SEVENTEEN WEEKS

Michael woke to his doorbell ringing incessantly. He groaned as he glanced over at his alarm clock. Who the hell had come by at 9 a.m. on a Sunday? It was his first day off in weeks, so they better have a good excuse. He padded barefoot over to the door and opened it with a scowl, which quickly changed into an expression of surprise when he saw who it was.

"Sorry for the early start." His aunt pushed a box of chocolates into his hand and made her way into his apartment without being invited. "Very late housewarming gift," she explained with a dismissive gesture, "since I wasn't around when you actually moved out and escaped the family's claws." She looked around the living area with a raised eyebrow. "Not bad for a first place." Michael finally managed to find words.

"Aunt Maria. I ... honestly was not expecting you. At all. Not to be rude, but why are you here?" The alpha shrugged, still examining her surroundings.

"I was in the area and thought I'd drop by, see how you and the pup are. Check if the daddy is here keeping an eye on things." The omega fidgeted slightly.

"Joseph is working today. And we haven't found a place together yet, so..." Maria looked him dead in the eye.

"Michael Adams, don't you try and lie to me. I'm a police officer. I know about you and Drake Burr. You and I both know that pup isn't a Robinson, and I don't know why you're trying to pass it off as one."

Michael sagged, knowing his time was up. "How long have you known?"

His aunt shook her head sadly. "Since I met you in the station. I could smell him on you still. Not recent, but... there. I'm around him a lot, Michael, I recognize my own officers. I knew that pup was his." She sighed. "I waited in the viewing room, next to where you and Drake were talking, and watched to make sure my suspicions were correct. I hope you can forgive me." Michael looked up finally and frowned at her.

"Forgive you?" She grimaced.

"I was in breach of your trust, I'm sorry. I shouldn't have listened, and I should have told you as soon as I knew. But I didn't know you too well... I didn't want you to panic and run off. My brother is a good man, but he's never exactly been supportive. I didn't want you having to go through this on your own if the Robinson boy wasn't there for you. I'm guessing he knows?" The omega nodded, slightly dumbstruck.

"You wanted to ... support me?" She shrugged awkwardly.

"Family is family, Michael. And I've got to say, I admire you. An Adams kid, going into nursing? That took balls." She grinned, showing sharp teeth. "You remind me of me. Shame you weren't an alpha, you could probably be running the damn place by now." She pulled out a cigarette from behind her ear, then remembered and tucked it back away. "Ugh, if I'm going to be a great-aunt, I guess I'll have to be healthy and responsible now." She pulled a face, before directly addressing him again. "How has Drake been to you? He's been all over the place at work recently; I've been cutting him some slack, since I figured he's going to be a dad and all." Michael couldn't help a small smile coming to his face.

"He's been ... great, actually. I never expected him to do this much for our pup, especially when he isn't even being acknowledged by the family. He's been going to my appointments with me, helped me shop for baby stuff ..." He shook his head slightly and cleared his throat. "Yeah, he's been very helpful." Maria fixed him with a knowing look.

"Helpful, hmm? Tell me, how *helpful* has your fiancé been?" Michael fidgeted nervously.

"He's been under a lot of stress recently. He's had to put in late nights at work, and I don't think –" The alpha snorted.

"That kid doesn't know late nights, I'll tell you." She turned to Michael, suddenly looking very earnest. "Listen, if you ever need support, or money, or even a place to stay, I want you to know you can come to me." She retrieved a pen from her purse and wrote her number on his arm. "Don't make me worry about you," she muttered, with a pained expression, "it's not good for my nerves. Come by more often so I can keep an eye on you. And your daddy doesn't need to know we even had this conversation," she added with a wink. With that, she was gone, letting herself out with a smile and a wave, and leaving Michael with emotions too jumbled to work out.

EIGHTEEN WEEKS

The recovery room was quiet for once, and Michael hummed to himself as he made his rounds. He only had three patients, and none of them had woken from their anesthesia yet, so he was surprised Nurse Haldon arrived back from her break looking flustered and uncomfortable. He tried his best to ignore the uncomfortable feeling he got when she wouldn't stop glancing his way over her desk. Eventually he gave up.

"Jess, is there something you want to tell me?" The beta reddened, and her discomfort seemed to grow.

"N-no, it's fine. I just ... Are you and Dr. Robinson still together?" Michael frowned.

"Yeah, we broke up a couple of months ago, but we got back together again the next day ... Why?" He had a pit in his stomach that was growing with every moment.

"Oh ... Okay. Cool, I guess." He fixed her with a glare and approached the desk.

"Jessica, what are you not telling me?" His colleague seemed like she was trying to sink into her chair as she did her best to avoid his eye.

"It's just ... I was passing by the staff room on the way back from my smoke break ... And I happened to see Dr. Robinson in there ..." her voice got very quiet as she spoke the next part of her sentence, "with Dr. Tarnov ..." A strange sense of calm came over Michael as he asked the next question.

"And what were they doing in the staffroom, Jess?" The poor beta looked terrified when she answered.

"They were kissing, Michael. I'm sorry." He took a deep breath. Of course Joseph was cheating on him. Joseph, who was so set on them getting married and having this pup together. He fought off a wave of nausea before he spoke again.

“Thanks for telling me, Jess. I appreciate that.” She looked mortified.

“I really am sorry, Michael. I can’t believe he would –” He cut her off.

“I have an hour of my shift left. I *really* don’t want to talk about it. On cue, a patient started shifting in the bed opposite of them. Michael plastered a smile on his face and made his way over to their bedside. “Good afternoon, Mr. Rhodes, how are we feeling today?”

Joseph sat across from his fiancé in the staff canteen, a frown on his face.

“What’s wrong, Michael? Is there something wrong with the pup? I’ve got to get back to my rounds soon –” The omega waved a hand to silence him, before taking off his engagement ring and sliding it across the table.

“I want you to have this back. For good this time.” The beta’s face changed from confusion to mild panic.

“Michael?”

“I know about you and Dr. Tarnov. Someone saw you two in the staffroom earlier and was nice enough to tell me. I don’t want an explanation, and I don’t want an apology. I just want to know how long it’s been going on.”

Joseph seemed to flounder for a moment before he sighed and answered quietly. “Four months.”

Even though he had been prepared, Michael still felt a dull pain at the thought. He’d been lied to for four months and hadn’t noticed a thing. Sure, the beta had been taking a lot of late nights, but... “Why didn’t you just tell me? Why didn’t you just dump me if you didn’t want me anymore?” His voice broke a little and he had to fight to hold back tears. He'd been counting on Joseph's love and support, for the both of them.

"My father –"

Michael scoffed. Of course. The family argument. "Your father can go to hell, Joe. I'm done with this. I'm done with your family, and I'm done with this relationship." He stood to leave. "And I want a transfer to another department. You're my boss, you can do that." The beta looked like he was about to say something, but just nodded, defeated, as Michael walked away.

TWENTY WEEKS

Michael lay on Dr. Mitchell's examination table for the third time, watching as his scan was examined with interest. Next to him, Officer Burr fidgeted impatiently in the chaperone's chair. Finally, the doctor spoke.

"Well, Michael, I can confirm that the pup looks healthy. Do you want to know the sex?" The omega stifled a laugh at Drake's strained expression.

"No, we agreed that we'd prefer for it to be a surprise." That was a slight exaggeration. Michael wanted it to be a surprise, and after some minor threats, the alpha had agreed to wait until the birth to find out. The doctor gave him a knowing look.

"Alright, then. Well, your Caesarean is booked in for week 40, and you've looked through all the literature I sent you?" He nodded. "Good, then we're all set. I'll let you get cleaned up and file these." He picked up their paperwork and exited the room, leaving Drake and Michael alone. The alpha wasted no time, pulling the pregnant omega into a gentle embrace. Michael held on tightly, letting the man's scent soothe the growing nerves he felt.

"I'm scared, Drake," he whispered, finally admitting it. "What if something goes wrong? What if –" The alpha let out a warning growl, shutting him up.

"Everything is going to be fine, Michael. You've got this." He gazed into the smaller man's eyes, deadly serious. "You are going to deliver this pup, and you are going to be a great father. I couldn't wish for anyone better to be carrying our pup." Michael could feel tears threatening and he dropped his eyes to the ground – or as much of it as he could see past the moderately sized bump of his stomach. It might have just been his hormones, but recently everything the alpha said seemed to be making his heart beat faster. Since he and

Joseph had split up they'd texted every day, and had met up several times. He wasn't even bothered when people mistook them for mates anymore. When he looked up he was stunned by the intensity of the alpha's gaze. His breath caught as Drake leaned in, pressing their lips together. For a moment Michael was too surprised to do anything, before it finally registered and he responded enthusiastically, almost pulling the alpha back onto the examination table. The kissing quickly turned into full-on making out as Drake gripped his ass and trailed kisses down his neck, making the omega moan quietly. "I've missed this," the officer whispered into his ear, before nipping his earlobe gently. "I haven't stopped thinking about that night – about you." Michael flushed, pulling his alpha in for another long kiss before responding.

"That makes two of us," he murmured, smiling shyly. Drake's face broke into a smile and they split apart, the alpha chuckling as he helped Michael straighten his shirt collar. "We should probably go before Dr. Mitchell gets back in here and wonders what we've been doing." The alpha shot him a mischievous grin.

"I'm willing to risk it if you are." Michael rolled his eyes, still smiling.

"Knot-head," he mumbled affectionately as they left the office. Once they were outside, Drake wordlessly took his hand and they walked together to Michael's tram stop. This time when they kissed goodbye, there was no hesitation.

WEEK TWENTY-SIX

Drake and Maria frowned at Michael as he stood in front of the mirror, attempting to stare down his own reflection. *It's okay,* he told himself, *it's just a baby shower. No one is going to hurt you.* His shoulders sagged as he admitted the truth. No one was going to hurt him, physically. But it was the first time he was seeing his parents since he and Joseph had split up, and they would finally be finding out the identity of the pup's real father. Apart from him. He knew he had Maria's support, but he was scared of how they would punish him, and terrified for Drake. He had warned the alpha about his parents, but the officer sounded doubtful as to whether they could really be that bad. He prayed they wouldn't scare him away, not when he was finally realizing how good this relationship could be. He finally turned away from the mirror.

"How do I look?" His boyfriend beamed at him.

"Hot as hell, as usual. Though in my opinion that shirt would look much better on my floor." Maria snorted.

"You two make me sick. Come on, we're going to be late." She flashed the omega a smile and he managed to send one back, despite the painful twinges in his lower abdomen. They'd been happening since last night; the stress was really getting to him. He made sure to breathe through it, slowly, fighting to remain upright. Drake's expression changed to one of concern as he watched the omega.

"Are you okay, Michael? You look kind of pale." Michael nodded, unable to speak as another wave of cramps made him threaten to spew his breakfast across the bedroom floor. Finally, it passed.

"Yeah, just stressed. You know how I get anxious. I think my body is telling me not to go to this." He chuckled weakly, but

Drake still looked concerned. Maria called to them from the hallway.

“Get a move on, boys, it’s time to go!” Michael managed a step forward, before suddenly feeling an intense, sharp pain in the definite area of his womb that sent him dizzy. He vaguely heard Drake shout to Maria, panic in his voice, before he blacked out.

The next few hours passed in a blur, as Michael faded in and out of consciousness. Some things he understood: the press of warm hands against his neck and stomach, the press of needles into his skin, the words “Caesarean,” “premature,” “placental abruption.” Other things were more confusing: the inside of a squad car, Maria arguing with someone, and the pain, *God, the pain.* He must’ve been crying at one point, because he could feel someone wiping away tears and stroking his cheek gently, but he wasn’t sure who it was. Throughout it all, there was Drake’s cinnamon scent, and the tight pressure on the alpha’s hand on his own. Others came and went, but the alpha never left.

Michael woke up when the room was golden, the sunset just visible out of the window by his bed. Next to him, his boyfriend slept, his hand still linked to Michael’s. Feeling hazy, the omega shifted slightly, and was rewarded with a sharp burst of pain in his abdomen.

“Oh, thank God you’re awake,” he heard from his left. He turned his head and saw Maria in another chair, her makeup in streaks down her face. She pressed the call button before reaching out and stroking the hand not currently occupied. “You have a daughter,” she murmured, answering his question before he even asked, “born at 3:14 p.m., 1 pound and 9 ounces. She’s tiny, and she’s being fed through an IV, but the doctors say she should be fine. She’ll have to stay in the hospital for a while. So will you, though.”

“What happened?” Michael asked finally. She sighed.

"Your placenta partially detached. They had to deliver her early or they would have lost both of you. I called in a favor and managed to get a squad car to take you in; it was the fastest way." The nurse arrived and began taking Michael's vitals. Maria waited until he had left before continuing. "The Caesarean didn't take too long, but they were worried that you weren't stabilizing for a while. Your parents were here, but..." She glanced over at Drake, a guilty expression on her face, and Michael understood. He hadn't expected them to accept him, not in such a short time. Maybe in a few years, but for now it was just the three of them. Michael, his alpha, and their pup. He felt a warm glow in his chest at the thought, and finally let himself relax. On cue, his boyfriend stirred, and Maria stood, stretching awkwardly. "I'll go get some coffee."

"Thank you," Michael called after her as she left the room, and she smiled back tiredly. Drake blinked a few times before realizing the omega was awake.

"Dammit, Adams," he mumbled quietly after a few moments of silence, "everything has to be a big surprise with you." Michael snorted, wincing at the tenderness in his abdomen again before receiving a gentle kiss on the forehead from his alpha.

"We never thought about names," he said eventually, watching the last of the sunset dip under the horizon, "guess that was kind of short-sighted." Drake nodded, then smiled.

"I reckon Maria might have at least one suggestion. And, uh," he shot a stealthy glance at the omega, "I quite like the name Lynn, for the record." Michael chuckled, remembering their conversation about parents earlier that week.

"Lynn Maria then, or Maria Lynn?" Drake squeezed his hand gently, his thumb once again comfortingly circling Michael's knuckles.

“I’m feeling Maria Lynn, to be honest. Is she going to be an Adams or a Burr?” Michael felt butterflies in his stomach, but eventually answered.

“If she gets to be a Burr, can I be too?” There was silence for a moment, before the alpha realized what he meant. Slowly he shook his head, but a grin was spreading across his face.

“Michael Adams, that was the worst damn proposal I have ever heard.” He kissed his omega softly, avoiding jostling him too much. “So you’re damn lucky I love you,” he whispered.

HUNGER

A WOLF SHIFTER MPREG BUNDLE

Preston Walker & Liam Kingsley

Disclaimer

This is a work of fiction. Names, places, characters and events are all fictitious for the reader's pleasure. Any similarities to

CHAPTER ONE

"Looks good on you, Darius."

"You think?" Lifting his arm, Darius slowly rotated his arm, staring down at the fresh ink that now stained his skin. A familiar band that every member of Hollow Rock knew - the symbol of the Alpha. A band that defined their role for all to see. It wasn't his first ink, but none of his past pieces came close to the importance of this one.

Darius was the new Alpha of the Hollow Rock Clan.

No one expected the previous Alpha to die. He was old, yes, but hearty and always eager to put those who spoke ill back into their place. Everyone within the pack knew their place and when to bow down. He was strong, determined, and wise. Yet, he passed in his sleep. The pack healer said it was from natural causes, that his heart simply gave out.

The loss was hard, but everyone moved on. They had a new leader: Darius, a proud young man who was the pack wild card. No one ever knew what to expect with him, which made the whole pack rather anxious about him accepting the title, but like always, he surprised them; Darius was quite a strong leader.

From the moment he accepted the title, Darius had been honoring his position. Setting up a proper burial for his predecessor, meeting with the elders, and properly branding himself.

Ryker stood beside the new Alpha, giving the young man a slow look over. Beta for several years now, he had not left Darius' side since he had been given the title, assisting the man with the transition.

"You've been doing good, kid."

Giving a weak laugh, the younger eyed him, a brow raised. "Really? I feel like that's just slightly condescending."

"Not entirely, no." Darius grinned, shaking his head. At least he was an honest man. "I am surprised, but also cautious. I remember what you were like as a boy, Darius. It would be completely foolish to not tread lightly and follow your actions closely."

As he spoke, Darius just laughed, standing now. He was a good image for an Alpha, well-toned and healthy. He was a handsome young man, with dark skin and thick curls that hung heavily in his face. Ink covered his skin, each carrying their own story. Ones that he told proudly during their feasts.

"Say what you will, but I know you're just angry at me. Honestly, I don't know why the hell Lazarus chose me instead of you. I mean, you're the Beta." It was strange, saying his name, rather than boss, rather than Alpha, but his title had been passed on and they all needed to move on as well.

"I'm not angry, idiot." He was one of the few who could get away with such names when Darius was a boy - without being challenged - and the only one who could do so now. "Lazarus made it clear that I was not fit to lead. If I was, I would have challenged him long ago for the title while he was weak - but I didn't. If he didn't name me, I'll respect his choice. Even if I'm not completely pleased with the fact he picked a boy, he was one of the wisest leaders we had in quite a long time. I trust his judgment. Even if I may question it."

Listening to his words, Darius chuckled a bit, shaking his head. Ryker had always been the long-winded type. A strong hunter, but he wasn't the best when it came to plans or strategies. That was always Lazarus' area, and now his own.

"As long as you don't hate me, I'm not here for some civil war shit," he teased and Ryker sighed, rolling his eyes.

"I wouldn't dream of it, kid. Now, there are some things we need to talk about. Such as planning the next hunt. As the new Alpha, you must lead your first hunt and bring us a prize for the feast. We also need to speak about other matters. Such as-"

"Ryker, I know. I'm not some wet behind the ear cub. I know what the hell I need to do and how to do it."

The man glared as he was cut off, a twitch of irritation marking his brow, and Darius just grinned, enjoying pressing the man's buttons. Now a step above the man, he didn't have to worry about getting smacked around for his back talk like when he was a boy.

"You're cocky, though, which is my biggest concern. I don't need you getting too big a head and ending up dead before the damn ink dries. The last thing we need is another Thorn."

The name was practically hissed, and Darius just laughed, shaking his head. He wasn't going to be a repeat of Thorn; he wasn't an idiot. While he never met the man - an Alpha before his time - the man apparently was always in over his head. Wishing to impress a mate, he went after a prey that ended up being more a predator than himself. He was ripped to pieces, and the funniest part to Darius was the woman admitting even the display, had it worked, wouldn't have won her over. A truly amazing story that always kept him laughing.

"I'm not going to be a fucking Thorn, Ryker. I know what the hell I'm doing, besides, I heard he was a terrible hunter. I know what the hell I'm doing, unlike some people." There was truth to his words. Since he was young, Darius had always been quite the hunter. This feast wasn't his concern, he knew how to hunt and he was confident in his ability to lead. There were other aspects that he was worried about.

"There are other things we need to discuss as well. You're still young, Darius, but you're our leader now." He already knew where this conversation was going and he had no interest in hearing it, but he allowed the other to ramble on, regardless. "It's time that you settled for a mate. It shouldn't be hard, you're quite desirable to the young members within the clan." As he spoke, Darius grinned, and Ryker already started to grow annoyed before the young man even spoke.

"Am I? Gosh, Ryker, I never thought you saw me that way. I'm flattered, honestly, but you're not really my type-"

His words were cut off as the man glared at him, a low growl to his voice that only made Darius laugh. "Shut up before I do cuff your ear, boy. Mind yourself. I might be a step below, but I'm still your elder. Keep that in mind."

"Oh, trust me, I do." As he spoke, he took a step and his body leaned forward, invading Ryker's personal space. He forced the older man to lean back to create some space between them. His teeth caught the light as he chuckled, sharp and straight - he knew better than to show them so freely, but he didn't really care. The young man was always a bit of a show-off, a fact he never hid about himself. Reaching out, his arm wrapped around the other's waist, yanking him close and speaking softly, eyes trailing over the older man. "You are older than me, more trained, but also more worn out. Those old bones and muscles are starting to wear on you. There's a shift when you step on your left foot."

Darius always noticed these small things, it was one of the many reasons he became such a strong hunter in the first place. Never rushing, always observing and listening, he tracked his prey better than most his age. He had been taught how to hunt by Lazarus himself, so his skills weren't shocking to many. Just how he boasted was. Most of those taken in by the Alpha were humble - he was anything but.

With a growl, deeper than expected, Ryker shoved back the young man, glaring at him for a moment before whacking his hand against the side of his head. A small yelp was heard, and Darius cupped his red ear, stepping back now. While such a strike could be viewed as shocking, Ryker still saw the boy for what he was - a young man with much to learn. It would be his responsibility to shoulder the burden of helping him learn. This view was obvious to Darius, from the way the Beta acted around him, even before he took up the title. A, begrudgingly, caring older brother.

"I will never know what the hell Lazarus saw in you, boy. Pull that shit again and I'll have you stepping with a limp, got it?"

Staring at him for a moment, Darius held his gaze in a challenging manner before just giving a grin, nodding. "I'll get you for that, one day. Right now, I have other matters to attend to, more important ones." Now that caught his attention. Looking over at the man, the clan Beta raised a brow, silently curious to learn more. Ryker was an expressive man, he didn't need to speak for Darius to understand what he was feeling or expressing. "When Lazarus was in charge, we lost a few of the pack members. I understand that he let them wander for different reasons, but this is a fresh start. Most of them wandered due to conflicting views with him, and I plan to bring them back. It doesn't matter how far they may wander, we are a pack, we are a family. I will bring them home and make amends to have them stay."

Ryker didn't respond, not at first. He just stared, a surprised look on his face. Darius continued to hold his gaze, confident in his words. He was speaking like a true leader, bold with his words and chin held high. There was no flicker of fear or uncertainty within his dark gaze. For that moment, Ryker almost looked impressed, something that filled Darius with more pride than he was willing to admit. "You sound confident."

"I'm always confident. I'm going to travel and find them. It won't take me long, I know where all of them reside. There are two to the east, in our old hunting grounds. One out west, living near the river with her cub, and the last to the north, within the human city."

Slowly nodding as Darius listed off the few, he took pause when he mentioned the city and quickly met the man's gaze, frowning. "You're going after him? What good does that runt serve our people? He cannot hunt, nor does any woman here wish to mate with him. Childless, lacking survival skills, and just damned awkward. What good will he bring to our people?"

As he spoke, Darius just grinned, chuckling. Laughing as if he knew the punch line to a joke that Ryker wasn't aware had been told. "I said, we are a family, and I will bring everyone back. Wrongs can be righted and views can change. Amendments can be done. We are a family, Ryker. Every one of us - even our little Omega. Now, do be a good boy while I'm gone and make sure this place doesn't burn down?"

"Why must you go? There is much to be done here, we could easily send others out. I could go."

"No. I must go. I want to show them their new leader - I want a chance to speak to them, on their grounds and terms, to prove I am willing to listen. Plus, I'm far more charismatic than you, old man. I can bring them all back, even our runt."

While he made a face for a moment, Ryker eventually sighed, rolling his eyes. "It's not like you'll listen to me, anyhow. I'll handle things here."

Reaching out, Darius gave the man a firm slap on the back, beaming. "See! You're getting the hang of this new order. I think we'll be just fine, old man."

"You are going to give me gray hairs."

CHAPTER TWO

The sun was finally starting to set, and Quinton couldn't be more excited. He always enjoyed the evenings more than any time of the day - it meant that he would finally take time to himself, in his home. Despite working within the city, Quinton was, quite honestly, not a very social man. If it was up to him, he'd much rather spend the day tucked away in his small abode with a book and a cup of tea.

The evening had grown dark very swiftly, thanks to the heavy rainfall. By the time Quinton made it back to his apartment, his jacket was already soaked through and his arms were trembling. Fishing out his keys, they jingled in his shaking grasp nearly falling from his thin fingers, he finally managed to open the door. Leaning his body against the thick wooden door, he used his shoulder to nudge open the stubborn piece, sighing as it swung up with a loud squeak. This place was cheap and the landlord didn't ask many questions - if his tenants didn't ask any in return.

Stepping into the dark apartment, Quinton gave a violent shudder from the cold, hand slapping against the wall a few times before the lights flickered on. The bulbs flickered a moment before casting a dull yellow light across the barely filled apartment. He had grown quite use to the interior of this building, from its tattered old couch to the plain laminate, on which a large black mass sat.

"SHIT!" Shouting out loudly, Quinton stumbled backwards, tripping over his own feet. His shoulders hit the door with a loud bang, rattling in its frame. Pressing himself flat against the solid piece of wood, he stared at the creature with wide, terrified eyes.

On his counter lay a large cat - a puma, to be exact. Its fur a sleek black, paws crossed over one another. Its tail flicked in a lazy manner, golden eyes locked on Quinton.

Following each move he made. Panting heavily, his heart started to recede from his throat and back towards his chest, giving him a chance to catch his breath. While it waited, the large mammal yawned, climbing down and stretching. Its large claws bore into the old wooden floor, causing deep and ugly scars against the surface. Able to see the creature up close, Quinton noticed a part of its ear missing. The color drained from his face and Quinton took a sharp breath, groping at the doorknob, shifting towards the edge.

Noticing the movement, the dark puma gave a low, deep growl, rearing back before lunging forward. During the forward motion, its form began to shift. The large, black form morphed, slimming. Outstretched paws melted into thick arms; the paw that slammed against the door became a rough, scarred hand. Bright, yellow eyes became dull, yet there was still a spark within them as the form became that of a man, now trapping Quinton against the door with a wicked grin.

"Evening, Quincy."

Darius stared down at the smaller man with a hungry look, his own nails still digging against the wood of the door. Quinton didn't speak, he simply stared at the man like a deer in headlights. His body was still shaking; trembling fingers wrapped around the doorknob. Reaching out, Darius grasped his wrist and slammed it against the door, pinning it beside his head while the lithe man pressed his hand to the other's chest, trying to create some type of space between them.

"D-Darius." His voice was trembling, unable to look away from those dark eyes that seemed to stare right through him. He was a stark difference from the man before him. A lanky young man who seemed as awkward with his own body as he was with other people. His complexion was a few shades lighter than the strikingly dark man before him, with wispy soft brown locks. They fell around his thin face, framing the soft details.

"You look...thin. Do you eat, man? I thought I would find you nice and fat here. Filled with meats and liquor from the spoils of these men. By the looks of it, you turned into a little bird since leaving home." His words were whispered, his hot breath falling against Quinton's face. His chest continued to rise and fall rapidly and he just swallowed.

He never expected to see a member of Hollow Rock Pack, but more than that, he never imagined that he would see Darius again. "W-what are you doing here?" His voice was meek compared to the others, still unable to meet his gaze. "This is pretty far into the city for you." Darius never liked humans. He thought them to be weak, spoiled. He prided himself on the rustic, traditional lifestyle of the pack. For him to be this deep inside the city, a place thick with man and without the pack, well, that was certainly strange.

"I came to find you." Quinton frowned now, unsure how to react. He was never sure how to respond or act around Darius, the man made him quite anxious, if he was being honest. "I'm sure you've heard, but I wanted to tell you myself. Lazarus passed. His heart gave out during his sleep." He did hear the news. Despite not being involved with the pack heavily anymore, he did keep his ear to the ground and information like that traveled through all the packs in the area. There was a small one that was living within the city, trying to forget their old ways and adapt to human life. Quinton had learned through them of the death of his Alpha.

It was heavy news, even for him. That old man was a constant figure in his life growing up. While he wasn't one of the more praised and adored cubs, he was still given special attention. Lazarus still praised him for his intelligence and encouraged him to follow the path he thought was best - even when it took him away from the pack. He had been a very calm, understanding man towards all members of the pack, including the runts.

"I heard." He spoke softly, his gaze falling away from Darius once more, shoulders slumping slightly. While death wasn't a new subject, that didn't mean Quinton enjoyed the conversation. "How…is everyone?"

"Holding strong. We're getting through this together - and have already chosen a new leader." As he spoke, Quinton didn't have to ask. His eyes were drawn to Darius' dark gaze, then towards his exposed arms, running along the ink. There was more than the last time they met, but none of those mattered. Just that intricate band that wrapped around his bicep. Quinton's gaze shot back to him, shaking his head.

"No," he whispered softly, and Darius just laughed, giving his trademark grin, with those sharp teeth and a mischievous glint in his eyes. Even when he wasn't trying, the man had a very powerful image, causing Quinton to press himself further against the door, heart rate picking up once more. The larger man always put him on edge, mostly because he was known to be skittish. As a child, Lazarus often scolded him for acting like prey, much like the deer they hunted. "You?"

"Who else?"

"Ryker!" Quinton answered a bit too quickly and swallowed back the rest of his words. Darius didn't lash out like he feared, just slowly shook his head.

"No. Ryker is strong and bold, but he is not a leader. He's wise and loyal, but not fit to lead the pack. It takes more than wit and good intentions."

"Then why are you here? To tell me that Lazarus has passed?" His question sounded as anxious as he felt, hands trembling slightly, even the one within Darius' grasp. He didn't enjoy being cornered, but being pinned by this man was the worst situation he could imagine.

Darius didn't seem annoyed at the meek actions, thankfully. Instead, he just laughed and dipped his head forward, thick curls tickling against Quinton's forehead as he bit back a squeak when the man came close.

"I came to bring you home, Quincy." That wasn't what he expected to hear. "You've been away from your family for too long - Lazarus was forgiving with your curiosity, but it's time for a new path for the pack. I'm bringing back everyone who left, to see if I can amend what had been lost between us. We're family, after all. You belong back home. With the others, with me."

His words caused Quinton to frown. Slowly shaking his head, he turned away from Darius, looking anywhere but at this insane man who broke into his home. "I can't. I can't go back, Darius. I never belonged, I never fit in. How can you expect me to just suddenly return? They don't want me; didn't you realize that?" A bit of anger seeped into his words and there was a small bite to his tone.

Darius didn't seem to notice because he just laughed and tugged Quinton away from the door now. With a small yelp, his thin form was easily tugged around by the larger man, stumbling after him as they walked. "Careful!" he squeaked out his words, only to be silenced when Darius grabbed his sleeve, roughly yanking it up. His skin was vastly different from the new Alpha's, clean from any scars and nearly flawless - except for the thin ink on the inside of his upper arm. The symbol of Hollow Rock. An imagine given to cubs when they live past their first decade when they proved they were strong enough for this lifestyle, to carry on the pack's legacy.

"You still carry the mark."

“Hard to wash off.” The words were mumbled and Darius snorted a bit. Quinton, while he didn’t voice it often, did tend to have some sarcastic thoughts. Darius was one of the few who ever heard them and always seemed to enjoy them, smiling or even laughing when the comments were voiced. It had been so long since Quinton heard that deep, charming laughter.

“Either way, you carry it. You are part of our tribe and part of our family. Come back. You belong with us, and as Alpha, it is my duty to ensure you have a place among us. Omega or not, you are our brother.”

Staring for a long moment, Quinton just blinked in surprise. It seemed that Darius had changed quite a bit in recent years - he spoke with the same confidence and pride, but it seemed he now had the maturity to back up his words. He was less boastful and more sincere. Too startled to respond, Quinton found himself struggling to speak, and in this time, Darius released the lithe man. Allowing him to have control of his body once more.

“I came all this way to a place I detest more than anything, just to find you. We need you back at the pack. You belong with us. While you’re certainly the worst hunter we have, you’re clever. Your intelligence is important to us. The others may scoff at it, but I can tell what you could offer us. Times are changing, the world is evolving - you know this better than us. I’m asking this of you, Quincy. Return to us, help me in leading our people. I’ll need your knowledge of the world to ensure our survival. To survive, we must adapt, and you know how to do that better than I do. So, come back with me. Please.”

He never once considered returning to the pack. Even when he struggled to find a place to live, made a fool of himself attempting to figure out how Man survived without hunting. Stores were a very strange concept, but he had learned to understand them. They were far too cluttered for him to enjoy them, but there were other creations he found to his liking: large buildings, filled with knowledge called libraries. He spent many days there, reading through as many books as possible -- which unfortunately meant that Darius was right. Quinton had far more knowledge than anyone in the herd, and he had a far easier time blending with man when needed.

Staring for a moment, Quinton swallowed dryly, looking away now. “Fine,” he relented after a long pause. “I’ll come back, but I am not promising to stay!”

Darius just gave his toothy grin, slowly nodding. “Good. Then, let’s go home.”

CHAPTER THREE

"You really did it. You brought everyone back. I don't know how you did, but I'm not going to ask questions. I feel like I'd rather just not know."

"That may be for the best." Darius winked at Ryker who grimaced at the action, turning away from the cocky young man. "The important thing is that everyone is here, back home where they belong. We're stronger now."

Raising a brow, Ryker couldn't help the slight smile, laughing himself. "You really put a big stake on family, don't you? You always call us a family, instead of a pack." Darius shrugged in response, but soon gave a low growl as the Beta ruffled his curls, glaring up at him. "It's cute, kid. Perhaps that's why Lazarus chose you -- to bring us together once more, fix what he had broken."

"You're speaking like the old man now. I can already see those gray hairs starting to sprout. We're going to have to start helping you hunt." Instead of answering, Ryker merely gave a firm pat to Darius' head, making him grunt lightly.

"Either way, everyone is back. I've already given them huts to stay in, though, I mean, some of them already had some." At least all, but Quinton, had a home they left behind. The one that was built by his parents had been taken long ago by a young family several years after they passed. For the time being, he was placed within Darius' old hut, since he now lived within the home of the Alpha.

It was strange, to say the least. These walls were unfamiliar to him, every sound and smell would take time for him to grow accustomed to but he had years to do so. Darius didn't plan to give up this title anytime soon.

"I won't disagree, you've done quite well, Darius. Just don't go getting a big head. That is the fastest way to fall." These were all lectures that he had heard before, but he listened with a low, drawn out sigh. "There are still important matters to be handled, such as the feast and having you settle with a mate-"

"Please, Ryker, not this again. I just got back last night, the least you could do is give me some time to breathe and relax. Just stop fussing for like, ten minutes. I've been putting plenty of thought into the hunt and a mate, so just calm down, old man." Ryker glared, but he said nothing as Darius stood and stepped close to the Beta, leaning into his space. It was clear that he cared little for the personal space of others.

"Give me the evening to myself, I'll come to you in the morning, ready to hunt." He didn't allow Ryker a second to answer, instead turning away and walking from the hut. The home of the Alpha was the largest in the village, though less for a means of boasting and instead to hold meetings. The elders often tucked away in the old building to have discussions that they didn't wish others to hear. Lazarus spent many of his final days hiding away in this home, but Darius was never the type to hide. He enjoyed wandering around the village, spending time with his people.

Today, he wasn't looking to mingle. Darius had a target; once he stepped from the Alpha's abode, he made a beeline through the village and towards his old hut. He knew the path well, memorized in his mind. Many times, as a child, he was dragged by the ear, scolded by his old Alpha and left to return home with his tail between his legs. The number of steps was memorized in the back of his mind.

Now this building he knew better than any in the village. Built by his parents and left to him as a boy. It was small, but comfortable. The door could be stubborn during the summer here, swelling larger than its crooked frame. Darius didn't bother to knock, instead grasping the door and pushing it open with ease. He stepped inside quickly, shutting out the winter chill behind him, silencing the howl of the evening wind.

As the door closed, he was greeted by warmth and the soft crackling of a fire. It seemed Quinton had settled himself in nicely. For a moment, Darius feared the man would be too awkward to touch anything and freeze during the night. "Quincy?" he called out gently but found the man shortly. It wasn't a very large building, but the man was thin and, honestly, easily overlooked. Sitting on the edge of the bed, his hands were outstretched, using a long, blackened stick to adjust the wood within the fire. Raising a brow, he slowly walked over, sitting down beside him. The bed creaked beneath him, and Quinton met his gaze, yet stayed silent until he spoke again.

"You're settling in well, I see."

"I remember your home." That was true. It wasn't the first time Quinton had been in his home. They played together as children and had had a few meetings as they grew older. Some weighed more heavily on his mind than others. "Thank you, for giving me it. I know you're a private sort."

"It was the only one available." Darius tried to justify his choice, but honestly it was a lie. Quinton was homed before any others, giving the lanky man his old abode without a thought. He wanted Quinton somewhere that Darius knew he would be safe and cared for. That was his job, after all, to care. At least, that is what he kept telling himself, in the back of his mind. Even if it was a lie.

"I'm still surprised, you know. I never thought that you'd become the Alpha."

"No one did, not even myself."

"It looks good on you, the band. Besides, everyone says you're doing great. Acting humbler, which is new." Quinton smiled now, softly, staring at the fire. "I heard you've been holding out on the hunt - and mating. I think the latter is the most shocking." Darius raised a brow, letting him speak. It was true, he certainly had a history among the tribe. Aware of his good looks, the young Alpha talked his way into plenty of beds during his youth. Many of the women in the tribe knew his body well, as he did theirs. It was a part of his history he wasn't ashamed of. "Some of the girls in the village seemed upset - each wanting to be chosen. Your pride must feel great."

"I don't want them." His response was a whisper, and Quinton stared at him a few moments, frowning.

"Ryker said as much, he seemed upset you haven't chosen someone yet. I thought it was because there are too many choices, but you don't want any of them? I thought you would have been mated after the first year I left, much less wait this long. What's holding you back?" he asked curiously, and Darius frowned, staring at him a long, hard moment.

"You."

The answer hung in the air, silence engulfing them. The only sound was the crackling of the fire. Quinton attempted to speak, but no words came out. He didn't need to speak, Darius already knew he was confused. That he would argue. So, he spoke first, speaking the moment while he could.

"Do you remember, before you left? That hunt, with Lazarus? You were hurt and licking your wounds."

"You came to check on me..." Quinton's words trailed off, and as he started to remember the details, his face began to burn. His attention focused on the ground, on anything other than the Alpha beside him. "I remember." His words were a strained whisper and Darius slowly nodded. He had heard that Quinton was harmed during the hunt, due to his own clumsiness rather than a true fight. Darius showed up to his abode, curious and concerned. They spoke for a short time, Darius tended to his wounds and brought him liquor to drink. He listened to Quinton recant the story of the hunt while they drank their glasses dry. By the end of the night, in their drunken stupor, the pair ended up in bed together.

"I never forgot. I couldn't. I tried, I've had others. Tasted so many, and yet nothing was the same. There was always this hunger, this need that no one seemed to fulfill. Not like with you." He tried, plenty of times, with plenty of people. Somehow, the spark wasn't there. Something was missing from each of them, that he had only had with Quinton. Of course, Darius had his suspicions as to why it might be. After all, during their youth, they had been rather close, though more so out of circumstance than choice. They had both lost their parents quite young. Quinton was much younger, during a storm that nearly took half their tribe when the river flooded. Darius lost his several years later, due to hunters. His parents had wandered too far during a hunt and some men from the outlying human cities shot them down.

This led to them both raising themselves, while having the Alpha always over their shoulder. Acting as a father where he could, gently pushing them in the right direction and helping to choose right from wrong the best he could, while still running their entire village. Their similar wounds helped the pair to get along - fairly - as children, though Darius did become quite the bully towards their later years, Lazarus often having to step in to scold him, while Quinton scurried off. It didn't seem much changed between their dynamic.

He still refused to meet his gaze, and Darius rolled his eyes. If he was going to continue playing naive, act as if he didn't understand, then Darius would have to be blunt with him: a specialty of his, so it worked out either way. Reaching out, he cupped the man's face and drew him in close, whispering. "I want you." The words were soft, but strong. Quinton shook in his grasp, but didn't have time to speak before Darius kissed him. It was soft, comforting more than anything. Keeping a firm grip on his face, Darius sighed against the affection, running his fingers back through the other's hair. He had waited so long for this moment - he wasn't going to let it slip away.

Darius would make Quinton his.

CHAPTER FOUR

His lips were still as soft as Darius recalled. He couldn't resist a slight smile at that fact, wondering if everything he recalled would be so accurate. Such as the feeling of Quinton's trembling thighs beneath his touch and his tight, warm muscles around his cock. It urged him on further, but Darius was mindful to take his time.

The affection was gentle at first, but deepened as the moment continued. Quinton didn't attempt to pull away from the other, instead, submitting to the advances. It felt as if he melted against Darius' touch, which was the approval he needed to push this further. Keeping his lips pressed against the other's, Darius shifted his hand to the back of the other's neck, sharp teeth carefully biting down against Quinton's full lips, giving his lower lip a playful tug. The action earned him a whimper and the darker man groaned in need. He missed that sound. While he had only heard it once, during their youth, he craved that sound every moment since. No one compared, not even slightly.

Using his weight, Darius pushed them both back against the bed, eager hands gripping fistfuls of the other's shirt, tugging at it playfully. He moved quickly, much quicker than Quinton seemed prepared for. As his shirt was tugged and nearly stripped, he uttered out a few strangled words. "Wait - Darius." His words did give the other pause, frowning as he stared down at the man beneath him. "W-what are we doing?" He stuttered as he spoke, his trembling hands gripping the man's biceps. The smaller of the pair looked terrified, but he looked terrified most of the time, so Darius didn't take it to heart.

"We're fucking." He spoke bluntly, earning a loud, protested squeak. "I've been craving you for longer than I want to admit, Quincy. There's no chance I can keep my hands to myself." He did take a pause though, frowning. "Do you want me to stop?” He would, if that was truly what Quinton desired, but he had a feeling this was just the other’s nerves getting the better of him. As if to prove his point, there was no response to his question. Just a soft stammer and then his head turning away, almost bashful. Grinning, Darius continued with his movements. Pulling away the clothing that hid away the details of their bodies. As he pulled away the layers, Darius realized how much darker he truly was compared to the other. Quinton’s pale skin already showed thin red marks from where his nails had run along while undressing him.

Leaning down, a soft kiss was placed against each mark, then up along his chest. He could feel the other’s thin body trembling beneath him, and Darius just sighed. His warm breath falling against his chest, dark eyes shifted away from the final details of his body and up towards Quinton’s much lighter eyes. For a moment, there was a pause as if he was going to speak, but instead Darius kissed the other. A firm, almost rough kiss as his partner moaned in response, parting his lips and allowing Darius to invade his mouth with his tongue. The affection that started out rushed, however, quickly became heavy and sensual.

As the kiss continued, his fingers wrapped around Quinton’s growing excitement, stroking him without hesitation. His rough hand caused him to gasp and buck in response to the touch, thumb rubbing circles against his hip. All while he touched him, Darius kept his eyes on Quinton’s face and his reactions. They were quite cute, even more so than he remembered. While the memory was still vivid, seeing it again was everything he had craved for so long. Shifting away from him now, Darius stood for only a moment, returning shortly with a small bottle of oil. While Darius prided himself on being quite a masculine man, everyone had their small pleasures, and his came through oils. It carried a strong scent and he used it during times like this, as a lubricant to keep from harming any of those he bedded. It was a scent that far too many of the young women within the tribe carried on them during his teenage years. He felt no shame; he rarely ever did.

Still lying on the bed, panting as before, Quinton gave little resistance when Darius adjusted his legs, spreading them apart so he could fit between them better, his hand dipping between his thighs as well. He kissed the trembling man once more, hoping that the sweet affections would help calm Quinton's nerves, while Darius started to work away at his partner's body.

With the oil spread generously across his scarred fingers, Darius rubbed two against the other's tight entrance for a moment, pressing and teasing before he slipped in a finger, a second following shortly after. Quinton responded instantly to the feeling of something pushing and stretching his body -- he whimpered, and grew louder as the actions continued. His light whimpers turned into intoxicating mewls and moans, testing every ounce of Darius' self control.

Curling his fingers, the larger of the pair explored and teased his partner a few moments longer before finally withdrawing his hand, laying a weak peck against the other's lips. Panting beneath him, Quinton just stared up at him, unable to form words. Though, there really wasn't anything to say in this moment, either way. Running his fingers through the other's hair slowly, Darius provided a soft smile, kissing him a bit softer this time, sweeter even, before shifting their position. Sitting up, he pulled Quinton up towards him and helped him move to his knees. Exposing his pale, smooth skin to his Alpha. A rough hand ran along the curve of his back and small pecks went down his spine. He truly was the worst hunter in their pack, lacking any scars due to his inability to even engage with prey. While it was certainly a flaw for a pack of natural hunters, the sight was hard to handle for Darius - he wanted to run his teeth against that smooth skin until Quinton begged beneath him for more, which was currently the plan.

Wrapping an arm around his thin waist, Darius pulled the pack runt toward him with ease, kissing between his shoulder blades and the back of his ear, speaking in a whisper. “I’m going to mark every inch of your body until you shake with as much desire as I have these last years.” The words alone caused Quinton to groan, and Darius smiled with pleasure. Using his hand from before, the oil was spread along his thick erection, coating each inch in hopes of easing the pain when he overtook the man’s body. He didn’t have to ask to know that the other most likely had no partners since they were last together and that he would need to go forward with caution. Darius didn’t want to hurt him; no, he wanted Quincy to enjoy every moment of this.

Trying to steady his breathing, the smaller male beneath him gripped the pillow tightly, tucking his face against the fabric as Darius pressed his head against his wet entrance, pushing inside only moments later. His cry was muffled by the fabric, biting at it softly, thighs trembling as his muscles were spread wide by the other man’s erection pushing deep inside his body. His entire body tensed and Darius took his time, waiting for the other to relax before starting to shift. He knew the other’s body would be unaccustomed to the large cock swelling up inside him. “I’ve got you.” The words were mumbled against his ear, both hands grasping his hips now, thumbs stroking against his backside as Darius began to move - slowly at first, gently rocking their hips together. Helping to loosen the other’s muscles before pulling back and giving a true thrust inside.

Quinton cried out once more, louder this time, and Darius groaned above him. Those sounds would be the end of him. The way his voice trembled with each gasp and whimper caused Darius’ cock to twitch with excitement, tempting him to forget himself, to pin down the other’s small hips and fuck him until neither of them could move. The thought was tempting, but now wasn’t the time. That could come later - for now, he needed to have Quinton grow accustomed to the feeling of Darius deep inside him, filling him completely and soiling his body.

"Darius." He managed to gasp out the man's name, his chest rising and falling rapidly now as sweat began to dampen his skin, legs trembling with need as his body rocked forward with each, deep thrust. The bed groaned in protest, but Darius paid little mind. Instead, he focused on his movements and the man before him, around him. Nails still biting into his hips, Darius allowed his forehead to rest between Quinton's shoulder blades, thick curls brushing against the other's bareback, lips occasionally brushing and teeth nipping at his skin. His movements began to grow rougher, his hips slapping against his backside with each and every hard thrust. Darius began to pant heavily, shifting his lips from the man's back to his ear, biting and tugging at his lobe. Quinton moaned and whimpered beneath him.

It was all too much for him. Whimpering loudly, Quinton began to plead Darius' name. To what end, he didn't know, but his name fell from his lips regardless, desperate and mewling. As he finally reached his climax, Quinton moaned his name loudly, finally releasing against the sheets. His body tensed and his muscles squeezed at Darius' throbbing cock and the man groaned in protest. He didn't want to stop - he enjoyed being deep inside the other, feeling the warmth of his tight muscles around his cock as he claimed his body. Yet, all good things came to an end, and so he thrust roughly several more times before withdrawing from Quinton's body. His own thick release made quite a mess against the back of Quinton's soft, quivering thighs, dripping slowly down until it stained his sheets.

Moving his hands from his hips, Darius wrapped both arms around the other's waist and kissed his back softly, along his shoulders and then to his jaw, whispering. "You're even more than I remembered. Sounds like that, it's amazing I let you escape me during our youth." At his words, Quinton softly whined, hiding his face against the pillow, and Darius just chuckled. Shifting his body, he came to rest beside the other on the bed, yanking Quinton off his knees and against his side, pressing their damp, naked bodies together. While he didn't resist the movement, Quinton did shift rather uncomfortably before settling against the other's side.

"You're a taste I'll never forget." Darius continued with a gentle tone, but Quinton frowned, tucking his face against the other's neck. It was clear he wasn't sure what to do in this moment, so he simply latched to the other, in hopes that it was the right answer. Darius didn't mind, either way. He was not one to cuddle, per say, but this situation was different. He enjoyed having Quinton in his arms. He simply enjoyed having him. Since that first night, during their youth, he had always wanted to make the other his. He didn't mind if it would take work - Darius enjoyed a challenge.

"I don't understand you." Quinton finally spoke, his meek voice slightly muffled by his position, tucked against the man's neck.

"Few do, but you will, in time." Tilting his head, Darius dared to nuzzle against the other's soft hair, sighing a bit as his body started to finally relax. "I'll make you mine, Quincy." A promise he made when they were just teenagers that Quinton had awkwardly laughed off, no doubt assuming it was the words of a drunk, horny boy. Which they were, but they were also the truth. He never forgot them. "Sleep. You'll need it - tomorrow is the big day." The hunt. Quinton attempted to argue, but Darius just kissed him, silencing his protest. This happened twice before the runt finally gave up, just closing his eyes and settling against his alpha. His friend - his Darius.

They could deal with the consequences later.

CHAPTER FIVE

Darius finally led his first hunt - going further than they did in the past. While the pack had always stayed to the same hunting grounds, their new Alpha was a curious sort and took them beyond the river, which they had considered the edge of their grounds for so long. The hunt had been swift and successful. Beyond the river, deep into the thick woods, they found a small herd of deer. Their sleek brown coats stood out drastically against the stark white snow. Flustered around each other with fawns between their thin legs, the pack cared little for the deer - they wanted the buck. Thick and cautious, it stood a few paces away from the herd, watching the woods as they approached.

Ryker had stuck close to the ground, but Darius took a different approach. His coat was black as ink, hunting on the ground was nearly impossible, so he went up. Moving slowly through the thick tree branches, each step was close and careful, mindful of the falling snow and the creaking of the branches. While those who joined in on the hunt circled the herd, slowly closing in, Darius came from above. His full weight slammed into the thick form of the buck and the herd scattered. Three of the deer were taken out by the awaiting hunters, while Darius was left to handle the buck. The struggle barely lasted long enough to be deemed a fight.

As he dropped down from the tree, Darius had latched onto the creature's neck with his sharp teeth, baring his claws deep into its muscles and using his weight from the fall to snap the animal's neck. For a moment, the quiet forest erupted in sound. Birds cried out and flew from their trees, a loud snarl echoed through the woods and snow fell from the branches. After only a few moments, silence engulfed the forest once more. The attack was swift and calculated; Darius had succeeded in leading his first hunt.

This story was repeated throughout the night, over the feast that the hunters had brought home. Upon their return, the celebration had begun. The entire pack gathered within the hall that the village was built around, the meat butchered and prepared. Two large fires were started near the ends of the table, helping to fill the hall with a comfortable warmth. Darius sat towards the end of the table, with Ryker beside him. The man spared him a soft smile, handing the young man a mug and ruffled his curls roughly, once more earning that low growl and glare. There was nothing he hated more than being treated like a cub, but he allowed Ryker to touch him without much bite. He was the only man who could do so without losing a finger.

"You did well. Amazing, really. We've never gone past the river before, that was quite a chance that you took. I'm glad you didn't come limping home, empty handed. That wouldn't have looked very good for you." Rolling his eyes, Darius sighed, taking a large drink. The liquor was harsh, burning his throat as it slid down but helped to warm his body. It wasn't often that the pack partook in the bitter liquid, only during feasts which were used for celebrations.

"Praise me all you like, but the glory isn't all mine."

"You had fine hunters at your side."

"That's not the reason I crossed the river, Ryker. I didn't bring our people over there on a hunch." He grinned as he spoke now, causing Ryker to raise a brow, arms crossing. He didn't say anything in response, allowing Darius to further explain himself. "I had some help from Quinton - I discussed with him the lay of the land, information about the area and its creatures. Quincy is far cleverer than we give him credit, this hunt wouldn't have been so impressive if he didn't help me."

Brows furrowed, Ryker looked down the table towards where Quinton sat. He looked terribly small compared to the others around him, squeezing his body as tightly into the chair as possible, trying to take up as little space as he could. "That boy helped you? Quinton doesn't know the first thing about hunting, I doubt he'd even bore his claws into another creature during this life."

As he spoke, astonished, Darius just gave a faint chuckle, rolling his eyes. "Hunting is about more than the kill, there is far more importance to be had beyond knowing how to sink your teeth into meat. Quinton has been living with Man for quite some time now. He's grown used to reading their books and learning the land. I asked him for advice, and he is the one who told me to go past the river. Apparently, that city still holds hunters of its own and they often find herds of deer around that area. Due to the snow, no man dares to wander as deep as us, so, there was no fear of wandering." Pausing now, Darius squeezed Ryker's shoulder, looking at him as he spoke, making sure the man heard each word. "It is not a location we can go often, only when the weather makes it safe for us travel without fear of being spotted. Quincy will help us with that."

"He's helped quite a lot, it seems."

"I told you, everyone has their part to play, their uses to the pack. Just need to keep an eye open and keep your head out of your ass." Ryker took a swipe at the young man, but he laughed, leaning out the way easily. "Quincy, come here!" He called out without hesitation, causing a few conversations to hush and several eyes to look towards the lithe man.

Paling as attention was drawn towards him, Quinton quickly stood and made his way towards Darius - which was for the best. If he resisted, Darius would have gone and dragged him, making the scene that much worse. As the lanky man approached, Darius stood now, motioning Ryker to follow him. With the pair in tow, Darius led them away from the long table and towards back area of the hall. From here, they could speak in private while still having the warmth of a fire. Darius didn't feel like trekking through freezing snow just to have this conversation.

Quinton shifted anxiously on his feet, his gaze moving between the two men he stood with. It was cute, watching the way he seemed to squirm in place, unaware what to do with his body most of the time. Reaching out, Darius draped a thick arm across the other's small shoulders, tugging him closer with ease. "I meant what I said, Ryker. Quinton is as much a part of this hunt as any of us. The woods around us have been growing thin. With his help, we can keep our people from starving, and perhaps, make some needed advancements."

"You wish us to move to the city?" Ryker spoke cautiously, and Darius snorted, rolling his eyes. No, not in the slightest. Even with Quinton's insistence that Man wasn't as horrible as they had showed themselves to be in the past, Darius wasn't going to take any chances. Not when it came to the safety and future of his people.

"Never, but I do believe we should change some of our old ways, adapt to the world we're now in. Quincy is our best option with that. He knows more about how the world has changed than any of us. I suppose having his nose buried in those books turned out useful after all."

Glancing at Quinton, Ryker narrowed his eyes for a moment, but soon gave a chuckle. "He was always quite a studious thing, preferred text over weapons. Lazarus always said you were smarter than us from the start - I suppose that's why he left. So, you could be happier elsewhere."

"But he came back, because we're family." With his arm still around the thin man, Darius gave his shoulder a firm squeeze, watching him. "I just hope I can make you feel like family again." Finally, he spoke to Quinton directly, bringing him into the conversation.

At first, Quincy didn't speak, but after a few moments found his voice, meek and uncertain. It seemed that being around Ryker had caused him to become quite nervous, which only made sense. He was the Beta, the second. A man holding a grand title who didn't often interact with the runts of the pack. That was left to the Alpha to handle. "I don't mind helping. I think it'll be good for us, for our people, to change with the world. It's always shifting and there is so much I learned while living within those cities. I'd be honored to share this knowledge with the pack."

He spoke with a stiff, practiced tone. Ryker frowned and even Darius glanced at Quinton, finally rolling his eyes and pinching at the man's side until he squeaked. "Don't act like such a stiff, Quincy! Ryker is harmless, I promise. If he was going to be any trouble to you, I would have done away with him long ago." As he spoke, Ryker threw him a look, followed by a gentle huff. Darius knew the best ways to get the man's nerves.

"Is that why you dragged us over here, Darius? To explain that Quinton has a good head on his shoulders, or simply to boast that you were right about bringing everyone home?"

"You always assume the worst of me, Ryker. I wanted to inform you that there will be changes in the future, but also that I've finally chosen."

Well, he certainly didn't need to explain further than that. The Beta's attention perked and he seemed to be hanging on to each word that the young Alpha was saying. "Have you?" His comment was nearly softly whispered, but even as he asked, his gaze shifted to Quinton. It seemed he was starting to put the dots together, but Darius quickened the process for him.

"Yes." Looking at Quinton, he met the smaller man's gaze, who took a sharp breath, quickly looking away. Darius laughed, leaning towards him and speaking against the smaller male's ear. "You." While it was whispered to Quinton, the words were easily heard by their third party and Ryker stared. It seemed he hadn't expected this turn of events, but it wasn't likely that anyone would.

"You can't be serious, Darius."

"You really enjoy questioning me, don't you?" He still held Quinton close, the man squirming nervously beneath his touch. During their youth, he was always surprised when touched by others, quite unfamiliar with physical affections. It seemed that was still the case, but Darius didn't mind. It was one of the aspects he found appealing about the Omega of their pack. His insecure, almost innocent reactions were cute. Darius enjoyed earning these little responses from the other; it stroked a hunger within him that hadn't been sated for several years now. "I said what I said, and I mean every bit of it. You pushed me to choose, I've chosen. Deal with it." A smirk followed the snap of his words, and Ryker rolled his eyes.

"You're going to have some very unhappy women within the pack. They have been wanting to snag you for some time now...but I suppose that just means more for the rest, less competition."

"Take it how you will. Tell who you must, but I'm going to retire for the night, with my mate." The words were cooed, and Quinton attempted to speak, but nothing came out. Instead, he just cleared his throat and stepped away from Ryker, eagerly, and fell in step behind Darius. It seemed Quinton was eager to step out from the crowded hall for any reason, even if it meant returning to Darius' quarters.

As they left, Ryker called after Darius, carrying an annoyed tone, but his words were ignored. The Alpha just grinned as he stepped back out into the freezing evening, grabbing

Quinton's wrist the moment they were alone. It seemed impossible for the darker man to keep his hands to himself, more so when around the other.

CHAPTER SIX

It didn't take long to leave the hall and find their way back to Darius' hut. As they stepped inside, he went straight towards the fireplace, stroking the dying embers and attempting to bring life back into the fire. Quinton lingered by the doorway, looking around quietly. Unlike Darius, this was a place that Quinton didn't attend often during their youth. The space was new and yet so familiar. Though he was gone, there was still Lazarus' touch within the building. Quinton couldn't quite tell you where, but it was there. A comforting sense, one that helped to calm the trembling man from both the cold and his nerves.

As the fire was worked back into life, Darius stepped over, gently pulling Quinton away from the door and towards himself - towards the warmth. "You're quiet." His voice was soft, eyes settled on the thin man as he spoke, taking in his details. It was unsettling at times the way Darius seemed to stare him down, memorizing every detail.

"Why did you say that?" He didn't mean for his voice to sound so pathetic, but it was hard when Darius was looming over him, invading his personal space. Chewing on his lower lip, Quinton attempted to take a step back, however, Darius reached out and wrapped an arm around his waist, pulling him close and ruining any chance of escape.

"That I want you as a mate?" His words were whispered as he leaned closer, lips brushing against Quinton's jaw now, causing a tremble to run through his body. After spending several years, alone, within the city, Quinton grew unfamiliar with physical contract. Yet, despite his, Darius seemed to struggle with keeping his hands to himself, even if only for a few moments. "I thought I made that clear last night. I want you, Quinton. I tried to forget that night, for months, years. I couldn't - nothing ever compared to you. Without you, I'll always been craving what you gave me, that taste no one else has."

"I don't even know what that means." His words were forced out, face burning. Quinton had settled for hiding behind his bangs now, eyes focused on the ground as Darius continued to speak. The dark arm was still securely around his waist, giving him no time to make an excuse and flee. "I'm barely worthy of this pack, much less you. That's what they're all going to say."

"Tell me of a time I gave a shit what anyone here thought. What they said about me, to me. I'm not frightened of what others think, Quinton. I know who I am, I know what I want and I go for it." Darius spoke with a slight smirk, his confidence never waiving. Perhaps that is why Lazarus felt he would be a strong leader. A man who always put actions before words and was firm in his choices. Quinton envied him when they were younger - he could barely hold a conversation with members of the pack without losing his ground, retreating at the first chance he was given. This was the behavior that made him the Omega. That, and his size. Unlike the others within his pack, Quinton was quite small and easily the worst hunter. These were the reasons Darius confused him with his choice of a mate. He had little to offer, but the other wouldn't hear of it.

"Your mate is supposed to help you, Darius. Be a support system while you guide our people. I'm not what you need. I can't help you lead anyone."

"I don't need help leading, I can do that just fine on my own." Finally pulling his arm away, Darius cupped the man's small face, frowning as he spoke, dark eyes locked on his own. "You can help elsewhere, in areas that no one else could. This hunt proved that, don't you get it? You're more aware of this land than anyone, by this point. The world around us is ever changing, but we don't see it. You do, which is why I need you by my side. To help lead our people, to help provide them with a better future."

"So, you want my intelligence?" Quinton spoke with caution, but eased when the other started to laugh.

"Yes, but I also want you." Leaning forward, Darius caught Quinton's lips in a gentle kiss, arms wrapping around him once more. He drew the other's small body up against his own, holding him tightly. He didn't fight the hold nor the kiss. Despite how nervous he felt around the man, he couldn't deny that Darius did have some power over him, a charm that made him surrender to the other. Allowing his hands to rest against the other's chest, Quinton melted into the affection.

"I don't understand you." The statement was whispered, having barely pulled away from the affection. Darius just laughed, his thumb stroking against the other's cheek gently. The touch was soft, comforting. Not something he ever expected from a man like Darius, who was often rough and aggressive most hours of the day.

"You will, in time. We'll understand each other." His words were strangely comforting, and Quinton gave a soft smile before accepting another kiss from Darius. Just as careful and tender as before. With each moment that the gentle affections continued, the younger could feel his walls begin to crumble. It was harder to keep them up when around someone like Darius, a young man who was ever present during his youth and even took a protective role as they grew, before he left the pack. There were many different sides to their new Alpha that their people had yet to see, but Quinton felt rather spoiled, seeing these rare shades. The gentleness, the soft and caring side that kissed him so sweetly, held him so close.

He wasn't going to place an emotional label of their dynamic, he was never that foolish, but Quinton wasn't going to deny that it felt good like this. Wrapped in his arm, engulfed in his warmth. Walking them backwards, Darius gently pushed Quinton down on the bed. Falling with a slight squeak, he shifted against the bed, looking up at Darius as he knelt against the mattress. His large figure shadowed over Quinton with ease, making him feel far smaller than he already was.

Pressing his hands on either side of Quinton's head, Darius dipped his head down to catch his lips once more. This time, the affection was accepted with an almost eager reaction. Running his fingers up and into those thick, dark curls, Quinton gently gripped them as he started to return the kiss. Parting his lips, Darius pushed his tongue passed the full, trembling lips and earned a weak little groan from the man beneath him. The small sound seemed to urge him as his nails dug into the sheets and his hips rolled against the other's.

Shifting beneath him, Quinton's eyes fell shut, submitting to the advancements and giving a low moan against the kiss. His legs parted, and he felt Darius smile against the kiss. Moving one hand down towards his hips, he tugged at the other's pants playfully, earning a whimper. Each touch felt like fire against his skin, and, while Quinton didn't wish to admit the truth, he knew how Darius felt. Since that evening, years ago, he too felt an emptiness, a desire that he never sought to fulfill, but now couldn't resist the roaring need. Each brush and kiss from the Alpha caused his body to tremble with such a great need he didn't even know he possessed.

Grasping his shirt, Darius pulled the fabric away from the other's body, tossing his own shirt soon after. Sitting back on his heels now, Darius just looked down at the man beneath him, a hand resting on his chest and moving down the curve of his side. His thumb running against his skin, other nails giving a teasing scrape against the pale surface of Quinton's frame. In the low lighting from the fireplace,

Quinton stared up at the other, taking in every detail. His defined muscles, dark ink, and telling scars. Between the feeling of his hands and the sight above him, he started to grow aroused beneath his lover, gently biting at his lower lip. This was still very new to him; Darius was the only lover he ever had. Something he didn't voice, but he was sure the other knew, more so with how gently he treated him.

Taking in as much of the sight as he could, Darius finally removed their pants, exposing their bodies to the evening warmth, thankfully warmed by fire still crackling brightly. With their bodies bare, his lips once more found their way to Quinton's skin. He trailed a line of small affections across his chest and shoulders, even daring to nip at his collar bone. While doing so, he reached towards the side of the bed, shoving aside several items before bring forth what he was looking for. A bottle of oil, much like the one he had in his home. Quinton didn't bother to ask questions - he already had assumptions. No doubt Darius celebrated his newly earned title for several nights and the oils were always a favorite of his. Still, he did give a slight smile and laugh, shaking his head.

"What?"

"You had that waiting? Were you planning this?"

Darius grinned, kissing him firmly a moment as he opened the bottle, allowing the cool, slick liquid to coat his fingers. "Of course, I wanted to celebrate and what better treat is there than my mate, squirming and begging beneath me?"

His detailed response earned a dark flush to Quinton's face, which grew to his ears as he watched Darius stroke himself. Still kneeling over the other, he provided a soft, low moan as his hand worked the oil against his skin. The sound of his voice stirred the smaller of the pair, his own erection quite evident. He attempted to provide attention to himself; however, Darius grabbed his wrist with his free hand, pinning it above Quinton's head. He stared down at him with lidded eyes, slowly shaking his head, dark curls drooping into his face.

He didn't struggle, allowing the other to pin his arm, parting his knees instead. Understanding the invitation, Darius pulled his hand away from himself and instead gripped Quinton's hip, slightly smearing a bit of oil against his skin as he drew the other closer. Giving a slow, careful thrust, his erection slid with ease into the trembling man. Gasping gently, Quinton closed his eyes at the pressure, the faint pain of the other pushing inside him.

Being without for so long made his body quite unaccustomed to this type of abuse, but he wasn't about to stop the other. Within the pain was pleasure, which he knew would win in the end. Darius was careful with his body, always good and gentle. He didn't want to hurt Quinton, this much he was certain. It was this knowledge that helped to keep him calm during this unprecedented situation.

Pushing deep inside, until their hips met, Darius groaned Quinton's name as he bit onto the man's lower lip. His hand stayed firm on his wrist, but the other squeezed his thigh and lightly clawed at his skin. He gave a few, light thrusts, each earning small gasps from the shivering man beneath him. With a soft, short laugh, Darius rocked their hips together, thrusting into Quinton's tight body as he began to build a rhythm. The movement was slow at first, allowing the other to adjust to Darius' thick size, before quickening. Their hips slapped together with the building force. His head buried inside his tight body, and Quinton couldn't help but cry out his name with every deep thrust.

As his body rocked from the movement, Quinton pulled his wrist free from the other's grasp, instead gripping his hand now, keeping it above his head. This time, he was the one to claw at Darius, nails digging against his grasp as he wrapped his legs around the other's hips. Breathless gasps of Darius' name filled the air, mixing with the crackling of the fire. Giving a rougher thrust, Darius rested his forehead against Quinton's, their gazes locking before he gently kissed him.

"You're beautiful," he whispered, but Quinton didn't respond. He couldn't even find his voice much less any words to say. His body was too hot, too electrified, for him to think of a single response. Darius grinned, tugging at the other's ear. "And mine." He growled the words and Quinton's body shuddered beneath him on instinct. That growl always sent shivers down his spine. It was always hard to resist him, but those words made him completely impossible -- strangely sweet, yet concerningly possessive.

Quinton did try his best to respond to it, but his voice caught in his throat once again and he could only manage a little nod, a weak smile between the soft, sharp gasps with every thrust. He squeezed his hand. It was hard to deny him in this position, that cloud of pleasure fogging his mind from any logic or concern, but it wasn't as if the thought crossed his mind. They both knew the truth - they needed each other. Two pieces that clicked perfectly. Quinton had longed for the other more than he was willing to admit and this moment was more than he could have ever hoped for.

He would submit his entire being to the other, be his mate, help him lead. He just hoped that he would be able to walk the next day.

Mending Malcolm

A Wolf Shifter Mpreg Bundle

Preston Walker & Liam Kingsley

Disclaimer

This is a work of fiction. Names, places, characters and events are all fictitious for

The man swung at Malcolm, and Malcolm quickly dodged the blow. He had been out patrolling the territory boundary when he had stumbled across the man laying partly unconscious on the Eastern boundary. Unfortunately, the man had roused up when Malcolm tried to pull him to his feet. Now the man was swinging wildly at him, desperate to get away.

"Calm down," Malcolm growled as he grabbed the man's right arm. The man let out a groan of pain as Malcolm swiftly twisted and held the man's arm firmly. Malcolm put pressure on the man's shoulder. "I said, calm down."

The man stilled, and his breath came in ragged waves. "Just kill me already."

Malcolm took in the man's appearance now that he was still enough for Malcolm to see him properly in the moonlight. He was just an inch or two shorter than Malcolm himself. The man's blonde hair was plastered to his head, and there was a dark stain along the man's cheek. Malcolm could smell the scent of blood on the man. "What are you doing in this territory? I don't recognize you."

The man shook his head dislodging a damp clump of hair. "Does it matter?"

"Yes." Malcolm released the man's arm, and the man slumped forward a bit. "Are you seeking sanctuary?"

The man growled, "I seek nothing." The next moment he spun on Malcolm, and he gasped out in surprise as he fell backward into the cold, damp leaves. Malcolm stared up at the man and instinctively went to grab his knife but found the man's boot on his hand. "Should have killed me."

Malcolm had to agree that he probably should have. He had always had a bit of a soft spot for the underdog though. Gregory would get a lot of enjoyment mocking Malcolm's latest screw up, barring that this man did not end him right now. He stared up at the man but did not speak.

The man leaned over, and Malcolm caught the faint glow to the man's eyes. His mind corrected his terminology. This was a wolf, a shapeshifter, probably from a rival pack than Malcolm himself. That did not bode well for Malcolm's survival.

"I'm not going to hurt you. Do you understand?" The wolf asked in a low whisper. Malcolm just nodded in silence. The wolf looked off into the distance as if he was checking for something then he looked back down at Malcolm. Malcolm did not see the blow that knocked him unconscious.

**

When Malcolm's eyes blinked open again, he was in a room. His hands wouldn't move, and he panicked for a moment before he registered the coarse rope around his wrist. "Damn it," Malcolm muttered.

"Language," A voice said causing Malcolm's head to snap around. Sitting at a wooden table was the wolf from earlier. "What was someone like you doing out patrolling? Couldn't they spare any real soldiers?"

Malcolm grimaced. The man was referring to the fact that Malcolm was an Omega. Within his pack omegas were looked down as weak, but that had never stopped Malcolm before. "Don't underestimate me." Malcolm could not stop the growl in his voice despite the circumstances. Luckily the man at the table looked more amused than offended.

The man's blonde hair looked like he had bathed. There was a gash on the side of his face, but it seemed to be healing, so perhaps it was an older injury, or perhaps a self-inflicted one to make himself appear weak. Malcolm could taste the iron tang of the man's blood in the air. The man eyed him curiously.

Malcolm grew tired of the silence. He realized that he was laying on a bed and struggled to sit up. His legs were tied together too. The man seeing his struggles came over and grabbed Malcolm's arm at the elbow. To Malcolm's surprise, the man hauled him into a sitting position. The man leaned over to look Malcolm in the face. "Better?"

When Malcolm nodded, the man paced away. There was a noise of feet on wood, and then a child of perhaps ten burst through a door at the far end of the room that Malcolm had not seen. "Papa!" The child said and threw her arms around the blonde man that held Malcolm captive. The girl noticed Malcolm finally and ducked behind her father quickly. "Who is that?"

"Good question. Who are you?" The last part was directed at Malcolm.

Malcolm cleared his dry throat. "Malcolm Garver."

The little girl relaxed a bit and spoke from behind her father. "I'm Trace."

Malcolm chuckled despite the situation and dipped his head in greeting. "Nice to meet you, Trace."

"This is my Dad," Trace continued as she stepped out from behind the man. "His name is Soren."

Malcolm nodded. "That's a nice name, too." Despite the fact that he was holding Malcolm hostage, of course. "I'd shake your hand, but I'm tied up at the moment."

Soren seemed to think this funny as he ushered the girl back out of the room. "Go back to bed, Pup." The man's voice was affectionate but firm. The girl let herself be guided out of the room but gave Malcolm a bit of a wave as she disappeared out the door.

When the girl was gone, the man sighed and turned back around to look at Malcolm. Soren walked over to stand near Malcolm, and he eyed the man. Malcolm's long, dark hair had been in a braid at one time, but now the strands were disheveled. Malcolm's brown eyes stared back into Soren's blue ones. "Guess we should talk now that you are conscious."

"Hard to talk when I am unconscious," Malcolm quipped despite his nerves.

Soren chuckled. "I see how you got put on patrol. You have a lot of fire."

Malcolm sighed and shook his head. "Actually, I'm only in this mess because of my father."

"That sounds like the start of a very long therapy session that I don't have time for." Soren leaned over and grabbed Malcolm's braid. He yanked backward, and Malcolm's neck snapped back with such force that the pain seared down through his shoulders. "Now, I'm under orders to find some of your packmates. I need to know where the men are who ordered and took part in the attack on Bottle Creek Village."

Malcolm's blood ran cold for a moment. His eyes met the blue eyes of his captor. "I don't know anything about it." Malcolm was lying, and the man could probably tell.

Soren growled. "Well, that wasn't convincing. I can smell your fear. Why are you afraid to answer a question?"

Malcolm gritted his teeth as he caught the glimmer of a knife blade. "I won't tell you what you want to know. You might as well kill me."

"Maybe," Soren agreed. "But I'm an optimist." The blade flashed, and Malcolm bit down on the howl of pain that wanted to come out as the man cut a gash across Malcolm's arm.

Malcolm growled through clenched teeth, "Why do you care about that battle? It happened years ago. Everyone involved has gone mad, has been disgraced, or both."

"They are still alive though," Soren said, and he gave Malcolm a smile. "Now tell me where they are."

Malcolm shook his head. "All the ones in charge are too old or disgraced to be any threat to anyone. The soldiers are mostly dead or not fit for duty. Knowing won't do you any good."

"You'd be surprised what a little optimism can do," Soren assured Malcolm. "Now tell me where are the ones that gave the order."

Malcolm had no love for the packmates that Soren was asking about, but he was certain it would not stop with the people who gave the orders. "What does it matter? You kill them. Then what? You go after every soldier that followed those orders? Then you go after the ones who didn't follow the orders? Where does it stop?"

"Just answer the question," Soren growled.

Malcolm sighed. "No. I don't even particularly like the men you are talking about, but none of them are even in power anymore." Soren's eyes were filled with sadness that Malcolm was not expecting. "Who did you lose?"

Soren shoved Malcolm down onto the bed and paced away. The man raked a hand through his blonde hair that brushed his shoulders. It looked like it had been crudely cut off. Malcolm realized he had cut it in grief. It was a custom among some tribes to cut off long hair to display grief after the loss of a loved one.

Soren took a deep breath, and the man's voice was barely a growl. "My mate."

Malcolm closed his eyes. He had never had a mate, but he could hear the keen loss in Soren's voice. It was plain that the man had loved his mate dearly. "I'm sorry. I want to help you, but I can't."

"Are you going to give the speech about it won't bring her back?" Soren sounded pained, and Malcolm opened his eyes to watch the man pace. "I know it won't, but I have my orders."

"You have your daughter," Malcolm intervened softly.

Soren looked at Malcolm but never got to respond. A knock sounded on the door. Soren let another man in. Malcolm struggled to see from the angle he was laying at on the bed. The man appeared to have long gray hair that was tied back. The newcomer eyed Malcolm with something akin to disgust. They spoke quietly, but Malcolm could not hear what they were saying.

The newcomer stepped closer to Malcolm. "If he isn't going to talk, then we should kill him, so he doesn't report back."

"Yes, Sir," Soren said with no emotion that Malcolm could detect. The newcomer laid a hand on Soren's shoulder then was swiftly back out of the door. Malcolm knew the man must have been the pack leader. The man had probably come for a report. Well, that was that Malcolm thought, as Soren dragged him to his feet. Soren reached down and cut the rope from around Malcolm's ankles so he could walk at least.

Malcolm did not resist when Soren led him outside with his hands still tied together. The damp cold seeped into his clothing quickly, but Malcolm paid it no attention. When they stopped deep in the forest away from the house where Soren lived, Malcolm just closed his eyes. A few moments passed before Malcolm felt Soren cut the rope from around his wrists.

"Go," Soren said in a low whisper. The man sounded tired, more tired than Malcolm had ever heard anyone sound, except maybe for his brother.

Malcolm looked at the man in surprise. "You aren't going to kill me?"

"Why would I?" Soren slid his knife back into his boot.

Malcolm rubbed his wrists. "But your pack leader told you to. What if I tell someone?"

"Tell them what? That we are asking questions?" Soren seemed amused. "I don't care if you tell anyone, Malcolm, and I don't follow orders that I don't agree with."

The last part seemed to have a double-edge to it. The men who had followed orders and had burned the village down despite the fact that the orders were obviously erroneous had done so blindly. Malcolm shook his head. "I'd prefer you kill me. I'm not going back to my pack either way."

Soren eyed Malcolm for a long moment. "Why?"

"I have my reasons," Malcolm spoke softly and then shrugged. "If I go back, I'll be branded compromised at best, a traitor at worst. My family's name will again be shamed. Don't think I can stand that look on my father's face again."

"Again?" Soren asked. Malcolm never got to answer as there was a sound of boot falls. The change was instant. Malcolm did not know why, but when Soren instinctively shifted, Malcolm had as well without a thought. The next moment their paws were racing through the forest as the trees blurred past them.

When they finally stopped, they both panted and listened to the sounds of the forest around them. Soren's light fur glistened as a ray of moonlight came down through the trees. Then they were shifting back. Malcolm groaned as he stretched his muscles. "What was that for?"

Soren grimaced as he stood up. To Malcolm's surprise, the man laughed. "Border patrol. Didn't think about what I was doing. Nice follow by the way."

"Thanks, I think. Clothes would be nice though." Malcolm started laughing.

Soren agreed. "True. It is a bit on the cool side to be out naked." There was a shift in the air that Malcolm and Soren both seemed to notice at the same time. They eyed each other warily at first then with a bit more interest. Malcolm tried to remember that this man was probably a bit unhinged, but at the moment all Malcolm could really think about was how good the smell of the man was.

When the blonde came near to Malcolm, he leaned his head to the side and eyed the dark-haired man curiously. There was a faint glow within the man's eyes as the adrenaline kicked in. Malcolm knew his own eyes were glowing as well. The blonde man took a deep breath as if breathing in the scent of Malcolm. That was the last sane thought that occurred to Malcolm.

The cold bothered neither of them with the blood pumping through their veins and instinct carrying them forward without any reservations. Malcolm submitted easily to the man. Soren was all alpha, and the omega side of Malcolm responded to it. He had pushed down that side of himself to be what his father wanted, but now it took over him with such a violent force that Malcolm shook with the want of it.

Soren's deep voice whispered into Malcolm's ear as the man's fingers slipped into him. The words were meaningless, but the intent was clear. Malcolm was his and Malcolm had to agree that he was. It was easy to give himself to Soren, so easy. It was the most natural thing he had ever done, and when Soren finally pushed fully inside him, the world seemed to snap into place.

They mated under the trees. Their breath ghosting out into the cold night as they panted out their passion. When they finally collapsed beside each other in the cold leaf litter, Soren wrapped his arms around Malcolm protectively to keep him warm. Malcolm felt drowsy and safe as he slipped off to sleep.

The safety fled swiftly as he was jostled awake by Soren only a few moments later. "Someone is coming." The words sent a spike of alarm through Malcolm. They pushed up to their feet but did not make it very far before they heard the boot falls.

"Well, this is a surprise." The gray-haired wolf stepped out of the forest. "I told you to kill him, not bed him."

Soren took an instinctive step in front of Malcolm. "It wasn't part of the plan, but things happen sometimes." A couple of wolves that Malcolm did not recognize came out of the trees as well. Soren seemed to recognize them. "I think, Don, can agree with that."

A curly-headed man laughed. "Yep. Life just smacks you with things sometimes. What do you think, boss?"

The gray-haired man chuckled. "I don't suppose there is much to do. They are mated. We can't very well send the boy off if he could be carrying Soren's pup, now can we?"

Malcolm startled. They had mated. He had forgotten for just a split moment the consequences of their actions. Soren agreed with the gray-haired wolf. "He's under my protection. He had already renounced his pack, so there should be no conflict."

"Then that's settled. How about a beer?" It was the other man who had been silent until this point. The man was stout and tall. He towered a good inch over even Soren. His voice had the rumble of thunder in it. Don seemed to agree with the bellowing man and headed off back toward the village. "You two might want to find some clothes," the loud man informed Soren and Malcolm.

"What a brilliant plan, Garrett," Soren said with sarcasm which caused the larger man to laugh heartily as he followed Don into the trees. The gray-haired wolf gave them a shake of his head as he turned to follow the first two into the forest.

After the others were gone, Soren turned to him and gave him an apologetic smile. "I didn't mean for this to happen."

"I never thought you did." Malcolm honestly did not think Soren wanted him as a mate, but instincts are hard to fight. "I know you weren't looking for a mate."

Soren nodded and walked back toward where they had left their clothing. "Not looking perhaps, but here we are all the same."

They walked in silence, and Malcolm felt increasingly awkward. He did not really want to stay here. This was not at all what he had pictured being mated to be like. This was just an accident. As soon as it was clear that he was not with child, he would break off the bond. This was a mistake after all.

***

Trace eyed Malcolm over the kitchen table with interest. Malcolm eyed her back with trepidation. The girl looked like she was deciding if he was good to eat or not. "Are you going to eat me for breakfast?" Malcolm asked the question warily.

Trace's laughter echoed around the kitchen. "I prefer eggs. Do you like eggs?"

"Yes," Malcolm answered nervously.

Soren's voice boomed into the room before the man appeared out of the back, "Trace, leave Malcolm alone. He needs to eat, and you need to go to school."

"But I don't want to go to school," Trace whined as she eyed her father with big pleading eyes. "Can't I stay here with Malcolm?" Malcolm's stomach tied up in knots at the thought of the little girl interrogating him all day.

Soren's clipped answer gave no room for disobedience. "No."

Trace sullenly ate her eggs and then dragged her feet to go get ready. When the girl was out of the room, Soren eyed

Malcolm as he drank a cup of coffee. Malcolm's plate was still just as full as it had been. "Are you not hungry?"

"I--" Malcolm started to say he was not feeling well, but thought the better of it. The man had been watching Malcolm like a hawk for the last few weeks. The last thing Malcolm wanted to do was to give the man any reason to do so more intently. "Trace was just making me nervous."

Soren chuckled. "She has that effect on people."

Malcolm gave the man a slight smile as he forced himself to eat a piece of egg. It was the vilest thing he had ever eaten, but he chewed it up and swallowed it with determination. "Going out?" Malcolm asked the question to redirect the conversation.

"Pack meeting with Mason this morning. Nothing major though." Soren took a sip of his coffee. "You really don't seem that hungry. Are you sure you are well?"

Malcolm avoided looking up. He did not want to see that hopeful and curious look on Soren's face. The man had been eagerly waiting to see if their mating had produced any offspring, but Malcolm only grew sicker thinking of it. If he were with child, then he would be stuck in this mistake of a bonding forever. No, he was not with child, Malcolm thought forcibly. "I'm fine," Malcolm choked out.

"You look like you are going to be ill," Soren said conversationally.

Malcolm grimaced and covered his face. "I think your eggs are poisoned."

"Yes, I lace them with poison every morning to weed out the weak ones." Soren's voice was light. Malcolm glared over at the man who merely gave Malcolm a smile.

Malcolm growled, "Shouldn't you be going?"

"Yep," Soren replied chipperly. "Trace!" Malcolm cringed as the man's yell rang out. The girl came skipping back out into the kitchen with her book bag over her shoulder. She gave Malcolm a wave which he returned before he looked down at his plate. As the front door shut back, Malcolm pushed the plate away disheartened.

The day passed slowly. Outside the frost lingered on the ground. Malcolm pulled on his boots and a warm coat that Soren had given him because his own coat had been torn when Soren had captured Malcolm on the border. "Hello, Mia," Malcolm said with a smile to the woman who was just coming out her front door as well.

Mia was a petite woman with brown-red hair that she usually kept in two braids. The woman's slight figure was complemented by the protrusion of her round belly under her coat. Mia had befriended Malcolm soon after it became known that he would be staying. Some of the pack members were still a bit wary of him, but Mia was a comfort with her easy-going ways.

"Malcolm. You look green." The woman walked across her yard and laid a warm hand on his cheek. "Don't feel fevered though. Are you well?"

Malcolm shook his head. "I can't eat anything. It might be nerves. Soren and Trace keep watching me like I am going to suddenly grow another head. It's enough to wear the nerves down."

Mia giggled, and they fell into step beside each other. "Well, they are anxious too. I'll warrant Soren will be very overprotective with you after what happened to his last mate."

Malcolm frowned. "Yeah."

"I know you think that this isn't a real bonding, but shouldn't you at least give it a try? Soren seems so much happier since you have come. That has to mean something," Mia said in her soft way. They walked toward the store and Malcolm merely nodded. Maybe it did mean something. Maybe it meant that he was excited about a pup that might not exist.

Malcolm helped Mia gather her groceries, and then they carried the items home. The woman was not far out from having her pup, and the walk itself was enough to wear the woman out. "Are you sure you are okay?"

Mia patted Malcolm's arm as she walked him back to the door. "I'm fine. This is what we do, what our bodies were made to do. Go rest and try to eat something. I've knitting to do before the wee one is born."

Malcolm sighed and made his way back to the quiet house. There was a plaque out front that read Connelly, which was Soren's family name. Malcolm frowned. He guessed technically it was his family name now too. Although they had not had a formal bonding ceremony, the age-old tradition of the mating bond had ascended that formal rite in their case.

In Malcolm's home range, there were lots of humans who lived intermingled with the shifters, but here there mostly seemed to be shifters with just the occasional human. Malcolm sank into a chair by the fire. His eyelids grew heavy as he warmed and he slipped off to sleep.

"Guess what?" There was a loud bang accompanying the voice, and Malcolm jolted awake. "Sorry," Soren apologized. "Didn't realize you were asleep."

Malcolm took a deep breath to calm his frayed nerves. "It's okay. What were you saying?"

"I was saying that Grey Timber sent a messenger requesting your whereabouts," Soren spoke conversationally as he leaned against the counter. "Mind you, the messenger was lucky we didn't kill him on sight as our two tribes aren't exactly friends, but Thomas was curious to see what message he had brought."

Malcolm did not know how to react to the news. He missed his mother and brother, but he had gotten used to the idea of never seeing his home range again. "And what does that mean exactly? I'm not going back, so what did Thomas tell them?"

"He didn't tell them anything. He wants you to come tell the messenger yourself." Soren watched Malcolm as if trying to see an answer that not even Malcolm had. "He's leaving the decision up to you as to what happens. You can tell them that you are staying here, or you can make arrangements to return."

"What about our bond?" Malcolm asked the question cautiously. Some alphas were volatile. He had learned that lesson from his father very well.

Soren took a deep breath and let it out slowly before he spoke. "I can’t make this decision for you. I never gave you a choice, to begin with. I guess, what I am trying to say is, if you don't want to stay then I'll understand."

Malcolm looked at his hands. "What if I'm carrying your child?"

There was silence for a moment. "Do you think you are?" Soren's question was a quiet one. "I know that you hope you aren't, Malcolm. Despite what you might think, I'm not blind to the fact that you are unhappy here."

"I'm not unhappy," Malcolm said with a sigh. "Okay, fine. I don't think this is what bonding should be. Waiting around to see if I'm with a child or not, and what if I'm not? Do we try again? Do we--" Malcolm shook his head. "I respect that you want to take care of me, but that's not love, and a bond should be about love."

Soren nodded his head slowly. "Then you'll go home then?"

"I told you, I can't go home. That is only made all the more obvious by this situation. If they find out that I was mated by my captor my father will probably kill me himself." Malcolm put his hands over his face. "I have no idea what to do, Soren. I don't belong anywhere."

Soren came to kneel down beside the chair where Malcolm was sitting. "You never did answer my question all those weeks ago. What did you mean when you said again?"

Malcolm looked into Soren's blue eyes. "My brother was there at the raid that killed your mate. He didn't follow orders. He couldn't. When he got home, he couldn’t do anything for the nightmares and memories of it. The doctors said it was post-traumatic stress disorder. My father said it was a weakness. He made me go into the home guard to redeem the family name."

The sadness in Soren's eyes was deep and clear to see. "I don't see any dishonor in a good man doing what he thought was right."

"You aren’t my father," Malcolm said softly.

Soren agreed with a nod. "Neither are you, and you don't have to hold up his standards. Stay or go, that's your choice, but don't do it either for fear of what others will think Mal."

It was the first time Soren had ever used the nickname for him, and Malcolm chuckled. "All I ever wanted was to be a teacher. I never wanted to be a soldier. That was my father's idea of what I should be. My mother told him it wasn't in my nature, but he molded me into what he wanted in a son."

Soren brushed his fingertips across Malcolm's cheek. "I'm sorry."

"For what? Mating me? I kind of had a hand in that too." Malcolm shrugged. "I would like to see my mother and brother again, but I don't know if they would even see me."

"Clearly, someone is looking for you," Soren said softly. "Do what you feel you must."

***

The walk to the pack leader's house had was one of the longest that Malcolm could remember. Soren accompanied him. The messenger was a man that Malcolm had only seen in passing back home. The man seemed relieved to find Malcolm alive and well.

"Mr. Garver I'm thrilled to see you unharmed." The man looked over at Thomas and then back to Malcolm, only barely glancing at Soren.

"Elton, isn't it?" Malcolm asked politely. When the man nodded, Malcolm continued, "I'm sorry to cause you all such worry. I was injured on patrol and found by Soren." Malcolm waved his hand at the blonde man who eyed Malcolm curiously. "I've been here recovering."

Elton smiled. "I am glad to hear that our neighbors in Bottle Creek have kept you safe. Given our packs histories, we feared the worst."

"You mistakenly hold us to the honor standards of your pack then," Thomas said with a sneer. Elton shifted uncomfortably at the open insult, but simply nodded along with the pack leader. "Malcolm is welcome to leave whenever he chooses, or he is welcome to stay. Our pack would be honored to have him."

"His father was most insistent that his son returns home," Elton said the words nervously glancing at the men. He gave Malcolm an apologetic smile. "That is if you are well enough to travel."

Malcolm looked down for a moment as he thought. He had intended to break off the bond with Soren anyway, hadn't he? There still was the matter of whether he had Soren's child growing inside of him, but that matter would take time to reveal itself. He worried at the sickness, but it could be merely his nerves. "I will return, but only for a short visit. I've grown accustomed to the pack here, and I would miss them dearly. I want to see my family though and make sure everyone understands appropriately."

The look on Soren's face was what Malcolm would have called relief. He gave the blonde man a smirk. Thomas spoke then. "Soren, you go with them." Soren nodded his acceptance of his pack leader's mission.

"That won't be necessary," Elton interjected.

Malcolm chided Elton. "It's their territory. They call the shots, Elton." The man relented and nodded his agreement. "Besides our two territories could do with some diplomacy instead of knives, don't you think?" Malcolm was looking at Thomas now.

The gray-haired pack leader eyed him with consideration before he agreed with a nod of his head. "It has been a long time to hold a grudge. We would, however, be most interested in answers. Soren can act as our ambassador in this capacity."

Malcolm and Soren exchanged a glance and Malcolm could tell Soren did not like the sound of that. "I'll go make preparations," Soren said in a clipped tone before he spun on his heels and left the room.

"I better go get my things." Malcolm did not really have that many things, but he was eager to make sure that Soren was okay. When the other two men agreed, Malcolm was swiftly off across the village to Soren's home. He found the blonde in the bedroom. "Are you okay?"

"Yes," Soren said without looking around. He opened the closet and pulled out a long red coat. The color was a deep red like the leaves in the autumn that shone across the meadow where Malcolm had grown up. Malcolm came over and laid his hand on top of the coat gingerly. The material felt thick but supple. It was a leather of some kind. "Formal coat," Soren mumbled.

Malcolm looked up to see that the man had turned to look at Malcolm. "I don't even have one. Just home guard, border patrols. You must be fairly important in the pack."

"Lead General." Soren's words were clipped again, and the man was already snatching things out of the drawers. "I'll have to see if Mia can watch Trace."

Malcolm nodded. "I could run over and ask while you get dressed?"

"Thanks," Soren said, and Malcolm wondered if that was an apologetic tone. Malcolm gave Soren a smile and then left to carry out his errand.

Mia was thrilled with the idea of tending to the girl. Trace would probably be a big help to the woman with her belly so heavy with child. "You make sure you come back to us, huh?" The woman's soft, lilting tone held sadness.

"Don't be sad. I'm coming back. That's why Soren is going with me. He'll accompany me there and straight back." Malcolm said softly. "Don't go having that kid until I get back, do you hear?"

Mia threw her arms around Malcolm's tall frame and hugged the man fiercely. "I'll miss ya."

"And I will miss you," Malcolm assured the woman as she let him go with an embarrassed wipe of her forearm across her wet eyes. "Damn hormones." Malcolm chuckled as the woman nodded her agreement.

Mia giggled. "Think your beau has come to collect you," she nodded behind Malcolm. Sure enough, Soren had left the house and was headed toward them. Malcolm must have eyed him for longer than appropriate. "He is nice to look at, isn't he?" Mia giggled again when Malcolm's cheeks flushed with color.

"Hello, Mia," Soren smiled.

Mia smiled back at him, "And you, Soren. I've told Malcolm that keeping Trace will be no problem. She'll be a right help around here. You two must leave now?"

"Very shortly. I'm afraid I won't get to tell Trace goodbye," Soren's eyes held that sadness again.

Mia reached over and gave the man's forearm a pat. "I'll pass on the message. You two just be safe."

***

Malcolm decided before they ever reached the border that he did not like Elton. The man was noisy, jumpy, and entirely more condescending than he had any right to be. Soren seemed to share the opinion as he barely acknowledged the man's existence. It would have been faster to use a motorcycle or car, but the borders did not share any direct roads or at least none that would not take days to traverse. It was easier to simply walk across the border.

Elton himself had walked in and did not seem keen on walking back out. Malcolm raised an eyebrow at the man as Elton stumbled over a log. Soren was close enough to stop the man's fall but made no move to do so. Malcolm bit down on a laugh as best he could. Elton glared at the blonde and Soren ignored him.

"There are the border markers," Soren said conversationally as he walked forward. "Looks like we have company. Elton, do you want to give our introductions?"

Ahead was a couple of the home guard who seemed to have been waiting on them. Malcolm smiled. "Barton!"

"Mal, is that you?" The baritone rang out as the sandy blonde-haired man came forward to clasp Malcolm's arm in a brotherly embrace. "Thought you had gotten yourself buried by those creek wolves."

Soren eyed the man with a touch of hostility. Malcolm intervened, "Actually Soren here saved me when I was injured while on patrol. I've been recovering at their village."

"Well, that makes them fine with me." Barton held out his arm to Soren who clasped the man's hand. Malcolm noted the wariness in Soren. He did not trust wolves from Malcolm's territory, and Malcolm could not blame him for that.

Elton dusted off his clothes as he broke free of the tree line. "Can we please get back to the city now?"

***

The territory was steeped in late autumn colors. Soren watched the scenery with curiosity. The capital of Grey Timber's range was a bustling city called Hearthton. The city seemed alive with people and vehicles. Soren had been in large cities before, and it did not impress him. There was a reason he chose to live in Bottle Creek and not one of the bigger towns in his home range.

Malcolm's lips were set in a grim line. Soren had watched the man get quieter the deeper into the range that they traveled. The car stopped outside Malcolm's home, and Malcolm thanked the man who had driven them. The man smiled at them, "Anytime, Mal. Tell your father I said hello."

When the car drove away, Soren stepped up beside Malcolm as the man eyed the house with trepidation. "We could make a run for it," Soren offered in a semi-joking way.

The corners of Malcolm's mouth twitched up. "I'd take you up on that, but you stick out wearing that coat."

"Are you insulting my formal colors?" Soren asked. Despite the tension of the moment, Malcolm had not lost his sense of humor, and Soren liked that about him.

Malcolm chuckled and walked forward. "No. I rather like them on you. I'm just saying you are too noticeable."

Soren fell into step beside Malcolm. "Did you just compliment me?"

"I let you bed me, and you don't think I find you attractive?" Malcolm's eyes slid to the side to look at Soren. Soren opened his mouth to reply, but the door swung open. A petite brown-haired woman ran down the pathway and threw her arms around Malcolm. Soren gathered that was probably the mother. Behind her was a man who was eyeing Soren as if he wanted to sell Soren's body parts on the black market. That must be the father.

The woman was rambling excitedly to Malcolm. "Oh, sweetheart we were so worried when you couldn't be found. Then they found a blood trail leading toward that awful place and--" Soren tuned the woman out.

The man's hand appeared abruptly in front of Soren's face. "Shelton Garver, ex-general of the eastern troops of this territory. Who might you be?"

Soren could not muster the enthusiasm to fake being impressed by that ridiculous title. "Soren Connelly," Soren replied simply and shook the man's hand.

"You wear formal colors," Mr. Garver remarked.

Soren looked down at his clothes. "I'll be damned. I guess, I do."

Malcolm intervened. "Dad, Soren is the one that found me on the border---"

"I've heard the story, son. I was talking to the man." Mr. Garver's tone with Malcolm made Soren bristle, but he tried to not let on. The man turned back to Soren. "So you are a general then?"

Soren smiled tightly, "Yes."

"Horrible what happened to that village," Mr. Garver said, and Malcolm's mouth fell open in disbelief. Soren narrowed his eyes at the elder Garver. "Were you there?" Mr. Garver looked very interested in Soren's answer.

Soren never got to answer as Malcolm's mother intervened, "Shelton Garver. This man is here on a mission of diplomacy, and you bring up such things." Her tone was scolding and harsh.

Mr. Garver did not seem to mind his wife's verbal lashing. "If they want to put the past behind them, then they can't flinch when talking about it."

"We are the ones who should flinch, not them." Malcolm's voice shook, and Soren could not tell if from anger or fear.

"We are the ones that killed their innocents not the other way around, father."

"Yes, I had heard you had defected to their pack." Mr. Garver did not look impressed.

Mrs. Garver turned her back to her husband. "Ignore him," she begged both Malcolm and Soren. "He hasn't been well since your brother left."

"Matthew left?" Malcolm's face fell. "I wanted to talk to him."

Mrs. Garver smiled at Malcolm. "I'm sure he'll be back around in time. He said he couldn't take it here anymore. He needed to go find somewhere that he could be free of the memories."

Malcolm nodded. "I guess that I can understand that."

"He had already gone when we discovered that you were missing. He must have left that same night." Mrs. Garver said and dabbed her eyes. "Thought I had lost both of you."

"Mom," Malcolm shook his head and gave the woman a hug.

She smiled against Malcolm's shirt sleeve as she hugged him back. "You just promise that you'll visit."

"He's not going anywhere." Mr. Garver boomed from across the room. The man was pacing in agitation.

Malcolm sighed at his father. "You have no right to hold me here. You can't."

Mr. Garver looked from his wife to his son and put his foot down firmly, "He's an omega, and he is under his family's protection."

Soren laughed. "You sent him to patrol borders, and now you want to coddle him?"

"Stay out of this," Mr. Garver rounded on Soren. "It's an old traditional law, but it'll hold up."

Soren did not look impressed. "If we are going to get traditional, Mr. Garver, then Malcolm is no longer your responsibility. He's mine." Soren had taken a few steps toward the older man as he spoke.

Mr. Garver eyed Soren for a moment then he looked at Malcolm with anger. "How could you be so stupid as to get bonded?"

Malcolm was so aghast at having his secret out in the open that he forgot to breathe. The next moment everything went sort of white. Malcolm stumbled backward and felt himself falling. He landed with a soft thud, and the smell of leather and a spicy scent filled his sense. "Soren," Malcolm mumbled.

Soren cradled the fallen dark-haired man and watched his eyelids close. "Malcolm? Mal?"

Malcolm's mother knelt next to Soren. "He's fainted. He's okay. Come on, can you get him to the sofa." Mrs. Garver stood up, and Soren hoisted Malcolm up into his arms. The woman led him over to a soft crème colored sofa where he gently deposited the dark-haired man. "Let him rest. Has he been ill?"

Soren nodded. "He hasn't had much appetite. He complains of everything tasting bad."

Mrs. Garver gave her son a look of concern. "He's probably just weak from morning sickness. I never could stand eggs, myself."

Soren eyed the man on the sofa. "Are you saying he's with child?"

"That's exactly what I am saying. It's a bit early for morning sickness, mind you, but sometimes in male omegas, these things develop faster than in females. Surely you knew there was a chance he would conceive when you mated him?" Mrs. Garver gave Soren a curious look.

Soren laughed. "Yes, of course. He was just so adamant that he wasn't that I--"

"No harm was done," Mrs. Garver assured Soren. "Darling, will you go get the guest room ready?"

Mr. Garver seemed to have deflated, and Soren watched the man leave the room with his shoulders sagging. "Is your husband okay?" Soren held no real concern for the man, but Malcolm would likely want to know of his father's health.

"Don't worry about him. We have lots of help to keep him in line. His mind hasn't been well for some years now, but when Matt and Mal disappeared it snapped something in him. I think it was the guilt of what all he put those boys through growing up." Mrs. Garver's voice was soft. "He was not an easy man to have as a father."

Soren replied gently, "I got that impression from Malcolm."

"I'm sorry if my husband's comments upset you. Most of the ones in charge of that dreadful time have died or are like my husband now. Still, the need for vengeance seems to breed a life into conflicts that should only be filled with apologies and condolences. We have very little blood left to give to the cause of vengeance, Mr. Connelly." Mrs. Garver eyed him astutely. "You might tell that to your Pack Leader when you return home.

Soren eyed the woman for a long time before he slowly nodded. His gaze fell back on the dark-haired man on the sofa. A few weeks ago things had been very clear, but now everything was muddied with instincts and feelings that Soren barely had time for, yet would move mountains to indulge in. Perhaps the time for vengeance had slipped away, perhaps it was time for something more.

***

Malcolm had come to his senses in his old bedroom. At first, he had feared that Soren had left him behind, but he had found the blonde in the garden. "Finally I find someone. I thought I had gotten left behind."

Soren looked up at Malcolm's words as if he had not been aware of Malcolm's approach. "Would serve you right for sleeping all day," Soren chided.

Malcolm sank down beside Soren on the metal garden bench. "So, I fainted then?"

"Big time," Soren said, and then he chuckled. "Your mother says you are with child."

Malcolm nodded. "Well, I should probably get that confirmed."

"Probably, but I've been thinking. You are right about bonding. What we did, it wasn't bonding. I don't know what it was, Mal." Soren's words were honest. The man shook his head slowly. "I thought I knew what life was about. I had a purpose. I had a plan---"

"And then you ran into me?" Malcolm interrupted.

Soren laughed, "Something like that." His expression turned solemn. "I meant it when I said that I would understand if you went home if you chose here. I still will, even with..." Soren paused. "I want you to be happy. That's the best thing for our child is for you to be happy."

"Yeah," Malcolm said softly. "I get it. I also get how much I screwed up things for you, even though I didn't kidnap myself."

Soren smirked. "Okay, fair enough."

"So, maybe we should start with being friends?" Malcolm offered with a shrug. "You don't have to adore me, after all."

Soren sighed. "I think it's too late for that."

Malcolm looked at the man and then laughed. "When did you find time to fall madly in love with me with all the plotting of revenge you and Thomas have had going?"

"That's more Thomas than me," Soren admitted. "He is finding it hard to let go. The tribe as a whole has tried to put it behind them, but it's hard when you live at ground zero."

"I get that," Malcolm acknowledged.

***

A few days later, Malcolm and Soren stood at the territory boundary. "Ready to go?" Soren asked as he looked over at Malcolm.

Malcolm nodded, "Why not?"

They stepped off into the woods. The walk back was surprisingly pleasant. The wind was frigid that occasionally swept between the trees. The leaves rattled overhead, and Malcolm listened to the sound of Bottle Creek in the distance. The sound of the creek grew louder as they neared the village. It felt very much like coming home. No one paid them much heed, other than lifting a hand in greeting as they passed.

Soren went to Thomas' house to report in, but Malcolm made his way to Soren's home. The trip had worn him out. He came in and collapse straight away on the bed in the front room. It was the bed where he had been tied up when he had awoken in Soren's house all those weeks ago. Had it really only been weeks? How many months had the weeks morphed into? It felt like a year, but Malcolm knew that it was only at most 12 weeks. He lay there until his eyelids slid closed.

Much later, Malcolm felt himself being lifted and he did not fight the arms that lifted him. He was much too tired for all that fighting nonsense. He snuggled closer to that leathery smell. The motion of the person walking made Malcolm blink his eyes open groggily. Soren deposited Malcolm on the bed and turned to get out of his formal coat and clothing.

Malcolm mumbled, "What are you doing?"

"I don’t normally sleep in formal dress," Soren informed him.

Malcolm laughed. "No. I meant why am I in here?"

"Because you are my mate and I've let you get away with not sleeping in my bed for far too long," Soren said conversationally.

Malcolm leaned up on his elbows. "I thought we were doing the friend thing first?"

"I think I am very friendly." Soren slipped off his boots and coat. The man looked very amused with himself.

Rolling his eyes, Malcolm gave up trying to talk to the man. He laid back and tried to go back to sleep. Just when he thought he might drop off the mattress beside him dipped. Malcolm's eyes came open as he got rolled into the man next to him.

Soren chuckled. "Why are you still dressed?"

"I don't strip at your command," Malcolm mumbled. He closed his eyes then opened one up to peek at Soren. "Are you naked?"

There was a moment before Soren said in a shocked tone, "Holy damn, I do appear to be. Who is responsible for this?"

"I'm going to sleep now," Malcolm informed the insane man, and he rolled away from Soren.

Much later, Malcolm's eyes blinked open at a draft of cold air. "Hey... what are you doing?" Soren was in the process of slipping off Malcolm's pants and underwear. At Malcolm's question, Soren laid down behind him, and Malcolm stilled as Soren placed soft kisses along his neck. The kisses felt so nice that Malcolm relaxed back into the blonde. "Okay, yeah. That's good," Malcolm mumbled unaware that he was doing so aloud. He felt Soren's chuckle against his skin and shivered at the vibration.

Malcolm practically crooned at the feel of Soren's cool hand wrapping around the length of him. "Please, Soren," Malcolm begged. "Please more."

"What do you want?" Soren's husky question against his ear made Malcolm thrust into the man's hand. "You want me to mate you?" Soren's lips brushed against Malcolm's ear, and he shivered.

Malcolm breathed out, "Yes."

Soren needed no more encouragement. Malcolm felt Soren's fingers leave his hard shaft. Malcolm gasped as Soren's fingers slipped inside of him and began stretching him gently. Malcolm's instincts were on overdrive due to the influx of hormones in his state, and all he could do was pant at the sensations that Soren brought out of him. When Soren finally pushed inside of him, Malcolm cried out in relief at the feeling of fullness.

There were mumbled words of appreciation from Soren, as Malcolm rocked back against the man to take more of Soren's hard length inside. Soren let Malcolm take the lead, but that only lasted as long as his patience. Soon enough, Soren was pinning Malcolm on his back. Soren peered at Malcolm in interest as he thrust into him at a leisurely pace. Malcolm's face was full of frustration. "Not enough for you?" Soren teased to the man below him.

Malcolm growled at Soren and the man relented by thrusting into Malcolm with abandonment. While he thrust into the dark-haired man, Soren fisted Malcolm's hard shaft. It did not take them long before they were both spent. Soren collapsed onto the mattress beside Malcolm. Soren took a deep breath. "I guess you really did want more," Soren panted.

Malcolm laughed. "As if you didn't have this planned when you brought me in here." He rolled onto his side and eyed the fatigued blonde.

"Guilty," Soren admitted. "I'm no saint, Mal. I can only be patient for so long."

Malcolm shrugged, "And if I had minded then I would have said so."

The next morning, Thomas came by. "It's good to see you back with us, Mal." Malcolm clasped the hand the man extended to him. "I know that with your condition that you might not feel able, but I want you to know that if you want a position with the home guard here, then we would gladly welcome you.

Soren eyed Malcolm with interest as Thomas waited for the answer as well. Malcolm looked at the kitchen table in front of him. The plates from breakfast were still there, and Malcolm could hardly look at the eggs there without feeling nauseated. "It's a kind offer, but I never wanted to be military. That was more my father than myself."

Thomas nodded his acceptance. "I've known fathers like that," The gray-haired man assured Malcolm. "If you change your mind then the position will stand."

***

Trace bounced into the front room and eyed Malcolm. "How are you feeling?"

"Well, I'm alive," Malcolm said. "Where's your book bag?"

Trace's mouth dropped open. "I can't go to school if you are going to have the pup today!" Trace clasped her hands together and gave Malcolm a pleading smile. "Please, can't I stay out? I'll help the midwife, and I can be really quiet."

"I thought your dad had already decided that you were going to school?" Malcolm knew better than to let the girl rope him into agreeing to something that Soren had already told her she could not do.

Trace pursed her lips out,"Well, he didn't exactly say that."

"Yes, he did," Soren quipped as he pushed the front door open. "You are going to school."

Trace howled with indignation. "You hate me!"

"I don't hate you. Go get your book bag." Soren gave his daughter a smile before she stomped out of the room.

Malcolm frowned. "I'm going to be a horrible father."

"You are going to be a great parent. You are the kindest person I know. Plus, you've been dealing with Trace for months now, and you haven't killed her." Soren said the last part as if it should be very encouraging while he got a cup of coffee.

Malcolm said adamantly, "I do not like you."

"That too is okay," Soren said as he grabbed a piece of toast off Trace's plate from breakfast. "You'll love me one day." Soren gave Malcolm a wink which caused Malcolm to laugh despite himself.

***

Mr. Connelly if you would please stop pacing," Mrs. Greene said sternly to Soren who complied. "Thank you."

Malcolm and Mrs. Greene were waiting for the surgeon to come. Male births were risky at times, and Mrs. Greene liked to be prepared. The whole idea of having a surgeon on standby made Soren more nervous not comforted. "I really feel like I need to push," Malcolm gritted out as another contraction hit.

Mrs. Greene checked and noted that the slit had opened that allowed male omegas to give birth. "It looks like you are ready. When you get the next contraction, push."

As Malcolm felt the next contraction hit, a man slipped into the room which he knew had to be the surgeon. Soon enough Malcolm was too distracted by the efforts of labor to worry about who was in the room. Soren had come over to wrap his arms around Malcolm's chest, and Malcolm leaned back against Soren for comfort. Mrs. Greene gave them encouragement with each new push and Soren whispered in his ear. Malcolm paid no attention to the words people said. He just listened to the tone of comfort in Soren's voice and pushed.

The world rushed back when he heard Mrs. Greene say, "He's out!" There was a flurry of activity as Malcolm dazedly stared at the small form. Mrs. Greene cleaned the small pup's airways, and a loud cry went up. "He's beautiful," Mrs. Greene preened as she brought the small pup back over to Malcolm. Malcolm cradled the child as best as he could against his chest, and Soren's arms enclosed both Malcolm and the child. Mrs. Greene smiled at them. "Mr. Connelly, would you like to come cut the cord?"

Soren nodded and moved away. Malcolm stared down into the dark little eyes that blinked up at him. "Hi," Malcolm whispered. "I'm your Papa."

***

One Year Later.

"Say that again slowly," Malcolm said as he swatted away the toy that his child was trying desperately to hit him with.

Soren reached down and scooped up the child. "Malachi, stop trying to hit Papa."

Malachi giggled and hit Soren in the face with the toy instead. Malcolm did not even try to stop his laughter. He pointed at Soren and howled with laughter at the look on the man's face. Soren rolled his eyes at Malcolm as he set the child back down on the floor. Malachi squealed with delighted and ran across the kitchen.

"As you were saying," Malcolm said as he watched the child disappear down the hallway.

Soren sighed, "I was saying that Thomas wants us to lend aid to your lovely home range. It's that new age of diplomacy that you wanted, Darling."

"I don't think I get why you are so upset over this." Malcolm picked up the dishes from where he and the kids had eaten earlier.

Soren followed him to the sink and then stopped Malcolm when he started to fill the sink up with water. "I'm not upset. I just want you to understand when you hear the orders tomorrow."

"What orders? There's to be an announcement at the tribal council?" Malcolm was interested now. He eyed Soren carefully. "It must be a horrible announcement by the look on your face."

"We are dispatching several groups of generals to help with some disruptions. That means basically that I'll be gone a lot, potentially for months." Soren sighed. "This is what being bonded to a general means. So far we've been through peaceful times, but things won't stay that way, Mal."

Malcolm nodded. "I get it. I mean, I do. I'm not going anywhere, Soren. Is that what you think?" Malcolm put his arms around Soren's neck. "I will stay here and tend to the children and work with Mia to set up that nursery school we've been talking about. When you get back, we are all going to be here. You just make sure that you come back in one piece."

"I didn't know you and Mia were serious about that preschool nonsense," Soren said with a grin.

Malcolm shook his head at the blonde. "That's because you don't listen to me."

"I listen to you sometimes," Soren said with a wink.

Malcolm rolled his eyes. "It doesn't count if all you ever remember is what I say in bed."

"You do talk a lot in bed," Soren said with a grin.

"Daddy!" Trace shouted from the back. "Malachi bit me!"

Malcolm and Soren laughed, and Soren went to sort out the pups while Malcolm cleaned up the kitchen. While he worked his smile faded. What if Sorent didn't come back? There was always that possibility when it came to war. He was just finishing up the dishes when Soren came back into the room.

"Soren, I've been thinking. We should get bonded, like official ceremony and everything." Malcolm said as he turned around to look at Soren who had come to lean against the kitchen table.

Soren looked puzzled then said, "If you want to then I have no objection."

"That was so romantic," Malcolm said deadpan.

Soren laughed, "I'm sorry. You caught me off guard. Why the sudden urge to make it legal?"

"I guess, I want to make sure our family stays together no matter what," Malcolm said softly.

Soren nodded slowly, "You mean in case I die."

Malcolm gave the man an apologetic look. "I'm sorry. It sounds so---"

"Reasonable?" Soren finished.

Malcolm shrugged, "Not exactly what I was thinking."

"It's responsible, Mal. You know how I feel about you. Or I think you do. Hell, I've loved you since you first found me on that border. I couldn't hurt you, so I brought you home..." Soren sighed and rubbed his face with the palms of his hands.

Malcolm smiled. "You couldn't kill me when your Pack Leader order either, so you mated me."

"You know that last part really wasn't part of my master plan," Soren said while shaking his finger disapprovingly at the man.

Malcolm shook his finger right back at Soren. "So you say," he said accusingly. They both smiled.

"So, when do you want to get bonded?"

"What's wrong with now?" Malcolm said with a wriggle of his eyebrows. Soren just laughed and went to get the children.

A half hour later found the whole family on Thomas' doorstep. "I feel like this is an ambush," the gray-haired wolf laughed at the family.

"It might be," Soren said in amusement.

Malcolm smiled. "We want to get bonded, and since you are the local authority we want to know if you'll do us the honor?"

"It's just a formality," Thomas began but stopped at the look on Malcolm's face. "Fine, by the power vested in me. You are bonded. Congratulations."

Soren sighed dreamily, "That was so romantic." Trace giggled at her father.

Thomas frowned at the young family. "You want romantic, plan a wedding in the spring. It's freezing, and it just started snowing. I'm going back inside." The grumpy pack leader closed the door, and Malcolm looked up at the sky.

Trace stood and stared up at the sky as well. "It is snowing!" The girl smiled as a white flake touched her cheek. "Malachi, look snow!" Malachi squealed at the soft white flakes that floated down. Malcolm looked at Soren over the heads of the kids and caught the man's eye. They shared a smile as the snow gathered in their hair and on their clothing.

***

"We need to go meet your Dad," Malcolm called.

Trace came racing into the kitchen. "Sorry!"

Malcolm gave the girl an indulgent smile and adjusted the bag on his shoulder. Soren had been gone for four months, and Malcolm was more than ready for the blonde to be home again. Malachi seemed equally excited as the little boy babbled on.

They just made it to the pack leader's home to see the last of the general's pack go inside to get their release orders so they could go home. Malcolm and the kids waited anxiously until they saw Soren come out of the house. Soren spotted them and smiled. Trace took off and leaped into her father's arms, Malcolm really couldn't run, so he let Soren come to him.

The blonde man let Trace slide down to the ground. Soren said, "Hey Malachi." The child needed no coaxing to go to his father and Soren hugged him fiercely before depositing him beside Trace who grinned over at Malcolm. "And you," Soren said to Malcolm as he pulled the dark-haired man to him. "I've missed you so much that I may never leave again." Soren hugged Malcolm to him then pushed the dark-haired man away from him abruptly.

Malcolm laughed at the look on Soren's face. "Did we surprise you?"

Soren broke out in a grin. "Is that what I think it is?"

Trace shouted, "Yes! Papa is having another baby!"

Both men laughed at the little girl's enthusiasm. Malcolm admitted, "She's been dying to tell you that for about a month now."

"I'm impressed. You must have bribed her very well to keep such a secret." Soren chuckled.

Malcolm shrugged, "I said she could help name the baby." Soren looked properly horrified.

***

That night as they laid in bed, Malcolm's head resting on Soren's chest. "Did you mean what you said earlier about not leaving?"

Soren stretched. "Yes. I already told Thomas that I won't take any more away assignments. I've also agreed to step down as lead general. It just doesn't mean that much to me anymore. I'd rather be here on home guard than fighting battles for other territories."

"I'm happy to hear you say that, but are you sure?" Malcolm ran his fingertips over Soren's bare stomach.

Soren admitted, "I haven't liked my job in a long while. I'm looking forward to the downtime."

"Me too, although with two little ones I think downtime might be just a fantasy." Malcolm sighed and gave Soren's skin a light kiss.

Soren laughed. "You kissing me like that is what leads to more pups."

Malcolm leaned up and gave Soren a smile. Malcolm leaned over and brushed his lips against Soren's lips. He whispered to the blonde, "I'm okay with that."

Soren laughed. "You should rest while you only have one little one."

"You act like you aren't going to be getting up in the middle of the night with the little one," Malcolm teased.

Soren sighed in long-suffering, "Why did I sign up for this?"

"Because you love me," Malcolm reminded him with a grin.

Soren returned the grin with one of his own. "Oh yeah, that's right," Soren whispered and gave Malcolm a light kiss. Just like the first time they had mated, the world felt right. The pieces were in their proper places, and they were home.

GRAYSON'S CAUSE

A WOLF SHIFTER MPREG BUNDLE

Preston Walker & Liam Kingsley

Disclaimer

This is a work of fiction. Names, places, characters and events are all fictitious for the reader's pleasure. Any similarities to

Chapter One

He first noticed them out of the corner of his eye in the raindrops—blue and red lights flashing in the pebbles of water that were dashed against the diner window.

He had been enthusiastically eating a portion of bacon and eggs, washed down with a coffee too black for any normal person's taste buds.

Though he was no normal person.

The waitress behind the bar raised her head, her fingers pausing mid-way through the act of counting her tips in time to see two men exit the police vehicle, and make their way through the door. A bell perched over the entryway gave a merry jingle, and the fattest one out of the two peered over the heads of chattering people.

The officer turned the entire way until facing him—the coffee drinker.

He elbowed his friend, and then they both sauntered over; cool in their approach.

"Hey, friend." One said. The other didn't speak.

The man continued to eat his eggs. They were rubbery, not much butter, too much salt. They jiggled like jelly on his fork, and he spooned them in greedily, swallowing silently as the two men made their further movements.

The policeman required some effort to slide into the booth, placing his badge on the table. The man glanced at it, and paused chewing. He reached for his napkin to dab at the corners of his mouth.

"How can I help you, gentlemen?" He asked, levelling indifferent eyes at the two men.

The fatter one grinned, all seven teeth showing. "We heard you been causing a little trouble up here." He said, rather accusingly.

The man shrugged a shoulder. "If sleeping on park benches and paying for my food is trouble, then arrest me."

The policeman's smile sunk into a cruel pull of the lips. The other already in the midst of standing was interrupted before things could get too heated.

"Where are you from?"

"Chicago, sir."

"Chicago." The fat one interrupted, grunting. "Then what are you doing in Phoenix?"

"Vacation."

"You're a smart one, aren't ya?" The fat one said.

The man didn't reply.

"What's your name?"

"Rebul."

"Rebul what?"

"Rebul Cause."

The second officer narrowed his eyes. "You being funny with us?"

Rebul looked rather innocent. "No, sir."

"Then your name really is Rebul Cause? As in... rebel with no cause?"

Rebul snorted a laugh.

“Listen now, son.” The standing officer said, leaning his hands on the table. He towered over the man, and made a threatening shadow on his bacon and eggs. It made for an amusing thought. “We don’t take kindly to wanderers around these parts of town, especially in a place like Phoenix... small areas are small, and they’re already overpopulated with people who were born, bred, and raised here. We don’t need no stragglers. You get me?”

“I got you.”

“Then you wouldn’t mind leaving now, would you?”

The waitress behind the bar looked a little embarrassed, Rebul noticed. She must have been the one to call the police. It provoked a sigh out of him.

“Not exactly, gentlemen.”

The fatter one widened his eyes briefly, the sparse hairs spread across his brows moving up with his creasing forehead. He opened his mouth to object, but Rebul continued speaking.

“I was born and raised here. I’m just venturing down from Chicago, on a family visit. Thought I’d stop on the way in for some breakfast,” he shot the waitress a glance, “and now it seems I’m defying the law.”

The second officer glanced to his colleague, and then back again.

“This here is a small town—”

“As you’ve mentioned.”

He shuffled his feet beneath the table; impatient. “Then what family are you from? I never heard of no Cause before.”

“*Arkwood* Cause.”

The fat one lifted his chin, eyeing up the man with intrigued eyes. He hadn't seen a member of the family this side of town for years, and the features then struck a few memories from his younger days—when his moustache was still bushy and his teeth hadn't decayed down to the gum.

The trademark mismatch of blonde hair and deep brown eyes accompanied by fair skin.

He was a member of Arkwood alright.

"We best let him go, bud." The fat one then said to his friend. "This boy here has a long trip up to the eastern sector of town."

His colleague glanced between them, and then nodded thoughtfully, slowly. The fat one collected his badge off the table and raised his hand in deference and apology, before disappearing somewhere towards the bar.

Hopefully to scold the waitress, Rebul thought.

He spooned another mouthful of eggs and bacon into his mouth, and then thought about what the officers had said. It *would* be a long drive up to the eastern sector of town, and afternoon was setting in—that hazy wash of yellow being tainted by sweeping clouds, potentially provoking a thunderstorm.

Rebul pulled his denim jacket closer around him, and laid four green notes on the table; crisp, unused. He couldn't remember the last time he had carried money, though in these parts of the world, you would be lucky to find an ATM machine, let alone a cash register that would store anything other than 10's.

Rebul slipped into his convertible, cranked up the radio loud, and set off onto the road, the destination in mind weighing like a heavy burden on his shoulders.

The first change he'd noticed was the slow thawing of green trees, forestry growing into the roads and the smooth tarmac shifting to rubble that made for a bumpier journey. The buildings disappeared, and so did the streetlamps and the typical green to red traffic lights. The change was sudden, and yet, authentic. He was just surrounded by the woods.

The trail took a sharp left, and away from a lonely road, he travelled down a lonelier one, flicking on his headlights to make sense of the darkness before him. The overhead trees had banded together to block out most of the light—even though the sky was overcast—and the shrubbery before him was blending into one twist of green.

Rebul bared his teeth in brief anger, and turned down the radio.

He thought of transitioning into his true form and running, though such a nice car couldn't be left alone.

He leant left, and tried to reach for the phone that was on the passenger seat beside him.

Maybe he could call someone to come pick it up.

Though as his fingers touched the screen, a blur of brown and beige leapt out before the car, illuminated by headlights and he was forced to slam a large foot down onto the brake pedal, swerving the car into a crowd of trees and crashing the lights into darkness.

It happened too quick for any normal man to notice, but Rebul immediately saw the deer that was darting off into the thickets, a wild animal—something he probably knew to be a friend—hungrily chasing after it.

He slammed his hand onto the wheel and the car gave out a rather weaselled beep, dying to a squeaky nothing where there, Rebul sat in the same darkness as before.

He took ten minutes to mourn his car, before cranking the driver's door and stepping out onto the shards of glass from the burst window. They crunched beneath his boots, and he sneered his nose in frustrated anguish for his totalled vehicle.

Rebul slammed the door, prompting another shake to the silence as further glass dropped to the floor, and relaxed against the bonnet for a moment. He leant his head back, looked up to the sky and thought.

Perhaps all of these mishaps were warning signs. Perhaps he shouldn't have returned at all, and let someone else take his place.

Though the predatory pull in him, the pride that stung like a snakebite... it was cage enough to not set him free. He couldn't abandon this. Not now, not ever.

Something in the distance drew his attention in this moment.

Rebul turned his head to the north, and saw there a small pair of headlights peering through the greenery. It was a truck, and it slowed to a stop just before his broken convertible.

The truck gave a honk, and sounded far superior in comparison to the relative squeak produced by his own ruined ride.

Rebul clenched his teeth, the muscles in his jaw pulsing out of frustration.

He pushed all reservations away, and strode down the dirt track he had crashed through. A light went on inside the cab of the truck, and there, a man with bright green eyes and dark hair could be seen. He was richer in skin colour, and an amused expression was plastered across his facial features.

He asked, “need a ride?”

To which Rebul yanked on the handle. The door didn’t budge.

“Is that a yes?” The man asked.

“I haven’t got time for this.”

“I’ll take it as a yes. Jump in, I’ll take you back to my place for some help.” He said, rather smugly.

The door gave a swift click, and Rebul slipped inside.

It was warm in the cab, and the heat toasted the rough skin of his palms; scuffed from the accident. He almost had the urge to raise them before the heater and warm them like you would before a fire.

He resisted.

The driver filled the silence instead.

“Been down here long?”

“Long enough.” Rebul grumbled.

“This place can get you like that sometimes. It isn’t so bad though.”

“You can’t have lived here very long.” Rebul laughed.

The driver shook his head. “Lived here my entire life, though went away for a few years and came back. I now live in the east.”

“You’re a part of the pack?”

The driver side-eyed his new companion, and looked rather wary. “Is that a shock?”

“Seeing as they don’t just allow anyone in. Yes.”

“I’m not just anyone.”

"To a leader you might be."

"Yeah, well the leader might as well be dead. He hasn't been around since I joined."

"And why is that?"

"Vacation, I think. He'd rather be doing business elsewhere."

Rebul nodded, and turned to look out the window.

It was black outside, practically a cloud of darkness that followed both of them—the only light for miles being the headlights, though even they couldn't part the shadows.

The wheels spun right at just the correct moment, and down a narrower path they ventured, until they reached a large gate that seemingly broached the darkness to provide different scenery from the never ending mesh of green and brown.

An intercom box was on the left hand side. The driver wound down the window and reached out to press a red button.

It crackled, spat static, and then a voice came through.

"Name?"

"Grayson."

"Position?"

"Omega."

"Enter."

A crackle of static sounded to end any communication.

The gates folded in on themselves, and a sizeable building came into view. It was three tiers of grey brick, and the roof held an odd shape—like an Egyptian pyramid. Two guards were at the door, sporting black costumes that were hard to see in this light.

The truck sped around the bend of the drive, and stopped just before the entrance.

"Come in." Grayson said, stepping out of the running vehicle. Rebul followed, and an unidentifiable man clothed in the same dark attire as the guards slipped inside the driver's seat and took the truck off to somewhere out of sight and more remote. They walked in union up the stone steps, and Grayson passed the guards with a nod. They didn't question Rebul's entrance.

In the light of the building, Rebul could see that Grayson was relatively tall and broad, wearing mainly denim, and a white t-shirt that clung to his upper body rather tightly. His hands were the feature that stuck out most, as they were the size of eating plates. He gestured out a hand to the surroundings.

"This is the boarding house of the east, rather notorious if you're lucky enough to stay here... I'd bask in the graciousness of it if I were you, traveller."

Rebul stifled the smile that tried to show. "Oh I will." He said, and continued to watch.

Grayson pointed to the upstairs, where a corridor could be seen running around the entire span of the building. "Bedrooms," he said, before directing his thumb behind, "and back there is the drawing room, where if you excuse me, I have to attend a meeting. Sit out here and I'll get one of the guys to fix up your car when we're done."

Rebul nodded, though remained standing.

He watched as Grayson opened the glass door towards the end—shielded by a curtain—and revealed a gathering of men around a circular table, they looked up as he entered, and then turned back to the speaker of the room.

Rebul relaxed against the wall and tried his hardest not to listen. Though it was just too easy and beyond tempting.

"... take action now." A distance voice said, disgruntled.

The room hummed in agreement.

"We can't make that decision." Another said.

"We're going to have to." The original speaker disagreed.

Another hum.

"Twenty four hours have passed since the warning was submitted. He hasn't come, we're going to have to make the decision without him."

Who, Rebul thought? Who are they talking about?

Some in the far back said something, though it was too far away to hear.

Grayson answered this time, his huskier voice detectable. "I say we vote without him."

Half the room disagreed. The other was silent.

The original speaker seemed to leap at the feeling of uncertainty within the room and said, "I'm calling a vote."

"They're talking about me." Rebul then said, answering his thoughts. A smug smile pinched the corner of his lips, and with a swift push, he opened the door Grayson had disappeared through.

The heads at the table turned, all turning in his direction. An amused twinge settled in him, one he hadn't felt in a while, and the leader of the table stood. Perhaps out of shock, perhaps out of pride, Rebul didn't know. Though it surely made for an interesting reaction around the table.

"Rebul." The standing man said—the one who had insisted on the vote, it seemed.

Rebul immediately noted him to be Bryson Berneem, a friend from his childhood, an Omega the last time he left. It seemed he had taken over the role of temporary Alpha whilst Rebul was away.

"I got the warning whilst I was in Chicago." He said, moving to the empty chair at the opposite end of the table. He sunk into it with watchful eyes, scanning the crowd. "I'm aware of the fact half of you believe I have no power here, or my position as Alpha is a feeble one,"

Grayson's gaze widened, and then fell.

"Though let me reassure you this. There are four packs in the town of Arkwood Cause, and we are the most notorious—despite being the smallest—because I'm handling the heavy stuff outside of the borderline. If it wasn't for me, this pack would have died off with our previous Alpha long ago. So, I would appreciate it as your leader, that I'm not spoken about in a manner that is so... disrespectful."

Silence filled the room, and at the opposite end, the other standing man lowered himself into his seat.

"Now," Rebul lastly said, "what is the emergency?"

Chapter Two

Light came through the curtains, and stirring in his sleep, Grayson turned to see the clouds had disappeared, and in return was a warm and welcoming sun. He gave a rather groggy groan, and pulling away from the sheets, he walked naked to the bathroom with a need of a cold shower.

He brushed his teeth whilst under the cool stream, and dressed in the same clothes he had worn yesterday.

It had been a stressful night, one that was mixed with an awkwardness he couldn't shake off. How could he have been stupid enough to bash the Alpha of his pack to the Alpha himself? It had been a foolish move, one where his mouth had gotten him in trouble—and this wasn't the first time.

Though how was he supposed to know? He had never met with the Alpha personally before, and although he looked a little too strange to be in these surroundings, it wasn't until he'd said his name was Rebul, that Grayson matched the blonde hair and pale skin with that of the original pack family.

Rebul was highways and landscapes of jawline and cheekbone, of ripped arms and thick legs. He was short—though anyone was short to Grayson—but made up for it in his muscle capacity. He was rather beautiful, and that made it all the harder for Grayson to accept how stupid he had truly been.

He stepped out of his room and tried to push his embarrassment to the side, opting out of breakfast and heading straight to the training field. Men today were testing the water to catch fish, others were attacking logs with their teeth—not entirely human in their form at this present moment.

A separate group of five rather burly men were situated around two bench racks of weights. Animalistic grunts and groans huffed as bars stacked with iron plates were lifted in a shaky rhythm.

And Bryson was talking to Rebul, pointing to the men out on the field and discussing something rather intently.

Grayson strode past all of them and began taping up his hands, winding them in thick bands of white tape. When suited up, he stripped off his denim jacket and went to practising his boxing on a tree trunk.

The sweat began to build though it only fuelled him more, he punched more with his right and served with his left, ducking occasionally in protection against nothing. Grayson jumped also, making way for what could be a potential attack for his training, and spun out a leg to jab directly into the trunk. It gave a lurch, and cracked under the pressure, swinging in the wind and crashing into the forestry.

"Free wood!" Grayson yelled rather tiredly, and saw the grins surrounding him. He wiped his forehead on the bottom of his shirt, and saw in that moment Rebul eyeing his exposed torso, quickly snapping away to discuss further with Bryson.

There was a flush of heat in Grayson's face, though he put that down to the workout, and went to join the boys that were gathering in a circle.

"Listen up!" Bryson said, taking charge rather annoyingly, "as you know, the emergency that's risen has been a pack in the north that has slaughtered a few of our men. Tomorrow, we go and charge them with the agreement of our Alpha, and take what we can."

"Like what?" someone in the crowd asked.

Rebul answered. “Resources... We’re a small town without much to eat save for sparse wildlife. Rather than kill for sport, take what they need to survive and in return, they can die off naturally or move onto another town. We’re not the type of pack that kills.”

Grayson nodded in unison with the others, though it appeared as if Bryson lagged behind in the unified motion.

“Any questions?”

“What are we ordered to do for the rest of the day, sire?”

“Train well and band together weapons. We need what we can get.”

The day slipped by without much sound, a steadiness in the wind that came through. Many were uneasy about tonight—abandoning the daily mantras of their normal lives in order to work together for the pack; that many had to sacrifice all for. It was different now than it was then. Men didn’t have to give up their entire lives in order to keep the tradition of the group in order.

You could have a job, a life, a family—and the necessities of being a Beta, an Omega, or even an Alpha wouldn’t be as strenuous or lonely. In fact, many men in the eastern quarter worked as doctors and nurses, as firemen and local librarians. Had daughters and sons that were destined to join the same traditions as they did—and even had grandparents who served among older generations like those around today; with the scars and stories to prove such a thing.

Grayson had heard the stories, the ones told around the campfire. He had listened to Bryson’s grandfather (before passing away) tell the story of how he hadn’t mated until after his forties, because pack life was so chaining. It made a few around the flames snicker—such a thing unimaginable to boys that were so hungry, so lustful for life and lively for lust.

Grayson had remembered in that moment blushing, and ducking his head when others elbowed and joked with each other. Stuff like that hit a sore subject.

Now, he held his head rather differently—high, proud. It remained that way as he passed through the field.

Night was approaching rather quickly, and whilst many worked on their psychical strength, Rebul was out in the barn filing down pieces of wood into forked weapons. He dragged his blade against the spine of some bark, and a curl fell on the floor.

Grayson entered, still sweaty from earlier, and yet, still cold from his shower.

“I’ve come to apologise—” He began.

“Don’t bother.” Rebul interrupted, sounding immersed in his work.

Grayson stopped, standing in the barn door with his dark hair covering his eyes.

“I didn’t know—”

“You didn’t need to.” Rebul interrupted again, still filing down the wood.

“Are you going to let me speak?”

Rebul stopped, glanced towards the barn door, and sighed. “No.”

“Why?”

“Because this conversation is irrelevant.”

Grayson was taken aback. “That’s a little harsh.”

“Not entirely. I haven’t been around since you were assigned the Omega position, and you haven’t been around since I’ve been Alpha. It’s an irrelevant apology. Plus, I don’t hold petty grudges. Life is too short.”

Grayson shifted his weight from foot to foot, deciding on what to say next. What he settled on wasn’t something Rebul could have imagined.

“Why did you become Alpha?”

Rebul continued to file instead, filling the silence until it became too suffocating. He stopped after the weapon had been crafted, dropped it, and picked up another.

“I didn’t. I was assigned by my father, and his father before him, and his father before him. We’re a long line of successors to the throne.”

“Wasn’t denying an option?”

“Not entirely.”

Grayson waited, and his patience wore off.

Rebul shifted his weight on the barrel of hay he was perched on, and filed at the wood some more. “The town is called Arkwood Cause for a reason. It’s named after me, and my ancestors. We took over the town after we became the biggest pack, and since then, it has carried on as a hereditary duty that we keep it in our name. Such a thing couldn’t be taken over.”

Grayson frowned, and then asked, “what if someone took it from you?”

“What do you mean? Like kill me?” Rebul responded, laughing at the implications of such an insult. “I doubt it. Us Alpha’s are pretty tough, or at least my family’s line has always been. The majority have lived to be old men, not young ones in a puddle of blood and pride.”

Grayson frowned again, wondering whether those words were spoken out of arrogance or certainty. He wasn't quite sure, though one thing he did know—all had changed since Rebul arrived. It was like the air blew a little differently, the sky shifted colours. He didn't like it. Grayson had never liked change. Though what could be said? His Alpha had returned, and maybe that made for the water running downstream different, and the birds swooping west rather than east. Maybe the town knew he had arrived again.

Rebul raised a brow. "Why the questions?"

It brought Grayson out of his reverie. He shrugged. "I guess I want to know who I'm serving."

Rebul smiled. "Someone who finally knows what they're doing, I promise you that."

Grayson felt his cheeks tinge a little again, though he hid it by bowing his head, rubbing the back of his neck with his hand. "I don't know."

Rebul raised his brows in response.

Grayson grinned. "You can't really keep a car in check... how do I know you can with your pack?"

Rebul smirked. "Very funny."

"I'm serious."

"You better hope for your head you're not, kid."

The dimples in Grayson's cheeks formed, and Rebul noticed them.

"You have a family back home, Grayson?" He asked.

He felt funny at the way his name weighed on Rebul's tongue.

“No.” He said. “Mom kicked me out when I was sixteen, dad kept me going financially until he died a few years ago. I’ve been on my own ever since.”

“I know the feeling.” Rebul said, and filed the last weapon down to the prick. He laid it aside and forced the knife into his cargo pants, where it would remain safe until the fight. He hoped it wouldn’t come to using weapons, though you could never count on such a thing. These altercations happened, and you had to be ready for them... not everything was business and first class airplane journeys.

“Any boyfriend?”

Again, Grayson rubbed the back of his neck out of embarrassment.

“Shit... I don’t know, man.”

“You don’t know?”

“He died last spring. I don’t know where that leaves me.”

“Lost, I suppose.” Rebul said. Grayson gave a slow nod.

The conversation took a turn, and the tension was almost touchable.

“Well, you know where I am if you need me. The Alpha has many responsibilities, counselling is one of them.”

Grayson smiled though didn’t quite know what to say. He remained silent, and they both stared at each other for a moment.

A howl in the distance broke their concentration—later, Grayson would curse it.

Rebul stood immediately, and the knife was back out and in his palm.

“That was an alert.” He said; a sense of urgency slicing through the tension. “Someone is hurt... something, something has happened.”

Just then a pair of footsteps came running down the dirt track, and the barn door was occupied by another silhouette. Grayson moved, predatorily protecting his Alpha out of devotion he didn’t know existed in him until this very moment. The air had shifted.

“There’s been an incident at the house. Come quickly.” The messenger said. All three of them set off in a run.

When they got back to the boarding house, it was full of an atmosphere that raised the hairs on Grayson’s arms. He entered the conference room and saw a circle of men huddled around the table. They lifted their heads to see that their Alpha had arrived.

“Sire,” one said, “look.”

Rebul sidestepped through the crowd and reached the table, finding on it a letter in cursive writing. It was stuck to the mahogany wood by droplets of blood. A few men peered over his shoulder out of greedy interest.

“Welcome back Alpha,” It read,

“You’ve finally decided to return after these many months away... doing what, us in the North wonder? Taking care of business and flying first class to get a richer tan? We choose the latter.

As a gift to welcome you back, we’ve decided to take the liberty of removing a certain problem from your way—Bryson, who has been an enemy of ours since the beginning of your absence. We hope you don’t come after him, as we might have to de-Alpha your pack once more if such limits are tested. I would suggest you and your band of boys move on from the east, and find haven elsewhere.

We are growing by the day and only becoming stronger as a pack, and as a family.

Take this as a warning, and don't go through with any of those plans you are discussing. We know everything. We will always know everything.

There is a mole in your field, Alpha."

It is signed by a large 'N' (from the north) and a bloody fingerprint could be seen by the edge of the page. There was a silence in the room and a pull on Rebul's brows.

"What happened?" Grayson asked.

"Bryson has been taken." someone answered.

"Why?

"To throw off our attack."

"But how did they get him? The gate..."

"That doesn't matter now," someone said, "we're screwed."

"No we're not." Rebul says, cutting through the worry that had managed to churn the air like butter, it spread quickly; infectiously. He felt guilty in that moment that he hadn't been there... He hadn't been able to reassure his men when times of trouble had arisen. How many people had died due to his foolishness? Due to his misconducted leadership?

Now was the time to take action. Now was the time to be the Alpha they needed—that he and his family's bloodline needed.

Rebul straightened out the tense muscles in his back, glancing past his shoulder to see questioning eyes burning into him.

"We move the attack to tonight. Ambush them. They think we're waiting... they think we're attacking tomorrow."

“But they spoke of a traitor in the pack,” another says.

Grayson looked alarmed, glancing from his leader to the note on the table.

There hadn’t been speak of such a thing in the group, he thought. And suddenly there was wariness in every pair of eyes in the room.

Rebul shook his head. “No one leaves this group; we stay together at all times until we leave. We attack tonight, and if I find out who has crossed my pack, prepare for your end.”

Chapter Three

He had never seen a pack of more vengeful eyes, burning holes into the side of his face as he waited, his nose pointed to the west. A small, yet, sharp wind blew, sharp enough to cut through the skin of his cheek. It swept left, right, brushed over the fine hairs of his nose, and settled somewhere on the back of his neck.

It was the wind of a moving animal, changing the course of the air as it darted closer, closer—at ease with the nature around it.

Rebul lifted his hand, tightening it into a fist—a signal for the others to hault, to stay where they were. Grayson shifted his weight between his two feet and looked out into the forest, where , a rustle of leaves raised the hairs on his arms.

"Steady." Rebul whispered to his men. They softened under his command, though continued to glare—their leader had been taken because of him after all. And who was he? To come back with such arrogance, to pretend to know what it was like to live like them, to serve like them... He was an alpha of idiocy, not of their tribe.

Grayson saw from the side a couple of the boys begin to bare their teeth at their leader, and in return, he himself growled. Now wasn't the time for a fight, especially with what they were waiting for.

An animal broke through the trees in this moment, and its reddish fur was accepted as innocent—nothing to be worried about. The great wolf shook into a human form, every spec of hair sliding into human skin; teeth disappearing and snout vanishing. A man stood in place of what once was the animal, and he stood, panting and frantic.

“Two men at the gates and three standing behind it. They’re wound pretty tight.”

Rebul um’d, frowning for a moment.

“We have to take them out,” someone from the back whispered.

“Killing is the only way,” another agreed.

Grayson interrupted, “We don’t kill.”

“We might have to,” Rebul said.

All turned to look at him, their piercing glares softening.

“You don’t mean that...” Grayson whispered.

“They have one of our men and they’ve bullied us into moving out of our territory. We can’t expect a bloodless path once we enter their land.”

Grayson lowered his head. He knew his Alpha was right, though it was hard to accept something that went against his morals.

“You must stay behind, Alpha.” A voice from the back said. “If you show your face, every member is going to go for you and we’ll be more bothered about you being killed than finding Bryson.”

Again, Rebul frowned. “I can’t not fight with my pack.”

“It might be the better way.” Grayson said.

Rebul turned and looked at Grayson with a strange mix of frustration—trouble settling between his brows and upon his forehead. He didn’t want Grayson to go either, though he couldn’t say such a thing. He only nodded, remaining silent.

“I’ll stay back in the east, half of you go, the other half come with me. We can go up to the high quarters and watch over the trees for a smoother path.”

The men halved themselves down the middle, and Rebul began to walk back the way they had come—through the shrubbery and dark oak. Though he stopped, and glanced back. Grayson was in the pack that would fight.

Rebul sighed, couldn't say much more, and sauntered on forward, going with his men back to the boarding house.

In this darkness, the three tiers of brick stood hauntingly through the clouds—the pin top of the triangular roof striking the sky that was becoming cloudier by the second. Rebul remembered when he first saw this place, back when he was only knee-high to what he was now, and holding the hand of his father.

"You'll become a great leader one day, my boy. You'll send tribes shivering with doubt and supply men with a true home and family. Sanity is with you rather than me, and it's something us tribe leaders lose as we get to a certain age—and the hair on our head turns grey... you have the capability to become everything we aren't, and everything we will. Take this lesson, and know that time will only bring you the finer things in life."

Rebul thought over these words as he climbed up the stone steps, reaching the path that would lead him further into the house. What was it that had made him leave, truly? Was it the business in the other areas of the globe... was it the promise of a finer pack? Was it his father's face he could see every time he looked at this house?

Rebul swallowed the tension in his throat, and went to the main room where the letter had been found. He placed his hands against the table and let all the muscles release their tight hold in his back.

The stretch felt good, and he released a groan.

Life was far different down here than he had remembered, and the loose threads he had left behind were hard to tighten again. He wasn't strong enough, he didn't have it in him.

Though being around Grayson made it a little easier… that was for sure.

Rebul moved his hands, wanting to run them through his blonde hair, though stopping just as he was about to. He thought at first it was the bruises on his knuckles—the red ones that never seemed to heal, no matter how much time he gave them—though the closer he looked, he noticed the glisten in the smudges on his hands.

He had pressed his fingers into the blood on the table—Bryson's blood that had stuck down the letter. He winced, made a face, and went to the kitchen.

The men had dispersed up to the high quarters, and were probably looking out for a potential attack. He would follow.

He rinsed the blood off of his knuckles and climbed the spiralling staircase that began in the basement and finished somewhere on the floor. There, a glass cube surrounded the men that were peering out into the wind with binoculars and red markers, making connections on a whiteboard that lit up under the beam of the moonlight.

Rebul sunk into one of the chairs around a small table, and looked out onto what was left of his pack. They were banding together to try and find their once-was leader, and what progress they were making. One of them peered over and saw their alpha, shaking their head and glancing forward.

They didn't need him.

Hell, Rebul didn't need them.

But they were here and that was all that mattered.

Rebul yawned, lent his chin in his hand, and allowed his lids to get a little droopy. He couldn't remember the last time he'd slept at night with the comfort of other people. He had been alone for so long.

He fought against his tiredness and forced himself to glance out into the night, it was starry and blue and the clouds were still moving. Sleep tried to drag him down deeper, and he yawned once more.

He fell asleep, though not before seeing something in the distance.

Rebul was awoken later, when the grey had spread far and wide across the sky. He opened his eyes to see someone dabbing at the hand he was sleeping on.

"What are you doing?" He grumbled, and shifting the weight of his body on the chair. A boy smiled, dimpled and kind. He had the face of a kid you'd buy candy from at the door, only this kid had stubble and scars on his left eyebrow and jaw.

"You were asleep for quite some time." The boy said. "I'm Dominic."

"Dominic... what's happened?"

"Nothing as of yet, just waiting... waiting and watching. Watching and waiting."

Rebul hummed and nodded again, feeling sleep try to get her claws on his weak moments. The wet tissue brushing his skin brought him back to reality again, and his falling head was brought back up with the reminder.

"What are you doing?"

"Washing the ink off of your hand." Dominic said.

"Oh," Rebul hummed, "right, yeah."

Sleep washed over again, or tried to. He nudged back up once more, and then the question surfaced. "What ink?"

"The red ink on your hand."

"That's blood." Rebul almost laughed. "The red blood of Bryson's that stuck the letter down."

Dominic stopped, the wet cloth dripping in his hand. He all of a sudden jerked Rebul's hand and brought it to his eyes. "This is ink." He demanded.

Rebul frowned, and then came closer to his own skin. He could see the smudge of red that wouldn't come off... and smelt the pungent smell of chemicals on his fist.

"I thought it was..." He mused off.

Dominic stood up instantly. "It's a trap!"

Grayson was prowling along the floor, the dirt between his feet being raked in large swoops as he pawed through the woods, desperate to reach the light in the distance. He plunged left, slamming into a tree, and yelped as he hit a thicket of wild thorns on the floor. They cut through his fur and made slashes of red on the dirt, churning it to mud as he rummaged around to his feet—all four of them.

Behind, he heard a scream—a yelping of a dying animal—and paused with shock. Should he go back...? Should he try and help the men that were ambushed?

Grayson couldn't bring himself to do such a thing, and knew the one person he could talk to, the one person that could make sense of this madness was his alpha... Rebul.

Grayson's eyes narrowed in fury, and whirled to the east. He pulled himself back to higher ground and began sprinting, running to the light that was yellowing against the tips of the trees and the edges of the mountains.

He sprung right and darted down a dirt road that pulled him closer to the boarding house, the glass roof above showing a group of people, all alert and watching the trees—watching for their movement.

Grayson identified himself with a howl and reformed himself into skin and smiled, grabbing a robe from the cloakroom as he did, marching up to the highest tier. A field of men were sitting around the table as he arrived, and there in the middle was Rebul. He got to his feet immediately, and embraced Grayson with a sigh.

It felt hot against the side of his neck, and it took all he had not to melt against it—the true powers of a beta and alpha worming deep into his bones. He had never felt this way about anyone (or anything) before... and he was sure it must be the animalistic genes in him, obeying to his true master.

Rebul pulled back and braced himself against the table, all seriousness in his brows as he leant over, exposing a red smudge against his knuckles.

“This is red ink... found by the letter left by Bryson’s capturers, thought to of been blood in the beginning. Sending you out there was a trap to begin with.”

“I’m aware.” Grayson said, still focused on his alpha’s hand.

Someone in the back—Dominic—spoke. “How? What happened out there...? Where are the others?”

“We got separated in the forest. Some of them were on the floor by the time I left. They were waiting for us. They knew. And there was someone controlling them, someone I hadn’t seen before.”

“What do you mean?” Another asked.

“There was a guy with a hood covering his face, telling them all to go after us just as we neared the river. If it wasn’t for the surprise of our attack—not that it was much of one—we would have been wiped out instantly.”

Rebul huffed, loud. He slammed his fist down onto the table and sent a thundering stroke through it. “How did they know of our plan!”

“The mole... the person on the inside.” Dominic answered, rather shyly. He faced his friends, his family by bond and not blood, and then glanced away. Grayson did the same.

Rebul couldn’t look away. He faced every person in the room and weighed intently on their stares.

“Who is it?” He demanded. His voice full of urgency.

No one answered, and Grayson did all he could to not cower beneath the power that surged through the room. It was electrifying, and at all cost, no one would challenge it. But his words, they bared an enriched meaning, something that licked like honey over the subconscious and made it for no man to lie...

A few dwindled on their speech, and then eventually, decided on saying nothing. The room was full of an uncomfortable silence, and then a voice broke it—glass sharded speech hitting the floor in such a crash, that it broke the confusion of every member.

“Rebul.” The voice said, stretching through the expanse of the room. A body stumbled forward, supporting something more limp. It was one of Rebul’s men, and he was carrying Bryson.

“Oh god.” Grayson said, and rushed to his side. He nursed Bryson’s head and there a fine line of sweat was prickling the skin. Blood came off in the same wipe.

“Is he...?” Grayson asked, leaving room to fill in the blank.

The carrier shook his head—his name was Jeff something, Rebul remembered —and heaved him up a little more. “Still alive, rescued during the mission... no one made it back alive but us.”

Grayson’s head sunk to the floor, and for a moment a sniff or two came out of him. Rebul immediately turned his attention to Bryson, and ordered someone take him to a comfier room—and for medical staff to get here right away. The storm would make such a thing hard—clouds and wind and rain gathering—though alas, Bryson would be seen to.

Chapter Four

Time jumped, in a kind of movie-like way. One minute Grayson was watching his old leader being swept out of the door, the next he was sitting in the glass hub alone, watching the trees for movement and odd shapes.

The wind came from the north, and rustled a few leaves. It was cold this time of year, so a few fell to the floor that would be hard to travel through in a few weeks time. The glass did little to protect him from the cold.

People were scared, and the likelihood of their clan being able to stay here—where the east was theirs—was wearing to nothingness.

Grayson poured himself a stiff drink and sat on the leader recliner, watching the wind some more, sipping and musing over his thoughts—his findings since joining the pack. It had been a good idea, perhaps at the time, perhaps for the future in mind... though now, did he really see anything other than mistreatment and mistrust there? He didn't know anymore. Hell, did anyone?

He pressed his elbow into the arm of the chair and began massaging at his forehead, the glass of whiskey balancing on his knee, the other leg extended out. He was a young man, not too young to bare no age on his skin—a few calloused edges on his fingers and thumbs—and a saltiness growing on the dark edges of his hair.

He had grown accustomed to the mystery that was age, but the thought of living (though not truly living) in a place without growth, and just eternal survival... it wasn't kind. Time wasn't kind to such a job.

And neither was betrayal.

Grayson had seen the look in Rebul's eyes as he scanned the boys earlier, looking for a figure to point the blame at. Though who, Grayson wondered? He truly had no idea. He couldn't think of a person who would dare cross a pack and receive such bad karma.

Alas, he drank some more.

Grayson eventually left the glass hub around midnight, and entered the second floor not drunk, but warm. He clenched his teeth and let the little muscles in his jaw bounce, his brows furrowing, his lips pouting as he thought.

He touched the doorknob to his bedroom and went to twist it... though heard a sound on the other side of the house.

It was a swift click of keys, of music. It rang against the walls in a smooth, relaxing tempo. It warmed Grayson further. He stepped away from the door and followed its rhythm, keeping to the corridors as he travelled further.

He met the music outside the parlour door, and peering inside, he saw a pair of equally calloused hands dance over the keys. White, black, pressing down together or darting left whilst the other remained right. They moved in sync with the notes on the paper in front, and didn't stop until the chorus had finished. The verse picked up then, and it was even sweeter.

Grayson swallowed, loud enough to be heard, and leant against the door frame, sounding a little creak on the floorboard. The music came to a swift finish, and then a voice, equally as buzzed though not quite drunk, said:

"Who is it?"

Grayson didn't answer, and stood in silence for a brief moment.

"I said who is it?"

The second time he noticed it to be Rebul, and felt his posture relax with the warmth of a familiar voice. Grayson pushed the door open after a while and smiled—no, he smirked. It was amused and yet cocky. It turned Rebul's stomach, and he pulled away.

"Oh, it's you."

"Disappointed?"

"No... just disturbed."

"I can leave you if you like?"

"No point in that." Rebul drank from a glass on the piano, and it went down smoothly. He hissed at the after burn and pulled away from the keys entirely.

"No. Don't stop. I enjoyed it."

"I don't enjoy an audience."

Grayson remained standing, watching as Rebul lifted off the piano stool and went to the back of the room to fetch another drink. When he returned the liquor decanter visible from the other side the room was down to barely dregs. He must have cleaned most of it off in the last few hours.

Rebul glanced aside toward the towering frame of Grayson, in a drunken haze reminiscing about a less stress afflicted time mere hours ago when it had been possible to gaze upon his bare torso.

As if the direction of his thoughts prompted reality, Grayson hummed in quiet contemplation, "How differently today could have turned out."

"Perhaps we can still savour the dying embers." Rebul mused.

“How would you suggest we do that, oh powerful Leader?” Grayson quipped, that ever present playful cockiness returning to his defined features.

The stretch of carpet between them seemed irrelevant as the temperature within the confines of the room seemed to become stifling, a hunger felt within Grayson built steadily.

That same hunger was reflected within Rebul’s blazing gaze, no longer a leader, more a stunning example of the male form.

Several strides sealed the act, large palms seeking the others body as lips collided in aggressive harmony. Grayson’s eyes slipped shut before moments later popping open, Rebul sliding his tongue between his lips and into Grayson’s mouth. A steady groan hummed between the kiss as the pair found themselves relaxing into the new ground of intimacy they both found themselves breaching.

Grayson demanded more, needed more, desired more. Slipping his large calloused digits beneath the hem of Rebul’s t-shirt he sought to touch the toned layer of abdomen hidden beneath the designer garment.

Halted in his tracks Grayson’s wrist was suddenly dragged aside, merely a taste of warm flesh granted against his fingertips. Rebul’s secondary hand sought purchase against the broad curve of Grayson’s shoulder, showing surprising strength as the chaste kiss was broken and Grayson was forced down to his knees before his Leader.

Without the need for communication in any form Grayson knew what Rebul desired, what his Alpha demanded, he desired it too.

Grayson’s thick fingers traced the buckle of Rebul’s belt, seeking to free the leather binding restricting entry into the denim prison of his jeans. Meaty yet nimble digits tugged free the buckle and proceeded to both eagerly and aggressively tug open the material that stood between him and Rebul's manhood.

Rebul's heated gaze searched downward, allowing his worries and fears to dwindle into nothingness beneath the weight of animalistic hunger.

Grayson gasped as the boxer clad rod of Rebul's dick breached the opening of his jeans, springing forth yet still restricted by the snug fit of boxer trunks.

A gleeful smirk twisted the corner of Grayson's lips at the sight, the prior need to protect Rebul transforming into an all-consuming need to please him absolutely.

Rebul aided with the removal of the remnants of his jeans, the heavy denim dropping to pool around his knees. Revealing a pair of well-defined and toned thighs, thick bands of muscle tensed and rippling before halting at the cusp of his knee.

Grayson could barely contain his delight at the sight, leaning forth to press a heated open mouthed kiss to Rebul's right hand thigh. Grayson's lips travelling upward to outline the base of Rebul's twitching and throbbing cock, the heat of the solid pillar causing a groan to escape between Grayson's parted lips.

Rebul's impatience was apparent in an instant as he removed his own boxers in one swift tug, catching Grayson off-guard and resulting in the large shaft of Rebul's manhood striking Grayson's defined cheek.

"At least I now know why you're Alpha." Grayson gasped as he admired Rebul's heavily veined cock, eyes roaming from base to bulbous tip.

Grayson's lips followed that same path, fastening themselves against the very base of the lengthy shaft before working his tongue across the stiff underside of Rebul's dick. The action drawing an appreciative moan of encouragement from Rebul, head falling back as his digits grasped a firm hold upon the back of Grayson's head to ensure he remained on task.

With one last greedy overly exaggerated flick of his tongue Grayson caressed the enlarged head before him, careful to tickle the sensitive flesh on the underside of the swollen tip.

Engineering a change of pace Rebul directed Grayson's lips to encompass the width of his cock, easing himself within the warmth of his Omega's mouth.

"Fuck..." Rebul cursed, a word suitable to describe the intense pleasure felt as Grayson's tongue left his cock slick with saliva.

Allowing for a few moments of adjustment Rebul merely watched with flushed features as Grayson went about familiarising himself with every inch of his Alpha's cock.

Rebul's hips began to twitch, easing into a steady thrusting motion to encourage Grayson along with his sensual actions. The flurry of gentle sucks, precise flicks of his tongue and gentle gags delivered ecstasy only rivalled by a singular act.

A final more adventurous inching forward forced Grayson to take almost every inch Rebul had to offer into his mouth, gagging abruptly as the large head of his cock struck the back of his throat, signalling the final straw.

Drawn back with a fervent yank on his short strands of hair Grayson found himself all but lifted to his feet before being directed toward the piano Rebul had previously been playing.

Bent over and left vulnerable Grayson gasped as his jeans were aggressively tugged down from his hips to leave him exposed and free for Rebul to exploit as he saw fit. Not that

Grayson was in any mood to object to any advances, he craved further contact and almost mourned the loss of Rebul's considerable cock from the depths of his throat.

Grayson felt Rebul grope at the muscular cheeks of his backside, slipping onto his own knees. An exhale of hot breath saturated the bare skin of Grayson's rear as Rebul leant forth to sweep an eager tongue across the entrance to Grayson's ass.

Slick with saliva Grayson's exposed anus clenched in anticipation, Rebul not halting in his attempts to stimulate his Omega.

The act didn't last for even a near the amount of time Grayson had wished for, Rebul only deciding to gift several lingering swipes of the flat of his tongue before alternative between a flurry of circular traces.

Left slick and glistening Rebul clearly could not deny himself any longer and wished for a more intimate alignment. Having ensuring Grayson was ready for entry Rebul stood and grasped a hold of his throbbing manhood, still damp from Grayson's saliva.

Directing the large tip of his cock toward the puckered rim of Grayson's exposed ass Rebul wasted no time adding pressure to the helpless entrance.

Grayson gasped out in desire, moaning in encouragement as he shifted his hips back into Rebul's motions. Grayson responsible more so than Rebul, as Rebul's rock solid cock popped past the tight rim of Grayson's ass and invaded his body.

Stifling a cry out of pleasure Grayson pressed his mouth against his forearm, biting down as Rebul roughly entered him. Allowing several seconds of adjustment before slowly beginning to roll his hips back and forth.

Tears blossomed in the corners of Grayson's eyes as a heady combination of pain and pleasure left his muscular back rigid and tense, clothes still clinging to their frames as desire left their removal a task far too time consuming.

Grunts of poorly disguised pleasure left Rebul's mouth with each careful thrust forth, in perfect sync with Grayson's low moans of pleasure.

It took perhaps thirty seconds of steady, deep, penetrating thrusts before Grayson was able to re-insert himself into proceedings and force himself back onto the rigid length of Rebul's cock.

Each greedy motion earned Grayson an encouraging squeeze upon his hips as Rebul drove his pelvis forward into the toned cheeks before him. The aggressive thrusts leading to a steady creaking as the piano shifted against the floor, the sounds of sex echoing around the room.

The steady pressure of Grayson's tight ass drove Rebul past the point of no return within minutes, the steadily building pressure halting only momentarily at the very base of his throbbing cock before flooding forth.

A staggered groan of pleasure was exhaled with a exclamation of joy, a load pumped directly into Grayson's backside moments before Rebul's body hunched over the bent form of the larger Omega.

"Oh fuck!" Rebul moans, Grayson nodding beneath pants of joy.

The pair remained entwined for several moments after the act, simply enjoying the tenderness. There wasn't much need for conversation, or sweetness. What they had done was a powerful exploitation of intimacy, and as beta and alpha, the waves along their shore had been timed just perfectly. It was meant, in many different ways of the universe, and they felt it in those breathing, panting moments.

Rebul eventually pried himself free, and ran a hand along the canvas of Grayson's back.

"You're perfect." He said, to which Grayson laughed breathily, sinking his red and sweaty face. He stood a second later, and touched the toned edging of Rebul's cheeks.

"No... *that* was just perfect." He corrected, proceeding to re-clothe himself. A moment later, he made for the door.

"Listen," Grayson mused, "after all of this is finished, and Bryson regains strength... are you leaving again? Are you going back to whatever business you're doing?"

Rebul couldn't retaliate with much emotion, but instead, shrugged as if it all was simple. "Not if you're around."

Grayson just smiled—a simple twitch of the lips—and slipped off to his room.

Stupid, crazy happy.

***

The light appeared as a small wedge on the floor, peering through the curtains and creating shapes across the room. It must have been mid-day, the sunlight seeming more yellow than anything else.

Rebul lifted his head off the piano—its body having swiftly cut metres out of the hardwood floor thanks to last night's doings. He yawned, stretched, and stood. Contemplating a shower or maybe just breakfast for now.

There was a lot to do today.

He went out onto the second tier of the boarding house and got steamy in the bathtub, soaping and rinsing his body—not entirely wanting to rid himself of Grayson entirely, but knowing that he would see him today... and all would be well.

He stepped out, dried his hair on the back of a towel and sobered up the gunk-liquor taste from his mouth with a bit of toothpaste. He foamed up the back and the front, spitting in the sink and then standing, wiping the condensation off the mirror with one swipe of the hand.

It cleared, only a strip though, and in the reflection he saw a figure behind him. Rebul whirled around, facing someone beneath a dark hood—the enemy of the other clan. He remembered everything up until the break, where the mirror was smashed to smithereens and somehow he ended up on the floor. Though when he awoke, after much time, he couldn't think about much at all.

In fact, many minutes passed until he realised where he was... or who he was.

He was still in a towel, bloodied and bruised. Whoever had left him did a poor job of ending his life, and as he stood, he noticed not much time had passed. The wooziness took him though, and Rebul fell against the sink with a groan.

"Grayson." He whispered, his mouth reminding him of his main priority.

He stepped from the bathroom once regaining his strength, and pulled on a pair of denim jeans. They were the ones from last night, and they smelt of bourbon.

He stepped out into the hall and debated whether or not to shift, though doing so would make him exposed once in transition, and he didn't want another weak moment to take his life entirely.

Rebul came from the corridor and moved down the staircase . His foot was on the first step when he heard a crash from upstairs, his head whirled, and he set out for the upper tier.

He made the first few steps before finding a foot, and a limp body attached to it. The body was wheezing, and for a brief moment, he thought it was Grayson. It wasn't...

"You're alive." The body said.

It was Dominic.

"Just about." Rebul answered, forever the comedic. He lifted Dominic's head and made a move to shift him lower. Though just as he did, Dominic snapped out a hand and grasped Rebul fiercely by the wrist.

"No." He demanded. "Leave me, I can sort myself out."

"You'll die—"

"He's still here, Alpha."

"Who?"

"The man in the black hood."

Rebul froze, looking up to the glass hub where more crashing was coming. He knew he would have to leave now if he was to catch this killer. Rebul gritted his teeth, groaning beneath his breath.

"Forgive me." He said, before jumping the staircase and making way for the glass hub.

At first, all he could see was flying paper. Though as he approached, eyes narrowed enough to make sense of the sharp wind—he saw the man in black.

He was standing in front of the glass window, except now there was no glass, and the air was forcing its way in.

"Hey!" Rebul shouted, grabbing a shard of glass from the floor, holding it up in a threatening matter. "What are you doing? Why are you here?"

The man in black froze, all of the muscles in his back setting. There was a moment where this stranger thought, and wondered what the possibility was that his greatest enemy was still alive... but no sense could come of it.

He turned, gradually, and the wind pushed the hood from his head.

It was Bryson.

Rebul in took a breath of air, and stepped forward.

"Not so fast." Bryson said, and made a move to the left. Rebul saw then what was in Bryson's fist, a scrap of leather, some that was attached to the jacket of Grayson, hanging out of the three story building.

Rebul made another move, and Bryson dangled him lower.

"Don't!" He snapped, and gestured out his hand. "Why are you doing this?"

"Why am I doing this?" Bryson snapped. "Because of you, because of your foolishness. The pack should belong to me!"

"Then why hurt Grayson?"

"He's seen too much, they all know too much... I need to start fresh."

Bryson lowered Grayson again. Grayson yelled and kicked his legs. The wind was coming in sharper now.

Rebul tried to get him talking more. "Let him and the others go, I'll give you anything you want."

"Oh, now you want to play Alpha? The humble leader? Please." Bryson snorted.

"I didn't know what it meant to be a leader until I returned. Please just let them go. We'll leave."

"You won't leave this pack, this land... it's in your blood to defend it."

Rebul didn't know what to say, he could only think back to what his father had said.

"You'll become a great leader one day, my boy. You'll send tribes shivering with doubt and supply men with a true home and family. Sanity is with you rather than me, and it's something us tribe leaders lose as we get to a certain age—and their hair on our head turns grey... you have the capability to become everything we aren't, and everything we will. Take this lesson, and know that time will only bring you the finer things in life."

He stepped forward.

"Don't do this." Rebul said, with genuine defeat in his voice.

"I have to." Bryson replied, and went to unwind his fist. A bullet came through the room in that moment, and pierced through his chest cavity. Blood spurted outwards, and Bryson collapsed to his knee. Grayson continued to fall from outside.

Rebul yelled and lurched forward, kept back by a set of hands he didn't know who they belonged to.

It was the officer from the café, from a few days ago. The fat one who had all the questions.

"Easy, boy. One of our men has your friend in a safety net below... breathe."

Rebul sighed, and collapsed to the floor. Police swarmed the glass hub, and outside he saw red and blue lights.

It was over.

***

The truck pulled to the curb and the motor was cut.

"Are you ready?" The driver asked.

Rebul turned and shook his head. He didn't want to leave, not really. Though he was needed elsewhere.

Grayson sighed, and dropped his head. His face was pretty mashed by the accident, but he still had that boyish charm that could make men envy such beauty.

Rebul reached over and grabbed him by the chin. The kiss was soft, reassuring. It was a 'I'll be back soon' kiss. Grayson relaxed into it.

"Do you really have to go?" He asked.

"Afraid so."

"You'll be missed. I'll try not to think too much about it."

Rebul smirked. "You can go and see Dominic in hospital. I heard he's low on balloons."

"You know he isn't after that delivery you made."

Rebul laughed. Grayson rolled his eyes.

"Promise me you'll message when you get there?"

"I will." Rebul reassured, and brushed his thumb over Grayson's lower lip. He took one last glance, and stepped out of the cab of the vehicle. It was cold out, he wrapped his jacket around him.

Grayson wound down the window, stretching across the seats to ask. "How many days will you be gone again?"

"Three." Rebul replied. "I'm only getting my car fixed, remember. That crash really did a number on it."

“Oh yeah.” Grayson said, rather cockily. “Did I ever apologise for that?”

Rebul turned. “It was you? You were the animal that jumped out...?”

“Aren’t you glad I did?”

Grayson smirked, and pushed on. The truck whirled off into the distance, and Rebul remained frozen, and amused.

He left Oakwood Cause, though temporarily this time.

Alpha Claim

A Wolf Shifter Mpreg Bundle

Preston Walker & Liam Kingsley

Disclaimer

This is a work of fiction. Names, places, characters and events are all fictitious for the reader's pleasure. Any similarities to

Marcella slowed the car, looking to Greg in the passenger seat. Rain pelted the window, distorting the shitty neon lights of the club. *Club Battle Blood,* the sign read. The sound of the windshield wiper dragging across the glass put Greg's nerves on edge.

"This is crazy, you know?" the woman said, her lip trembling. She slowly handed him a small plastic disk, no bigger than his thumbnail. "That's a tracking device. I recommend you put it in your shoe, just in case they search you."

"We're witches, remember? You can always find me with a spell," Greg said optimistically. Raising his leg, he did as she said, putting the device between his sock and shoe.

"Being a witch didn't prevent you losing your job yesterday, and it won't prevent a club full of werewolves from eating you," she said evenly.

Greg sighed and nodded. "I'll call if I think I'm gonna die," he said and dipped his head as he pulled the latch on the door and jumped out into the cold rain. He ran to the curb then to the alley behind the club. He passed dumpsters full of foul trash, a few parked vehicles, and doorways to businesses.

A fire escape made an easy, but wet climb to the balcony on the second level of the building, he knew, the thighs of his jeans were dark with water. He tested the door on the balcony and sighed with relief to find it was unlocked. Letting himself in, he went down a flight of stairs towards the beating sound of heavy metal music.

The first door marked *fire exit* he came to led into the bar. He stepped from fluorescent white light into the dark of the club, punctuated by flashes of colorful lights synced to the music. A sea of shifters milled around the dance floor and socialized at the bar. Some even eyed him as he walked in. Greg gulped.

The fragrance of body odor mingled with spilled beer (making the floor slick) and the citrusy perfume of a stepped on lime. Probably from someone's abandoned vodka tonic. It was like any other bar, except that at any moment these patrons could morph into an army of rabid wolves. He reached into his jacket pocket and wrapped his fingers around the pair of syringes he found there.

"It's rather wet out, ain't it?" came a voice thick with the drawl of plantations.

Greg turned to find a man with blonde hair, cropped short on the sides, spiked and messy on top.

"What?" Greg said stupidly.

"The rain looks like it caught you. Or you got caught in it," the handsome man mused. His smile was genuine, and Greg knew that though the joke was at his expense, it was in good humor. Greg couldn't help but grin.

"Yeah, it's embarrassing, but oh well," Greg said, attempting to act as natural as possible.

"Almost as embarrassing as a witch being caught in a shifter bar," the stranger replied. He shuddered and looked over his shoulder.

"You won't tell anyone?" Greg said.

The man smirked "Let's talk in private," he said and motioned for Greg to follow.

They wound through the dance floor and to the door through which Greg had entered. They went up the stairs and to the rainy balcony that gave him access to the club.

"This is how you got in?" The man asked.

Greg folded his arms over each other and hunched his shoulders. "Yeah."

"What brings you to my club?" he asked. The tone of the question sounded curious and friendly rather than accusatory. Greg couldn't help but eye him suspiciously. He just claimed to be the owner of this club, after all.

"I'm a journalist. Or, was a journalist. I lost my job yesterday," Greg said, rubbing his scruffy chin.

"I'm sorry to hear that," he said. *This stranger is damn attractive*, Greg was alarmed to find himself thinking. Truthfully, the man was at least six inches taller than him. His broad shoulders and bulging pecs strained against his flannel shirt. A wolfish grin played across his blonde bearded face. There seemed to be an irresistible pull to Greg's hands, wanting to run them up and down the man's massive thighs.

"Sorry? I'm sorry." Greg said, feeling silly as he emerged from being distracted.

"Don't be," he strode forward. He put a broad hand on the back of Greg's neck, running fingers through the short dark hair. He inhaled deeply through his nose. "I'm Joseph," he said, smiling as he savored whatever scent he'd caught.

Greg knew that Joseph was a werewolf; he wouldn't own this bar or act this strangely if he wasn't. "You're smelling me," he observed.

Joseph's other hand wrapped around Greg's waist pulling him closer to the big man. "Apologies," he said insincerely, putting a nose to Greg's neck.

His heart fluttered, and his stomach felt like bottoming out. But he watched every muscle move in Joseph's neck and could smell his cologne mixing with fabric softener and sweat. How softly Joseph touched Greg's skin despite the rough calluses of his hands. It sent a shiver up his back.

The mustache of Joseph's beard poked at Greg as he placed a first gentle kiss on his lips. Raindrops pelted his head, and the street lamp flickered above the alley below. Greg sighed and tossed his head back.

"Is this ok?" Joseph said, not releasing him.

“More than ok,” Greg said, bringing his lips to Joseph’s. Their tongues joined, passing eager lips. They explored each other's bodies with their hands. Greg obsessed over the thick thighs, feeling them through Joseph’s jeans. Joseph grabbed at Greg's ass, first running his hands over it, then beginning to knead at it lustfully.

Greg moaned as their erections met and began to buck into each other, their kissing becoming more heated. He could feel the rock hardness of Joseph’s massive cock through both their pants. He desired it so badly.

Joseph took Greg by the shoulder and guided him around in a circle so that he faced the opposite direction. Greg grasped the railing of the fire escape, rain wetting his hair and face. His skin had begun to burn; the cool precipitation felt amazing.

Joseph put his arms around Greg from behind, hands finding Greg’s belt buckle. “When I saw you downstairs,” Joseph said, unbuckling him. “I knew I wanted you.”

Fiery adrenaline pumped into Greg’s cock, and an itch began deep in him. Hunger.

Joseph unbuttoned Greg’s jeans and pulled them down around his knees. Rain began to weigh down Joseph’s flannel shirt, sticking to his ripped body. Greg’s heart quickened as Joseph went to his knees, soaking his jeans further. He spread the cheeks of Greg's ass and inserted a thumb. Greg moaned.

“You’re perfect,” Joseph said, kissing and nipping at his butt. His tender caresses and affirmative needy bites were only serving to arouse Greg even more, though he told himself he should feel terror.

“Oh my gods,” Greg sobbed as Joseph went deeper, kissing the puckered hole. The hunger reeled inside him, demanding more. As Joseph's' tongue swept circles around his asshole, Joseph massaged the tip of Greg's searing cock. Greg could only bite his lip and sigh in pleasure, gripping the railing and getting more drenched.

Joseph lifted his face and stood. “You taste amazing.”

Greg gasped as Joseph pulled his huge cock through the zipper of his jeans and rubbed the tip of it teasingly against Greg’s hole. His hunger was boiling over.

“Are you going to dose me with the sedatives in your pocket?” Joseph said.

Greg blinked. His mind blanked. Color drained from his face.

“No, I wasn’t going to, I—” Greg stammered. A lie, of course.

Joseph bucked forward, the head of his dick almost penetrating Greg. He yelped in surprise and delight, breathing heavily in excitement—and fear.

“I want to make you mine,” Joseph said, grinding into Greg's butt. Greg moaned, feeling the denim, leather belt and buckle, and soft flesh of Joseph's cock. “Alphas claim what’s theirs.”

Gritting his teeth, Greg whimpered.

Joseph growled and humped again, grabbing Greg by his dark hair. “What do you say?”

White hot fuzz filled Greg’s thoughts. A small voice urged him to think about the empty syringes, about the drugs to sedate this overpowering alpha, and about how he had to sell the proof that werewolves existed. But all he could think of was the pull of every instinct to accept this man into his body.

“Fuck me,” Greg demanded.

Joseph shook his head, unsatisfied. He spat in his hand and eased a finger into Greg’s hole slowly, Greg groaning ecstatically.

“Please, yes,” Greg pleaded, the hunger itching at him fiercely.

Joseph’s jeans and flannel were soaked, water dripping from his blonde beard, but he spat again into his hand and lubed up his big dick. This time, he lined up the head, and Greg felt him ease just inside him. Joseph growled, gripping Greg’s hips. Tilting his head back, the two men kissed, Joseph’s prick sliding in deeper.

His ears hummed, his heart sang, and Greg's body unclenched in relief as Joseph’s cock scratched the itching hunger inside, drawing backward, and easing forward. Joseph placed a tender kiss atop Greg's head, sighing as though he savored the sensation. Greg leaned back, fucking himself on Joseph’s dick, urging him to go faster.

“Harder,” Greg whispered.

Pedestrians were visible beyond the mouth of the alley, and the glare of passing headlights illuminated Joseph’s face as his brows set in resolution, and he gave Greg a solid pounding.

Greg licked his lips. “Yes.”

“Fuck yeah,” Joseph said, thrusting into his lover’s ass.

Joseph seemed to hone in on Greg’s prostate, spearing it relentlessly, drawing a loud moan from Greg.

A wolf's growl answered. Joseph, veins bulging, guided Greg to stand upright, wrapping his arms under Greg’s armpits, cupping a hand over Greg’s mouth.

“You’re mine,” Joseph whispered.

Greg never wanted to be claimed before, to be someone else’s. He avoided relationships entirely. But at that instant, in the white fire of the moment, he turned his head over his shoulder, lips meeting Joseph’s.

Breaking the kiss, Greg whispers. “I’m yours.”

Joseph howled a growl. He thrust forward with finality and buried his face into Greg's shoulder. The head of his cock felt as though it expanded, a bulb of glowing indulgence. Shuddering as cum spurted from Greg's cock and down two stories to the alley floor below, Greg sighed. The hunger subsided, and Joseph still clung to him, was still mounted inside of him.

"That was amazing," Greg grinned.

Joseph gyrated his hips, stirring his still engorged erection inside Greg's ass. "I don't want to leave here."

They kissed, and Greg savored the feeling of this gorgeous man's flesh locked on his own, but Joseph grunted and pulled out the still dripping head. He tucked it back into his jeans and zipped up. Greg realized he'd been watching the man's every move instead of dressing himself, so he awkwardly stooped to bring his pants around his waist.

A stirring of the air blew against Greg's face, and he realized that Joseph was standing over him. His hand shot for Greg's pocket, but Greg shoved it away.

"Give me the syringes and sedatives," Joseph growled.

Greg looked up at Joseph. Defiance flared in him. The intimacy of moments before felt ages away.

Joseph pointed to Greg's pocket. "Why needlessly harm someone?"

"I need money. It's survival," Greg said, furrowing his brows.

Joseph lowered his hands and smiled at Greg.

"Why the hell are you smirking?" Greg demanded.

"Nothing. It's just that—Well. How fiery you are really turns me on," Joseph said, shoving his hands into his pocket.

Greg cleared his throat and gave the werewolf an apprehensive side eye.

"You can move in with me," Joseph offered.

"Wha...what?" Greg stammered.

"Even if only for a little while."

Greg buckled his belt and tucked in his shirt. "I can tell you think I meant everything about being yours, but let's be real. It was just sex. Why should I move in with you?"

"You wouldn't have to see or talk to me if you didn't want to, I have an entire carriage house for guests."

"It sounds nice, but—"

"If you think I'm hiding some agenda, I'm not," Joseph said plainly. "When I saw you, I knew I wanted to be with you. Also, I genuinely don't want you to sell proof of my existence to the media." Joseph gave a baritone laugh, and Greg couldn't help but chuckle a bit as well.

"What do you say we go out for coffee tomorrow night?" Joseph said, coming closer to Greg. He lifted his big biceps and put them around the Greg's shoulders. .

"A coffee date? I'm flattered! Seeing as how I can barely buy it for myself, then yes. Let's."

"Perfect, I know an amazing joint with the most interesting latte choices."

"Well, then, I suppose this is where we should exchange numbers?" Greg asked.

Joseph nodded and reached into the back pocket of his jeans, where his phone was miraculously a bit drier than the rest of him. Greg did likewise.

"I should let you get back to your work, I'm taking your time," Greg said.

"You're not at all. In fact, I don't want you to leave."

Greg laced a finger through the belt loops of Joseph's jeans. "You're sentimental, aren't you? And dominant, protective, rugged."

"We're called alphas, though only one usually claims superiority in a single pack. Along with the alpha's mate, that is."

"And we just mated?"

Joseph snickered. "Yes, though my body reacting like it did with you usually only happens with other werewolves. I wonder what that could mean."

"Because I'm a witch, perhaps?" Greg offered.

"Maybe, but I prefer to think it's just because you're you," Joseph grinned.

Greg leaned into him, feeling safe and valued. Joseph ran a hand adoringly up and down his back, the damp of his clothes causing Greg to shiver. Joseph's beard scratched at Greg's face as they kissed.

Greg's hand shook. It rose during their lip locking and slowly guided a needle into Joseph's neck. He broke the kiss and stared at Greg wide eyed, but his pupils rolled back, and he fell to the balcony floor with a thud.

Greg stooped over the handsome man crumpled at his feet. He'd loved the dominance that Joseph exerted over him, and the feeling of him cumming inside him. God. There wasn't a sensation like it. He felt uniquely drawn to Joseph, intrigued, and compelled to know more. He was floored by the proposition to live with him, and also felt like the shittiest person: being so low as to repay his kindness by sedating him with drugs.

But, it must be done. Greg needed his independence, and this was the way to get the money. With an empty syringe in hand, he searched for a nice vein on Joseph's arm, which wasn't hard at all. He winced as he inserted the needle and drew back on the plunger, filling it with red ichor. He freed the needle from Joseph's flesh. Putting a cap on the sharp end, he slid it in his pocket, but his eyes lingered on the beautiful unconscious man. Lifting a hand, he placed it over Joseph's. They felt sturdy, unyielding. Then he intertwined his fingers with his, sighing wistfully.

"If our lives were different, perhaps we could've fallen in love," Greg said.

The door to the club slammed open. The flood of artificial light almost blinded Greg. He threw up his forearm in front of his face, turning away from the brightness. Silhouettes of men stood there, hunched over and massaging their knuckles. Four of them.

"What's this, then?" the biggest one said. He was bald with bulging muscles.

There was no reasoning with these people, Greg knew that. He stood over an unconscious member of their pack.

"I think I smell us a witch," said another, lifting his nose to the air.

Turning over his shoulder, Greg bolted for the ladder. He put his hands on the first rungs and began to dive downward. His momentum came to halt when strong hand grabbed him by the leg. Screaming, they banged his head against the metallic framework as they dragged him back onto the balcony, blood beginning to drip from Greg's temple.

"Take him to Dakota," instructed the bigger burly one.

They opened the door and hauled him back inside the building. He yelled, as loud as he could. So loud that stars began to dance in front of his vision. But the thumping of the bass and the flight of the guitar strings of the music playing drowned him out.

They took him through the corridor as he kicked and clawed at the smelly man holding him.

They shoved him to the ground, and he fell painfully to his side, in front of a man with straw straight gray hair, down to the small of his back. The burly man handed the gray-haired man the syringes that he'd discovered in Greg's pocket. This stranger twisted his mouth with disapproval upon seeing Greg, and spat on the ground before him.

Heart rapping against his ribs, Greg gulped.

"The fuck you doing in Battle Blood territory, witch?" Pack Leader Dakota Wiseheart said.

Greg cleared his throat. "I was coming to be among fellow magical folk, like my—"

"Bullshit," Dakota interrupted. "You know that our species don't get along. He held up the syringes. "What's in these? This one looks like blood."

Greg opened and closed his mouth, dry as a desert. He'd have killed for a glass of water.

"Seems to me you're intruding on pack business. The Battle Bloods have no desire to be in the public eye. Which is why we have a private club such as this," Dakota explained.

"I'll be quiet about everything I saw here, and where it's located. You'll never see me again," Greg said, stumbling over each word. He berated himself for letting his voice tremble.

Dakota smiled. He put his hands on his hips and hinged forward so that his face was closer to Greg's.

"What is this I smell on you? Joseph, for sure—but something else. Something more?" Dakota said, tilting his face.

"Please, just let me go," Greg pleaded.

"Ha, I can't do that!" said Dakota clapping and rising. The men around them all chuckled and held their bellies. "You've seen plenty; you know my face and the faces of my comrades. Plus, you have the smell of a broodmare to you."

“B-broodmare?”

Dakota grinned wickedly. “Oh yes. I can build a wolf dynasty with a mate of fertile stock like yourself.” He bent and smacked Greg’s ass, drawing cheers from the men around them.

Greg shook his head. “No. No.”

“Let’s get these wet rags off our new bitch, eh?” Dakota proposed, pulling a dagger from his belt.

Iron strong grips took hold of Greg’s wrists and ankles, forcing him down face first. “Stop, stop!” he cried.

“That’s enough,” said Joseph. Greg’s heart leaped, but tension was strung through the air. His handsome lover stumbled down the corridor, wiping a hand down his face and pulling at his shirt, watched by the werewolf pigs.

Dakota raised a hand and waved. “Joseph, Joseph, glad to see you up and at ‘em. What do you say we all share in a little fun?”

“That is my mate,” Joseph growled in a husky voice. He shoved his pack mates to the side, standing over Greg and kneeling next to him. Greg shook with fear and sat upright.

“He’s a witch, we can all share a bit,” said a man to the side, licking his lips.

“I’ve claimed him!” Joseph roared. He stood, hurling his chest against the rotund belly of the speaker. The man took three significant steps back from the force of Joseph’s assault.

Dakota clicked his tongue in his cheek. “Give your old dog of a pack leader a taste of the treats you’ve already gnawed on. It’s just brotherly courtesy, man.”

“Don’t do this,” Joseph said, pointing a finger at Dakota. “This is my place, one of the only establishments you don’t have to pay off anyone to keep. I’ve mated with him, he’s bound to me now, and you will honor that.”

"You son of a bitch, telling me what I will do? This is pack. My pack. I'm your king."

"Some king and his harem of canine whores," Joseph said, motioning to the group of pack members.

"Take him away," Dakota breathed venomously.

Joseph yelled as broad arms wrapped around his throat and torso. Two of the men struggled to lift and carry him away. His screams echoed down the corridor, crying out for Greg.

Greg felt pale. He flinched as Dakota knelt over him.

"Now that we can have some alone time," he said, though two Battle Blood pack members lingered. Leaning forward and inhaling through his nose, Dakota went to all fours and animalistically walked forward. Prowling, as though Greg were prey to pounce upon.

"Mmm, no wonder Joseph is crazy about this nectar for the gods. You must be some lay," Dakota snarled.

Greg yelled as the werewolf crawled closer. "Stay away!"

Lifting a foot and punting as hard as he could, his heel collided with Dakota's nose. The pack leader yowled and recoiled, holding a hand to his face. Crimson leaked through his fingers.

"Get him!" Dakota snarled through his hand. The two men bounded forward, their bodies warping as they came running towards them. Greg sprang to his feet, watching in horror as their noses extended to snouts, and their fingers curled into claws.

Turning, Greg ran. The soles of his sneakers squeaked on the linoleum floor, his breath and racing mind taking over his awareness. He needed to find a door out. A bark and growl from only yards behind him let him know he was being closely followed. He huffed and lifted his thighs to try and speed ahead, towards a door at the end of the hall.

He looked over his shoulder. The massive wolves lunged at Greg, mid air, maws open. Pulling an elbow close to his body, a wolf's mouth snapped shut where it had been. Lowering himself, he rolled to the side of the hall, the wolves sailing over him. Their nails scraped at the waxed floor and they slid even further down the hall. Wanting to extend the distance, Greg rose and sprinted the opposite direction. Back towards the kneeling Dakota.

In hot pursuit, the wolves resumed their chase with aggravated yelps. Greg, racing at top speed, lifted a foot and kicked Dakota a second time as he passed. The werewolf snarled and fell to the floor, unconscious.

Sides aching, and lungs feeling raw, he turned a corner, then another corner. Coming to a door, he closed it as the werewolves bound around the corner and jumped at the glass portal window. Greg quickly flicked the locking mechanism. They barked and scraped at the door, even pulling at the lever.

Satisfied they would no longer be on his tail, he continued down the corridor. Around a few more corners he crept and stopped, hearing voices ahead.

One of the Battle Blood werewolves snickered. "Boss is gonna put a pup in that street kid."

"Then you'll be farther down the chain of command when that pup can walk and talk," observed the other with him.

"Fuck off."

The room was a kitchen, populated with ranges, stoves, and deep fryers. Beyond the talking wolves, who rummaged through shelves of food, loud bangs came from a shut door. It must be Joseph. Joseph yelled, but through the heavy steel of the door the sound muffled into nothing that Greg could understand.

Greg lifted his hands to his chest, interlocked his fingers and closed his eyes. He focused on the pulse in his palms, the pattern of his fingers, and the cadence of his breathing. *Mudras*, they were called—the magical hand positions.

Stepping over the threshold of the room, he closed his eyes.

"What do you think will happen to the asshole, Joseph?" said a werewolf.

"He's toast. Boss is gonna slice him if he lasts in there."

"What a dumbass."

Greg's hand closed around the handle to the locked room, and he opened his eyes. An industrial refrigerator. He could see Joseph beyond the glass, smiling, but shivering. Looking the other way, he saw the doorway he'd just spelled himself from, and the occupied werewolves were still bantering, unaware.

Slowly and carefully as possible, he opened the heavy door to the fridge, putting a finger to his lips as the cold air blasted him. Joseph gave a stiff nod of his head, remaining silent, and stepping out of the frigid room.

Breaking through the terror, Greg couldn't help but glow, seeing his gorgeous wolf. His golden wolf. Greg wrapped his arms around him and nuzzled his face into his neck against the chilled skin.

"Oh what've we done?" whispered Greg.

"You... have no... idea," Joseph stammered, but rubbed his hands together, color coming back to his face. His expression turned stony, he pushed gently against Greg's shoulders. "Stay," he whispered.

Greg lowered himself toward the fridge door, and Joseph crouched, making his way around the corner, towards the kitchen as the two club wolves broke into laughter.

Then there were yelps of surprise and grunts of pain. Greg came around the corner; he found his mate huffing over the two men. One was unconscious, and one of the Battle Bloods had a broken wrist and tried to army-crawl towards the door.

Joseph's muscular chest rose and fell with his heavy breaths. "You and me. We need to get out of town." He picked up a big 36-ounce can of tomato sauce and strode to the still conscious werewolf, clubbing the can against his head. He slumped to the floor, out cold.

"I just drugged you and took your blood to expose your kind to the world. Then, I basically got you expelled from your own pack while within walls you own. You sure you want to stick with me?" Greg asked.

Joseph replied, wrapping his thick arms around Greg. "I want you."

***

His head sunk in a plush pillow, enveloped by the arms of his lover, Greg stared at the ceiling while the fan spun. Morning peeked from behind drawn curtains. Traffic outside the hotel was beginning to pick up as horn honks became frequent, and the chatter of pedestrians made their way to the open second-story window of their hotel room.

"What thoughts are you having?" asked Joseph. Greg could feel the rumble of his voice in his chest.

"That everything is going to change," Greg said.

Joseph intertwined his fingers with Greg's. "What do you mean? Everything is always changing."

"I know, but... I've never done anything like last night."

"What? Fighting werewolves and fucking in the rain?"

Greg smiled. "Yes, fighting. I don't do that."

"Well, why don't you—I" Joseph began to say, but he stopped abruptly as a gurgle in Greg's stomach must have become apparent on his face. "What's wrong?"

Greg held up a hand and ran to the bathroom. His knees smarted as he dropped to the floor in front of the toilet and vomited.

He lifted his head, his eyes watering, reaching for toilet paper to wipe off his face when a wave of nausea once more rolled over him. He put his face further into the toilet, retching.

"Oh no," said Joseph from the doorway.

Turning his head, Greg looked at Joseph painfully.

"Oh no—what?"

Greg turned before Joseph could answer to vomit again into the toilet. Joseph ran his hands over his beard and looked sadly at Greg.

"Why do you look like you're going to tell me something I won't like?" Greg said.

Joseph bent at the knees and dropped to the floor, sitting beside Greg. He took Greg's smaller hand into his and looked deep into his eyes. "When I saw you at the club I knew in my mind that the draw to you was some sort of pull, a magical side effect. And that's because witches have long been able to mate with werewolves, our magical blood gels as if we were of the same species."

Clearing his throat and resting his head on the seat of the toilet, Greg croaked, "So what are you telling me?"

"What I'm saying is that I've impregnated you," Joseph said, squinting his eyes closed. He opened them again, Greg staring at him.

"You're not joking."

"Not at all."

Greg laid back on the bathroom floor, his head on the tub. A fog had settled over him, which seemed a perpetual effect of his decision making for the past twenty-four hours. His hand rested on his belly, and over his knees, he could see the concerned face of his mate. His mate... Still so strange to think.

“I am happy,” Greg said finally.

Joseph’s brows lifted. “You are?”

Sitting upright, Greg inhaled deeply and took Joseph’s hand in his own. “I just don’t know you yet.”

Joseph pulled Greg into a bear-like embrace. “We can fix that.”

“What if you dislike me? I’m crazy; I’m messy, I have momentary ideas that take me off into the sunset. *Husband material* doesn’t describe me at all.”

“You also drugged me,” Joseph interjected, but his smile let Greg know he was joking.

Greg cleared his throat and shifted within Josephs' arms. “That was a bad decision, I agree. I regret that.”

“I like your fire. In fact, it makes me desire you even more,” Joseph assured him, nestling his forehead against Greg’s cheek and smelling his shirt. “You’re unpredictable and full of life.”

Massaging his back, Greg smiled. This wasn’t at all how he expected his plan to turn out. He’d lost the syringe of blood, he’d been caught by the Battle Bloods, and now he sat pregnant on the bathroom floor with his new werewolf baby daddy.

“I’m scared,” Greg admitted. “This is unbelievable. But, perhaps in the best way possible.”

“I’m worried too. You should know, this won’t be easy. But it will be worth it.”

Tears welled in Greg's eyes. “We have to not give up on each other.”

“Never, I’ll never give up on you,” Joseph said, his grip around Greg hardening.

There came a knock at the hotel room door.

Joseph tensed, and a knot formed in Greg's throat.

“Who could it be?” asked Greg.

Joseph shook his head. He released his mate, and they both stood. Creeping as silently as possible, they went to the door. Joseph peered through the peephole and looked to Greg in confusion. Pushing on his shoulder, Joseph stepped to the side, letting Greg have a look through the hole.

“Marcella,” Greg said, spying the brown-haired girl outside the door.

“No shit, I could hear you breathing out here,” Marcella said, her voice muted through the door.

Greg swung open the door and let her stomp inside.

“You... are friends?” Joseph said, pointing at her quizzically.

“Joseph, this is my best friend, Marcella. Marcella, this is Joseph.”

“Pleasure,” she said unconvincingly, measuring him with a critical stare. “Werewolf?”

Joseph nodded.

“Well, Greg, you know how to get extra credit. We agreed to get some wolf DNA, and you bring the whole man. A hot one! I sure hope you got DNA of some kind.”

“I’m sorry I didn’t reach out to you, everything spun out of control really fast,” Greg explained.

“Luckily, we thought ahead and had the tracking device, so I could find you wherever you’d end up.”

Greg’s stomach turned, and he bolted for the bathroom, barely making it to the toilet in time.

Marcella appeared in the doorway, crossing her arms. “Shit, did you get laid and wasted? No fair.”

“I’m fucking pregnant,” Greg said, blinking away tears.

"Very funny."

Joseph spoke from the bedroom. "He's not kidding."

A moment of silent exasperation came over his best friend. "What?"

"Magic," Joseph explained with a shrug of his shoulder.

Marcella groaned. "Oh, of course. *Magic*. I'm a witch, and sometimes that explanation just gets to me."

Greg looked at her expectantly, mopping at his face with a towel.

"Oh! Oh. And, congratulations. I'm so excited for you both. Are you going to get married?"

Joseph coughed, and Greg put his face into his palms.

"I'm gonna run to the store, see you kids soon," said Joseph. He kissed Greg, shuffled to the door, and was gone.

"Oh my god. How can you screw up so royally and yet be so fortunate to end up with hotness monster?" Marcella said with a smirk.

Greg shrugged. "I'm convinced there's a stellar guy under those pecs."

Snorting, Marcella playfully hit Greg's shoulder. He told her everything that transpired the night before.

"So now we need to find out where to head, somewhere far away that Dakota can't reach," said Greg.

Marcella chewed on her lip. "But there is a werewolf pack leader after your witchy man-womb."

"Shut up," Greg said, though he admired her creativity. "I'm thinking Montreal. It's cold, there are woods for Joseph to run in, and I can use my six years of French training."

"Montreal? You'll seriously leave?" Marcella asked incredulously, pouting a lip.

"It's not just the pack leader, Mar. The whole pack is going to come to help him, I'm sure. We've really screwed him over."

"When he does come he'll have two very talented witches waiting for him."

Greg shook his head. Her confidence warmed him. His best friend looked at him with a smile, though he felt the weight of anxiety in his stomach.

"Do you really want to have a baby with a complete stranger?" Marcella asked with her usual directness.

Greg swallowed a knot in his throat and blinked. "It's pretty hard to believe when you put it that way. But, yes. I've been a mess; my life's a series of punctuated misfortunes. I feel so sure about this, more than anything else I've ever attempted."

Marcella turned to look up at the ceiling. She sighed wistfully. "I'll be here to help, whatever I can do. You lucky bastard."

Greg grinned. "Lucky to have you."

Marcella put her hand on top of Greg's.

"Please," she said, "don't leave. Stand and fight for what's right."

"But what about the baby—and the Battle Bloods?"

"We can take on both, I promise you. If the werewolves show up—"

Joseph slammed open the door to the hotel room. "Turn on the TV," he sputtered.

Marcella grabbed the remote and flicked on the flatscreen at the far end of the room.

The perfunctory voice of a reporter filled the room. "A blaze rages downtown, started in the early morning hours. Club

Battle Blood seems to be the origin of the conflagration, though numerous buildings are affected...”

“Oh my gods,” Greg said, as a picture of raging fires pouring from the familiar windows of the club displayed on the screen.

Joseph sat down on the bed, hands on his knees. He stared blankly out the window. “Dakota did this.”

A cloud of smoke could be seen rising through the vista.

“What can we do?” asked Greg, going to Joseph’s side, and putting a hand on his shoulder.

“We can take them out when they come looking for us. We have to be smart,” Joseph said through clenched teeth.

“An entire pack of werewolves? We’re only three in number,” said Marcella. “And battle magic is not recommended in urban areas.”

Joseph cracked his knuckles. “We don’t have to take on the entire pack. I just have to kill Dakota in one-on-one combat. That’s what men do. That’s what alphas do”

Greg lowered his head, dying inside at the prospect of his mate fighting another battle.

“But if we just leave... and start over.” Greg said. “That way we can have a fresh patch of ground to grow on. And raise our child in peace.” He put a hand to his belly.

Joseph’s face set and he stood, putting his hand over Greg’s stomach. “I can’t wait to raise this child with you. But I won’t be driven from our home.”

Greg felt tears well in his eyes, and fear sent a chill down each vertebrae.

“I’m going to protect you,” Joseph assured, pulling Greg close.

Marcella sighed. "Cute. But what are we going to do about the werewolf pack?"

***

Marcella left to acquire spell components, and find food. The two men stood by the window, looking at the smoke rise from the fires burning through Joseph's business.

"I feel horrible for involving her in any of this. She should've just let me try to collect unemployment."

"But then you wouldn't have made the decision to break into my club. And we wouldn't have met." Joseph pointed out.

Greg pressed his lips to Joseph's. "You're a teddy bear. Large and burly, but so sentimental."

Crying out in surprise, Joseph lifted Greg and dumped him on the bed. They tangled in the sheets and each other's arms. He laughed and let the vision of the man before him dominate his thoughts. When he was alone with Joseph, the world around them faded to black. He knew when looking into the fierce icy blue of this man's eyes that a potential joy lay in wait, an untouched happiness that seemed completely alien. How could that be? A sense of foreboding set upon him, stealing the smile from his face.

"What's the matter?" Joseph asked, squeezing Greg.

Greg resumed his smile, though less sincere than before. "Nothing."

"What a liar you are," Joseph chuckled and kissed his cheek.

Biting his lip, Greg ran a hand along his mate's bicep. "Tell me something."

"Tell you what?"

“Tell me something. Anything. About you. I want to know more,” Greg said.

“Well,” said Joseph. “My favorite thing is fishin’.”

“No *g* in that word?” Greg teased.

“None at all. Dad used to take me out into the state park, and we’d pack a huge lunch. All day we’d muck through the stream and find the best spot to cast out a line. It was simple and wonderful. I loved being away from the lights and stench of the city and getting in the shade of trees with the smell of loam and honeysuckle.”

His voice sounded like poetry, ringing with the plantation accent.

Greg leaned over and kissed him, the softest meeting of their skin.

“You're incredible,” Greg said.

“Not so,” Joseph disagreed. “But I feel like a better man when you’re with me.”

Joseph kissed him, snaking his tongue into Greg’s mouth. Greg moaned at the wet warmth and aggressiveness. Joseph’s rough hands slid underneath Greg’s shirt and over his chest, hovering over his nipples. Greg could feel himself getting hard, pushing against the zipper of his pants. He writhed beneath his alpha’s touch, the hunger from before beginning to nibble at him from his core.

Taking hold of the hem of Greg’s shirt, Joseph rolled it up his chest and over his head. Joseph went to his hand and knees on the mattress and seemed to inspect his pregnant mate. Locked in eye contact for a moment, it broke when Joseph moved lower to look over Greg’s bared chest. He bent and put his lips to Greg’s nipple, placing silken kisses on the raised flesh. His beard scratched at Greg’s skin a bit, but he didn't mind. In fact, it served to make him even harder. The warm velvet of Joseph’s mouth moved lower to Greg's abs, and then to the V section just above his groin. Thick fingers worked with dexterity, and he undid the belt around Greg's waist and pulled down his pants. Exposing the erect cock within.

Joseph's hot breath drove him nuts as he kissed inside Greg's thighs. He moved higher to the side of his balls, and Greg thought he could blow a load without his dick being touched. But when the velvet of Joseph's mouth swept over the head of Greg's cock, he groaned loudly.

Grinning, Joseph took a hold of his manhood. "You're a perfect fit."

"You fit perfectly inside me," Greg said, rising and massaging at the crotch of Joseph's jeans. Joseph smiled and pushed against Greg's chest so that he had to lay back down.

Joseph enveloped Greg's dick in his mouth, holding his balls gently in hand. The other hand slid up and down the shaft, as he sucked off Greg.

While the ecstasy of this intimacy was real, the hunger inside Greg knew what he wanted. Greg put both hands on either side of Joseph's face and guided him upward, to awaiting lips and passionate kisses. Greg's chin almost felt raw from rubbing against Joseph's facial hair.

"I want you more than ever before," Greg said, lifting his legs and wrapping them around Joseph's waist.

Joseph tenderly kissed Greg's forehead. He broke from Greg's embrace to stand and pull his shirt over his head and shove off his jeans. Leaping, he tackled the already prone Greg, showering him with more loving nips. Greg laughed in delight.

On top of him, Joseph pushed his dick against Greg's ass, eliciting a moan from him.

"Let's have twins," Greg smirked.

Joseph spat on his hand and massaged Greg's sphincter. He greedily inserted a finger, Greg shuddering in approval.

Joseph curved his finger and kneaded at Greg's spot. The hunger flared.

"I need you," Greg pleaded.

Joseph grinned. Greg thought it must feed the alpha part of him to be wanted so badly.

Lifting his legs, Greg spread apart his ass cheeks. Joseph squatted on the mattress, working the head of his big dick into Greg's awaiting hole. Watching his mate's expression, Joseph eased forward. Greg felt the release as Joseph slowly buried his cock to the hilt in his ass, itching at the point of hunger.

"Ah, yes," Greg chuckled.

Joseph brought himself lower so that he was face to face with Greg. "It is a perfect fit," Joseph said, starting to fuck Greg with a steadier rhythm.

"C'mon, fuck me, Joseph," Greg urged, feeling the hunger welling up again.

"I'm gonna put another pup in you," Joseph growled.

"Yes," breathed Greg.

Joseph entirely unsheathed his cock from Greg's ass before plunging it back in, balls deep. Joseph gyrated, his massive manhood rubbing Greg's insides before removing it again and then burying himself in Greg once more.

"I'm gonna cum," Greg said urgently. Ropes of semen shot from his dick onto his chest.

"Fuck," Joseph said, pumping in and out of his mate.

Despite having orgasmed, Greg felt the hunger pulling at him. It still held him captive with urgent need.

"Cum inside me, babe," Greg pushed, breathing hard.

Sweat dripped from the tip of Joseph's nose onto Greg's face. Joseph was truthfully as drenched as he'd been the night before. His thighs bulged, and his veins protruded from his skin.

Greg cried out as he was lifted. Joseph's face turned red from strain as he held Greg against him, still embedded in his ass. Greg held on with his arms around Joseph's shoulders, and his legs wrapped around his waist. Joseph led him to the window, putting Greg's back against the glass for support. He regained his former rhythm, plowing Greg.

Greg felt he was floating on a cloud of ecstasy. Cum from before dripped down his chest, but Joseph was relentless. He wasn't satisfied yet. And neither was the nagging hunger within.

"Fill me up," Greg ordered, leaning forward and nipping at Joseph's ear.

"Not yet. I'm not done with you," Joseph growled.

Joseph removed his dick from Greg, and set him on his feet. He pulled Greg to the bed, and lay him on his back, but so that his hips hung off the edge of the mattress. Joseph ran his tongue along Greg's torso, lapping at the semen, and working his way down to Greg's groin. He lifted Greg's legs, and put pressed kisses to Greg's ass.

Greg moaned.

Standing, Joseph teased his head into Greg's hole again. He fucked him with only the tip of his cock, groaning as he inserted and pulled out.

"Give it all to me," Greg said.

Joseph opened his mouth and howled as he drove his dick deep into Greg, where he felt it become even more engorged. Joseph emptied his seed into him. Groaning, his cock spasmed inside of Greg, drawing more waves of ecstasy. Greg felt the itch reach a climax, and more semen spurted from his member into a slick puddle on his chest.

Joseph remained inside Greg, eyes locked together as much as their bodies.

"I think that we're going to have an amazing life together," Joseph said, kissing Greg.

Greg ran his hand over Joseph's back. "I know we will."

***

Marcella came back to the hotel room with wire hangers, scissors, and unlabeled cloth pouches in plastic grocery store bags.

"Just thought we should be as prepared as possible." Marcella shrugged. She cut the wire hangers into L-shaped rods. "These are called dowsing rods; they will help us find Dakota. These," she motioned to the pouches, "are for when we find Dakota.

"Then let's go," Joseph said anxiously.

Marcella held the rods in front of her as she led the group. Holding them by the short part of the device, they would swivel either way, as though honing in on something.

"The trail might be warded," Marcella said. She walked in a circle, the rods going every which way until she faced west. The rods crossed.

"Ah ha, this way," she said and started down the boulevard at a fast walk.

Joseph and Greg trailed her several blocks. Sometimes the rods would uncross, and Marcella would have to circle to find the new direction to turn.

Joseph stopped after they had been walking for a half hour.

"I know where the rods are taking us. The old club the Battle Bloods used to use," Joseph said.

“What do you know about the club?” Marcella asked, pointedly.”We need to know how to seclude Dakota.”

“Not good news. They took over an old school house on the west side. Dakota stays in a room on the top floor. It will be heavily guarded by the most elite wolves in the pack.” Joseph explained.

They came to an intersection, the derelict brick school directly across from them. Either side of the building had an alley separating it from two apartment buildings.

Joseph pointed to a neighboring building of the same height as the school. “I’m going to the roof of that apartment building and jumping over. Otherwise, we’ll be fighting our way up.”

“I’m going with you.” said Greg.

“Then I will create a distraction to get the wolf goons away from you and Dakota,” Marcella said.

Pulling Marcella into a hug, Greg tensed his jaw with worry. “Be careful.”

Marcella squeezed him. “You too.”

Joseph and Greg entered the art deco-style apartment building to the school’s left side. They ascended the spiraling staircase until they reached the roof access and let themselves out.

“This looks a lot higher up than it did from street level,” Greg said.

Joseph went to the edge, the toe of his boot just over the edge, causing Greg’s palms to sweat and his pulse to quicken.

“I-I dunno,” said Greg.

“You stay here, and I’ll be back for you,” Joseph said, striding to him. Joseph took Greg’s hands in his own and kissed him.

“No way,” Greg said when the kiss was broken.

An impish smirk stretched across Joseph's face. He turned, got a running start, and vaulted himself out into the open air. Greg's breath caught.

Joseph seemed to hang there in mid air. Greg's jaw was tight and his hands clenched. Joseph came crashing into a heap on the roof of the school. He stood and wiped sweat from his brow and dusted his dirtied clothes.

Greg took steps back and paced. He stared at the edge of the apartment building—and the void separating it. Perhaps only his legs would break if he fell?

He gulped and took even more steps back away from the ledge before starting into a sprint. His arms pumped, and he inhaled heavily. Coming to the ledge he sunk into a squat before pumping his thighs upward and forward.

Air.

Just seeming to hang there. Greg saw the alley below, and the trash in the dumpsters. He flew closer and closer to Joseph, and before he knew it, he was wrapped in his arms on the rooftop, the landing rattling his bones.

"That wasn't so bad," Joseph said, grinning.

They found the door to access the building and let themselves in. Creeping through the hallway, they descended into the school's interior, floored with original hardwoods that had warped with time. Wallpaper peeled in strips from the wall, and the ceiling was buckling in places.

"Fire!" came a shout from below them. "Fire!"

Greg and Joseph looked to one another and said jointly, "Marcella."

A door opened down the corridor from them and out stepped Dakota. His nose was bright red and looked broken. Appearing frantic at first, he then caught sight of the pair. A beaming grin breaking onto his face, he gave a deep bellied laugh.

"Ah, the great Joseph and his new puppy. How fortunate that I may enjoy you both a second day in a row."

"Stay back," Joseph said, stepping forward. Greg hesitantly did as he said.

Dakota folded his arms. "Your fucking hero complex pisses me off. You think you're here to kill me?"

Joseph stood squarely raising his fists. "Yes. We're going to settle this like alphas."

"And the winner gets the baby maker?" Dakota said, looking to Greg. A pallor of terror set into Greg.

Snarling, Joseph launched himself at Dakota. Dakota, quick as a cat, shifted to the side and landed a punch to the side of Joseph's face. Grunting, Joseph flew against the wall from the force of the blow.

"Joseph!" cried Greg.

"Ha! Joseph!" Dakota yelled, mocking him. "Shut up, you."

Joseph staggered to his feet, ran across the hall towards Dakota, and tackled him head first.

To the floor they tumbled. Joseph's elbow drew back, and he sent a fist colliding with Dakota's face. Dakota bucked up his hips, throwing Joseph from on top of him. They both got to their feet and began circling one another.

Blood colored one side of Joseph's beard from a cut on his lip, and his flannel shirt was torn. Dakota formed another fist and seemed but a blur as he crossed the hallway, punching Joseph's stomach. He doubled over to his knees. Blood speckled the floor as Joseph coughed. He writhed there in pain.

"This is what you would prefer to me?" Dakota asked, motioning to the heap on the ground.

"A million times over, I would," Greg snarled.

Dakota took a slow step towards Greg. “Then you are really only good for the one thing I need from you.”

“Stay the fuck away,” Greg ordered. He took steps backward

Joseph appeared behind Dakota’s shoulder.

“You can’t run from me, Greg. I’ve caught your scent.”

“You’ll never have me willingly,” Greg said.

“That’s alright. Sex will be all the sweeter,” Dakota said disgustingly.

Joseph lunged then. His handsome face transforming mid-motion. A snout sprouted with whiskers and sharp canine teeth, and ears tufted by a golden coat. Joseph’s werewolf mouth clamped down on Dakota’s neck.

Greg heard a snap. A bone break. Dakota went limp to the floor, Joseph standing behind him, the front of his flannel colored with gore.

They rushed to one another and wrapped arms in a tight embrace.

“Are you alright?” Greg asked, putting a hand to the side of Joseph’s face. He was roughed up with blood through his facial hair and a bruised cheek, but Joseph looked upon Greg with an intensity that made the hunger flare.

“Now that I can hold you, kiss you, fuck you as I please—I’m perfect. We’re pack now, Greg. I want you to know that I will always protect you and our family.”

It couldn’t be explained, but at that moment tears fell from Greg’s eyes, and he placed his head on Joseph’s shoulder. He felt fulfillment, completion of something, warmth, and love. Greg wanted nothing more than to make Joseph as happy as he felt in these moments. This responsibility he bestowed on himself. It felt new and frightening, but organic and powerful.

Marcella came down the roof access stairway. "Good, you were successful?"

Greg smiled at her, "Yes, thanks to you." He broke from Joseph to wrap her in a hug.

"It was nothing; I just cast a fire spell on the dumpsters along the eastern side of the building," she explained.

"Let's go downstairs," said Joseph, though Greg and Marcella shared anxious side glances.

They found the grand staircase and soon came across a brigade of Battle Bloods in the main lobby.

"It was these fuckers who set the fire," roared a man with a bandage over a side of his head, who Greg thought must be the man that Joseph clubbed with a can.

"It was. And now, Dakota is dead," Joseph said to those congregated. Marcella and Greg stood by his side at the landing above the lobby.

A murmur rippled among them.

"That makes me your new pack leader," Joseph continued, taking hold of Greg's hand, "and Greg as my mate. You will be following us now."

The crowd before them stirred and seemed to hesitantly look at one another before the man with the bandaged head came forward. He stood before the first step of the staircase and sunk to his knee.

"I welcome you, pack leader," he said.

Another came forward and knelt beside the first man. "I, too, welcome you, pack leader," he said, before bowing his head.

A small number of men threw up their hands and spat on the ground, but several more werewolves came forth before the staircase and knelt in homage to Joseph and Greg.

Greg watched Joseph's tense gaze. The objectors soon realized they were outnumbered as more and more wolves went to their knees. The dissenters backed away from the group and left through the front door.

Joseph released Greg's hand and stepped down the stairs to address those remaining. "No one who wishes to be elsewhere is forced to remain a pack member, and no one is to ever harm pack members or anyone else for that matter. This band of wolves has forgotten honor and loyalty, but these things you'll remember. We stick together, look out for one another, and give back to the community instead of living like cowards in the shadows.

"And a new coalition is to be formed between wolves and witches. Our bloodlines are compatible, and needless conflict serves no one," Joseph continued, looking up to Greg. "A new generation of werewolves will be nurtured within our ranks, who know adoration and virtue."

"Then what are your first orders as pack leader?" asked the man with the bandaged head.

"Our first action together as the new Battle Bloods will be to help those affected by the fire Dakota set at the club," Joseph stated resolutely.

The crowd of wolves nodded reverently, looking upon their new leader with wide eyes.

Turning back to Greg, Joseph ascended the stairs to him. Placing a passionate kiss on his lips, he grinned. "How did I do?"

"Excellent, my love," Greg said.

"Oh no," Joseph groaned.

"What?"

"You said the *L* word."

"As in, *I love you*?" asked Greg.

Joseph smiled and put a hand on Greg’s belly. “I love both of you.”

THE END

His Alpha

A Wolf Shifter Mpreg Bundle

Preston Walker & Liam Kingsley

Disclaimer

This is a work of fiction. Names, places, characters and events are all fictitious for the reader's pleasure. Any similarities to

Chapter One

Frantic, urgent knocking woke Christopher from a dead sleep, and he raced for the front of the house, the hair on his arms standing up in alarm. As he clutched at the handle, he couldn't help the yawn, and covered his mouth as he pulled the door open.

Justine and Adam, two members of his pack, stood in front of him, worried and panicked, and they wasted no time in urging him from his home.

“Chris, it's Theo!”

Annoyed with the vague explanation, but not awake enough to argue, he pulled on his jacket and slipped on his shoes. They said it had happened just a few blocks down, so he didn't bother shifting.

It's probably another fight, he thought to himself. Theodore and his mate, Harley, had been on the rocks lately, especially with Theo's hormones, and his partners' reasonable frustration with work. A recent dip in the economy had cost a lot of people their jobs. Several of his pack members had gotten demotions, or had been laid off. While the aggravation of it was justifiable, Harley should have just counted himself lucky that he still had a job.

But it wasn't another fight. It wasn't even close.

Chris didn't know what he was staring at, at first. A crumpled mess of metal, plastic, and rubber, there was smoke, and the sour smell of gasoline made his sensitive nose burn. As the sleep from his eyes cleared a little more, he started to recognize the finer details. Two cars had smashed together on a quiet little corner, right next to a family owned convenience store. There were a couple dozen people there, and almost everyone from his pack.

They were frantically digging at the car, and Chris was almost confused as to why, until he heard the heart-wrenching cry of an infant, and then he remembered.

It was Theo!

His instinct kicked into overdrive. He bolted to the side of one of the smashed vehicles and tore away pieces of metal to try and see them. Theodore was pinned and unconscious, a dribble of blood running down his forehead and bruises already turning his supple pale skin blue and purple. His daughter, Olivia, was more or less fine, save for the little cuts and scrapes that adorned her small, round face. She was scared, and the one person she trusted more than anyone else in her little world couldn't help her.

Cutting up his arms as he pushed away spider-fractured Plexiglas, Chris reached as far as he could to undo the safety buckles that kept Olivia from going anywhere, the only thing that had saved her life. He took her arm and pulled her toward him until he could get a good grasp around her and pulled her from the confines of the car. He handed her off to Justine, who rocked her, trying to shush her.

The sound of blaring paramedic horns caught his ear. He could have stopped and waited for them. They would be able to pry Theo from the car with their hydraulic tools, but as he watched Theodore breathe, his breaths ragged and pained, his slightly rounded belly moving slowly as he inhaled, Chris couldn't bring himself to wait that long.

He went around to the other side of the car, and with the help of a few other people, started yanking on sheer metal pieces to clear the way to the door Theo was pinned against. The locks were jammed, and he punched at the mechanism until it popped and the door sprung open. Theo's leg was jammed underneath a section of the ceiling that had collapsed inward from the crash. Chris pushed on it until the metal warped, and let him wriggle Theodore out from its constraints. He supported the young man, carrying him carefully away from the vehicle and setting him down on the grass nearby.

Justine swayed Olivia back and forth next to him, trying to soothe her fright. Chris smiled slightly at how she cooed and doted on the little girl. She had never been able to have kids of her own, and she was absolutely dedicated to protecting the little girl.

“How the hell did this happen?” he demanded, glancing back at the wreck. He only had two people accounted for. Theo hadn't been in the driver’s seat, and the other car also needed a driver.

Justine looked at him with haunted eyes and shook her head. She didn't know. No one knew. The one person who could tell them was unconscious, the other two...

It took him a moment, but Chris saw it. Harley's body, limp and battered, ejected from the windshield and launched over twenty feet away from the accident. The other car's driver hadn't been from their pack, and as Chris drew closer he could smell the alcohol. The man had died, trapped and frenzied in his vehicle. The man set his jaw.

Harley and the driver of the other vehicle had been pronounced dead on arrival when paramedics finally got there. Theodore and his daughter had been rushed to the hospital. Olivia had been cleared of anything major, just some cuts and bruises. Theo, on the other hand, had broken almost everything. His left leg was fractured in two places, several ribs were broken, there was a hairline fracture to his clavicle, his shoulder blade was shattered, and his left wrist was broken. He would be bed ridden for at least two months, and wouldn't be able to walk without help for the next three.

He was in an induced coma for two weeks to soften the blow. Chris wanted to be there when they woke him up.

Theo groaned in agony, his head lolling back and forth uncomfortably, and he winced as he opened his eyes.

Chris swallowed thickly. “Theodore?”

He turned to look at the Alpha, tired and weak, and pain ripping through him with every motion.

Theo watched Chris, examining him, and his eyes welled up with tears. “Harley...” he croaked.

Chris shook his head slowly. “I'm so sorry. Olivia's fine,” he gestured to Justine, who stood beside him feeding the little girl a bottle of warm formula.

“The... the baby?” Theodore tried to move his arms, and he softly grunted in pain. He looked down at his abdomen, not really able to focus on it. His vision was blurry and the room was spinning.

Chris softly patted his shoulder. “The baby's fine. Healthy and unharmed. But you have to take it easy. They said it was a miracle you didn't miscarry from the stress of your injuries alone.”

Theo shut his swollen eyes, tears making his cheeks wet. He cried quietly, his breath quick from the pain. Justine took Olivia closer and she put her small hand on his bruised cheek. He let out a pained sob and looked up at her. “Daddy's here,” he whispered. “It's okay baby, daddy's here.”

For two months, Chris took Olivia to the hospital to visit Theodore everyday. Not just so she could see her daddy, but so that Theodore wouldn't give up hope that he would get better, so that he wouldn't give up on his family, the people that needed him the most.

Each day, Chris saw a little more light die inside of the Omega. The man had lost his mate, the father of his children, and his freedom, as there was a chance he would never shift again. Theo was breaking.

Chapter Two

“I don't know why you're bothering,” Colt crossed his arms in annoyance. “All this effort, just for an Omega,” he scoffed.

Chris rolled his eyes, focused on making sure everything was in place. “Because, Colt. *I'm* the Alpha. It's my duty as the pack leader to ensure the safety and well being of my people.”

“But he's just an Omega! Why would you go *this far* for *him*?!”

Straightening his back and turning to the man, Chris growled low in his throat. “I don't know what makes you think he isn't worth taking care of, but you better start thinking otherwise *right now*.”

Colt backed off a little. He may have been Christopher's best friend, but it didn't mean he was allowed to forget his place. He was still just a Beta, and talking down to his Alpha like he was above him was a punishable offense.

“He lost his mate, Colt. He has no one right now, and with his injuries still healing, he can't look after his daughter. Not without help.”

“I just don't understand why you're letting him live here.”

“Because,” Chris snapped. Colt jumped back a little, and with a grumble, turned and left.

Chris, in the meantime, had rearranged his office to accommodate Theo and Olivia. He'd brought over Theo's twin sized bed, and his daughter's crib and toys. He tried to make it as homely as possible, with as many personal items as he could fit in the room. Pictures of the family, clothes, blankets and small trinkets that seemed of value. Anything to remind them of home.

Theo arrived in the cab Chris had sent for him only a few minutes later. The Alpha helped him into the house and showed him to where he'd be staying until he could take care of himself on his own. The young man was silent as he was given a tour of the house and told to help himself to anything.

"Justine will be over with Olivia within the hour," Chris explained. "I have lunch prepared too, if you're hungry? It's nothing special. I didn't have much time to go shopping so it's just macaroni and cheese..."

His voice faded into the background as Theo looked around. Why was he here? Why did he have to be here? As he stepped, the uncomfortable tightness around his leg reminding him of his current limitations, his throat swelled with emotion, and a tear rolled down his face. He quickly reached up to wipe it away, trying to hide any evidence of his seemingly unending sorrow. He was grateful that someone had reached out to him like this, that the Alpha, of all people in his pack, was helping him, but it was too much. It felt like a cruel joke.

Without a word, Theo left Chris to his ramblings, and slipped into the bedroom quietly and unnoticed. He hobbled toward the bed, curled up under the covers, and stared at the wall. Chris' study had built in bookshelves, and from the ceiling to the floor, there was dozens of books on every shelf on every subject. The universe, science books, cook books, books on the management of various businesses, text-books, even books on parenting and anger management. Theo wondered what kind of person Chris truly was. He was an enigma to the entire pack.

Christopher had become the Alpha through succession. His mother had been the Alpha before him, and after she'd stepped down, the role had come to him. He'd had a sheltered childhood, and while it was obvious why the man was the Alpha, with his attuned instincts, natural power and strength, and his raw ability to command, not a single pack member had ever really taken the time to get to know him, with the exception of Colt. He kept everyone at a distance, addressed problems as they made themselves apparent through paperwork, and knew a lot about every single person in his pack, though never reached out to form ties or make bonds. He'd never taken a mate, or expressed interest in starting a family.

Christopher was a mystery, and even the very act of Theo and Olivia being accepted into his home for an extended period of time, was a riddle in and of itself.

Eventually, when the Alpha had noticed his guest had disappeared, he peered into the bedroom, and found him fast asleep. He shut the door and sighed. Collecting the bowls of food he'd prepared and stuffing them into the fridge, he went to wait for Justine, and they talked quietly in the living room while Olivia watched cartoons.

"Is he here?" she asked.

He nodded, gesturing to the bedroom. "He's very depressed."

"Wouldn't you be?" she stroked Olivia's head with the utmost affection. "Losing your mate, the father of your children... that would devastate anyone, Chris."

He furrowed his brows. He understood why Theo was upset, why he was feeling the way he was. But he'd never felt such pain or sorrow. He didn't know the intricacies of having a mate, or feeling such an overwhelming sense of love that it blinded and deafened you to everything else. The love of one's parents, no matter how strong, was nothing compared to the love a mated pair shared.

"I think you need to let him feel the way he needs to," said Justine. "He needs to feel bad for himself, and think that this world is ending. That's the only way he can overcome it."

"Which means..."

"That you'll be Olivia's primary guardian until he's back on his feet," Justine nodded. "I would take her, but it's not fair to Theodore. He needs her here, even if his attention isn't completely devoted to her. She's all he has left."

Taking a deep breath, Christopher looked at the little girl. Barely a year old, with Harley's night black hair and chocolate brown eyes. She smiled at him and giggled, and he felt his breath catch.

He would do what he had to do.

For the first few days, Theodore was absolutely miserable, and moody beyond belief. Chris had been around pregnant pack members before, but they were nowhere near as vicious and callous as Theo was being. He was six months along, and as his belly grew with each day, there would be more, and more problems to overcome, not only for Theo, but for Chris as well.

One evening, the misery grew out of control, and Theo had locked himself up in his room for what Chris considered an absolutely ridiculous reason.

"Come on, Theodore!" Chris banged his hand on the door. "Don't be like this!" Olivia cooing from the living room made him turn his attention briefly to her and he made a face. All of these theatrics simply because the little tyke had refused to play with her daddy.

He called at the door once more. “Olivia needs her space just like you do. You can't force her to do something and get upset because she doesn't want to do it.”

“Yes I can!” Theodore shouted, and that was that. The end of the argument punctuated by the sound of a heavy feather pillow being chucked at the other side of the door.

Chewing the insides of his cheeks in frustration, Christopher went to put Olivia in her playpen and with his arms crossed, thought about what he could do.

He remembered a long time ago, that his mother used to make rabbit stew. She'd catch the animals herself, and the resulting pot of deliciousness would be passed around to many of the families expecting children. He recalled asking her one day why she only gave the stew to the pregnant pack members.

“Because,” his mother had said, happily stirring away at her thick soup. “A full wolf, is a happy wolf.”

He rummaged through his cookware in the kitchen, and found the biggest pot he could. He put in his vegetables and spices, and a little bit of beef bouillon, and set it on a low simmer. Then, after Olivia had some crackers and a sippy cup of juice, he slipped out the backdoor and stripped. He folded his clothes neatly and set them on one of the chairs to his patio set, and taking a deep breath, he shifted.

His blood pumping faster, his body began to rearrange itself. His bones popped as they moved to manage his wolf form, and his nose elongated into a slender snout. His dark hair grew thick and course, and he was forced down onto four enormous paws. He shook, renewing himself with the part of him he hadn't been in touch with for many weeks, and without wasting a single second, set out on his hunt.

Rabbits were easy prey, stupid but easily panicked. Chris had hunted them for as long as he could remember, along with mice and the occasional squirrel. Mom had taught him the ways of stealth and cunning. He could track his prey for miles based on the cues of the nature around him. He could take down anything bigger than him on his strength of intelligence alone. He could outsmart anything he trained his hazel gaze on.

The rabbits were betrayed in the colder months, as it grew brisker and more freezing with each day, but not a single snowfall had graced their little city. So, their bright white patches of soft fur gave them away as they grazed on grasses and berries among the bushes and trees of the secluded little patch of forest nearby the neighborhood. Christopher hunkered down low, feeling the rough, dry earth beneath his foot-pads. He inhaled slowly, his breath like a whispering wind against sweet, honey brown blades of dying grass. They hadn't caught his scent yet.

He picked his targets. Two would do, and he watched his plump victims take their last few nibbles of frost endowed foliage. He sprung from the shadows, pouncing on the first of his take. He made quick work of the poor hares suffering, then raced for the second that he'd chosen. The little creature darted for its burrow, its heart beating hard enough for Chris to almost hear. He drew closer, and closer still, and just as the terrified animal took its last bounds before reaching the freedom of the hole it called home, Chris' paw swiped it sideways and he jumped on it.

Grabbing up what would soon be dinner into his maw, he trotted home, and placed the two hares on the back deck before shifting back, and changing into his clothes again.

After skinning and preparing the meat, he started the real work on the stew, adding thickening and a couple more dashes of spice. It wasn't even an hour later that Theo was curiously peeking out from his room, looking around wildly with hungry eyes.

"It's not ready yet," Chris warned from the living room, Olivia bouncing merrily on his lap and giggling with joy.

Reluctantly, Theo withdrew himself from his bedroom, and waddled over to the couch. He sat down in a tired huff, and watched the Alpha across from him tend to the child *he* should have been caring for. It was odd to see such a reclusive man spend so much time with anyone, let alone a child. Let alone *Theo's* child.

"Why did you... help me?" he Omega asked quietly. "We aren't... I'm not anything special. I'm just-"

"An Omega," Chris nodded, holding Olivia's sides as he pushed his knee up and down rhythmically, her little voice playing with how it made her garbled words sound. "You are the third person to ask me why I'm helping a lowly Omega." Justine had questioned him as well, asking him why he would do so much for someone of such little standing in their tight knit family.

Theodore liked to think himself anything but lowly. He'd once had a beautiful family, a wonderful husband, a gorgeous daughter, and a baby on the way. They hadn't been well off, but they'd been comfortable. He'd felt that despite the place the pack hierarchy had put him in, at the very least wasn't *lowly*.

"Omega's are as apart of any pack as any other member. Alpha. Beta. Omega. We are all apart of the same pack, the same family."

"So you're helping me just because I'm apart of the pack? Doing your 'Alpha Duty'?"

Chris nodded hesitantly. "You don't really have anyone else right now."

"So it's pity, then?"

"Theodore, don't be difficult."

The young man was quiet for a moment, and his voice was small when he spoke again. "I'm just trying to understand."

Chris's gaze was soft. "Understand that I'm here if you need me. Whether it's because it's my job as an Alpha, or because I pity you, what does it matter? *I'm* here."

Theo didn't respond, and Chris got up to check on the stew. Olivia followed him toward the kitchen, and he returned with two steaming bowls of thick, rabbit stew. Mouth watering, the Omega tried not to seem so eager to eat the food he was offered, but couldn't help scarfing down spoonfuls after initially burning his tongue.

Chris watched contently from the corners of his eyes. Theodore was the physical manifestation of what you pictured when you heard the word 'Omega'. He was short, unassuming, and would blend into any surrounding without trying. He had strawberry blond hair, naturally fair skin, and freckles that decorated the bridge of his nose and tops of his ears. He was boney, and gangling, and being pregnant did nothing but make the rest of him look sickly.

But through the hormones, there was something humble about him, something likable.

Chris hid a little smile, and jumped in surprise as Olivia reached out her hand to try and take chunks of tender rabbit meat from his bowl. He laughed, and gave her a spoonful to try. She struggled for a moment, unsure of the flavor and texture, and then was rearing her head for more. He chuckled, and got up to get her a bowl of her own.

After two bowls each, and still over half the pot left, Theodore and Olivia were up to their necks with stew, and were falling asleep together on the couch, color returning to their pale cheeks. Chris plucked them up and gently placed them in bed, pulling the thick quilt over their slumbering forms. He stood to watch them from the doorway for a moment, and his eyes scanned the pictures he'd put around the room that he'd gathered from Theodore's house. They would be a family again, even if it was without Harley. It would be hard to push through, a difficult rock to climb over, but they could do it.

Chris would help them get there.

Chapter Three

On the one day that Christopher couldn't ignore his other duties as Alpha, Colt hung around him like an abandoned dog begging for food. With Theodore's mood swings having Chris walking on eggshells half the time, he noticed that his best friend was more annoying to him than usual on this particular Friday, and as the day went on, it started to really grate on his nerves.

"How's the mutt doing?" the brass Beta snorted.

"Great," Chris muttered, going through some of his paperwork. Since his study had been taken up by a pregnant Omega and his cute daughter, he'd had to move most of his files elsewhere, and Colt's spare bedroom had been the best place for it. He sat in a circle of manila folders and went through files as Colt rambled on about how silly it was to have an Omega living with an Alpha.

When the headache started to settle in, Chris rubbed his eyes tiredly.

"You're basically breaking the entire hierarchy of our pack. Of packs everywhere, Chris. It's not natural."

Chris grumbled. "I am so close to demoting your ass to an Omega, Colt, you have no idea."

This seemed to get his attention, and he straightened up, like he was being accused of a crime. "You wouldn't," his voice was small, and scared.

"I would. Maybe then you could learn some humility about the importance of family. We are not *natural* wolves. We *do not* follow their way of barbarous disregard of our pack members. We are just as human as we are wolf, and first and foremost, we are family. Family protects and loves one another, even if we aren't too happy to be doing it."

Colt crossed his arms, annoyed, but defeated. "Let me guess. 'Mommy' is moody."

"Of course he is."

"Maybe he needs to get laid," Colt wagged his eyebrows.

Chris glared up at him, his dark eyes fiery with warning. Even Colt knew the gravity of Chris taking a mate. Wolves, even shifters, were monogamous animals. It would mean that Theo would no longer be an Omega, and while that may have meant a significantly less troubled life, it meant a lot of official litigation and red tape. Although shifters may have not followed the completely inhumane treatment that took place in purebred wolf packs, there were still several things that they were bound to as a society. And an Alpha taking an Omega as a mate, was unheard of.

"I wouldn't tell anyone," Colt shrugged, leaning against a wall, his eyes downcast to his friend. "Promise."

"I'd believe you saying you were in love with Theodore faster than I'd believe that load of crap," Chris frowned.

Colt raised his eyebrows, surprised, and bit the insides of his cheeks. "I'm just saying. It might be possible. Pregnant people can want sex too."

Chris muttered to himself incoherently, and ignored his friend as he went back to work. When he was finished, he organized the files, and set them aside in a neat pile to deal with the next time he could spare some time. He thanked his friend for letting him use his spare room as his temporary work room, and walked home, denying Colt's offer for a ride.

Hands in his pockets, Chris was solemn as he trudged home. He knew exactly what to expect from the expectant. Insane mood swings, weird cravings, unusual requests, unrealistic reactions. He knew that sex was also something a lot of people wanted when they were pregnant. He remembered traveling with his mother to all of the homes of the pack members who were with child. She had been so kind and caring, devoted to helping them get through the worst of their problems. She tended to some of their needs, answered some of their questions, aided them through some of the worse bouts of their pain or discomfort.

Christopher's mother was why he was doing this. She had taught him that just because he was a man, he wasn't above the kindness and affection that they were all capable of.

He stopped just outside his house, and through the front bay window, watched Justine and Theo laugh as they played with Olivia, and he could hear her giggling with absolute delight at the attention. He had neglected his pack, forgotten that they themselves were people who needed the same kind, nurturing attention he'd been giving Theo and his daughter. His pack were more than just requests and concerns submitted on pieces of paper. They were people, and they were wolves, who needed just as much tending to as anyone else did.

Theodore's accident was the stepping stone to Chris reuniting the bonds that his mother had once had with her pack, the very bonds that Chris himself should have held onto and cared for.

Inside the house, he could smell the remnants of re-heated rabbit stew, and scraped the bottom of the pot for what was left, joining the others in the living room as he ate.

“Does Olivia speak yet?” he asked Theodore.

The Omega shook his head. “Not yet. She thinks she can, though. She could tell you stories all day in her own little alien language,” he smiled down at his little girl, kissing her forehead. “Harley and I were...” he took a shaky break. “He and I were working hard to get her to speak. We'd say words over and over again to see if she'd pick it up. We started sounding like parrots,” he gave a sad little chuckle, and then turned Olivia around and let her walk in whichever direction she wanted.

She came to Chris, and he picked her up and set her in his lap. She chewed on the collar of his button down shirt, and hummed.

“Well, I better go,” Justine patted her thighs and got up.

“Thanks for keeping me company today,” Theo smiled at her.

She gathered her coat and nodded happily. “Any time. I love seeing Olivia. She's such a precious girl. You two play nice tonight, okay?” she pointed at the both of them, and with a laugh, shut the door behind her.

Theo and Chris shared a curious look.

Chris carefully balanced Olivia on his lap so that he could finish his bowl of lukewarm stew, and then leaned back on the couch with a content sigh.

“I uh,” breathed Theo. “I wanted to thank you.”

The Alpha peered at him through tired eyes.

“I never really properly thanked you for helping us. For helping me,” he gestured to his wrist, which was covered by an air-cast. “I never would have been able to do anything by myself.”

“Justine would have helped,” Chris said honestly.

"But *you* helped. Which I'm sure everyone in the pack thinks is insane. An Alpha and an Omega. What a pair are we."

"Well, it's only temporary. So I'm sure things will settle back down once you're back at home."

Theo's eyes narrowed, and his shoulders dropped. He looked down at his hands, his fingers worrying themselves. "Oh," he whispered. "Well, yeah. I guess... that would help. No need to really worry."

When Chris realized how insensitive what he'd said had sounded, the damage had been done. He reached out to put a hand on Theodore's shoulder, but the smaller male pulled away, like he was expecting to be hit. Chris slowly pulled back his arm and swallowed.

"I didn't mean for it to come out that way."

"No," Theo got up, putting his crutch underneath his arm and scooping up Olivia. "It's alright. It's the truth, right? I can't stay here forever," he hobbled back to his room, thanked Chris again for the stew, and shut the door quietly.

Chris groaned and put his face in his hands. Angrily, he washed the stew pot and chopped some fresh vegetables. He went out the back door and threw off his clothes, shifting silently in the dark of night. A hunt would ease his vexation, and more stew would ease Theo's.

A peace offering had never been simpler.

Theo watched from the window as his Alpha clambered down onto all fours and took off into the brush. The man was beautiful when he shifted, the motion swift and clean. He tucked Olivia in, and once her small eyes fluttered closed in exhaustion, he slipped out of the room and took his own tour around the house.

Christopher had pictures of his family here and there, hanging on the walls or propped up on bookshelves. His mother, one of the strongest Alpha's their pack had known, had been part of the same enigma her son was entangled in, but she was a much more open person. She went out of her way to be attentive to her pack members, and he remembered seeing her deliver bowls of the same rabbit stew Chris had made for him to pregnant neighbors when he'd been a child. He remembered her kind smile, and the wink she'd given him when he'd caught her eye as a young boy.

He'd once wondered if all Alphas were like that, but when Chris had taken over, he'd learned otherwise very fast. Chris wasn't a cruel leader, however he had never put the same effort into his role as his mother had.

Theo looked around the living room. Being here, though, was a step in the right direction. He sat down on the couch to give his aching leg a break from standing. It didn't feel too good to be here. He felt like he was a burden. Chris was always watching Olivia, always feeding them all and making sure they had what they needed. He put up with Theo's terrible cold shoulders and even worse mood changes.

Harley would always fight him. Always make it about how Theo *wanted* their relationship to be the way it was, that it was a pain in the ass to be together because they wanted a family, and Theo had difficult pregnancies.

The Omega rubbed a hand over his belly, feeling the little one inside of him twist and turn. He sighed and returned to his room. As soon as he could walk without his crutch, he would be returning to his home across the neighborhood, far away from Chris. It was better that way.

Chapter Four

Over the next week, Chris made himself available to all of his pack members. He went to each house, talked with every person, and listened to every story. He recognized some of the concerns he'd received and had been reading on a file. He understood them much better when they were being told to him face to face.

People were reluctant at first, unsure as to why he would suddenly want anything to do with them, but after the third day of making his way around the neighborhood, they started warming up to him. They kept their boundaries, however, and maintained their places as Beta's and Omega's, not once stepping too far out of line. But Chris didn't care about breaking down their social pecking order. He laughed and made friends, made connections and strengthened bonds he hadn't cared for in years. He even visited Colt's home and talked with him. It was less about their friendship, and more about understanding his plight with the pack. The problems he had, the concerns he wanted to voice.

"We're secluded to this neighborhood," Colt said. "The last thing your mom did before she stepped down as Alpha was move us all here, and a lot of us are confused why."

Even Chris didn't know why, but an idea came to him as Colt talked about how it felt like they had been segregated by their own kind. "I'll ask her," he blurted. "I'll see if she remembers why."

Colt's eyebrows furrowed. "You know she won't tell you," he said softly. "Chris, her mind has been gone a long time. She might not even remember who you are."

He didn't care. He had built up in less than one week what his mother had worked to create over a series of years, and he planned to keep it that way. Besides, he had other questions for his mother, and just because her mind had been torn up by her disease, didn't mean that she was gone forever. Just gone sometimes.

"You aren't the first person I've talked to who's had that question," Chris explained. "I want to know too."

Colt watched him, his eyes searching Chris for any sign of uncertainty, but he'd never seen his friend stand so firm about something. This was the most Alpha Chris had ever acted, and Colt liked it.

"I can drive you," Colt offered, smiling kindly.

When Christopher's mother had stepped down alongside his father, they'd retreated to a home in the country, just outside the city limits. The property was overgrown and under-managed, and many of the animals that his parents had kept to keep themselves busy with something while they weren't running a pack, had been sold off to surrounding farms for the better of their well-being.

His father had been dead for years, so his mother had been left on her own, with only a few visitors to her home each month.

"This place has seen better days," Colt muttered, locking the car doors as they approached the shamble of a home.

Chris knocked, and got a grunt in response. He pushed open the door and there, in the living room, his mother was sitting quietly on the old tattered remains of a blue couch, with a cup of cold, half empty tea sitting on the coffee table in front of her.

“Mom?” he drew close to her, sitting down and at an adjacent chair. “Mom, how are you?”

She put down her book, her silver eyes watching him cautiously. “Do I know you?”

He took a strained breath, his lips tight together. It had been years since he'd last seen his mother. A combination of hurt, from the blatant disregard of her Alzheimer disease, and ignorance, the same ignorance that had caused him to ignore his pack members for so long.

He exhaled, preparing for the worst. “I'm your son.”

She suddenly smiled. “Of course you are, baby. It's been awhile since you came to visit. If you had called first, I would have made something to eat.”

He felt warmth flood him. This was the first time in years she'd actually remembered him, but he knew it wouldn't last.

“I have a few questions for you, I thought you might be able to answer.”

She nodded, eagerly sitting forward. “What is it?”

“Why did you move the pack to Sherwood? I was talking with some people, and a lot of them want to know.”

“Well,” she sighed, almost seeming embarrassed. “It was so we could hide.”

“From what?” Colt busted out.

From what Chris could remember, they'd never had many enemies. Of course there were always rival packs, but these days, they were few and far between. Their city was semi-secluded and very low on the list of places that other packs desired to control.

“Oh honey,” she leaned her face in her hand. “I never told you. Well, Chris, your father and I were... an unusual pair.”

Chris nodded. “Alpha's are usually the male,” he muttered.

“Not just that. You see, we fought for a long time to get the Society to change its mind, and they wouldn't listen. So we reached out to our pack members, so that they could help us change the tide of our social construct.”

“What were you trying to convince the Society of?” Chris blinked. This was the first he was hearing of this.

The elderly woman seemed surprised, and then laughed to herself. “Oh, darling. I really never told you anything, did I? Your father was an Omega, dear.”

Chris and Colt exchanged stares of disbelief, then, the Alpha's expression changed to one of eager challenge.

“He was a rogue, before I took him in,” she recalled. “He had no pack, but unfortunately taking him into mine meant he would have to start at the bottom. He adjusted to Omega life well, but, well, he was just so charming whenever we spoke. Of course, the Society would never allow it, so we pleaded with them to try and get them to change their minds, or make an exception.”

“That's why you went around and spoke with everyone all the time,” Chris connected the dots. “You wanted to get everyone in your pack on your side to you accepting an Omega as a mate.”

She nodded, sighing sadly. “Everyone petitioned on our behalf. They helped us try to pave the way to a more open hierarchy.”

The hope that had flared up in Chris' heart started to deflate like an open balloon. “It didn't work, did it?”

She shook her head. “The Society was still opposed. They wouldn't allow Alpha-Omega pairs because it broke down the careful social constructs that shifters had upheld for hundreds of years. They would not change their rules. Not for all of us.”

“So, what did you do?” Colt asked, sitting down next to the woman and eagerly awaiting her story.

She looked over to the last image that had been taken of her and Chris' father, before he'd passed away. “They told us we could keep our company, as long as we did it away from the other packs. So, I moved us all here, to this small little neighborhood, and lived happy and free with each other,” she reached out, softly touching the picture, framed in cherry wood with gold engravings. “I knew it would cost the pack some of their freedom, but they all supported us, and said they'd remake their lives over if it meant the pack was happier as a whole.”

Colt folded his hands in his lap, appearing to feel a little bad for being so insensitive to the idea all this time.

“I'm sorry darling,” Chris' mother reached out to take his hands, patting them. “I should have told you, after all this time.”

“It's okay,” he said, his voice barely above a whisper. “You've forgotten a lot of things recently, so it's alright.”

She seemed confused, and as she reached to grab her cup of tea, her attention focused elsewhere for just a moment, she looked back up to him, and smiled brilliantly. “How can I help you two lovely gentlemen?”

Chris' heart ached, and he deflated a little in disappointment.

Colt sucked in a breath and patted her back. “We were just checking in on you.”

“Oh!” she said. “How lovely.”

“But we have to go now.”

“Come back soon. If you call me, I'll put on tea.”

Christopher nodded, and stood up, signaling their leave. Colt drove them back to his house, and they sat in the car silently for several long minutes.

“So, now what?” Colt asked. “Are you going to take my advice?”

“About having sex with Theo?”

He nodded.

“No,” Chris shook his head, frowning. “He's still grieving over his mate. That would be insensitive.”

A little mischievous smile curled Colt's lips. “But you are thinking about it.”

Chris would be lying if he said the thought hadn't crossed his mind. He looked at the house. “Maybe,” he replied in a small voice. “But not right now,” gathering his coat, he thanked Colt for the ride, and headed inside.

Theodore watched Chris from the window as he finished talking with his friend and then made his way for the front door. He scrambled to sit forward on the couch, and ran his fingers through his short hair, smoothing out his pants and fixing his shirt.

Instead of coming to sit with him, like he usually did, Chris gave him an acknowledging look, and disappeared down the hall to his bedroom.

Theo slumped over and rested his chin in his hand. What was eating Chris all of a sudden? Usually he was a little more social, especially when he was gone for most of the day.

Getting up, the Omega limped down the hallway and knocked gently on Christopher's closed door. “Hey?”

“Yes?” the Alpha's quiet voice called.

“Are... you still okay with taking me to get my x-ray done this weekend?”

“Of course.”

Theo nodded, leaning against the nearby wall. He looked down at the air-cast around his wrist, and leg. When they were healed, he'd have to leave. He rubbed a hand over his belly, and felt the familiar kick of his unborn child reacting to his touch. “Hey,” he spoke out again. “Did you... want to feel him?”

There was silence for a few seconds, and then the door opened. “Feel him?”

Theo gestured to his abdomen. “Have you ever felt him before?”

Shaking his head, Chris eagerly reached out his hand, gently placing it against Theo's swelled tummy.

“Oh, of course,” Theodore mumbled. “He has to stop when you want to feel and make an ass of me.”

Chris laughed, moving to crouch in front of Theo and placing his other hand on him as well. “That's okay. I can wait. I have nothing better to do right now anyway.”

It took a few minutes of them being together, awkwardly waiting in the quiet of the hallway, before the little body started kicking out again, pressing his hands and feet against Chris' palms.

"He likes you," Theo whispered. "Olivia used to get so excited when Harley would talk to her," his voice was soft as he remembered his mate.

"I like him too," Chris said firmly, looking up at Theo. "He's been such a trooper through all of this, just like his daddy."

Theo felt his breath catch, and a shiver made his skin prickle with goosebumps. Chris stood up, pulling his hands away from the smaller male's belly.

"How's your leg...?"

"Sweaty," Theo replied with a laugh, then it disappeared. "It's going to be strange being alone," he grasped at his arms tightly. "Just me and Olivia, and whoever this little one turns out to be."

Chris searched Theodore's face, the hurt and concern that twisted his features was evident, and he took a shaky breath.

"Maybe... when everything is said and done," he started. "You could stay here?"

Theo's expression lit up. "But... we're..."

"An Alpha and an Omega living together isn't that strange," he shrugged. "Wild wolves do it all the time."

Theo swallowed. Was it too good to be true? Some kind of cruel joke? Pity?

"I can move my files back here and switch the rooms around a bit, so my room is the study."

"What about Olivia? She needs her own room eventually."

He shrugged. "This house is simple to add onto. I could easily just build a new room off of the living room."

Theo chewed his lips tentatively. “How long would I be here, then?”

Taking a slow breath, Chris lowered his eyes to Theo's soft blue ones. “As long as you'd like.”

Theo searched for the lie. He searched for the give that would tell him that this was just some gag that Colt was having Chris put on. But there wasn't one. The Alpha's dark eyes were clear and genuine.

He pushed himself up, stumbling a little, and met his target dead on with quivering limbs. Lips forced together, Theo took a chance on rejection. He didn't know much about the kind man in front of him, other than the sad loneliness with which he lead the majority of his life. But the unadulterated benevolence that Christopher showed him in his time of need was more than enough to foster the growing affection Theo had for him in his heart.

Whether it was the final stages of his grief begging him to move on, or the urges from his raging hormones asking him for some release, Theodore didn't care what it was. He clenched his fists at his side and shut his eyes tightly as he kissed Chris, hoping that, at the very least, he wouldn't be shoved away in disgust.

Surprised, and pleasantly so, Chris leaned into him, pressing him gently up against the wall he'd been leaning against, and reached down to untangle the clinched mess of his fingers to entwine them with his own. He pulled back for a moment, parting their lips for just a few seconds, so he could adjust his stance and tilt his head a little better. Then he dove back in, their tongues mingling and exploring uncharted territory as they got to know each other in a different way.

Theo was breathless. The scent of the Alpha – *his* Alpha – before him was intoxicating, pheromones making it feel like everything between his ears had been replaced with cotton.

Chris nibbled at his neck, sparking renewed passion within Theo that he hadn't felt for a long time, even with Harley. The last few months had been so lifeless with his beloved mate, Theo had almost forgotten what it felt like to be touched and kissed and *wanted.*

Theodore's hands reached up to grasp Chris' biceps, squeezing tightly as teeth gently grazed his jugular and long fingers slipped underneath his shirt and groped at the supple muscles of his back.

Heat welled up within him and his breath grew heavy and wanton. He pulled Chris' head back up to kiss him again, harder and fervent. He wanted this so badly, he ached for it, and reached to shove the bedroom door open.

"Fuck," Theo said breathlessly, pulling away from Chris in exasperation. Olivia cried from her crib in the makeshift bedroom down the hallway, spoiling what would have been, albeit a very short however very wanted, sexual encounter.

Chris was laughing, wiping at his mouth and huffing. "I got her, it's okay," he started down the hall and disappeared into the room. Only seconds later, she was soothed, but refused to return to sleep, and the two were awake until dawn when she finally settled down to sleep for a few hours.

"My daughter is a homewrecker," Theo mumbled.

Too exhausted to even continue from where they'd left off, Chris snorted in agreement, getting comfortable in the love seat adjacent to the Omega, and they slipped into a peaceful sleep.

They'd rekindle the fire later, Chris thought as he drifted off. For now, they'd gather their strength.

Chapter Five

Around noon, when Theodore woke, he braved the kitchen to make a small lunch for the slumbering Alpha still in the living room, Olivia, and himself. Once it was prepared, he took out his phone and gave a quick call to Justine.

“Hey,” she said happily. “How is everything?”

“Great,” he replied honestly. “I had a favor to ask.”

“Sure!”

“Are you busy tonight or tomorrow?”

Seeming to sense the reason for his request, she started to giggle. “Nope. I'm free. Need me to take Olivia?”

He sucked in his bottom lip and bit it. “If you didn't mind.”

“Of course not,” she snickered. “Did you want me to bring a bottle of wine and some chocolate over when I come to pick her up?”

Theo hissed. “That's a little extreme.”

She cackled. “Just call me tomorrow when you plan on wanting her back. She could live with me forever and I'd be just fine with that.”

With a smirk, Theo chuckled. “Maybe I should find someone else then, if you're so keen on kidnapping her.”

“Oh come on! Don't be mean. So, five?”

He nodded. “Perfect.”

“See you then!”

Hanging up, and hastily stuffing his phone into his pocket, he got Olivia out of her crib and put her in the living room, then served the simple little lunch of meat sandwiches and fruit.

"Thank you," Chris said, almost surprised when he was woken with a plate of food. It had been a long time since someone had prepared anything for him, and while it was nothing more than a few sandwiches and some fruit salad, it tasted amazing.

Sitting down with a plate stacked high of food, Theodore nibbled at his sandwiches. "Are you going to Colt's today?"

Chris shook his head. "He's been a little annoying lately. So I'm taking a break from him."

"What about the rest of the neighborhood? You just started building bonds again."

He smiled slightly. "They don't need to be pestered everyday. A couple times a week, or a couple times a month is all anyone needs. Why the sudden interest in how I spend my time?"

"I just noticed that you've been working a lot recently, not really doing much for yourself."

Chris paused from eating for a moment. "A few months ago, all I ever did was do things for myself. I put everyone else's needs on sheets of paper, and treated them like that's all they were, pieces of paper to either read or throw away. I've worked hard to start going somewhere recently, so a day off is needed once in a while."

Theo grinned, nodding happily. He hoped Chris didn't regret last night, and as the day progressed, and they grew closer to when Justine would be by to take Olivia overnight, the excitement built up within him. He put on something nice, even though their night would likely be spent naked and in ecstasy, and packed a little bag full of his daughters things.

Chris answered the door and furrowed his brows in confusion when Justine waved jubilantly and came in to collect the little girl playing quietly in her playpen in the corner of the living room.

“Right on time,” Theo greeted her from the couch. “Everything's packed for her, she's ready for her sleepover.”

“That's good,” Justine plucked her up and tossed her gently into the air. Olivia giggled and the Beta tickled her, watching her wiggle in delight.

“I'll call you when we can pick her up tomorrow.”

“No worries,” Justine put the little backpack over her shoulder, winked at Chris, and closed the door behind her.

Blinking in confusion, Chris took a breath. “Okay. Is no one going to tell me what's going on?”

“I thought... we could use some alone time,” Theo said shyly. “Unless you don't want to.”

He scanned the Alpha's face, looking for the contrition, and waiting for the 'no thanks'.

Chris just smiled softly. “Why didn't you tell me?”

Relief flooded him and his tense shoulders relaxed. “I wanted it to be a little surprise.”

The taller man came and hoisted the Omega into his arms, pecking at his forehead. “I like your little surprise,” he carried him down the hall to the bedroom and ceremoniously placed him atop the cool sheets. Not bothering to close the door, Chris tore his shirt off and bent down over Theo to kiss him.

Theo threw his arms around Chris' neck and held him tight, gasping for breath when the other pulled just far enough away from him to separate their mouths. Chris suckled down his pale neck, and started undoing the buttons to Theo's shirt, revealing his slender chest and enlarged belly.

Suddenly, Theodore was covering his face and holding his legs tightly together. Chris frowned, sitting up. “What is it?” he breathed, fearing the worst. Was he in pain? Or was Chris just so horribly awful at his attempts to seduce the man he treasured?

“I-I'm sorry!” Theo called out.

Chris watched the tiny motions in the man's abdomen, as the little one inside of him protested. He tried to hide the grin that curled his lips and made him laugh lowly, and ran his hands over Theodore's stomach. “Don't be embarrassed,” he said. “I love this part of you as much as I do the rest.”

Slowly, Theo unwound himself, and although he wasn't able to completely relax under Chris' intense gaze, he felt less self conscious as the man ran his fingers down his chest lovingly and gently urged the shirt off of Theo completely. His pants were a different story. Nowhere as easy to remove because of the air-cast encircling his leg. But Chris was patient, and each inch of skin he pulled fabric away from, he kissed, delicately savoring Theo.

With his excitement more evident now that his clothes were gone, Chris treated him like fragile glass as he explored him, nipping at bits of his pale skin playfully. Theo felt completely exposed, and the heat that ran ragged within him took more control of him than he wanted. He would have loved to let Chris learn his nooks and curves, what made him growl with lust or howl in pleasure, but the craving was so intense, he pulled the Alpha back up to him and kissed him hard.

"Please," he begged. "Don't make me wait much longer."

Desire rumbled low in Chris' throat as Theo's thin fingers pried open the button and zipper on his jeans. His own hand reached around to the lithesome male's rear, and he made quick work of preparing him. He'd wanted to make this a little more special than just giving into the deepest and most hungry of their wishes, but it appeared that, despite still being more human than wolf, the animals within them yearned something else.

The satisfaction needed to happen now, not because of pregnancy hormones, long lost lovers, or loneliness, but because they *wanted it*.

Pushing into Theo roughly, the ragged moan from the young Omega's lips made Chris shiver with avidity. How long had it been since the body of another had positioned themselves so delightfully beneath him? Long before his Alpha years, at least.

Theodore was already gyrating in release, his fingers marking the skin of the man he clung to with little red crescent shapes. "Don't stop!" he pleaded, his voice husky and desperate.

Chris was happy to oblige, and pounded into the tender flesh without regard for anything except his own satisfaction. He was rough and dominating to the small form he attacked with hungry passion. He carefully draped his body across Theo's, cautious of the body between them who protested their love making with kicks against the thin bit of skin and membrane that separated him from the world.

With a huff, he gave it all he had, Theo's jumps and twitches as his body responded to Chris' firm touch driving him wild. He drove himself home, unforgiving thrusts making Theo call out in unbridled rapture. The scratches on his back, the one good leg hooked around his waist and pulling him as close as he could get. His breath was heavy and hard, and though it had only been a short few minutes since they'd begun, sweat glistened on his forehead.

Theo grabbed at the sides of his head, yanking him down and kissing him hard as he gave the last few thrusts he could manage. Theodore was shivering again in climax, as the Alpha spent himself, and pulled out to flop to the side on the bed.

Breathless and hot, the both of them laid still for several minutes, basking in the afterglow of sex and passion.

A twinge of pain in his lower back made Theo wince, and he rubbed at his stomach, feeling annoyed fists press back against his fingers. He struggled to push himself up, looking down at Chris' half naked appearance and biting his lip.

"Was this... okay?" he asked.

Chris cracked an eye open. "You mean us having sex?"

Theo nodded.

"Of course it is. If it wasn't, I wouldn't have done it."

"I think it was more of a mutual decision," Theo snorted, raising his eyebrows. "But what about the pack? You and me... Alpha and Omega... What about that?"

Chris shrugged his shoulders. "I guess they'll just have to deal with the fact that I want a cute little Omega as my mate."

Theo covered his mouth in embarrassment, his cheeks burning more than ever.

"Too much?" Chris grinned, sitting up and snaking his arm around the Omega's lithe body. "Too bad," he pecked at his neck softly. "You're stuck with me."

Another thrum of discomfort rang out from his back and Theo groaned in irritation. He stood up, careful about his air cast, and the pain exploded from his abdomen. "Shit," he stumbled, using the nightstand next to him to brace himself. "Uh, well. As absolutely awesome as this whole thing was, it seems you've thrown me into labor."

Chris started up at him unblinkingly, mulling over the words he'd just been handed. When the gravity of it dawned on him, he flipped like a switch. "Are you serious?"

"There are a lot of things I would like to joke about," he rushed for the door. "This, unfortunately, is not one of them."

Stuffing the aftermath of their toils in bed back into his pants, Chris yanked his shirt back on and ran to get his car keys. Theo calmly packed a bag and got re-dressed, breathing slowly through his increasingly painful contractions. Chris carefully escorted him out to the car, trying not to show his panic as he raced them to the hospital and were admitted to a room. Theodore's doctor was female, and she was very pleasant, even if Chris felt that she was being incredibly invasive as she examined Theodore's rump, inspecting how dilated he was, if at all.

"How's Olivia doing?" she asked from behind the privacy blanket mantled over his legs.

"Great. Eating great. Growing great. Great," Theo hissed through a contraction.

She smiled, removing her gloves as she came around from probing him. “Beautiful. You're coming along quickly. Should be a much simpler birth than little Olivia. Did you want an epidural this time?”

Theo shook his head furiously.

Nodding, the doctor placed the gloves in the nearby trash bin. “Alright, so. It looks like it will only be a few minutes until you're ready, but we all know what labor is like. I'll have a nurse in here to monitor you until we're all set,” getting up, she disappeared outside the door and in walked a young man in pink scrubs, who immediately came around to adjust some nearby equipment.

Chris was over attentive. Hyped up on the renewed feeling in his life, and excited over consummating the taking of a mate with his beloved Omega, he was protective and snippy with everything the nurse and the doctor did.

Theo was laughing and patting his arm when Chris growled low in his throat as the nurse adjusted the stirrups Theo's feet would be in when he gave birth.

“Calm it down a little,” he huffed. “It's fine.”

The rest of his labor only lasted about twenty minutes at the hospital, and although it was spent in occasional agony, it was more or less peaceful.

Chris was allowed to stay, but only if he put on some scrubs, gloves, and a facial mask. He stayed by Theo's side, holding his hand tightly through it all, and when the beautiful sound of a crying newborn echoed into their ears, Theo cried in joy and relief, and collapsed exhausted on the table as the baby was preened and wrapped snug in a soft little blanket.

“Another little girl,” the doctor announced, offering the red-faced, pink bundle to Chris. He hesitated, looking back and forth between the woman and Theo, who nodded in encouragement. Uncertain and cautious, he held out his arms and cradled the small body close to his chest, and she quickly fell asleep against him.

"She looks just like him," Chris said, smirking at the little tuft of black hair and her deep brown eyes. "What are you going to name her?"

Unbelievably weary, Theo watched the Alpha as he held and rocked the tiny baby. He smiled to himself. Such a big, strong guy holding something so delicate and frail, and treating it like it was the most important thing in the world. "Haley," he said.

"Haley... I like that," Chris grinned.

"Haley's a wonderful name," the doctor added, finishing up her tidying and urging the other nurse out. "You can take all the time you need," she whispered softly, and shut the door behind her.

Chris leaned close to Theo, allowing him to reach out to softly touch the rosy cheeks of his daughter. She cooed, squinting at him, and held onto his finger tightly. He chuckled and rested his head against Chris' shoulder, sighing contently.

"Thank you for helping me, for everything."

Chris laughed softly. "I should thank you too. You kind of usurped my life for the better."

Beaming, Theo lifted his head. "You're welcome, then."

Chapter Six

When the air casts finally came off, Theo was told to take it easy for at least two weeks, and despite his urgency to try and test the limits of his newfound freedom, he sat at home and tended to Haley and Olivia diligently, and even started helping more around the house, something he wished he could have done more of earlier.

They switched around the bedrooms, so that Olivia and Haley shared the room that used to be Chris's, and the Alpha and Omega shared the study. It was cozy, if a little cramped, and Chris made it so that he rarely had to leave the house for his work with a little makeshift corner desk. Though, after a pile of books fell on Theo, he still promised he would add an additional bedroom within the next year.

Justine and Colt were over visiting one day when Theo seized an opportunity while they were deep in conversation. He slipped out the back door and stripped down, placing his clothes on the nearby patio chairs. He took a deep breath, and just as he was about to shift, the sound of a door closing made him jump and turn around.

Chris was smirking at him, eyeing him up as he stood naked in the chilly weather on the back porch.

"What?" Theo asked shyly.

"Not going to invite me? I'm a little hurt."

Theo shrugged. "I was just going to see if I even *could.*"

Chris started pulling off his clothes. "Won't know until you try. Take it slow."

He did. He inhaled slowly, rolling his neck as his body worked through almost a year of not shifting. Joints popped, his skin was stiff as it elongated. His wrist was a little uncomfortable, and his leg resisted the hardest as his wolf form pushed him down onto all fours. When he exhaled, he looked down, examining his paws and making sure everything turned the way it was supposed to. Tail, check. Four legs, check. Cold nose, check. He shook himself out, enjoying the way a cool breeze blew through his thick beige fur, with hints of his strawberry blond hair here and there.

Chris nuzzled up against him, getting his attention, and he happily jumped down off of the porch, play-bowing to his Alpha mate and wagging his tail.

Seeming unimpressed, Chris just stared at him. Theo whined in protest at the rejection of his invitation, and then Chris pounced, sending them in a rolling mass into the brush.

They ran for miles, playfully snipping back and forth at one another. Chris chased Theo, then turned tail and was chased. A few of the young children in the area who caught their scent came to join them, their half as big forms running and jumping in play around the Alpha and Omega. Theo smiled internally, and laughed to himself.

Returning home, they both yanked their clothes back on, and breathlessly headed inside, were their two unintentional babysitters were having a quiet, and obviously private conversation. They cleared their throats and moved a few inches apart on the couch when Theo and Chris came to sit down.

"Oh," Theo looked toward the hall. "Haley's up."

"I got it," Chris stood back up and headed to the bedroom. The crying culprit hushed when she saw him, and he picked her up. "Someone needs a bum change," he grinned, and took her to the changing table. She watched him with silent fascination as he cleaned her, and put her in a new diaper.

"Hungry too?"

She made a noise at him. He laughed and cradling her in the crook of an arm, he went to the kitchen to warm a bottle. Unfortunately, despite the century long adaptation male shifters had developed for carrying their own children, they never evolved mammary glands, and so their babies were fed high protein, high nutrient formula developed especially for them.

He held the bottle for her, and she sucked hungrily, slurping away as he headed back into the living room to join the conversation about some Beta teenagers causing trouble on the north side of the neighborhood.

"Need me to take her?' Theo offered.

Chris shook his head. "You carried her for nine months, I can hold her for a few minutes."

Justine laughed. "You seem to be taking on the 'daddy' role rather well, Chris."

He gave her a smile. "That's what happens when you take a mate with kids."

"You guys are gross," Colt said in jest. "Too lovey dovey. Hurts my teeth."

Theo opened his arms toward the man. "I can spread the love. Maybe it'll help."

He made a face and leaned back. "Maybe you and Chris can switch places so he can carry the next kid."

Theo paused, a slow, devilish smile curling his lips as he turned to the Alpha. "Hey, that's not a bad idea."

"I'm not responsible for your first two pups," Chris said hastily. "I don't think I need to be punished for it!"

They laughed, and he moved Haley so that he could burp her, patting her back while she hung over his shoulder.

"Honey," Theo started. "Not so hard or she'll... oh."

Colt and Justine burst out in uncontrollable giggles at the look of mild disgust on Christopher's face.

Theo covered his mouth, sucking his lips inward and trying to hold back a laugh of his own.

"That's okay," Chris muttered. "This shirt was old anyways," he pulled Haley back to look at her little pink face, and she just stared back at him adoringly with her big brown eyes. Joyed with her existence, but still a little grossed out, he passed her to Theodore. "There. *Now* you can take her."

Theo was glad to hold her, and watched as his currently less than jovial mate stood up to go change shirts. This was his family. And even though a part of him would always love and miss Harley, he wouldn't change how his life had ended up. In the arms of a man who treasured him, who not only loved him but both of his daughters. They would have to talk about having a giant litter of kids, as Chris had so happily thought out loud one day, but it was the least of Theo's concerns.

His happiness was simple, and in his grasp, and he wouldn't have this any other way.

Omega's Touch

A Wolf Shifter Mpreg Bundle

Preston Walker & Liam Kingsley

Disclaimer

This is a work of fiction. Names, places, characters and events are all fictitious for the reader's pleasure. Any similarities to

Chapter One: Derek

Derek Farthing adjusted his jacket for what seemed like the millionth time that evening. It was too hot to be in a full tux, but the Gathering started as a strictly black tie affair. Derek hated them. It was a yearly event that brought all the packs together, giving a chance for the original packs to reconnect with their offshoots and each other. In theory, it was an occasion for wolves to meet and mingle freely and be who they were without questions. To be fair it was- for everyone except the Alphas.

For the Alphas it was much more political, all about strengthening alliances, demonstrating power and lobbying for matters to be brought to the Council - the Alphas of the three original packs. Which meant that Derek, as Alpha of the Moonstone Wolves, was forced to make small talk with bigoted assholes and simpering boot lickers.

He shook his head, trying to focus on the conversation with the new Alpha of the Redwood Wolves, an offshoot of the Bloodstone Wolves. The man was a foot taller than him, more obviously muscled, and clearly thought that Derek was beneath him.

Derek suppressed a growl, his wolf pushing closer to the surface, demanding he put the man in his place. It had been a long time since anyone had been so stupid. The only people who dared treat him like this, were morons who thought his being the youngest Alpha in a century made him an easy target. They were the people who hadn't seen or heard of the fight that had won him the title. The scar across his back twitched in reminder.

"What were you saying?" Derek asked, staring long and hard into the man's eyes.

They flashed angrily before he looked away. Derek smiled; the man wasn't a total idiot.

"I was saying that the Council needs to do something about the Omega problem."

Derek raised an eyebrow, "I wasn't aware of an Omega problem."

"Surely you can't be as stupid as you lo-" but the man never finished his sentence.

Derek had moved forward. Raw power emanated off him, his rage filling the space like a mist. His usually grey eyes flashed gold and his teeth were fangs. Wolves nearby whimpered and shuffled away. The Alpha cowered as Derek rested a hand firmly on the man's neck, drinking in the fear that rolled off him in waves.

"I wouldn't finish that sentence if I were you," his voice was calm and quiet but the man winced as if he'd been hit. "I'm the Alpha of the Moonstone pack, Council member, do you really think you stand a chance?"

The Alpha didn't respond. Derek could tell his pride and his wolf were at war. The wolf was begging to submit to the stronger Alpha, but his pride wouldn't let him. He took a breath, concentrating hard as the hand on the man's neck partially shifted, his fingernails growing into razor sharp claws. The smell of blood hit the air as the man cried out. Partial transformation was something only Alphas could do, and even then it was a rare ability. Derek smirked as a wave of pure terror rolled off the man.

"I'm sorry Alpha," the man hung his head, tail between his legs.

Derek threw him to the ground, watching him scuttle away. The wolf in him roared its approval as his eyes turned to grey. Maybe the evening wouldn't turn out to be a total waste.

"I never get tired of watching you do that," a woman's voice said.

He whirled around, a smile across his face. "Alyssa."

Alyssa was the Alpha of the Sunstone pack and as the only female Alpha to ever sit on the Council, she'd dealt with more than her fair share of idiots. Incredibly gorgeous, even by Alpha standards, she was one of Derek's closest friends. She hugged him and he noticed the woman she'd brought with her.

Alyssa caught Derek's look and smiled. "This is Tara Argent. She's my mate."

Derek beamed, but didn't move closer to the woman. She was Alyssa's mate and friends or not, Alpha's were fiercely protective. "You're Adolfo's daughter? Nice to meet you."

"I live in hope that my mother had an affair," she quipped, frowning at the mention of her father.

Derek and Alyssa both laughed.

"Hope springs eternal," he said grinning. "I'm glad you two found each other."

"So am I," Alyssa said, an arm around Tara. "Things are changing you know."

Derek did know. The old school Alphas expected everyone to be straight, to play by their rules. From day one he'd refused to do that. Alyssa was the same and as two of the most powerful Alphas they got their way more often than not.

A few people were trying to attract his attention, but there was no challenge in it. He blew a kiss and turned back to Alyssa, enjoying their eyes on him.

"You can be a real dick, you know that right? What's the point of teasing them like that?"

"I'm not doing anything. Besides, you know me. It's too easy."

Alyssa sighed. "You're never going to find a challenge, much less a mate, if you don't give them a chance."

Derek shook his head, "I'm not looking for a mate."

Alyssa opened her mouth, but at a look from Derek she closed it. This was a discussion they'd been having as long as they could remember. She knew what his life had been like, and knew the reason he refused to take a mate.

"Fine. Well it's a Gathering. You should at least have a little fun." She glanced around meaningfully. "You could have anyone you want Der, let your wolf out to play."

Derek let out a bark-like laugh as he scanned the crowd. He trusted Alyssa. She'd been helping him secure secret one night stands for years, feeding fake gossip to the world at large. There were so many rumours about him. He was gay, he was bi, no he was obviously straight. He didn't mind, the mystery worked for him and it let him do as he pleased. He caught sight of someone at the bar and it jerked him from his thoughts.

He'd never seen him before, but his wolf rose up as soon as their eyes met. He was the same height as Derek, with a beautiful face and emerald green eyes. His hair was short, and black with a streak of silver that shone out against it. Derek felt a thrill run through his body, every muscle tightening. His wolf began to prowl.

Someone bumped lightly against him and he whipped round, snapping and growling, causing the young shifter in question to stammer out an apology, and start to shake and whimper.

When he'd turned back, the stranger had disappeared. His wolf was furious. *The one interesting person at the party.*

"That was a little harsh," Alyssa said so that only he could hear.

Derek's wolf sprang up again, still frustrated that the stranger had apparently vanished. "What?"

She nodded to the kid still standing in front of him.

Derek flushed. Alyssa was the only person in the world who talked to him like that, and as it was it took a moment to calm his wolf down. Most Alphas ruled with an iron fist, recognising only the need to dominate the others. Derek was dominant and expected that deference, but his parents had taught him that the best Alphas ruled by more than fear alone.

He reached out, grabbing the nape of the boy's neck and shaking gently. It was a gentle reprimand. As soon as the boy stopped whimpering, Derek ruffled his hair and smiled. It was a clear exchange, all was forgiven but don't do it again.

"Go have fun, George." Derek said.

Alyssa was still watching him and he shrugged, trying to shrug it off. "I'm not sure why my wolf's so on edge."

An unreadable look crossed her face, but she didn't say anything else. They both knew that a look from him would've sufficed, but his wolf had reacted like someone had stolen something prized from him. Derek was one of the most powerful and measured Alphas around. It wasn't like him to lose control so easily.

Chapter Two: Alex

As soon as he'd made eye contact with the man across the room, Alex Fleet had felt his wolf rush to the surface. He'd never seen anyone so attractive. His tux was well tailored, just highlighting his muscled body. His silver hair was completely at odds with his young face, but somehow it suited him perfectly. His grey eyes rooted Alex to the spot, his entire body spellbound.

As soon as the man had been forced to look away Alex had taken off. He left the ballroom, walking into the grounds and the cool night air. He shook his head firmly, trying to calm his wolf and his body down. His hole was already wet and ready, and the guy hadn't even touched him.

It took him a moment to calm down, the panic in his chest rising. He'd been raised a Silver wolf, one of the most old school packs in the world. His father, the Alpha, ruled through fear and aggression. The only reason he hadn't killed his son for being an Omega was because pack law forbade killing a wolf without cause and existing as an Omega didn't count. It didn't help that Alex was gay either.

Gradually, his heart beat slowed down and he stared out at the stars in the sky. He'd left the pack a few months ago, but it was hard getting used to freedom. He'd been living in neutral territory and avoiding shifters since he'd left. After all, a lone wolf was more often than not a dead wolf. He'd only come to the Gathering after his sister had begged him to, reminding him that the Gathering was a time of peace. Legally, no one could hurt him.

He wasn't sure how long he'd been standing there lost in his own thoughts, when he heard yells and cheering coming from somewhere off in the distance. He cocked his head, his heightened sense tuning into the world around him. It was coming from a little way below him. Carefully, he made his way towards the noise, his curiosity getting the better of him.

He found a crowd of shifters, cheering as two men fought at the centre. This wasn't a blood match, just something for fun. That was obvious, but it was also clear neither contestant was giving it their all. With a jolt, he recognised one of the men in the ring. It was the man from the ballroom.

The crowd cheered as the match ended and Alex found himself pulled into it, forced further and further forward with each match. By the time he was at the front of the crowd, the man had defeated five more challengers and was gesturing for more.

He was a good fighter, and it was obvious that he was just showing off at this point, flirting with the crowd. As Alex watched him, he struggled to place the energy coming off him. Sure he was cocky, he was one of the most amazing fighters Alex had ever seen, but there was something else. He was bored.

Alex wasn't sure why that goaded him, but as the sixth fight ended and the challenger was sent limping slightly away, his wolf roared to the surface. He struggled, surprised by his own ferocity and then realised it wasn't aggression. His wolf wanted to play, to challenge but ultimately to submit. His Omega nature made him equal parts dominant and submissive, but he was always bad at submitting in a fight. It had gotten him in trouble before. Now here was his wolf, spoiling to play and even more surprisingly, to submit to this total stranger.

"Any others?" called the stranger his arms folded across his well muscled chest. His voice was deep, almost musical and sent a thrill down Alex's spine.

"I'll do it." The words escaped from him before he could stop them.

The crowd parted to let him through. He stripped off his jacket and shirt, laying them on the ground as he faced the man. Someone grabbed his shoulder and he turned around.

"Tara?" He gaped at his sister's worried expression. "Where've you been?"

"With my mate." She pushed on before he could question her further, "Alex you can't fight him."

"Why not?"

"He's an Alpha. Not just that, he's Derek Farthing. You know, *the* Derek Farthing."

Alex glanced at Derek who had just turned around. He could see the telltale scar from his ascendancy stretched across his back. It was weirdly sexy.

"So?" Alex asked, knowing exactly what Tara would say.

"Don't be an idiot. You're an Omega. I know you. You'll give it your all and you won't submit until he makes you." She sounded frightened.

Derek was watching them, his head tilted slightly. A grin spread across his face, and Alex knew it was an invitation. He doubted he'd be able to refuse, even if he wanted to.

"Move away, Tara. " Alex moved his sister aside, the wolf in him roaring its approval. He could smell her fear, but he didn't care. All he wanted to do was play with Derek Farthing.

"Let's do this," he said, dropping into a fighting stance.

Chapter Three: Derek

As soon as the man had stepped into the ring, Derek's wolf had howled its delight. All through the fights he'd been bored. The people who'd come at him were either holding back or at best adequate fighters. He wanted a challenge. At least that's what he told himself as his wolf called out to play.

The man stood there, his shirt off and Derek couldn't help but admire his body. His arms and chest were beautifully toned, with rock hard abs pulling the picture together. Derek had a sudden vision of those arms around him as he crushed the man to him and claimed him. He forced the image far from his mind. It wasn't the time.

"What's your name?" he asked, his voice coming out a soft growl. His wolf wanted to play, to make him submit.

"Alex Argent." He was obviously related to Tara. His voice was strong and clear, a hint of a challenge in it. It wasn't aggression so much as an invitation and it drove Derek wild.

His wolf was too wound up to think. Instead he spread his arms, sending his own unspoken invitation to Alex, who lunged forward without hesitation. Derek ducked out of the way, brushing against Alex as he did so. He was faster than he'd thought.

Alex deftly switched course, aiming a kick at Derek. He deflected it and countered with his own punch and kick combo only to find himself blocked. His wolf growled, he'd found a decent opponent. His excitement building, he began to lash out with more complicated moves.

The intensity of the fight mounted, and Derek felt the heat soar through his body. Every now and then Alex would surprise him, lashing out with something and managing to make contact. He would have a few bruises in the morning.

He'd landed some good blows against Alex too. This was like nothing he'd ever done. There was nothing to prove to each other. He knew that Alex wanted to submit to him, that he wanted him to claim him, without knowing how, but he wasn't just letting him have it. He was making him work.

Surprisingly, his wolf wasn't angry. It was thrilled. He lost focus briefly and Alex managed to land a solid punch to the jaw. Derek snapped back to reality as Alex danced away grinning. His entire body humming, his muscles tense, Derek let out a howl and faked right, luring Alex into his trap. As Alex made to move away, Derek caught him, kicking his legs out from under him and pinning him to the ground. He lay on top of him, his wolf howling its victory.

All he could see was Alex. His throat exposed, his lips soft and so close. He breathed him in, letting his scent wash over him. Alex smelled like earth and forest, and something else. He could smell the excitement coming off him and it drove him crazy. He wanted him then and there, his cock hardening in his pants. Alex's eyes widened. The crowd erupted, breaking the spell.

He stood, subtly hiding his erection as he helped Alex to his feet. He could see the hunger in his eyes and it took all his self control not to claim him. He shook his head trying to clear it. No one had ever affected him the way Alex did, and he knew it was dangerous.

He took great pains to keep any sex he had private. He'd grown up watching his mother deal with the constant threats to her family just because she was next in line for succession. His father had been killed in an attempt to convince her not to run, and it had worked. As soon as he'd become Alpha, his mother had been put in greater danger, especially as he tried to lead the shifter world into the 21st century. He needed to be in control at all times which meant that Alex was the last thing he needed, no matter how attractive he was.

Chapter Four: Alex

Alex was still shaking from the fight. At least that's what he told himself. His heart pounded painfully against his chest and he could tell his hole was wet. The feel of Derek's cock against him had turned him on more than he'd thought possible. He'd had difficulty hiding his own reaction, slightly disappointed with how quickly Derek had seemed to recover.

As soon as he'd moved away Alex's wolf had protested, wanting more. He swallowed the rising panic in his throat. He was allowed to be attracted to him. Nothing had to happen. Besides, if Derek's reputation was anything to go by, at most they'd get a night together. Not to mention the fact that he was supposed to be keeping a low profile. Sleeping with one of the most powerful Alphas in history was hardly likely to help.

Alex couldn't help but watch Derek, desperate to touch him. His wolf strained at the surface, urging him to go to him. Alex shook his head. He was being an idiot. He pulled his clothes on ferociously, deciding to leave before his wolf could get him into any more trouble.

A hand caught him and he turned to find Tara smiling up at him.

"You weren't trying to leave were you?" She gave him a hard look before continuing, "Come on, I want you to meet my mate."

Alex hesitated, but could see his sister's excitement as she lead him over to the gorgeous woman talking to Derek.

"This is Alyssa Fleet, Alpha of the Sunstone Wolves and my mate." Tara put her arms around her, beaming.

"Alpha," he said, lowering his eyes.

"Call me Alyssa, you're basically family." Alyssa voice was husky but warm and Alex glanced up, taking the hand she extended to him. "That was some fight you put up. It's been a while since I've seen someone give him that much of a challenge." The way she said it sounded casual, but Alex had a feeling she knew more than she was letting on.

He blushed. "Thank you."

Derek stood to the side, silent, with a thoughtful look on his face. He was almost impossible to read, but Alex got the sense that Derek was wrestling with something.

"So you're Adolfo's son?" Alyssa asked. Alex saw Derek's eyes narrow suspiciously. He felt cold.

"I left the Silver Wolves a few months ago. I..." he trailed off. He didn't want to bad mouth the pack to these strangers.

However, Alyssa and Derek both seemed to understand. Alex realised that they would've met his father. After all, his pack was an offshoot of the Moonstone Wolves. Alex didn't want them to think the entire pack was full of dull brutes like Adolfo so he continued. "It just wasn't for me. There are plenty of decent wolves in the pack, it just wasn't where I belonged."

Alyssa squeezed his shoulder lightly and Alex was surprised to hear a soft growl escape from Derek. Tara growled back until Alyssa put an arm around her, looking thoughtfully from Derek to Alex. He turned away, his arms folded, not meeting Derek's gaze.

Alex wondered how long he had to wait before he could make a suitable excuse to leave. He could feel Derek's gaze on him, tracing his body. It felt like he was on fire. His own wolf prowled, itching to be closer to him, but the man was in control and he knew better.

"I should -" Alex started but Tara cut him off.

"Where are you staying tonight?"

"I hadn't really thought about it." The truth was Alex had planned on pitching camp in the forest, and leaving at the first sign of dawn, as soon as the Gathering was officially over. Tara seemed to know that.

"We have one of the wings of the house. Derek and I hired it for our wolves, you're more than welcome to stay. It'll beat trying to get a cab out of here." Alyssa smiled kindly. "Besides, we were thinking of having a small after party, why don't you come? The night's still young."

Alex didn't know what to say. He knew he should leave, but he couldn't bring himself to. He glanced at Derek who nodded. "I guess I can stay for a while."

Tara and Alyssa exchanged looks and beamed and the four of them set off for the house.

Chapter Five: Derek

He'd only agreed to the party because Alyssa had vetted all the guests. A select few of their closest wolves, completely devoted to their Alphas. As they entered the hall, they greeted their wolves affectionately, the slightest touch letting them know they were welcome. It wasn't a sexual touch, more a greeting: re-establishing ties and reminding them of their places.

The room was dimly lit, with numerous shifters already dancing. Alyssa pulled Tara onto the floor, kissing her fiercely and winking at Derek. He could feel his wolf prowling around, desperate to be close to Alex. He'd almost lost control when Alyssa had touched him. Now his body was tight, tense and he knew what he needed to relax. He refused to give into his wolf. He walked away from Alex, and instantly had two companions dancing with him, grinding against his body. It felt good, their bodies against his. He glanced up, locking eyes with Alex. He could see hunger in them.

Derek turned away. He could have anyone here. Why did his wolf need to have the only person in the world who made him lose control? One of the men dancing with him, a wolf of Alyssa's, kissed him, and Derek heard a growl. Alex stood a little ways away, glowering at the man and the woman touching Derek. The growl sent a thrill through him. His wolf rushed to the surface, he wanted Alex and no one else would do. Derek flashed his golden eyes, an invitation which Alex took, stopping just in front of the group.

Derek growled softly at his companions and they retreated, scowling at Alex. He smiled, and pulled Alex to him. As soon as they touched, he felt the same spark as before. He wanted him, wanted to make him submit again, to feel him under him, around him. He could smell Alex's desire, knew how badly he wanted this too. He wanted to make this count.

He began to dance with Alex, their bodies close, pressed against each other. He moved his hips against him, his cock growing hard as Alex curled his fingers through his hair. Their lips were inches from each other. Time seemed to slow, the music faded away and it was just him and Alex. He cupped the nape of his neck and kissed him.

The world exploded, his wolf taking control. He wanted Alex, wanted him beneath him, to empty himself into him and claim him as his own. He shook his head, trying to get back control, but Alex slipped his tongue into Derek's mouth, and he was left with instinct alone. He ripped Alex's jacket and shirt, discarding the rags as he felt his cock straining against the fabric of his trousers.

Alex's hands were at his shirt, tugging off his jacket, undoing the buttons. It was too slow. He needed his skin on Alex's, needed it now. He ripped his own shirt off, throwing it aside, pulling Alex towards him and cupping his cock through his pants. Alex moaned and Derek growled.

He kissed his neck, tasting him, drinking in his rich scent. Alex's hands were in his hair, pulling him closer. His balls grew hard and heavy, and he pressed himself against Alex, pinning him against a wall, nipping at his neck. Alex moaned as Derek worked him through his pants. Alex kissed him again and he lost all control.

Chapter Six: Alex

Derek growled hungrily, pulling him into a nearby room. It was empty except for a bed. "Take off your clothes." It was a command and every fibre in Alex wanted to obey him, but the Omega in him knew how to bend the rules and it knew what an Alpha like Derek needed. He wasn't about to be just another notch on this gorgeous man's belt.

He kicked off his shoes, and socks, glad he'd worn the shitty loose ones. He moved his hands to his belt buckle, working it slowly. The pressure of the fabric against his swollen cock was almost painful, but he knew it would drive Derek wild. That the slight challenge would set his wolf on edge. He smiled, the look in Derek's eyes almost overwhelming him. How was it possible for someone to get him so close with just a look? He caught the satisfaction in Derek's smile and knew he understood exactly what he'd done.

Alex growled and slipped off his trousers, taking his time. Derek stood, watching, the bulge in his own pants driving him wild. Alex's balls tightened, aching. Derek let out a low growl and Alex pulled the rest of his clothes off without hesitation. He was shivering slightly, but the room was warm. He stood there, watching Derek watch him.

Without speaking, the Alpha stood stripping off his own clothes. Alex gasped. He'd figured Derek would be big, but not that big. He was practically quivering with excitement, his hole wetter than it had ever been. Alex held still, letting Derek prowl around him, a finger tracing the lines of his body. He shivered, his balls so hard and heavy he thought he might explode. His hole was wet, and he quivered as Derek traced a finger across it.

Then Derek was standing in front of him, letting Alex touch and explore his body. Alex kissed him greedily, tasting the salt on his skin as he traced his way down his chiseled body. It was only now that they were close that he noticed the scars that lined his arms, back and chest. The one on his back felt thick and twisted. Derek growled as he felt it, and Alex stopped kissing his way down Derek's stomach.

He felt sadness welling up in him. The thought that someone or something had done that to Derek, that some of those clearly still caused him pain. He wanted to comfort him, but Derek was an Alpha. Alex doubted he'd be that vulnerable with him. The feel of Derek's hands tangled in his hair snapped him out of the train of thought. He looked up, his mouth inches from Derek's swollen cock.

Alex was surprised at the softness in Derek's eyes, the understanding, as if he knew what Alex had been thinking. Tenderly, Alex took him in his mouth, his tongue swirling the pre-cum across the head of his cock. He tasted so good. It sent another jolt to his balls and Alex knew he needed to cum. His wolf refused the release, knowing instinctively that Derek was in charge. He worked his thick cock with his mouth, taking it deep inside of him, glad his gag reflex was so ineffective. Derek began to guide his head, working Alex up and down his shaft at the pace he wanted. Alex wanted to drink him in so badly, wanted Derek's seed to fill his mouth. He began to play with his balls as his Alpha guided his head along his cock.

When did he become my *alpha?*

Now that he'd thought it he couldn't stop thinking it. It sounded so right. Derek growled, looking down at Alex with glowing gold eyes. He felt a jolt in his stomach and Derek said, "When I cum, you cum."

Alex had no doubt he'd be able to do that. He was barely hanging on as it was. Derek's cock was thick in his mouth, his balls hard and ready in his hands. His cock pulsed and Alex's mouth was full of the taste of Derek. It flooded him, trickling down his throat. He couldn't contain him all and he felt his own release a second later. His cum spreading across the floor. Derek pulled out of him and guided him up, kissing him fiercely.

Alex loved the way he tasted, so salty, so smoky and that faint taste of whiskey. He moaned as Derek picked him up, and brought him to rest on his hips. Alex wrapped his legs around his waist, revelling in how strong Derek was. His muscles rippled and with a jolt of excitement Alex realised Derek was hard again. He wasn't surprised, Derek was an Alpha after all. He felt his hole respond. He wanted Derek inside of him, filling him.

Derek nipped at his neck and Alex felt like his skin was on fire. He could feel the tip of his cock pressed against his hole, just teasing the entrance. Alex put every ounce of self control into not sliding onto it. Derek was in control, and Alex wanted him to claim him.

Slowly, Derek eased into him, giving him time to get used to his hard cock. It filled him so well, hitting his prostate perfectly. He cried out, barely holding on. His hole was even wetter now, his cock hard again, pressed against Derek's hard stomach. Derek thrust into him, hard, filling him completely. Alex couldn't help but moan in ecstasy. Derek's growl of need drove him close to the edge again. Derek was thrusting hard now, working Alex's hole. His muscles clenched around Derek's hard cock, working it, while his own cock spread pre-cum all over their stomachs. Derek spun and moved them onto the bed in one movement, landing gently, but staying inside of Alex.

The feel of Derek's body against his, his weight pressing down on him drove Alex to the brink. He was going to cum again, but Derek reached out and squeezed his shaft with his hand. The signal was clear, not yet. He kissed him deeply, his tongue sliding into his mouth as he thrust into him yet again, filling him with his cock. Alex pulled him closer, his fingers digging into Derek's perfect ass, wanting all of him. He felt Derek's cock throb and knew he was close. That he was going to cum again, inside of him. Alex whimpered, desperation getting the better of him. His balls ached, his hole was full of Derek. He needed him, wanted him more than he'd wanted anyone before.

Derek came inside of him, releasing Alex's shaft as he filled him with his seed. A moment later, Alex came, moaning into Derek as he bit hard into his shoulder. He did it without thinking, acting on instinct, his wolf urging him to mark him, to claim him. A moment later, Derek had pulled out, flipped him over and pinned him to the bed, still lying on top of him.

Alex felt Derek's lips next to his ear, his hard cock pressed against his hole and heard him whisper a word that made him cum again. "Mine."

Chapter Seven: Derek

He lay on top of Alex, the mark in his shoulder burning. His wolf cried out triumphantly as he pressed his cock into Alex's hole. He knew what Alex had done, even if Alex didn't fully understand. He should've been angry, should've been furious, but he wasn't. His wolf wanted him to bite Alex back, to cum inside of him and fill him, completing the mating.

He'd already come dangerously close when Alex first bit him. The only coherent thought running through him was "mine". Every fibre cried out for it, was desperate for it, but he couldn't. He wouldn't do that to Alex, wouldn't put him in that danger.

The smell of Alex's need brought him back to the present. His cock was hard, his balls tight and heavy. He needed this release as much as Alex. He thrust into him hard, filling him completely, loving how ready Alex's hole was for him. He'd never been with someone like him.

Sure, all wolves could self-lubricate, but few of them had ever matched his stamina. Alex seemed to know exactly what he wanted before he did, exactly how to please him. He listened to the silent commands Derek gave without needing any further explanation. Derek wanted him, wanted to claim him. He'd already submitted to him, exposing his neck happily. His fangs grew in response, but he forced himself away.

He couldn't let himself do it. Instead he kept thrusting into the gorgeous man under him, harder and harder, Alex moaning with pleasure. His balls were aching, full again and ready. He emptied into him, fighting for control of his wolf. He stopped just short of biting him, his talons slipping into Alex's shoulder instead. He came hard and lay on top of Alex, enjoying the feel of his hard body. His back was a beautiful maze of lines, surprisingly unscarred. He supposed that Alex had never had to fight, never had the chance to be wounded.

The thought of anyone trying to hurt him made Derek's wolf howl in rage, and he rolled over, pulling Alex into his arms protectively. He was only dimly aware of Alex stroking him, talking to him and calming him down. No one had ever managed to calm his wolf before, not like this. His muscles relaxed and he held Alex close, breathing him in. Why did his wolf respond so readily to this man?

They lay breathing heavily in each other's arms. Every so often, Derek kissed Alex softly and Alex continued to stroke him. Derek had never let anyone touch him like this before. It was nice, but dangerous. They drifted into a comfortable silence, quietly stroking each other.

"Are these all from the fight?" Alex asked after a while. He'd been stroking the scars on his arms.

Derek tensed. He didn't like to talk about his fight for ascendancy. Alex seemed to sense his reluctance and looked into his eyes. "It's okay. You don't have to talk about it if you don't want to."

The problem was that Derek did want to. He wanted to tell Alex about the fight, the lead up to it. Everything. He hesitated. He knew next to nothing about Alex, but his wolf trusted him. Out of nowhere he heard his mother's voice. *You've got to trust.* He took a breath and started to explain.

He told Alex about the way Blake, his uncle, had forced his mother to give up the ascension. How he had spent most of Derek's life threatening her through his father and himself. He explained how he had trained, the months and months of the most gruelling regime he could imagine and the days that lead up to his final challenge. Blake was twice his age, more experienced, with the power of an Alpha behind him. Derek had been barely 18, and half his size.

Blake had almost killed him in the fight, slicing his back so badly it had almost severed his spine. Alex gasped, but Derek continued. He needed to explain. "Blake turned his back on me. He thought I was finished, and maybe I would've been, but just before he turned he told me that he was the wolf who'd killed my father. That if he could get away with it, he'd kill my mother too. I lost control. It was like he'd woken some part of me I'd never known existed.

"I leapt up, onto his back. I couldn't feel pain, couldn't feel anything. I just wanted him to bleed. I tore at every part of his body I could reach, my wolf fully in control. If you ask people who saw the fight, they'll say my eyes glowed gold as I did it, but I don't know how true that is. It makes a good story though. By the time I'd come to my senses, he was lying in front of me. I'd defeated him, but he wouldn't back down. I didn't want to kill him, just wanted him to submit. But I should've known he wouldn't. He was too proud. In the end I killed him, and broke my mother's heart. He was an asshole, but he was still her brother, and he'd turned me into a monster."

Derek turned away from Alex, breathing hard. "The thing is, I don't regret it. It kept my family safe, and the pack's been thriving for nearly a decade. His supporters were driven off, although I'm sure they're just biding their time. They've got support with the more old school packs, but for now, we're good. We're safe."

He turned to Alex, defiance in his eyes, but to his surprise he saw Alex looking back at him with understanding and tenderness. "It was the right decision. Alphas like that... There's no reasoning with them."

Alex's eyes clouded over and Derek knew he was thinking about Adolfo. "It must have been hard for you, growing up a Silver Wolf."

"It wasn't too bad. I had my sisters. Tara, who you've met, and Cam. We were all close as kids, but dad never had time for the girls. You know what he's like. Women are for breeding, that's it." Alex scowled as he continued, "It wasn't too bad, not at first. I was his only boy and he was determined to leave his pack to me. He trained me relentlessly, he's the reason I can fight the way I can. It was only once I'd hit puberty things started to go south."

"Is that when you realised you like men?"

Alex laughed bitterly and Derek was surprised. "I'd known that since I can remember. I've only ever been into guys. No, that was just the straw that broke the camel's back... What started it..."

Derek could smell the fear coming off Alex, and tried to comfort him. What was the secret he was so desperate to keep? Derek kissed him softly, the wolf in him growling wanting to know what was causing him so much pain and how to fix it. When Derek drew back, he gasped. Alex's eyes were bright green, the colour of an Omega.

For a moment, neither wolf moved. Understanding dawned on Derek. The control Alex had over his wolf, his perfect mix of dominance and submission, the way his wolf wanted to claim him. Of course he was an Omega. How had he not realised? His wolf renewed its effort to claim Alex, to make him Derek's Omega, the perfect mate.

The fear in his eyes stopped Derek short. Alex really thought he'd leave him, that he'd hurt him for who he was. Growling, Derek kissed him fiercely. "Your father is an idiot. Trust me, he's one of the least powerful Alphas I've ever met."

Alex's eyes were wet and he kissed them softly. He had heard tales of the Adolfo's ways, seen how vitriolic he could be first hand, but to see the damage he had done on his own flesh and blood. It made Derek's blood boil. His wolf clawed to the surface, wanting retribution. Alex stroked the bite he'd left on Derek's skin.

His wolf calmed instantly, and Derek looked at the man in his arms. It would be so easy to bite him, to slip inside of him once more and finish claiming him as his own. He'd never wanted anything as much as he did now, but he couldn't do it. He wouldn't do it and something inside of him broke.

Alex seemed to sense it. He didn't say anything, just pulled closer to him, nuzzling into his chest. "We'll have tonight."

Derek nodded, his wolf howling against the statement as they fell asleep in each other's arms.

Chapter Eight: Alex

It had been a few months since the amazing night he'd spent with Derek. He'd been consumed with thoughts of him, with the need to finish whatever it was they'd started that night. Every now and then he got strange stabs of emotion that he was sure weren't his. On top of that, he'd vomited continuously for nearly two weeks after and now it was like his wolf was in overdrive. He could barely control it or any of his senses. Everything was overwhelming.

That's how he ended up sitting with Tara at the doctor's office. As a lone wolf, Alex didn't have access to any of the pack facilities. Tara had agreed to take him to one on neutral ground, a shifter doctor Alex had found online. She was sceptical, and as they stared around the dingy waiting room, Alex could see why.

"You could've just come with me. I'm sure Alyssa would let you into the pack and then you could've just used one of our clinics." Tara gave him a hard look.

Alex just shrugged in response. The truth was, there was only one pack he really wanted to be part of and if he joined Alyssa's pack he'd never be able to. You couldn't leave an original pack. If he was going to be a pack wolf again, he wanted to be a Moonstone Wolf and sadly it wasn't an option.

"Have you heard from him since?" Tara asked as if reading his mind.

"We've talked on and off." It was true. He and Derek talked most days about almost anything.

A part of him was surprised how much he enjoyed the conversations, how easy it was to talk to each other. They hadn't met in person since that night, both knowing that if they did they wouldn't be able to keep from finishing what they'd started. Each conversation ripped through Alex, but he couldn't stop. He needed Derek in his life, and he would take whatever he could get. Derek had made his decision, and Alex doubted he would change his mind. Alex saw how worried Derek was about his mother, how much he still blamed himself for his father's death. His wolf might not agree, but he understood how much of a liability he'd be.

"He's just playing you," Tara said.

Alex growled, his wolf forcing its way to the surface, desperate to defend its chosen mate. "You know that's not true." His voice was strangled with rage.

Tara sighed and nodded. "I still think he's being an idiot. You can look after yourself. You guys either need to suck it up or move on. It's killing you."

Alex knew she was right. Whatever was happening between the Alpha and him, it wasn't going anywhere. All it was doing was hurting both of them. He sighed and at that moment the doctor called him into the office to talk about his test results.

He was a thin balding man with a weedy, rat like look about him. He was definitely a shifter, but Alex's wolf bristled at the sight of him. The man smiled sickeningly.

"The problem, Mr. Argent, is quite simple. You're pregnant."

Alex felt his jaw drop. "What?"

"You're pregnant. It's not unheard of, although many deny it. It happens when an Alpha and an Omega couple."

"There has to be another explanation." Even as he said it Alex knew there wasn't. He'd heard of Omega males in other packs getting pregnant, read stories about it.

"I'm afraid there isn't. I suggest you tell the father, Alphas like to keep track of their young."

A jolt shot through Alex. He had the sneaking suspicion that this doctor knew about him and Derek. He got to his feet, his wolf growling. Tara stood beside him, a hand on his arm.

"I can see why you're a neutral doctor." Tara sneered, her father coming out in her for the briefest second. "My brother has never slept with an Alpha."

The doctor smiled and shrugged, gesturing to the door. Alex and Tara left the clinic together, Alex's mind whirring wildly. Pregnant. He was pregnant. What the fuck was he going to do? Absentmindedly his hand went to his belly, stroking it. His baby, Derek's baby. Their baby. He needed to tell him, but he didn't want the baby to be the only reason Derek chose him. What if he didn't? What if he wanted nothing to do with them? What if he thought it was a trap?

He glanced at Tara. "Tell him."

Alex called him, but it went to voicemail. Derek was probably in a meeting. He texted him asking him if they could talk, in person. He'd just have to wait for a response. His wolf was frantic, a mix of fear and happiness soared through him. He was only a few blocks from his apartment when he calmed down enough to hear the footsteps.

He and Tara whirled around and saw five of Adolfo's thugs behind them. Alex's mind shot back to the doctor's office. He could dimly remember hearing the sound of voices on the phone as he left the clinic. He knew why they were here.

"That bastard," Tara breathed, her pelt beginning to shine through.

Alex grabbed her hand. "Don't. You need to get out of here."

"I'm not leaving you."

"Get Derek, he'll know what to do. Don't worry about me. They'll have to catch me first." He felt strangely calm. His wolf was in charge and it knew what to do. They needed to keep the young safe, whatever the cost.

Tara hesitated and Alex growled at her, "Damn it Tara, go. I'm more valuable to them alive, you know that. Just go. Find Derek."

Finally, she nodded and sprinted away, shifting into a brown wolf as she raced off. Alex turned to face the men. None of them had sped up, why would they need to? There were more of them and he had nowhere to run. His wolf pressed to the surface. He wasn't going to go down without a fight, and he wasn't going to let these men hurt his baby. He whirled round, sprinting into a nearby alley, vaulting the wall, shifting into a black wolf mid leap. He hit the ground with all four paws and raced into the forest. He would keep their baby safe.

Chapter Nine: Derek

The months since the Gathering had been some of the most frustrating of Derek's life. His wolf, usually so carefully controlled, was riding close to the surface, desperate to claim Alex as his own. Sleeping with other people hadn't helped, just made it worse. The other Alphas were trying to push anti-Omega bills through to the council, bringing enough signatures to force them to debate the idea which only made a bad situation worse.

Thankfully, he and Alyssa had the majority vote, but some of the offshoots were starting to get restless. Rumours were spreading of offshoot Alphas campaigning together, saying they needed to go back to their roots. The whole thing made Derek sick.

To cap it all off Alex was sick and Derek couldn't even be there to help him. He growled in frustration, gripping the back of the chair so hard it shattered in his hands. He scowled and called his secretary.

David answered right away, "Yes Alpha?"

He sighed, "Order me another chair David. Thank you."

"Right away Alpha."

The line disconnected and at that exact moment Derek felt a jolt of fear that shook him to his core. His knees buckled and he clutched his chest. This wasn't his fear. This was Alex's. Something was wrong. Caution be damned. He needed to find him and needed to find him now. There was a scuffle outside his door and he heard a woman's voice yelling.

"If you don't get out my way I will rip your fucking head from your shoulders, pack rule or not." It was Tara.

Derek flung the door open and waved down his wolves. "What's happened?"

"They took Alex, well I'm not sure if they've got him yet. There were five of them, we were almost back at his apartment. He told me to come get you and then he ran."

"Do you know where he is now?" Fury rose in Derek. Someone was trying to hurt Alex. His wolf was calling for blood and he agreed completely. Whoever had done this would pay.

He could feel his pack reacting around him, their aggression palpable. He needed to get his rage under control. He would bring his fighters, his pack, and destroy the scum who'd tried to hurt his mate. *My mate*. He knew it was true, whether or not they'd finished the ceremony. Alex was his. He'd been an idiot for staying away so long. He shook his head. If he brought his pack, it could start an all out war. Which would be exactly what Adolfo and his cronies wanted.

"Stay." He didn't need to shout. The power reverberated through his voice, stopping his wolves in their tracks, a few of them whimpering.

He moved towards the door and as he did so Tara moved close, whispering something in his ear. Alex was pregnant and the thugs knew it. Derek's wolf howled in anguish as another jolt of fear shot through them. He couldn't tell if it was his own or Alex's, but he couldn't wait. His stupidity might cost him two lives.

He turned to the room at large. "If I'm not back in three hours, come to me. We'll fight together." He nodded to Tara whose eyes widened, and then he leapt through the window, smashing through the glass and shifting mid air. He hit the ground a gigantic silver wolf. Pain shot through his paws and he began to run as fast as he could towards the Alex.

His wolf guided him, catching the faintest scent of Alex on the wind and pushing him harder. He howled in rage, determined to find his mate. The scent of blood filled his nostrils and brought him up short. He inhaled, his wolf brain piecing the puzzle together. Alex had been here. His assailants had attacked him, but it wasn't his blood. Derek turned and saw the body of a red wolf lying a short distance away. He felt a surge of pride and bounded forward, breathing in the scents. There was more blood. This time though, it was Alex's.

He'd been hurt, and from the look of it badly. Derek roared and thundered through the undergrowth, ignoring the branches and trees that lashed out at him. Pain didn't matter. He needed to find his mate. The smell of blood was overwhelming as Derek leapt into the clearing, snarling and growling. Alex was lying there, no longer in wolf form, clutching his side which was bleeding profusely.

He sprinted to Alex, nuzzling against him, pressing his nose against any part of him he could reach. Alex held his fur and Derek heard his rasping breath. With difficulty, he gasped, "I knew you'd come."

The sound of applause rang out behind them and Derek whirled around, snarling, his hackles raised. Four men appeared, dropping the knives they were carrying and shifting into wolves. Without thinking, Derek lunged at the closest wolf, but Alex cried out. Derek pulled up short, confused. His wolf cried out for blood. For vengeance. Alex was stroking his fur and whispering something.

"I need you to breathe. Use your nose. Scent what's in the air."

Derek took a breath. He breathed in Alex's blood, his fear, but beneath it all was something else. It was new, both him and not him. He tilted his head, glancing at Alex. "You don't need to fight them. Can't you smell how scared they are? They need a real Alpha."

One of the wolves growled at Alex's words, his hackles raised.

Derek ignored him, focusing on Alex. He could smell the fear. He knew what he needed to do. His wolf somehow understood and he shifted, standing in human form. The wolf closest to him lunged at him, but Derek caught it by its throat, his hand half transformed as he pinned it to the ground.

"Stop." He didn't yell it, but the command in his tone was unmistakable. The wolf pinned beneath him whimpered, and two of the three remaining ones stopped, their ears flat against their head. The last one continued advancing.

"Stop," Derek growled, his muscles tensing, his eyes glowing gold. The wolf jerked, and lay down, head on the ground.

"Listen to me." His voice was still soft, but there was no mistaking the anger in his tone. " Adolfo is a weak Alpha. He rules with hatred and aggression, matched only by his incompetence."

One of the wolves growled, but Derek quieted him with a look. "Do you remember the Moonstone pack before I came to ascendency? Do you remember the price you paid for our failings?"

The wolves whined. Before Derek had ascended, the Moonstone wolves were in constant skirmishes. Blake hadn't wanted to waste his own wolves, so he'd pulled from the offshoots, sacrificing Silver Wolves, Moon Wolves and countless others. Their packs had been ravaged, their Alphas letting it happen. The raids had continued amongst the offshoots, fuelled by weak Alphas who let their wolves die for them without risking their own skins.

Derek could see the thought bubbling in the wolves' minds. He knew what they were thinking. Their Alpha was sitting safe while they were out here being risked like their lives didn't matter. Yet here was the most powerful Alpha in the world, standing before them without his wolves, ready to defend his mate alone. " My wolves know I would die for them, can you say the same?"

The wolves whined, crawling onto the ground and exposing their bellies. They recognised his superiority. He knew he'd planted a seed within them. "Go back to your territory." He let the wolf beneath his hand up and took a step forward. "Come after my mate again, and it will be the last thing you do."

Derek roared and the wolves fled, tails between their legs. Derek watching them go, the rage and fury coming off him in waves. Then he turned to Alex, pulling him gently into his arms.

"How badly are you hurt?" he asked.

"It's not too bad. I think I can walk." Alex tried, stumbled and fell down.

"Don't move." Derek's eyes glowed yellow as he lifted Alex into his arms. "I'll take you to a doctor."

"You can't. I'm not pack."

"You're my mate. You're a Moonstone Wolf and you're carrying my child. You're pack, and as soon as you're better I'll give you the mark to prove it. I'm sorry it took me so long."

Alex shrugged and winced. Derek's eyes glowed gold. "Let's go home."

"Sounds nice," Alex murmured weakly, as Derek carried him back to Moonstone Wolf territory.

Chapter Ten: Alex

Alex had been badly injured more than they'd thought. He spent months in and out of the hospital, his recovery complicated by his pregnancy. Derek was no help. The Alpha in him refused to compromise, to risk anything happening to Alex or their baby. Alex had had to accept that he'd be in the hospital until he was 100% recovered. The only good news had come when Alyssa had told them the Silver Wolves had revolted. Cam was the new Alpha.

It didn't make hospital life any more fun though.

"I'm bored." Alex growled. "I want to go home."

" We need to stay here until the baby comes."

"Can it hurry up already? I mean come on, I'm huge, hot and horny."

A grin spread across Derek's face and Alex looked at him quizzically. "What?"

"Well, we could try and jump start labour." Derek had a wicked look in his eyes.

Alex could smell his arousal and it fuelled his own. They hadn't been able to have sex because of Alex's injury, which meant that Derek hadn't finished the bond. Alex's wolf growled. "Are you serious?"

"Apparently it can help. The doctor was the one who suggested it. You should be okay, as long as I'm not too rough."

Derek was incredibly close to Alex now. Gently, he turned Alex over, lying against his back. He heard the sound of a zipper and felt Derek's cock pressed against his hole. Alex had never been so glad for backless hospital gowns. He felt Derek press into him slowly, filling him. He moaned as Derek reached around and started to rub his shaft in time with his thrusts. Alex could barely control himself, his balls were already tight and heavy, his cock leaking pre-cum as Derek fucked him. It had been months, and he'd wanted this so badly.

Derek growled, and Alex felt his breath against his neck. His cock was throbbing inside of him as Alex worked his muscles around it. With a final thrust Derek came, biting Alex's neck hard. It was pleasure like he'd never imagined. He came hard, barely able to breathe. They lay there, wrapped in each other, and Alex drifted in a post-orgasmic stupor.

A sudden pain in his stomach brought him to his senses. He cried out and Derek leapt up, ignoring his nudity. Alex could smell the panic coming off him, but before he could reassure him, another wave of pain ripped through him.

In a few seconds the room was flooded with doctors, and Derek was clutching his hand tightly. The baby was coming, and Alex finally had an answer to what hurt more, getting kicked in the balls or going through labour.

"Stay with me?" He looked at Derek.

"Always." Derek shot a look around the room, daring anyone to challenge him.

No one did. A doctor leaned over and put a mask on his face. "Count backwards from 10."

Alex barely got to eight before he lost consciousness..

When he woke up his mouth was dry. He looked around, trying to remember what happened.

"You're awake," Derek's voice was barely a whisper.

Slowly, Alex's brain started to work. "Where's the baby?"

"He's here." Derek moved closer and Alex gasped at the tiny bundle in his arms.

"He's so small." Alex choked up as Derek slipped their son delicately into his arms.

He was beautiful. He had Derek's grey eyes and silver hair, but Alex's face. He breathed in, Alex had never smelled anything so wonderful. He turned to Derek.

"Have you thought of a name?" He asked.

Derek shook his head. Alex hesitated, and after a few moments he said, "I thought Luca, after your dad."

There was a sharp intake of breath and Alex turned away from their new son to look at his mate. Derek kissed him, deeply. He didn't need to say anything more.

They broke apart and Alex brushed the soft hair on top of Luca's head. "Welcome to the world baby boy."

Derek wrapped them both in his arms, kissing Alex softly. "I love you."

"I love you too."

"Let's go home."

Alex nodded and finally, after months of waiting, their family was ready to go home.

BREAKING THE RULES

A WOLF SHIFTER MPREG BUNDLE

Preston Walker & Liam Kingsley

Disclaimer

This is a work of fiction. Names, places, characters and events are all fictitious for the reader's pleasure. Any similarities to

Chapter One

Ainslie stretched and yawned as he rolled out of the tent. The air was crisp and caused goosebumps to crawl up his arms as an early morning breeze cleared his sinuses. He smiled wide as his rough batch of five o'clock shadow itched in the breeze. He shook his head to clear it and scratched his face as he looked around to see most of his hunting party spread out on the ground. Apparently, they slept outside of their tents around the smoldering fire they should have put out the night before.

He sighed and cleared his throat loudly. He expected them to wake up or at least stir, but when no one moved he arched a brow and started barking out orders.

"Alright guys, up we get. Let's go. We need someone to wet the ashes, Ben needs to take down the tents. Sam put up the cooking pots. Ash make sure all the food is packed. We don't have time to sit and waste this morning. I don't even know why the tents were even put up if you all slept outside." Ainslie grumbled as he walked around nudging some awake.

The loup garou dragged themselves awake and grumbled the whole time. They looked at their future Alpha and huffed loudly about him ordering them around. They would have his back in an instant if he so needed it, no matter what, but right now they were half asleep and just grumbly in general. They didn't outright challenge him, but if Ainslie wasn't busy making sure things were in order he would have playfully turned and challenged them for talking back.

"We slept pretty close to the territory line." Sam mumbled and pointed towards the sign that split the woods on this side of the town in half.

"Yeah, well, we didn't have much choice with how you were all grumbling and complaining. I don't see anyone from over there... we should be fine." Ainslie hummed. He pulled at his shirt, feeling as though he had ended up sweating all night rather than freezing with some of the plants. He took his shirt off and tucked it into his back pocket while the others finished packing up.

He wanted to be extra limber today. They had to bring down a big elk or something good to show their training wasn't a waste. The feeling of being watched prickled the hairs on the back of his neck, but he didn't look around. Not yet, anyhow. His eyes narrowed though and he fought the urge to growl. He finished breaking down his own tent and had his things packed and ready to go before the others.

"Alright guys, it's time to go," He said as he clapped his hands together for attention. He stood to his full height of six foot five and turned around seeing *most* of the packing and clean up done. He gave them a look which made them work faster.

"I'll scout ahead then, since you're taking *forever*. Catch up soon." Ainslie huffed and started walking with his bag slung over his shoulder in a slouchy way. That feeling of being watched followed him. He knitted his brows together as he fell deep in thought over what was watching him. An elder? Someone from the other territory? He swallowed down a growl. When sticks broke ahead of him he ducked down carefully and set his bag to the side.

The trees were thick in this area, but not thick enough that the sun didn't trickle in between them. The fog of his exhale puffed through his nose as his eyes dialed in on where the noise had come from. Ainslie tilted his head very slightly while sniffing the air as another gentle breeze brought him a delicious scent. He smirked as his skin melted off slowly, his body expanded, bones elongated and teeth fell out and grew anew only longer and sharper.

With his muddy yellow eyes fixated on the rustling of bushes he launched himself into the air, gripping the tree in front of him and hurling through tree after tree until he landed on the back of a large male elk. It started to bellow, but his training had it down and silent before the gurgle in its throat finished into a full bellow.

"Damnit that was mine!" A stocky blond growled as he stepped through the bushes, finishing a slow shift back into his human form.

“Too bad *pup*.” Ainslie growled, his voice strained and guttural in inhuman form.

“Not too bad! That’s mine.”

“Are you really going to fight me over *my* kill?” Ainslie arched a brow, he sniffed the air and stepped closer to him.

“You are on my territory.” The male snarled.

“Not by the smell pouring off you, *Omega*.” Ainslie narrowed his eyes.

“*That* doesn’t mean anything.” The wolf growled back.

“And actually, that elk is on the border. So, if you want it we *have* to fight for it.” He turned back, the thick hide and fur melted to the ground in exchange for a naked muscular brunette.

The blond glared at him in silence. Obviously thinking over the situation carefully and taking the moment to look his opponent over.

“My wolf would destroy yours. You wanna fight we’ll fight human forms only. Nothin’ dirty.” Ainslie offered.

“You’re not worth the fight. Take the elk and stay away from *my* territory.”

“Boy, I’m going to make *you* my territory if you don’t shut up about that.”

“Wooooo! Look at Ainslie!” Sam snorted off in the distance. “Throwing that Alpha status all around.”

“Fight him!” Ash hollered from behind Sam.

Ben sighed from where he was as they walked up to the edge of the clearing they found Ainslie in.

Ainslie turned and set his sights on the blond once more. He tilted his head slightly with his brow arched. He looked relaxed but he was ready to fight. Ready to take the other down and keep his “honor” over the elk he had killed and make sure his hunting pack knew not to mess with him.

He saw the blond narrow his eyes and in quick movement the male darted forward and swung at him. His fist connected to Ainslie's jaw sounding close to a gunshot.

"Whoa!" Ainslie's hunting party hooted and hollered on the sidelines.

Ainslie was taken by surprise and stepped back, but it didn't last long. He stepped forward with two quick jabs to the others face to distract him. After the other backed up to avoid them he tackled him into the brush and out of view of the howling entourage.

"Ainslie you're such a show off..." The wolf beneath him huffed and was visibly glad none of those punches had connected.

"I think you like it, Michael." Ainslie whispered as a smirk pulled at his lips. "Concede."

"I want that elk." Michael lifted his hips, throwing Ainslie off him and rolled them over to pin him down.

"*You* concede."

"How bad do you want that elk?" Ainslie growled beneath Michael. Their fingers tangled together he lightly squeezed.

"Bad enough to actually fight you in front of your pack..." Michael murmured and tilted his head to the side with a smirk pulling at his lips.

"You knew they were there didn't you."

"I did." He pouted but fought to keep Ainslie pinned.

"Yours isn't far away, is it?" Ainslie mused aloud and barely put effort into pushing the other off.

"Nope."

"Stop talking and fight!" Sam snarled. He was unable to make out what they were mumbling to each other and not pleased that there was not enough fighting going on over that elk.

Ainslie snarled and flipped them over, rolling them out of the brush and pulling Michael up into a choke hold. He was waiting until Michael tapped out to release him as the snarls of his pack made him realize he had pulled the other out of his territory instead of staying on the line. Michael crawled back into his own territory after he was released and glared back at him as he shifted into his wolf form and trotted off.

"Stupid shifters... maybe you'll get lucky, Ainslie, and you'll get paired with a were instead of one of *them*." Sam grumbled as they picked up the elk and started to walk off. The elder shifters snorting and glaring at them to make sure they didn't cause any more damage.

Chapter Two

Ainslie had been praised for bringing that elk back and he was proud of that. What he wasn't happy about was the look his mother gave him. She sat across from him at the kitchen table with her hands folded neatly before her. He ducked his head and stared at the ground rather than look up at that expression again. He was not going to like what she had to say. He never did.

"Ainslie Grey Etchinson. I heard you got into a fight on the border of the Johnson's pack and our own."

"Yes Mother..."

"I heard you won." She sounded pleased about that, but it didn't look like he was going to get off the hook for fighting with someone in the neighboring pack.

"I did mother."

"I also heard you pulled him onto our territory." She half snarled. Ainslie looked up to see just how upset she really was.

"It was an accident. I wasn't paying attention and I should have."

"Fights like that stay on the border. There's a reason for this you know."

"Yes mom..."

"Do not let it happen again. They will not push the issue... but there is no territory crossing allowed."

"I know mom, I'm sorry."

"Next time you'll regret it." She narrowed her eyes and made him feel small. Ainslie wiggled in his seat and pursed his lips.

"I know..."

"Other than that, you did good taking down the elk yourself. You have training today after you're done with classes. I want a report of some kind... I want to see your grades if we're going to pay all this for university."

"Yes mom, I'll send you the grades."

"They better be A's." She growled.

"They are."

"Good." She half growled and half huffed, but after a sip of her coffee her features smoothed out and she smiled lightly. "Are you looking forward to fair?"

"Kind of..."

"Are you going to take someone?"

"No, what would be the point?" Ainslie looked up and arched his brow.

"Ah, your dad told you didn't he?" She pouted a little.

"Yep, I already know I'm set up for an arranged... thing."

"I just wish we knew with who. That hasn't been discussed yet." She sighed heavily and sipped her coffee again.

"Yeah, I know. We'll find out this weekend though, won't we?" Ainslie stated more than questioned as he stood up and grabbed his bag.

"Have a good day in class."

"Mmhm." He headed out the door and down the street. It wasn't long until he bumped into the shifter from the day before.

"Ugh, you." Michael snarled.

"You." Ainslie growled in response.

"You going to steal my grades too?"

"You going to get in my way?"

"Maybe."

They stood at the public bus stop and waited quietly until the bus turned the corner down the road. Ainslie could easily afford a car of his own if he really wanted to. He wanted to save his money though and he refused to let his parents buy one for him. He looked around to see that as usual the bus stop was empty save for the two of them.

Ainslie's pack didn't have school until the afternoon. They worked until then so he wouldn't see them until later that night. Michael was usually by himself when they headed to campus anyway. Ainslie always thought it was weird, but he had never pushed the issue to find out why.

Ainslie thought about how he knew the other while he stared across the street with a half glare. His mind lingering on thoughts of their childhood; always playing in the festivals together away from elder eyes while the ceremonies were taking place.

"You get in trouble?" Michael asked quietly as they climbed onto the bus.

"Nah, just a stern talking to. You?"

"Yep. I'll be hearing about it for the next month."

"Shifters are weird." Ainslie grumbled. "It was just an elk. There are others out there."

"You didn't back down though..."

"The elk was on our territory..."

"Half of it was on the border when you took it down..."

"Are we really going to fight about this or are you going to tell me how you did on your math test last week?" Ainslie had helped him study for it on the bus ride all last week. He had told himself it was only to keep him from whining about if he failed. They sat side by side, acting as though they couldn't even stand to look at each other.

"Oh, *that...*"

"Don't tell me you failed..." Ainslie snarled as his eyes snapped over and meeting the others and keeping his gaze.

"I... passed. Flying colors." Michael smirked, having seen the look of pure irritation in the other's eyes when he paused for dramatic effect.

"Better have. How you managed to get into this school I'll never know."

"Oh, like you're the best student ever... I had to help you with your history." Michael rolled his eyes.

"History puts me to sleep." Ainslie grumbled defensively.

"*You* put me to sleep." Michael glared at his feet, Ainslie looked back out the window for the remainder of the ride.

"Stop that." Ainslie snorted.

"Stop what?"

"Being cute." Ainslie stood when the bus stopped and headed off to his first class, leaving Michael to just stare after him. Ainslie didn't bother to look back over his shoulder to find out his expression, but he felt his eyes on him.

***

Ainslie spent the day studying, learning, and listening while trying not to snap at the teachers for telling him what to do. When he was finally free from classes he went straight for the main park in the middle of town. He didn't have to listen to anyone and could just run through neutral territory. It also gave him an excuse to look at Michael whose small pack liked to run through the trails trying to bulk up even the Omegas. His pack did things differently and Ainslie wasn't sure how he felt about it. Omegas were generally treated poorly just because they were not strong enough to take down most Alphas.

But Michael, even listed as an Omega in his own pack could pin him for a minute and *he* was an Alpha in his pack. The strength was there but it was just not utilized... and Michael was the Alphas son. Ainslie either couldn't understand or he was refusing. He was stuck in his own pack's line of thinking as he shook his head as he saw them in the large field beside the running path he was on running drills.

It wasn't until the familiar foot pattern of Sam catching up to him did he focus on what he was supposed to be there for. He looked over his shoulder and smirked then took off in a challenge for Sam to follow him and keep up.

They were not delicate with each other. The whole point was to go out do the other. Sam had always been faster but that didn't stop Ainslie from pushing and growling to slow him down. It also didn't stop Sam from taking those challenges as fighting words and fighting back. He didn't want to challenge for Alpha but that didn't mean he would back down.

"How long have you been playing nice with that shifter?" Sam growled at him after getting a rough push.

"What?"

"I saw you staring at him."

"Doesn't mean anything. Was just trying to figure out what the point of their training that way is. He's too weak to ever get out of his position."

"That's not how you were looking at him." Sam snorted. Their pace had slowed to a light jog.

"This is the kind of fight you want to pick today?" Ainslie sighed. He couldn't hide his annoyance and didn't bother trying.

"Yup."

"Why?" Ainslie groaned.

"You could have torn him apart in the woods. You didn't. You're always just fussing at him and never putting an end to the fussing. You think we're blind, don't you?"

"There's no point in getting into that kind of fight over an elk and he knew that too."

"Did he? Or was he just trying to be close to you. You're going to be paired with another Alpha this weekend. Like you *should* be. Don't let that Omega stink cloud your nose." Sam warned as though he'd challenge him over it.

"Do I need to fight him again?"

“No, but if you two do fight again you need rip his head off or I will.” Sam snarled and started running at his usual pace. It left Ainslie to look after him confused as he jogged a bit slower through the slender trees of the park.

Chapter Three

Michael stretched out over the rocks at the edge of his packs woods. He was glad this little hiding spot was barely in the neutral zone so he couldn't get fussed at for being in the wrong spot. He yawned and started to doze off. After a long morning of being yelled at for even sneezing wrong, he just wanted to hide. That was, until he heard the gravel move, suggesting someone was climbing up into his hiding spot.

"What do you want?" Michael asked as Ainslie's handsome face popped up into view with a large smile.

"I think you know what I want..." his voice purred, sending goosebumps crawling across his skin.

"Oh really? That all you want?" Ainslie tilted his head as he sat up the rest of the way.

"Maybe... maybe not... you never know with me. I might change my mind after," he growled playfully and finished climbing up.

"Were you followed?"

"Nope. I never am." Ainslie crawled over to him, lightly pressing his forehead against Michael's.

"So..." Michael giggled.

"So, kiss me." He purred and pulled Michael close. He cradled his head as he laid him back on the rocks while they kissed making the butterflies in Michael's stomach flutter. Michael met his eyes and smiled wide as he broke the kiss.

"Did you bring..."

"Yes, I brought it. So impatient." Ainslie stood up and walked over to the edge. Picking up a backpack he had left for suspense.

He returned and sat beside Michael as he opened it.

"I like Edna's cookies," Michael purred.

"I like you." Ainslie had Michael snorting with slight laughter.

"Good," Michael chuckled and pulled him for a kiss as the cookies were brought up.

"After this we go for a quick run? These things always make me feel sluggish." Ainslie stretched and yawned, having not been thinking too far into what it would mean to be out of the hiding spot together.

"Only if we stay in the neutral area, Ains, we can't get seen together without fighting..."

"I know. It's okay though. I can always fight you."

"Not another fight... not today anyway. I just want to eat the cookies and relax for what little while we have left for today," Michael pleaded.

"*Fine*, take the fun out of everything." Ainslie teased him lightly. He opened the jar and handed it over, then pulled out his tablet.

"Movies too?" Michael blinked in surprise. He tilted his head to the side and eyed him carefully.

"Yep, your favorite one too. Even though it's gross. I figured since you were in trouble forever you weren't getting to watch your movies," Ainslie said softly, trying not to look like he was being considerate on purpose.

"I don't think I'm in trouble forever any more... but thank you," Michael murmured and scooted closer, ducking under his arm so they cuddled up in the chilly autumn afternoon. While he nibbled on cookies and they watched his favorite movies, Michael looked up at Ainslie. He wondered why the other was being overly nice today. It wasn't often that he was, maybe it was just to keep him from regretting being close to him? Michael ran his hand along Ainslie's abs, his shirt being the annoying barrier between him and those chiseled muscles.

"You're going to start something you can't get out of," Ainslie growled playfully.

"Well your shirt is in the way. I can't really enjoy this if your shirt is in my way."

“Then move it.”

“You want me to?” Michael couldn’t help but smirk as he leaned in, their lips inches apart.

“Do it,” Ainslie demanded against his lips.

Michael nipped playfully and pulled his shirt up and over his head. His own shirt didn’t stay on much longer as Ainslie pulled it off quickly after. The tablet and cookies forgotten as they laid down on the rocks.

“We’ll meet again tomorrow, right?” Michael asked softly. He frowned lightly and turned his face away from Ainslie’s soft kiss.

“Yea, why?”

“I just... I dunno.”

“Are you scared we’re meeting up too much?” Ainslie frowned and softly ran his fingertips over Michael’s cheek.

“Yea... a little bit... but I also feel like I never see you smile anymore unless we’re here.”

“They won’t smell us on each other if we...”

“That’s not what I mean Ainslie. What if we get followed?”

“You’re worrying too much about too many things.”

“Alright...” Michael relaxed back against the ground. His brow wrinkled as he worried. He couldn’t help it though. He didn’t want to lose Ainslie.

“What’s that face for?”

“Whose idea was it to make a secret spot in a rocky place?”

“It’s high enough up to where we won’t just be seen... there’s enough flat surface on this rock...”

“So, you did,” Michael teased and leaned up to kiss him again.

“Mmhmm, but you like it... since it’s just us.”

“I... want it to always be just us.” Michael pulled away and scooted over to the side. The air around them changed, he knew Ainslie wasn’t a fan of how things had to be either. Often as children they had talked about just running off together and never coming back.

“Look, Michael...”

“You can’t. I know. It’s fine. At least we have right now. Right?” Michael murmured, his chest starting to hurt from the reminder that they couldn’t just keep each other.

“Hey, don’t make that face,” Ainslie demanded and pulled him close, nuzzling into his neck and wrapping his legs around him from behind so he couldn’t escape.

“You’re not changing my mind...” Michael started but stopped as he was interrupted with laughter when Ainslie started to chew on his neck and hold him close so even though he squirmed he couldn’t escape.

Michael loved this side of Ainslie. He couldn’t help but enjoy when Ainslie was being playful. His stomach flip-flopped as Ainslie nipped at his ear and wrapped his arms around him tighter, he kissed his cheek, and murmured in his ear sweet words that Michael believed more than anything.

“You’re beautiful.” Ainslie nuzzled into him as Michael hugged his arms a little tighter around himself.

“Yea? You’re not so bad yourself...”

“Mmhmm, you taste so sweet...” Ainslie smirked and licked Michael’s cheek, causing him to laugh and rub his face.

“Eww!” Michael laughed and squirmed in his arms. He turned his head to nuzzle and kiss where he could. His lips connected with his Ainslie’s throat and kissed up to his lips. He turned in Ainslie’s arms and smiled as he wrapped his arms around his shoulders.

“I want to spend the night with you,” Ainslie murmured as he broke the kiss and pressed his forehead to Michael’s.

“You want to what?”

“You heard me.” Ainslie sighed and pulled away a bit. He looked down and ran his fingers along Michael’s arm slowly.

“Why? We could get in a lot of trouble...”

“I don’t have much longer of being able to even just look at you... Michael, please?”

“Oh... that...” Michael looked down, following Ainslie’s eyes to his arm.

“So, you’ll sneak out?” Ainslie was close to pleading.

“Yea, I’ll meet you here tonight.”

“Good, I’ll see you here.” Ainslie smiled softly and kissed Michael again. Michael’s world feeling right when they kissed.

“Better,” Michael said, his voice muffled against Ainslie’s lips.

Chapter Four

Michael's silent dinner with his father was almost painful. He sunk further down in his chair just waiting for the chance to say he was finished so he could sneak off and go back to see Ainslie. He wasn't even hungry, but he ate everything on his plate and all but ran to the kitchen to clean his plate.

He started to his room with a simple, "Goodnight Dad," but was stopped.

"Any plans for tonight?" His father asked quietly.

"Going to go to bed..."

"Yeah? You so excited about going to bed you have to nearly trip over yourself several times to get there?"

"I'm just tired, I have a test tomorrow at school and I wanna make sure I'm rested well enough to get a good grade," Michael lied, but he had no choice in that matter. It wasn't like he was going to tell his dad he was going to go out and see Ainslie. He knew better than that. He'd probably get locked in his room with his window nailed shut... again.

"I think you're lying..." The elder hummed and tilted his head.

"Why would I do that?" Michael asked quietly.

"I don't know, are you running off to go meet someone?"

"No..."

"I think you are... someone from that college?"

"Dad..." Michael groaned and rolled his eyes. This was not what he wanted to talk about, this wasn't what he wanted to do. He pursed his lips and sighed heavily as he tried to get his dad to just leave him alone. That thought of moving out passed through his mind for what was possibly the millionth time.

"I'm going to take that as a yes... why won't you bring them home?"

"Dad..." He murmured and turned his head to the side, trying to get him to just leave him alone.

"Yeah, fine... go have fun." The old man waved and let the surprised Michael slip out of the room and into his own room. He shut his door and packed a quick overnight back and just went out the window. He didn't feel like facing his dad again and after making sure his door was locked he just ran off as fast as he possibly could.

Michael went as far as to cover his tracks, hide his scent, and leave random trails to keep people from following him. He was lucky that as an omega he didn't have to worry about anyone following him, anyone caring about whether or not he got lost out in the woods and never seen again. It was the only time he was glad to be an omega. He could blend in and hide. That's all he needed in life sometimes it seemed.

Not that it mattered once he got close to Ainslie. He could feel it in his bones that he was getting closer to him. He ran faster, his bones popping and cracking as fur burst along his body, his clothes vanishing but his backpack staying on and in place. He darted up the rocks and bound into the arms of Ainslie who caught him with ease. Michael growled playfully and licked Ainslie's cheek before wiggling free and climbing up the rocks as far as he could in his wolf form.

Ainslie had shifted as soon as Michael had gotten out of his grasp and climbed up after him, his large claws digging into the rock as he growled playfully in response, lifting the small wolf by his backpack and jumping up the rest of the rock wall without hurting Michael.

Michael shifted once they were up there, he laughed and rolled onto the ground as he dropped away from his backpack and looked up at Ainslie with a wide smile staying on his lips.

"I see you're feeling a bit... playful?" Ainslie teased after he'd taken a minute or two longer to turn back.

"Little bit," Michael smirked and nipped at his lips.

"Why is that?"

“Dad practically gave me his blessing to be out tonight.”

“What?” Ainslie looked at him in pure disbelief.

“He doesn’t know I’m out here with you though... He thinks it’s someone from school.”

“Technically... I am from the same school... so it’s not a lie.” Ainslie mused and pulled him close.

“*Definitely* not a lie...” Michael murmured, he nuzzled into Ainslie’s broad chest and smiled as he closed his eyes. He peeked up at him from under his lashes and smirked before he playfully bit him.

“Hey now, you’re going to start something if you keep that up,” Ainslie warned playfully. He leaned down and kissed Michael’s forehead, chuckling at the others noise of laughter.

Michael leaned up and kissed Ainslie, his hand sliding up slowly into the others thick locks. He growled playfully and pressed his body close. He relaxed against him, his eyes half closing as he smiled up at him, just glad they had this and they didn’t have to rush off any time soon.

“I brought my tablet again, it has a full charge. I was thinking after we watch the stars we might could watch a show or... just... I don’t know, exist together?” Ainslie rambled for a minute, he seemed to be uncertain, but he made Michael giggle softly and arch a brow.

“You wanna exist together?” Michael’s voice echoed as he teased him, he tilted his head as Ainslie pulled back and instantly pouted to be out of his arms.

“Yea, I do.” Ainslie grumbled. He picked up his duffle bag and pulled out a blanket for them and a small pillow, but Michael knew he’d probably end up sleeping mostly on top of Ainslie. He helped Ainslie spread the blanket and curled up with him as they looked up to the sky.

“You think... we could maybe... no... never mine. It’s a dumb request...” Michael had started but stopped. He knew what he was thinking was wrong. He couldn’t keep seeing Ainslie even after he was married off. No matter how bad he wanted to.

“I don’t know...” He frowned gently. Michael regretted starting that question, watching as Ainslie’s expression changed completely. He reached out and ran his hand over Ainslie’s chest, stopping over his heart. He loved the strong, warm beat of it. How it always seemed to change when he moved closer to him. Michael closed his eyes as he felt it.

“I shouldn’t have asked Ainslie, I’m sorry...”

“I want to... I would rather be here with you forever. But... we can’t. We have these little moments only.” Ainslie looked up at the sky. He frowned as he held him close.

“I’ll treasure these little moments forever. Even though I won’t be able to look at whoever gets you...” Michael mumbled without realizing it until after the last word trailed off. He buried his face into Ainslie’s neck, clinging to him tightly.

“I don’t expect you to. I wouldn’t be able to look at you with anyone else. The thought just pisses me off.” Ainslie admitted.

“Well... I guess after the festival we just can’t look at each other,” Michael murmured against him.

“We shouldn’t, but I’m still going to look at you.” Ainslie admitted, “I mean, I get yelled at by my pack anyway for looking at you now.”

“You do not...” Michael tried not to laugh.

“I do. Anytime someone notices that I’m not paying attention they notice you’re in the same area.” Ainslie smirked.

“Now I know you’re lying. You don’t lose focus for anything.” Michael moved to roll away from him but was trapped in Ainslie’s arms.

“Oh no, no running away from that one. I am always watching you. I always will.” Ainslie guided Michael’s lips to his own.

Michael melted. He could always tell when Ainslie was watching him. That feeling deep in his chest always stirred his heart, it always skipped and caused him to ache with the memory that those eyes belonged to Ainslie and Ainslie wasn't able to do more than stare at him.

"You remember when we were little?" Michael murmured in sudden thought.

"I remember a lot of things from when we were little, what memory?"

"The one where you told me you were going to kidnap me and run away to another country?"

"Oh yea, I remember that. You told me to stop being dumb and fight you." Ainslie arched a brow.

"I didn't tell you to fight me... I just told you to stop being dumb. It's not my fault you decided to tackle me and steal my first kiss." Michael snorted.

"I stole our first kiss... I hadn't kissed anyone either."

"I'm glad," Michael said selfishly. He leaned up and kissed him again.

"Yeah?"

"Yes. Now, I need all the kisses I can get until the festival."

"Just... kisses?" Ainslie smirked playfully.

"Hmmm..." Michael purred playfully and looked up at the stars for a long few minutes.

"I'm going to say that means more," Ainslie murmured, he pulled him close once more and kissed him until they rolled over.

***

Michael stared up at the stars long after Ainslie had fallen asleep beside him. He saw a shooting start and closed his eyes tightly. He knew it was foolish to wish on them, but it didn't stop him from hoping that maybe, just maybe this time his wish would work. *I wish Ainslie could be mine.*

He kept his eyes closed for a few more minutes, tiredness slowly rolling through him so he rolled over and wiggled his way carefully into Ainslie's arms, smiling softly as he was rewarded with a half-asleep kiss and a gentle squeeze of a hug. His heart fluttered as he considered this night just lucky for him. Tomorrow would be rough.

Chapter Five

Ainslie stretched, the sun woke him up as soon as the first few rays peeked over the rocks. He wrinkled his nose and grumbled. Forgetting for a moment that Michael was perched in his arms with his face already hidden from the sun, he moved to sit up and realized he was stuck without dumping Michael over.

He arched his brow lightly and tried to peer around to see if Michael was awake, but feeling his smile against his neck he knew he was. He ran his hand down the others back, enjoying this. Even though he could feel the soreness from sleeping on a large flat rock in the same position all night...naked.

"Don't move so much," Michael grumbled playfully.

"You're too cheerful in the morning." Ainslie wiggled a bit and finally pulled Michael fully on top of him. Michael sat up and smirked, his hands on either side of Ainslie's head as he held himself up.

"Me? Cheerful? Whatever do you mean?"

"Being all... playful and stuff."

"What? I don't know what you mean. Where's my coffee? I need a shower, I can't function right now." Michael teased as he sat back fully, pretended to grumble, and rub his eyes.

"*So sorry,* I must be mistaken. Look at this grouchy man here! My life is in danger." Ainslie rolled his eyes and sat up, wrapping his arms around Michael.

"What's that look for?" Michael asked before kissing him, keeping him from answering for a few minutes.

"What time do you have to go?"

"I don't know... should probably crawl back into my window soon..."

"Wanna go for a swim?"

“I would love to, but I can’t... we should probably go home.” Michael frowned, trying to shed the logic on this.

“But we absolutely stink of each other...”

“You stink.” Michael pouted.

“You smell just like me... so you stink too. We should take a swim in the river.” Ainslie nibbled on Michael’s earlobe softly, his grip tightening.

“It’ll be cold though.” Michael wrinkled his nose and leaned back trying not to get excited from Ainslie’s nibbles.

“Yea... I’m going to need a cold bath after waking up next to you.” Ainslie let go of Michael, watching him stand and resisting the urge to pull him back down.

“Yeah? Does that mean I have to start waking...” Michael stopped and frowned looking at the ground. He shook his head and muttered something incoherent.

Ainslie didn’t respond to it, though he would have liked to smile and tell him he demanded that they start waking up next to each other he knew he couldn’t say that.

“Hey... did your dad tell you who you’re supposed to marry yet?” Michael mumbled.

“No, either way it’ll never be someone I want.” Ainslie said as he stood up and started to pack up. He’d get away with taking the bag back smelling the way it did since his parents would be at work by the time he got back.

“You don’t think...” Michael trailed off again and sighed heavily before he pulled his pants on and started the climb down the rocks. His lips pursed, his heart heavy.

“Tomorrow night... do you want to come back here?” Ainslie asked, his voice more hopeful than he meant.

“I highly doubt my dad will let me get away with “sneaking out” without bringing the mystery person home. Especially since I won’t smell like anyone different after this bath in the river.”

“Michael...” Ainslie bit his bottom lip as he stopped his descent and rested his forehead against the rock in front of him.

“Ainslie, let’s not think about it. Okay?”

“It’s all I think about sometimes.” Ainslie growled almost incoherently.

“It’s fine. Let’s just clean up.” Michael said, trying to brush everything off. Both of them knew that talking about it didn’t solve anything. It just made it worse.

“Fine.” Ainslie finished climbing down, Michael grabbed Ainslie’s hand and pulled him to look him in the eye.

“Don’t... don’t mistreat whoever you get paired with. Treat them right... please?” Michael pleaded.

“I’ll treat them like a living being. I’ll be as nice as I can, but I can’t...”

“Just promise me you won’t hurt them.” Michael blurted out.

“The only person that I’m going to hurt is you.” Ainslie said and pulled away. He headed for the river with Michael following behind him, tears washing down his face. Ainslie hated himself. No matter what he did he hurt Michael. For his benefit, Ainslie ignored Michael’s tears. He didn’t want to add insult to injury by trying to fix them, since they both knew Michael would be crying during the festival too. Ainslie knew he’d end up crying. He’d never admit it out loud, but he knew he’d run off to hide somewhere and throw a fit of some sort.

No one would even sort of come close to Michael in his eyes. He already knew it and didn’t need this to prove it to him. The river wasn’t far and they made it there in no time at all. The water was cold, Ainslie could smell it in the air as they got to the bank. He dipped a bare toe into the water and winced.

“Are you sure you still need a cold bath?” Michael taunted.

“I’ll give you a cold bath.” Ainslie took a deep breath, a few steps back and ran, then jumped into the water. The breath was knocked out of him but he surfaced, glad it was a deep and lazy river. He smiled out at Michael, not expecting him to even sort of get into the water. Michael smirked at him, stripped free of his pants and mimicked Ainslie's jump into the water. Surfacing with a gasp and staring at him wide eyed.

"It's freezing!" Michael pushed at Ainslie shivering beside him.

"Come here then," Ainslie said and pulled him close, smirking as he nipped at his ear lightly.

"You're warm," Michael breathed and wrapped his arms around him.

Ainslie kissed him softly, enjoying the reaction he got, the way Michael held onto him tighter and pressed even closer to him. He whimpered softly against Ainslie's lips, that needy feeling resonating in his chest.

"You're soft," Ainslie murmured and caressed Michael's cheek with his thumb, smiling softly before kissing him again. He ran his hand down along his chest, not wanting to let him go just yet even as Michael lightly pushed him to get him to let go.

"We gotta clean up and get ready to go home..."

"I don't want to." Ainslie growled lowly in his chest.

"We have to... I'll try to sneak out again tonight." Michael murmured.

"Really?" Ainslie let him go, wondering if he was only saying that to get him to release him.

"Yeah, I'll try. I can't outright promise, but I'll try to come spend each night with you that I can. I'll text you when I'm free."

"I can accept that..." Ainslie murmured in thought as he worked on rubbing the smell of Michael off of him. He dunked in the water and rubbed mud on his person only to wash it away just moments later.

"What are you going to tell your parents?" Michael asked curiously.

"I'm probably going to tell them I went for a hunt, or I was restless and just needed to be outside for a bit. They usually fall for that each time I come see you."

"Really?" Ainslie saw Michael's look of disbelief and nodded.

"Yep, I always come back with the smell of dirt and mud instead of you, so it's not like they can really assume it's anything else," Ainslie said with a shrug.

"You really don't think they know you've gone off to meet someone?"

"Michael, as far as they know I've never had interest in anyone. I don't show it, I respond negatively at the mere mention of someone liking me, my mom doesn't know any of this and always tells me it's good I don't have feelings." As much as he hated saying those words he knew they were true and Michael winced about as bad as Ainslie wanted to.

"That is terrible."

"Yeah, it is."

"I'd never put my child through this mess," Michael mumbled with a soft sigh.

"Me either. I'd figure everything I possibly could to keep them out of this kind of poison."

"I know you would," Michael murmured and sighed heavily. He had finished scrubbing and was starting to walk up to the shore.

"I..." Ainslie stopped what he was about to say and just followed him. They laid out in the soft grass together, far enough apart to not accidentally touch. He tilted his head to the side and pursed his lips in thought.

"You're making that face again..."

"I'll show you a face." Ainslie rolled away from him and sat up on his knees. He looked at the trees, stretching and feeling Michael's eyes on his body. He smirked and peered at him from the corner of his eye.

“I bet you would,” Michael licked his lips, sitting up as though he were about to pounce.

“You know we’d have to take another muddy bath...”

“It’s worth it for you,” Michael said before he lunged forward, Ainslie moved quickly to dodge and roll out of the way. He crouched on all fours and grinned playfully at Michael.

“Oh, really now?”

“Yeah, now come here.” Michael growled and jumped forward again, shifting in time to land carefully in the place that Ainslie vacated.

“That’s cheating,” Ainslie teased.

Michael flicked his tail behind him and lunged again, getting caught in Ainslie’s arms. Ainslie chuckled and buried his face in Michael’s fur. He had always liked that Michael’s fur wasn’t as coarse and scratchy as his own was. The humanoid wolf form he took on himself was not a creature built for snuggling, but Michael was built for it. His soft fur, the warmth he put off... it was all definitely for a snuggling creature.

Ainslie heard footsteps as Michael’s ears twitched back. Ainslie set him down carefully and returned to the water while Michael darted into the bushes carefully to hide and stalk out whoever had come this far into unmarked territory.

As time passed, they realized it must have been just a hiker. No one had stopped or gotten close enough to mess with them. They had to quickly descent themselves and head home anyway, that had been too close... now was not the time to get caught.

Chapter Six

The weekend was coming fast. Ainslie felt the insanity of it as his pack started to prepare for it. The fairgrounds at the very edge of town was being worked on and Ainslie had to help set up for this year's fair. He set his face and spent most of his days after school there instead of looking for Michael... even though that's where his mind tended to wander. He sighed heavily after he finished hammering in the last nail for a random booth he'd been set to work on.

"You sound irritated." Michael's voice filled the air as he carried stuff over to the booth.

"Little bit."

"You stink." Michael wrinkled his nose.

"I've been out here all day working. Where have you been?"

"In the air conditioning... sorting boxes."

"No wonder you aren't sweating yet... get the easiest job." Ainslie rolled his eyes.

"Don't tell me you're trying to pick a fight again."

"Shut your mouth."

Michael frowned and narrowed his eyes. He licked his lips like he was about to start something anyway.

"We can't fight... can't even sound like we're trying to fight. Take my word on it." Ainslie hissed as he started to pick up his tools.

"Uh-huh..." Michael looked around, "What's it to you if we do or don't?"

"If we do, you won't make it."

"Oh, because you're some big Alpha that-"

"Shut. Your. Mouth." Ainslie warned and shot him a look. "We can argue on the bus tomorrow but not here."

"Fine." Michael growled and set the stuff down on the edge of the booth. "You did a good job. Should work in construction instead of trying to be a lawyer."

"And you should become Captain Obvious instead of an elementary school teacher."

"That was a *terrible* comeback..."

"I'm tired... I'll have a better one tomorrow." Ainslie grumbled.

Others walked passed them, glancing at them curiously as Ainslie walked near Michael to gather more supplies for the next booth. Michael had to walk in the same general direction for another box.

"Fine..." Michael mumbled and glanced over at Ainslie, noticing there was a lot of things on his mind. He ducked away back inside without another word. This left Ainslie to have to continue to refrain from looking after him as he grabbed what he needed. He couldn't let Sam or Ash notice him looking at Michael anymore, no one could notice. That kind of thing had to stop. Whether he wanted to or not.

The way his parents had spoken to him the previous night said more than he ever wanted to hear again. He had to keep hearing the same thing over and over each night and even though he promised, he'd keep casting glances at Michael and he knew he had to stop. He pursed his lips

Ben moved to help him with the next few booths. They got the work done in silence, then again, Ben didn't always like to talk and make noise. This it made it much easier to get everything done. Once they were done Ben pulled him aside as they were leaving and looked him in the eye, almost as if challenging him.

"You uh... you sure you're okay with giving up your fated mate?" He asked quietly and toyed with his hands idly. His body language suggested he didn't want to deal with this too much, but Ainslie wasn't really all that sure of what he would expect.

"That's just a load of bull parents tell their children to keep them from 'playing around'. Ainslie leveled him with a glare.

"I dunno... I kind of like the idea everyone has someone they are supposed to be with."

"Yeah, a lot of people do. It's drilled into us. But we should also keep in mind the Alphas might chose a different path for us. This arrangement is just something we must deal with. I can forgo that to keep the peace and our family honor."

"*That's* bull and you know it. As soon as that shifter rolled over for you you'd take him in a heartbeat."

"This isn't about him being a shifter, is it?"

"No... he's an Omega. You deserve better if you're about to start a pack war over *it*."

"He might not always be an Omega you know." Ainslie grumbled.

"That's not how that works and you know it." Ben sighed.

"I know..." Ainslie mumbled.

"Stay away from him. Unless you know for a fact that he's about to be who you're arranged to. Stay away. It's not worth it Ains."

"I *am* staying away from him. Nothing's happened and nothing will happen. I don't even like him. I just don't understand how their packs work is all. It's weird."

"Mmhmm. You know we've known you since we were all young. We know what you're thinking."

"Not as much as you think you do. Now stand down." Ainslie growled lowly and made Ben back down. He pursed his lips and shook his head as he left him alone. He had no idea why everyone was thinking he had feelings for Michael. He did everything in his power to stay away from him. He didn't look at him, he didn't get seen talking to him, and being nice...

Not unless someone saw him on the bus tutoring him in math... It was very possible. Ainslie shook his head and walked towards home. It'd be a long walk and he'd have plenty of time to spend thinking about everything. He turned his head when he heard footsteps behind him and arched his brow as Michael tackled him into the trees. He wrapped his arms around him as he cushioned their fall.

Their lips met eagerly.

“You weren’t followed?” Ainslie asked worried.

“Nope. Neither were you.” Michael smiled against his lips.

“You’re going to get us in trouble.” Ainslie teased.

“Shut up and kiss me, Ainslie. We don’t have a lot of time.” Michael demanded, it was almost a challenge.

“Mmhmm...” Ainslie flipped them over and pressed close to him. “Now’s not the time to get caught like this...”

“You were picked for certain, weren’t you...” Michael frowned as he realized. It had been talked about that he was more than likely going to be picked, but he hadn’t really felt it was set in stone. Each time the festival had come around they talked the same way, this time apparently all that talk had been for real this time.

“Yeah...”

“Why didn’t you tell me?” Ainslie watched as Michael’s expression turned from his usual happy smile into a terrified and upset frown.

“I couldn’t... think of how.” Ainslie murmured. “We don’t have much time together when we are together and I don’t like ruining it by making you frown.”

“We’ve kept this secret well enough they don’t know? Your mom doesn’t know you’ve found me?”

“Even if they did, I doubt they’d care... Alphas are a big thing... I can’t pass it up.”

“You’re a big thing.” Michael huffed out trying not to sound as hurt as he was.

“You weren’t picked... were you?” Ainslie murmured quietly in question.

“No.”

"I'm sorry..." Ainslie wasn't sure what else he could say. He was certain there wasn't anything he could say to make it feel better.

"I'm an Omega. Unless a clan pisses off another one enough... I won't get picked for that."

"At least you'll get a mate... that you might like."

"No, I won't." Michael pushed him off and got up, walking off through the trees where Ainslie couldn't follow without breaking rules.

"You really do like pushing it, don't you..." Ainslie sighed and rubbed his face, rolling over onto his back as he pushed the heels of his hands into his eyes. He growled and got up, darting after Michael and pinning him to a tree.

"Now we'll really get seen... I at least put us on the ground..." Michael murmured, his lips about an inch from Ainslie's.

"Shut up and kiss me," Ainslie demanded, his lips centimeters from Michael's.

"No." Michael turned his head to the side.

"Why?" Ainslie started to lightly kiss along Michael's neck instead, nipping his jaw playfully.

"Because I want to." Michael moaned and closed his eyes as he arched up against him.

"Best reason to kiss me then, right?" Ainslie growled against him, he tangled his fingers with Michael's, his hands sweaty with anticipation and fear of being caught but his heart was calm with the ability to be so close to Michael.

"Not if I can't have you. I'm not a toy. I'm not useless... I do have feelings you know," Michael snapped he felt weird inside. Something was wrong and he couldn't help all the sudden eruption of feelings and upset.

"No, you're not... You're...I..."

"Ainslie!" His mother's voice snarled through trees and struck him as though it were the back of her hand. He froze mid-sentence.

Michael stared up at him terrified. What could Ainslie do in this moment? He had been about to say something that would have gotten him in trouble with his mom, with the pack, and with everything. He stared at Michael and couldn't figure out what to do right away. His whole world was breaking as Michael's fear seeped into him. He licked his lips and opened his mouth to speak but Michael's eyes told him not to even try.

Nothing could be said to save them in that moment.

Chapter Seven

Michael's heart pounded in his chest. Just being close to Ainslie always had him running laps while standing still, but right now that was not the only reason. Because he wasn't just sitting next to him on the bus or talking to him about trivial things like math or why they didn't finish a fight in public. Right now, his heart thundered in his chest painfully as Ainslie's mother stared at him with his legs wrapped around Ainslie's waist! He could only have been more embarrassed if they'd been caught naked. This was bad enough; any more embarrassment would have killed him.

What had she seen? What had she heard? Did she know about everything in that moment? Michael's head could not take it. He was close to tears as it was because he was pretty sure Ainslie was going to say something he shouldn't. His breathing was shallow, he wasn't sure what was going to happen now, but he knew it couldn't be good.

Ainslie was searching him for help. Michael could see that much as Ainslie tried to open his mouth but he didn't know how to respond to this either. They had been so careful! Until now. He licked his lips and very slowly put his legs down and straightened up, lightly pushed Ainslie away from him, and cleared his throat.

"I uh... I have to go..." Michal breathed finally. He started to take a step away. He nearly jumped out of his skin as his dad appeared before him.

"You bet you do." Michael's father's voice snarled as he walked through the woods, having seen just the end where they were caught by Ainslie's mother.

"Marcus." Ainslie's mother glared at the greying male on his own territory.

"Mary Ellen." The man responded.

"I apologize. My son shouldn't be *attacking* yours..."

"I suppose you do. He shouldn't be."

"It won't happen again."

“It better not. This is your last warning.”

“I’m sure.” Mary Ellen said. Her voice nothing but ice as Ainslie walked back over to her.

“You’d think a twenty-three-year-old adult male would know better.” Marcus motioned at Ainslie and wrinkled his nose in disgust.

“And you’d think your twenty-three-year-old adult male would be able to fend off an attacker instead of getting pinned against a tree.” Her voice was getting dangerously cold at this point, any colder and she’d be attacking him.

“Mom, let’s go. I’m sorry… I *attacked* your son, Mr. Johnson.” Ainslie was just trying to get them to stop this and leave, he didn’t want to deal with this right now. It was always the same with them.

“I’m sure you are.” Marcus half snarled as he grabbed his own son and pulled him away. He was growling at him almost incoherently.

Michael winced as he followed his father, having no idea why they were calling this an attack. It hadn’t been an attack… it had been much more. It had been… he realized they were calling it an attack because if it had been what it really was it’d have started a war of some sort. He pursed his lips and stared at the ground.

“What the hell were you thinking Michael?” His father growled in a constant low hum of irritation. He glared at Michael and made him feel smaller than he already felt having been under the gaze of Ainslie’s mother.

“I… I’m sorry.” Michael wasn’t sure what else to say. He frowned and couldn’t bring his eyes to meet his father's. He winced slightly and gave a slight side glance as his father started to scream at him.

“You can’t be messing around with Alphas. Especially *that kind* of Alpha. What if he knocked you up? I can only guess that’s what was starting before you two were interrupted. He can’t raise a family with you. He has much bigger things planned for him. Things that do not involve you. I’m sorry son. Stay in your role.”

"Dad..." Michael started, he looked up at him as his heart practically stopped. How could anyone tell their child to stay in their role rather than reach something that was obviously good for them?

"Trust me. Stay in your role. Otherwise, you'll hate life as much as he does right now."

"He was..."

"He wasn't, Michael. He really and truly wasn't."

"I know... but it was a nice thought." Michael mumbled quietly and rubbed the back of his head.

"I'm sure it was. You'll have extra sprints tonight... No arguing. This is going to hurt and you are going to be sore in the morning. You might miss the bus in the morning."

"No, I won't. I'm going to school." Michael insisted.

"That doesn't mean you'll make the bus. You'll still get to school though."

"I'll make the bus," Michael said. He frowned as he looked at the ground.

"You think we don't know you take the same bus? This is a tiny town for as big as it is. No matter what you do, what you think... people can see you."

"You saw me go into the woods?"

"I saw you getting caught by his mother. Not the brightest thing to do if you're breaking rules." The old man pointed out, grumbling. He had let too much slide by not just driving Michael to school, or so he thought was the least of his worries.

"It's technically not breaking rules though... he was not officially promised to anyone and I'm definitely not. He technically isn't promised right now, it's just he was chosen to get promised."

"And you should be happy for not being promised to someone. You can choose your own."

"Why? I can't have who I want," Michael murmured softly. How was he supposed to enjoy that? How could he take on someone else in his life when Ainslie was his special someone?

"It's not about who you want..." Marcus seemed to have trouble thinking of how to explain what was on his mind. He wasn't figuring in how long the two had been seeing each other. He didn't know what Michael knew, only that he thought it was a simple crush, a lustful attraction they both had that had recently come up with having to spend so much time together.

"Fated mates... fated this... fated that. That's not how this works. That's not how any of this works. He must forgo his own 'fated mate' as all the elders call it, well what about his fated mate? What does that person have to do just because of this peace?"

"Do you really want a pack war? We can't handle that. None of us can. The last one took out a lot of us. That's why so many humans moved in here and we have to be more selective of how things work around here." Marcus was struggling with this. He hadn't thought he would need to struggle so much with it.

"So, six people get punished for peace?" Michael hummed as he questioned everything for the millionth time.

"Six?"

"Ainslie's fated mate, the person he's with after the fact, their fated mated, Ainslie, the people their fated mates end up with trying to fill the void?" Michael pointed out, making a mess of things as his thoughts rambled on. "It'd be the same for each pairing. Why can't we just all agree to not attack each other?"

"Well you see how well hunting goes already. We can't agree on anything. Everyone wants to be the Alpha of the area." Michael's father sighed heavily as he spoke.

"Then people need to *stay in their role*. That's what you said, right? Right. Why is that so impossible?" Michael snarled lowly. He was upset, probably more upset than he thought he would be over this. More so this time than he had been last time he had argued about this. It seemed to happen more often than when he younger.

"I don't know, Michael. I don't know how to explain this. Stop questioning it and just accept it." Marcus snarled at him and glared at his only son.

"Or what?"

"Or I'll find someone to marry you off to so I don't have to hear it anymore." The threat was ignored. Michael wouldn't just marry anyone. He had his mind made for what he wanted and if he couldn't have it he was going to just be alone.

"That does not, by any means, mean that you'll stop hearing about it." Michael looked over to his father, their eyes met and he was ready to lunge and rip the man apart... but this was his father and he couldn't do that. He couldn't fight family, let alone the alpha of the pack.

"Your mother always asked these same questions. She just hated the idea of all of this... just accept this." Marcus growled as he stormed off, leaving Michael where he stood to frown and just look at the ground. Any time his mother was brought up, that was the end of any argument.

***

Michael headed home after a few hours of just wandering around in the woods. He wanted to know what Ainslie was going to say. He wanted to hear those words. After all this time... all the time wasted and waiting for Ainslie to admit any sort of feelings more than just liking him. He wanted to know he was loved. Michael remembered when they were small and in the same classes together, before their parents started to drill into their head that they had roles to play and they couldn't just be nice to anyone.

They had been the best of friends, and now they were forced to pretend they were strangers riding the bus together every day and occasionally helping each other out with their homework... strangers that tackled each other in the woods when they were alone and that shared kisses by the lake or in secret hide away spots. Michael just went to his room, to bed, to hide his shamefully tear-filled face from everyone in the large pack housing. He didn't want to think about it, he didn't want to deal with it but his mind didn't want to stop.

He thought of all their usual shows of hating each other. How many times had he been pinned to a tree by Ainslie in front of their hunting parties? Their packs? Their families? How many times had he allowed himself to be scorned by the other's friends and family only to rush to him in the middle of the night to be doctored and held close? Made comfortable by his smooth words...

Michael felt his phone buzz and peered through the blurry tears at Ainslie's text.

"I'm sorry." Was all it said. That's all they ever said. Michael just let his phone drop to the bed as he rolled over. He didn't care what Ainslie had to say. He wanted to see what he did to fix it this time. His phone buzzed again. Then again. Then again... then it didn't. When it stopped Michael though that was the end of it.

A tap or two on his window woke him enough to look over to the window and growl. Michael hadn't even realized he had fallen asleep. He pursed his lips as he crawled out of bed, opening his window only to stumbled back in surprise.

"What are you doing here?!" he hissed at Ainslie who almost looked a little lost himself.

"You're mad at me... I don't like it."

"We're always mad at each other... that's what we do!"

"You're going to draw attention."

"You can't just come here, this will get you killed!" Michael panicked as he only imagined what his dad could possibly do finding another alpha there on their territory.

"It'd be worth it. Since I get to see you, and talk to you."

"No... no it won't. We're done. You need to leave me alone."

Michael's heart shattered into thousands of pieces at the look Ainslie gave him. After all these years, he had never expected that reaction from him... he looked... hurt. And then he didn't. Ainslie nodded and backed away from the window, he nodded again and headed back to the street to hit the back-roads and leave.

Michael couldn't breathe. That one look from Ainslie had torn him in half. He sunk to the floor and stared after him. He couldn't believe that was what had come out of his mouth. Ever since they were little all he had ever wanted was for Ainslie to show up and tell him he loved him and before he could give the other a chance to say those words he shunned him. He turned him away and as Ainslie left, he could only stand there and cry in shock.

"Good boy. You did exactly what you should have." Marcus said from the doorway.

"Dad?!" Michael jumped, having not even realized.

"I heard the tapping on your window. That boy ain't bright."

"He..."

"Don't make excuses for him. You did right." The old man stepped forward as he insisted and closed Michael's window. He made sure to lock it and pushed Michael back to his bed.

Michael didn't feel like that was the right thing to do as his chest throbbed with an unfamiliar pain. He looked down at his hands and nodded while his lips pursed in quiet contemplation.

"Get some sleep. We've got a busy day tomorrow."

"Sir." Michael tried to sleep. He couldn't get comfortable enough to sleep and it wasn't until he reached down and grabbed his phone that he realized what exactly he had done. Ainslie's last few texts were simple.

"Don't be mad at me please?"

"I love you."

"Don't believe me? I'll come prove it."

Chapter Eight

Ainslie stood with his eyes narrowed at his mother as they walked to her car, she was fuming and he could see it in the way she was staring at everything but him with a stare of pure death. The rage rolled off him in waves. As they sat down in her car, buckled, and she started it, he waited for her to explode into some sort of rage. She didn't, not right away, but he could feel it continuing to build. He shrank back towards the door and stared out the window, trying to do anything but acknowledge that his mother was so angry.

"Do you realize... how much trouble you're in?" She asked very quietly. Her voice hoarse with rage.

"Mom..."

"Do not mom me."

"But," He started but she held her hand up, he looked away from her again.

"How long has *that* been going on?"

"We've been friends for ever... we've been dating..."

"You've been what?" She hissed, interrupting him.

"We've been boyfriends, dating, whatever you want to call it since like fifth grade."

"Ainslie, what the hell..." She snarled, her grip on the steering wheel tightening to the point of leaving indents.

"Mom..."

"There couldn't have been a single other person for you to chase after like that? You couldn't have wanted anyone else? You just *had* to have him?" She turned and looked at him, shaking her head she stopped for a stoplight.

"Mom, I didn't want anyone else. I don't want anyone else. I only want him," Ainslie mumbled.

“Say that again,” she dared. The light had turned green but she ignored the person who honked behind her.

“I *only* want him.” Ainslie said a little louder.

“Do you not realize that you are supposed to be meet the person that has been arranged for you this weekend? You’re going to have to get married to someone other than him. Do you really not realize what this could do to everyone?” Her lecture had started but Ainslie was ignoring her.

He had been battling the thought of being chosen to get married since he was told he was chosen for the festival this year. He didn’t want to be that person. He didn’t want to be the one to harm his fated mate. He turned, snarling low in his chest suddenly.

“Excuse me?” His mother narrowed her eyes at him.

They had started moving again, but she was slowing down like she was going to stop the car again. Ainslie watched as his mother flipped on her blinker and parked so that she didn’t end up in an accident. He was ready for this.

“I don’t care. I want Michael. I will have Michael,” Ainslie said, he sat up straighter, opened the door after his seatbelt clicked and darted out of the car. He turned and looked at his mother.

“Get your ass back in this car. Right now. Your father will hear of this!”

“No. I don’t care if he does. Let him. What is he going to do? Yell at me? Fight me? It doesn’t matter!” Ainslie shouted and ran without looking back. He had his mind made up. First though, he ran to their secret spot, wondering if Michael would come and meet him there. He sat down after the rough, his phone in hand while he debated on whether or not to just go to Michael’s house.

“So, this is where you two go?” Ainslie looked up to see his mother climbing up the rock wall with his father in tow, they both glared at him; apparently, they planned to *talk* as the look in their eyes suggested their fury.

“What are you doing here?” Ainslie asked, his acts of defiance wouldn’t be overlooked and although he could see it, his heart pounded in his chest. He mostly felt anger, but fear formed a lump in his throat as he stood and glared back at them.

“We’ve come to find you and talk sense into you.” His father’s deep voice used to fill him with dread, especially because the old man was hardly around. There were always others in the pack that had needed him more than his family it seemed. Well, until his father spent an entire day with him just to tell him that he will be married off for the festival.

“There is no sense in trying to talk to me. My mind is made up.”

“Ainslie, if you refuse this you will put the packs into war.” His father sighed heavily as he tried to stay calm.

“I’m sure that things can be worked out much differently,” Ainslie said, he rubbed his face, taking a deep breath to keep from being rude while being defiant.

“No, things can’t be worked out, they are the way they are for a reason Ainslie, there is no changing them.” The look on his father’s face told Ainslie he was just being difficult. His well-worn creases around his eyes were furrowed deeply while he squinted at him. The old man seemed to just age right in front of Ainslie’s eyes.

“If there isn’t a way then I can’t help you. I want Michael.”

“Ainslie, please listen to your father,” Mary Ellen pleaded.

“No, Mom. There is no listening any more. You’ve always told me that I am an alpha. I get what is mine. Right?” Ainslie questioned, his skin slowly starting to rip and tear as he was losing control over his human form.

“Ainslie, settle down,” His mother growled at him, her hands clenching into fists as her own skin started to break and tear slowly.

“Both of you settle down,” His father demanded in a roar as he slammed his hand on a rock nearby.

“No! I will not be told to calm down, I will not be told what to do anymore!” Ainslie screamed as he shifted and lunged forward, he didn’t bare his teeth though since he wasn’t aiming to attack. He just wanted to get away from them. He crouched between them, darting passed and jumping over the edge of the rocks.

He landed hard, the heavy thuds behind him told him both of his parents were after him. He had never out run them before, but tonight he was determined. If he didn't out run them, then he'd have to fight them and Ainslie was smart enough to know he couldn't take them both on at the same time. They'd tear him to shreds.

Ainslie took a deep breath and plunged through the trees. He ripped through bushes, branches, and low hanging limbs. His ignored that primal urge to turn and attack his pursuers. It was there, burning in his chest to just turn and dig his teeth into them, their heavy footfalls only serving to anger him further.

He stopped just on the other side of the border and turned to roar at them, spittle flying past his lips. He tilted his head to the side and watched them as they stayed bound by their invisible lines of scent. He growled at them, snarled even. But he wouldn't go back to them, no matter how much they swiped at him.

"You're a disappointment." His father's voice was thick with the sentiment, but Ainslie didn't so much as bat an eye. He turned and started to walk away.

"Don't you dare, ever come back here again." His mother's voice was barely noted as he stalked off, shifting back into his human form, bones and flesh popping back into place. He stopped to grab a bag he had hidden in the other territory, pulling on some old and partially torn clothes, he checked his phone, which he'd just barely remembered to tie to his arm again for the run.

"I don't need your place. I need my own place," Ainslie grumbled to himself. His voice raw as he reached up and ran his fingers through his hair. He took a deep breath and started to walk towards Michael's house.

He stared in disbelief once he was rejected. Michael was serious... and he didn't want him... He walked off into the night, uncertain...

Chapter Nine

Ainslie didn't know how he was supposed to feel after that. He'd been turned away. He had never been turned away from Michael before. He winced and held his hand over his heart as everything hurt following that initial wave of pain. He didn't go home, he didn't know where to go from Michael's house to begin with. Ainslie just ran, leaving the pieces of his heart in his wake.

When he couldn't run another step, he collapsed on the ground. He could hear the busy hum of cars not far from him, but didn't bother to care enough to figure out where it was coming from or even where he was. His eyes closed and the world went still. He didn't hear the honking people in the city screaming at each other. He didn't hear the unfamiliar voices of people walking by him that didn't even notice he was there. He didn't even feel the sun start to scorch his skin until well into the evening.

His eyes opened slowly, his body slow and sluggish still trying to process the run from the night before. He coughed as he tried to breathe and a leaf stuck to his nose. Shaking his head and clearing his throat to get the phlegm from his chest he looked around with blurred vision.

Ainslie didn't recognize anything. He stood up slowly, a few pops here and there as his body screamed for him to stop moving and just lay down. He rubbed his face, that morning grime from sleeping outside did not feel good to the touch. He shook his head again and ran his fingers through the mop on his head before he started to dig in his pockets looking for phone and wallet.

Luckily, those hadn't walked off and he was able to turn his phone on to see he was nowhere near his pack lands. He wasn't even in any of the surrounding areas of the main town he lived in. He looked up, seeing a sign not far that told him he'd run clear to the next city.

"That's... unexpected..." He murmured. His phone started to buzz wildly as all the calls and messages he missed exploded across the screen. He winced but walked towards the city. He wanted a hotel first and foremost so he could have a shower. His growling stomach could wait until he figured something else out. His phone directed him to the nearest one. It wasn't the prettiest of places, but it would do for what he wanted.

After a hot shower he sat down on the bed in his room and started to scroll through the messages. Mostly his mom telling him to come home because he had stuff he had to do. One of his teachers had sent him a message... he sighed and sent an email to his instructors on campus he would be out for a few days. He lied, saying he was sick and asked if they'd send him any work he was able to do.

He laid back on the bed after having not seen a single call or text from the one person he wanted to hear from the most. He dug the heel of his palm into his eyes, his heart throbbed as he thought about Michael telling him they were done. They were done. He had no reason to go back... besides school anyway. He could transfer to a different college. He could get a job in the city and just stay away... he didn't need to go back. He could form his own pack, have his own territory in the city.

Simple. Decision made.

Ainslie would not return home for anything, not unless Michael showed signs that he still loved him. After Michael sent him away like that, Ainslie wondered if there were any feelings there to begin with. He had to have just been in it for the sex. That had to be it. Ainslie was certain of it now. Although he was sure at this point that his love was misplaced, he still wouldn't go back. Deciding that after a nap he needed to go searching for the necessities he closed his eyes and once again fell asleep.

***

Michael had no idea where Ainslie went. He tried to look for him when his father's intense gaze wasn't on him, but everywhere he looked there was no sign of him. He even went as far as to go up to Ainslie's hunting pack while everyone was doing the finishing touches on the festival.

Sam just blinked at him, Ash tilted his head confused, and Ben wrinkled his nose.

"Look, I just... I... have you seen him or not?" Michael asked. It had taken three hours that morning to hide the smell of pregnancy from everyone.

"Why should we even tell you?" Ash asked.

"Because... I messed up and I need to fix it."

"What'd you do, tell him to leave you alone?" Sam snorted.

"Yeah. I did, actually... he didn't take it well..." Michael looked down at the ground before him. He took a deep breath and looked back up at them, about to speak again but Ash held his hand up to stop him.

"You need to just leave it. He'll run out of steam and come back when he's done."

"What do you mean come back?" Michael blinked.

"I mean, he hasn't gone home and he isn't answering calls or texts. He'll run out of steam wherever he's hiding and come back in time to be married off like he's supposed to. He's an Alpha, after all. He's just... confused when it comes to you. So... go away. You've ruined enough don't you think?" Ash growled.

"That's... I don't think he'll just cool off by the time the elders get ready for council..."

"And why not? Sam snarled. "What'd you do?"

"I... I told him to go away after he said he loved me."

The three stood in silence, the rest of the world went about its business, but they froze.

"He said... He said what?" Ben asked quietly.

"He told me he loved me and he'd prove it. He came to my window and I told him we were done. I... I sent him away."

"Did you call him?" Ben frowned.

"No, I wanted to talk to him face to face."

"Then call him and set it up! Duh!" Ben growled with a heavy glare at the other.

"I swear, I don't know what he sees in you." Ash wrinkled his nose.

"Obviously something he likes enough to be this hurt over me being an asshole to him. I've tried calling him. He... he disconnected his phone." Michael growled back.

"Are you challenging me?" Ash was close to snarling as he ignored the part about the disconnected phone.

"No, I'm just trying to call your Alpha. Shut your mouth please." Michael stalked away from them with his phone glued to his ear, he might as well try again. It just rang and once again told him it was disconnected.

He couldn't help but start to cry when his call was ignored. He hit the ground and didn't even realize it until he looked up and realized people were staring at him. He could hear the murmurs, something about Omega's being over emotional and weak. He ignored it though, not bothering to care who it was from. Did they not realize that an Alpha was missing? That an Alpha was having a heavy emotional reaction to what *he* had done?

Michael stood and ran to the woods. He wanted to see if Ainslie had gone to their usual spot for some reason. That quiet place in the neutral zone no one ever went to because of how hard it was to climb up there. He swallowed hard, slipping on his way up the rocks once he got there. Usually Ainslie would turn around and help him up if he'd gotten there first or they were climbing together. He reached up in the usual spot and remembered with a heavy stone weighing his heart down that Ainslie wasn't climbing with him this time. And he had to be extra careful with the baby growing inside.

He finished climbing up the rocks and headed down a small path worn down by their feet to a clearing in the middle of large and small rocks with etchings that Ainslie had carved into them... there was no Ainslie. Michael could cry here, though. He could cry properly and just hide there until he died. Or so he decided.

Chapter Ten

Michael yawned softly, he was at the doctors for his normal checkup and hadn't slept well the night before. Maybe he just needed to take some time off or something. Hide away from his father and just take the punishment later. He yawned and chewed over his bottom lip as his doctor returned. He always had his blood drawn since his mother had had a rare blood disease and this time had been no different. He just waited to be told the initial blood count was clear so he could go home.

"Hi there, Michael." The doctor that had treated him his whole life walked back into the room with an odd frown.

"What's wrong?" Michael wondered if it was the same condition that had taken his mom. Starting to panic he gripped his pants legs and pursed his lips tightly.

"Your blood count is fine, don't worry about that... it's... well, I have a personal question for you. Have you been having unprotected sex?"

Michael couldn't answer, his face flushed red and he felt light headed. His stomach churned and flipped as he tried to focus on the implications of that question. He swallowed hard, fighting the dry knot in his throat.

"I ask because your blood came back with a high amount of hCG in your blood, that's human chorionic gonadotropin... it's a hormone that a body puts off during pregnancy."

The doctor might have been rambling, however the only thing Michael heard was *during pregnancy*. He was pregnant? He was pregnant with Ainslie's child... He pushed the man away and the only thing he could think of was that Ainslie would never come back. Even for the child! And what was worse, Marcus walked into the room. Staring up at his dad who had already been upset with him to start the morning out, now looked as though the veins in his forehead were going to burst.

"You're pregnant? With whose child? How did you... are you kidding me?" The old man shouted nearly at the top of his lungs.

Michael sunk back in the chair, trying to hide but he had nowhere to go.

"Uhm... dad... I've been dating Ainslie since fifth grade. He was my first and my only. It's his child." Michael mumbled. His doctor blinked at him in shock as his father exploded in incoherent stutters.

"I want it out of him. We'll need to set up an appointment. Do you do that here?" Marcus asked. His voice was uncomfortably quiet.

"Yes, we do. However, it's not up to you... it's between Michael and..."

"No. It's not between them. It's between me. *My* son cannot have anything to do with that boy. *Ever again*."

"Dad... we don't have to tell anyone it's Ainslie's. I don't want to lose my baby."

"I didn't ask you what you wanted, Michael. I told you that you cannot keep it. You didn't even know you were pregnant till just now!"

"But... this is your grandchild... it's my child and Ainslie's... He'd come back if he knew."

"How far along is he, doctor?" Marcus asked, his eyes boring into the other. He ignored Michael's pleas at this point.

"Almost two months, going by the..."

"Alright, it's not even formed much yet. It's not a grandchild. I don't even think there's a heartbeat. Let's go ahead and get this scheduled as soon as possible." Marcus said and stood up straight with his hands clapping together.

"Dad, please you can't do this!" Michael sobbed, he couldn't believe anything. He protectively wrapped his arms around himself, protecting his stomach as he looked at the doctor in horror.

"We don't have any openings for a while..." The doctor let his sentence trail as he considered how to help Michael.

"Whenever the earliest time is. Set it. You'll thank me later Michael."

"No, I won't," Michael murmured. He stood up and walked passed the doctor and his father. He walked passed the car and headed out into the woods trying to get his mind set and clear on what the next course of action should be.

He started to run once he heard footsteps behind him. He moved carefully to avoid being followed and climbed up the tall rocks back into his hiding place. He stared at the wall, silent tears fell while he debated on if he should try and call Ainslie. He shivered at the thought of Ainslie turning him away, but he wouldn't blame him. Not after the way he behaved the other day.

His phone went off, but he ignored his father's call. He had no desire to talk to him right now. Instead he called Ainslie just to make sure that he knew... he had to know! The line had been disconnected. Michael couldn't hold back his sobs. He was alone, and his dad was going to make him get rid of the only thing left he had of Ainslie.

"Just answer..." Michael pleaded and tried the number again, but again the message of the phone being disconnected played again. He closed his eyes tightly and took a deep breath trying to calm himself down as his soul sank to the rock beneath him. He curled up with his knees to his chest and his face pushed down into his knees.

"What am I supposed to do?" Michael asked himself as his vision blurred no matter how much he blinked. He couldn't run away. He couldn't let his dad push him through a... an appointment... he couldn't even think of the name of the procedure he was so afraid of it.

After a little while, he was able to rub the tears from his eyes and scroll through the various social medias and see what was going on out there. He still didn't want to go home, but he didn't like being out of the loop of everything. Even if it meant people probably knowing what was going on already.

He got the idea to send Ainslie a message after reading that his pack couldn't get ahold of him either. His page was full of people telling him to give them his new number or call them and just talk to them. He wasn't going to make his plea desperate and out in the open in case Ainslie didn't care or didn't respond. He pursed his lips and typed slowly. It took five minutes to send it as his fingers trembled in fear of never hearing from him again.

What did he expect? This child to be a miracle baby that brought them both together again? That's not what children were for. He couldn't help but start crying again. He wanted the child. He wanted Ainslie. He just couldn't have anything he wanted in life, could he?

After a deep breathe he stood up again and started to go home. He knew it was a bad idea, but he had nowhere else to go. At least for now. He wanted to figure something out. He needed to.

Chapter 11

Ainslie had gotten what he needed. It had taken a week and a half but he had the transfer papers, an interview for a job, and his own car. He made sure his parents still couldn't access his bank by going in and letting the bank know he was currently staying in a different location. That way, his parents couldn't say he was a missing person. On top of all that, he had his phone number changed.

This isn't running away like a coward... this is exploring new territory. He thought to himself as he walked down the street, having left his new car at the hotel so he could just go across the street to the burger place. He just needed to find an apartment and he'd be set. While he waited for his food, he toyed through his phone. His social media had blown up. People asking where he was, if he was okay...

Moving on to better things. There's new territory to discover.

He posted on his main page after making sure that the location on his phone was turned off so people didn't find him. He watched as the replies came in, the inbox blew up, but he shrugged it off. It's not like he was truly far away... but he was shirking all responsibility and hated himself for it. Pursing his lips, he lost his appetite as soon as the food was set down in front of him.

"Thanks..." He murmured to the waiter as he walked off, seeing the eye he gave him he wondered if his libido was broken. He tilted his head in thought and tried to picture himself picking the other up... but it wasn't the same. He looked down at his steak and baked potato... the seared onions and peppers smelled good, but he just didn't want it now.

It wasn't until a particular message caught his attention that he picked his phone back up instead of just staring at his steak.

I'm two months pregnant. –Michael.

Ainslie stared at the message, his heart broke even further. How did he respond to that? Michael had sent him away. Michael had... Michael was carrying his child. Growling he stood up and dropped enough money to pay for the uneaten meal and a tip on his way out, then he just drove with the phone up to his ear.

"Hello?" Michael's confused voice hummed through the device.

"Where are you?"

"I'm... I'm at home."

"Pack your stuff. I'm coming to get you."

"What?"

"I saw your message. I'm coming to get you."

"Ainslie?"

"Who did you think would call and tell you we're leaving?" Ainslie arched a brow as he took a turn a little sharper than he normally would have. His black challenger purring at his fingertips.

"We can't just leave... my dad set up an appointment..."

"I'll set up a better one... for healthier things in the city," Ainslie insisted.

"I can't... he's..." Michael's voice hissed as he nearly dropped the phone.

The phone hadn't shut off, but it wasn't by Michael's ear any more. He couldn't hear very clearly but he could tell Michael was upset, his voice was just barely there but the tone made him sound as though he was in danger.

Ainslie growled, hung up and drove faster. He thought the worst of the appointment. Whatever it was couldn't be very good if it was his father that had made it. He wasn't going to let that old man hurt Michael any more... if Michael would let him defend him anyway. They had technically broken up and he didn't know what to expect. He screeched to a stop out front of Michael's house and stumbled out of his car, standing to his full height he stormed up to the door and instead of breaking it down like he wanted to, he knocked on the door.

The few minutes wait felt like a lifetime.

Marcus opened the door, not expecting Ainslie to just be standing there looking like he was about to rip him to shreds.

“What do you want?” Marcus snarled at him. Ainslie wondered if he really understood that he had only left because Michael had told him to, not because he wanted to. And right now, Michael was carrying his child. He would not leave him alone that easily.

“I'm here for what's mine. Michael *is* mine and so is that child.” Ainslie narrowed his eyes, a low growl threatened in his chest.

“That child won't be there much longer, mangy mutt, putting your filthy hands on my son! You're lucky I don't skin you alive.”

“Skin me then.” Ainslie grabbed Marcus by the throat and backed him up against a wall, snarling loud enough for Michael to *finally* come out of his room. He had not wanted to deal with any fighting, but hearing it Michael had to see what was going on.

“I. *Said.* That. I. Am. Here. For. What's. Mine.” Ainslie repeated making sure each word was clear even though he did nothing but growl .

“Ainslie... stop.” Michael said, catching his attention to the point he dropped the elder. He frowned, not sure how to respond to being told to stop.

“Come on, we're leaving.” Ainslie reached out for him, he lightly waved him to come to him.

“I can't just leave Ainslie.” Michael was almost breathless. His eyes were wide and blood shot, heavy bags under them showed he hadn't slept, and even his breathing was ragged as his shoulders heaved with each panicked breath. Ainslie hated to see him like this, but he was determined to calm him down and get him somewhere safe.

“Yes, you can, we can.” Although he sounded calm, he did not feel calm. His insides were swirling with a mixture of confusion and irritation. How had he been so dumb to just leave him when he was freaking out. He shouldn't have left even though he had been told to go, he shouldn't have. He wondered if Michael was just telling him to tell him or if he wanted to keep it, keep them together.

"Why?" Michael asked, tears poured down his face. "So, you can just run off again and stay away from me?" He was worried. Ainslie had run off and just left him even though that's what he told him to do.

"No, so we can actually be together. We don't have to worry about our parents being snotty assholes anymore. We don't have to worry about them just... we'll have each other," Ainslie said, as he realized that was why Michael was had been so different, why he had told him to just go and why he had been so different at their meeting place. He had been pregnant. They hadn't even smelled it somehow! Could see it in any sort of glow or whatever his mother told him.

"Is that really what you want? You, me, and a baby?" Michael asked, his lip quivering in a mixture of fear and excitement. Tears poured down his face as the stress from all the emotions started tearing through him on top of the anticipation of Ainslie's answer.

Ainslie blinked at the way Michael was behaving and frowned. He tilted his head to the side as he readied himself for the worst possible answer that Michael could give him. He held his breath as he preemptively winced.

"I can't... I..." Michael's words were breaking; his composure long since broken.

"Yes Michael. You, Me, and the baby. Just us. No stupid rules, no stupid festival that I'm pretty sure I missed anyway... just us." Ainslie said and walked over to him, pulling him close.

"But... I'm an Omega, you deserve an Alpha..." Michael breathed those wretched words that had been drilled into their heads since childhood. It pissed Ainslie off to no end.

"No. I deserve you, because you are my mate and I will not lose you again." Ainslie retorted, his words weren't in the nicest tone but he wasn't as angry sounding as he felt. His features instantly smoothed into a softer expression.

Michael broke down in Ainslie's arms, babbling almost incoherently about how much he hated him but he loved him, but how dare he just leave without a word! Ainslie was sure he'd be hearing that a lot for the next few months.

"Come on, let's get your things." Ainslie murmured a little softer once Michael seemed to calm down enough to not need to lean on him to keep him up.

"If he's leaving with you, I'll be damned if he takes a single thing out of this house." Marcus snarled from his place by the door. He stood up and stepped forward as though he were going to attack them.

"Fine, I'll buy him all new stuff. Bye." Ainslie growled, holding Michael's hand he led him outside.

"Don't you dare take him! You can't have my son! You don't have my blessing!" Marcus screamed and took another step forward to actually attack this time but was stopped by Ainslie's words.

"I don't need your blessing. I'm an Alpha. Once an Alpha lays claim on someone, as I just did, gets it. Or else it is an act of war... do you *really* want to go to war?" Ainslie said and stood tall. Michael looked at him with almost pure fear, figuring he was about to fight with his father.

"Ains..."

"Because of Michael being here and already stressed, I will not fight you right now. His health and our baby's health is far more important than *you*... trying to shove dominance where it's clearly not going to stop anything anyway. He's mine. I'm his. No one has any say over this matter except us, and we've made our decision," Ainslie said and motioned for Michael to keep going.

"That's your car?" Michael asked and looked up at Ainslie in shock as they stepped outside and Ainslie lightly pushed him towards the car.

"Yep. For now, anyway... I guess we'll be trading it in soon."

"Wow... I wouldn't imagine that would be the car you went for..." Michael teased him, trying to not look as stress as he felt inside.

"Eh, it has a nice shape to it... It gets me around... and it's kind of the nicer of the cars that was there. It'll be traded in for something more family friendly though. Unless you want a car of your own..."

"You know everyone here is mad at you..." Michael murmured as he got into the passenger side and buckled his seatbelt. He finished drying his tears and yawned, having not had a single good night's sleep in a while. He looked over at Ainslie and wondered if he even sort of wanted to see his parents. He knew they had never had the best of relationships with them to begin with, or even if he was concerned for his hunting pack.

"Let them be mad. I've done everything for them, sacrificed a lot of time and blood for them. They can't let me have the one thing I want, they can lose me." Ainslie shrugged, knowing his mother had left several voicemails on his phone with various emotions and threats. He didn't even drive by there. He just headed back to the city, as far as he was concerned it was unnecessary to see anyone from his pack.

He reached his hand over and lightly took Michael's hand in his own. They weren't keeping them apart any more. He probably wouldn't have been able to go through with the festival anyway. He had tried to keep it in his mind while he had been sneaking around with Michael, but he just could not handle that kind of situation now. He would not be away from him anymore.

"I'm hungry..." Michael mumbled as if he were afraid Ainslie would tell him he couldn't eat.

"What did your dad do to you?" Ainslie asked quietly, wondering how long the old man knew, how long Michael had known before he told him.

"He wasn't happy when he found out... that's for sure"

"When did you last eat?"

"Last night..."

"It's almost dinner time now..."

"I know." Michael frowned and just looked down at the floorboard. Ainslie growled lowly, he drove to the first restaurant he saw.

"Do you think you can find something here or is there somewhere specific you want to go?" He asked.

"I'll find something here... you don't have to do anything special you know."

"If you want something specific, you'll get it. We're together, I'm going to treat you how I should have been all this time."

"Do you really mean it?"

"Yes." He murmured softly. "Look, I've been mean to you around others before. It won't happen anymore. I'm surprised you put up with me so long, but I love you and we'll figure everything out as we go along. You can help me look for a place that's big enough for us... they have plenty of little houses and places... We can get you transferred to the school over here, we can do it... we will do it. As long as you are by my side."

"I love you too," Michael said and leaned across the console to kiss him.

"Good..." Ainslie smiled and kissed him back.

"You're cute.... You know that?"

"Only when you tell me," Michael murmured against his lips.

"Then I'll have to tell you every day... you and our little one. Now let's go get you something to eat." Michael smiled at Ainsley's words.

"You're not mad at me?" Michael asked quietly as he stood up.

"No, I'm not mad at you. I was hurt, yes... but I'm not mad. I should have put my foot down a long time ago... I just... I was listening to my family and you know..." He murmured and frowned.

"Please don't beat yourself up... I was doing the same thing..."

Ainslie stepped forward, taking Michael's hand and leading him into the restaurant.

"Good, then no regrets."

“Not a one.” Michael smiled, making Ainslie feel warm and happy.

Chapter Twelve

Neither Ainslie nor Michael had thought they'd be parents anytime soon… but watching his first-born child coming into the world had Ainslie happier than he had ever been before. He cut the cord, eagerly watched as they cleaned up his son, and went back to his husband's side. He smiled at Michael as they handed him the baby.

"Gabriel is so beautiful," Michael cried. Ainslie nodded and kissed Michael happily.

"I'm so proud of you…" Ainslie purred as he softly ran his thumb along their little one's arm.

"I didn't think we could do it… I didn't…" Michael murmured. His eyes twinkled happily as he looked at their baby.

"Our Gabriel…" Michael looked up, "My father isn't here is he?"

"No. Even if he is, we don't have to let him come in." Ainslie reminded him.

"Is your mother here?"

"Nope. Neither of my parents are here. Your dad isn't here. There are no elders, it's just us." Ainslie reassured him. Most of the pregnancy had been Michael coming home scared he'd seen one of their parents or an elder somewhere watching him. Watching as drove his new car to and from where Ainslie had gotten a job and was just building extra money to support them in the long run. He liked to go and get lunch with him.

Ainslie didn't want Michael to worry as the nurse took Gabriel to get him cleaned up while Michael rested, so he watched as they helped Michael change beds and then he climbed into the bed with him, holding him close and watching as nurse after nurse came in and out to do something or other. Check this, check that… he was losing track of what all they were doing, but once their son had been returned they both calmed down.

"I can't wait to just go home…" Michael murmured.

"Soon, I'm sure they'll let us go tomorrow."

"I hope so..."

Ainslie smiled softly and watched as Michael relaxed enough to drift off to sleep. Though it was obvious the sleep was an anxious one. They both knew that they could receive an unwelcome visit by anyone... He didn't want Michael freaking out if one of their parents came since he didn't trust they would just want to talk after the way they behaved and ran off.

He traced little shapes into the other's arm softly with his index finger and eyed the door. Nearly snarling and waking everyone up when there was a faint knock on the door and three familiar faces poured through it.

"Hey..." Sam mumbled, Ash just looked down feeling ashamed, and Ben said nothing as per usual.

"Hi..." Ainslie half hissed.

"Look, we're not here to be hostile... I promise. We just... we knew your kid was due today. We wanted to come show support. You might be exiled from the pack forever now, but you're still our Alpha..." Sam said softly.

"Cute." Ainslie growled, not believing it. "Do not wake up my mate."

"We will be quiet, I promise." Ash said softly.

"Alright..."

"Your mom is outside..." Ash muttered.

"She can stay there." Was all Ainslie said about the situation.

"Fine... fine... but she would like a picture of her grandkid... that okay?" Ben piped up, but not loud enough to wake the sleeping Michael.

"No. She lost all rights to seeing any of her grandchildren when she told me I couldn't be with Michael. Same with Michael's father. They can all stay away from us." Ainslie whispered harshly.

“Okay...” They agreed and held their hands up to show they meant no harm. They stepped a little further into the room, but this time Michael snarled.

“Get away from our child.” Michael glared daggers at them. The three stopped and just stared, uncertain what to do and it showed.

“Look, you can see him from there. You don’t need to get any closer.” Ainslie said. That’s all he said about it too.

The three nodded.

“Michael... we’re sorry for the way we acted.” Ash said. “I... wanted what was best for Ainslie and didn’t realize that was you.”

“That’s because you didn’t give me a chance to prove myself.” Michael grumbled.

“We didn’t, and we’re sorry.” Sam looked up from the floor at Michael.

“They kicked you guys out, didn’t they...?” Ainslie murmured.

“Yeah, because we wanted to be here. It’s why you’re mom’s down stairs. She wants to know if you’re going to take us in or if she should find somewhere else for us to go. We’re good for things, you know that... and she doesn’t want us to go but your dad...”

“I see...” Ainslie looked at them each in turn and then to Michael who looked up at him in return.

“I don’t want to talk about it in front of them.” Michael said simply and Ainslie glanced at the trio, sending them outside with a look.

“You know... they’ll have to listen to you like an Alpha...” Ainslie smiled softly.

“That’s not what bothers me... what bothers me is your mother is here.”

“I know... that bothers me too. Do you think we should give those three a chance?”

“They never gave me one, Ainslie... not once.”

“Then I’ll tell them to go.” Ainslie sat up slowly.

“No, they can stay near us. We’ll help them get up on their feet over here in the city, but... they aren’t in our pack. Not until I see they are worth it... I’ll give them a chance, because they never gave me one. I’m not like that. I don’t even sort of want to be like that. So, they can stay... for now.”

“Really?” Ainslie was shocked, but he leaned down and kissed his mate.

“Really. Now, go tell them and hurry back. We’ll need help getting everything home anyway... They can help with stuff.” Michael smiled and kissed back. Although he wasn’t sure about this, he decided it’d be okay. Gabriel could be safer if they had more people around... he’d be able to grow up in a sort of pack instead of just the two of them... and whatever brothers and sisters he got in the future. The thought of giving Gabriel brothers or sisters made his heart swell and the amount of emotion that ran through him made him almost giddy.

“Alright... I’ll let them know.” Ainslie said and stepped out of the room slowly, almost as though looking for a reason to fight them. He didn’t need to though. His mother stood not far from the trio and although Ainslie growled she just held up her hands.

“Boy or girl?”

“None of your business.” Ainslie retorted and looked at the three. “If you’re joining us that’s fine. You can help us out. We’ll need some things done and done quickly... but we’ll discuss it in the morning. First, make sure she leaves. There will be no communication between us and them. Ever.”

Sam, Ash, and Ben nodded as they moved to escort his mother out the door.

Chapter Thirteen

Gabriel giggled loudly as Michael and Ash took turns making silly faces for the toddler. After a year of being a pack, Michael was glad he had made the decision to let the three stay. They didn't once act up, they didn't bother to argue with anyone. They did what Ainslie told them to and they had each managed to get houses close enough they could just walk over when needed.

Ainslie had instructed them to stay over for the weekend while he went away for work, because even if they didn't have contact with their families Michael and Ainslie both still feared the packs would come after them and bug them. Michael was still certain sometimes that he was being followed, being watched by someone other than Sam, Ash, or Ben. Though the three did a great job at keeping them from trouble. Potential muggers? Avoided. Door to door salesmen? Covered.

All Michael had to do was take care of Gabriel and he couldn't have been happier. Never in a million years had he thought he would be a stay at home mom, adoring the little one more than absolutely anyone. As he cleaned up the dishes he checked the clock. Hearing Gabriel go on and on babbling he turned around to look at the door.

"Da da da da da da..." Gabriel was kicking and fighting against his high chair, fussing and starting to squeal until Michael picked him up and headed to the door, which instantly got a giggle from Gabriel as a car door opened and out stepped Ainslie, dressed nice in slacks and a dress shirt.

"Good meeting, my love?" Michael called.

Ainslie shrugged and walked up, wrapping his arms around them both. He kissed Michael and then Gabriel. "Eh, good enough. How's everything been here? Everything okay?"

"Of course." Michael smiled sweetly and pulled him into their house. "I got something to show you, you're going to love this." He said and made Ainslie stand there in the doorway. He walked away for a few steps and then set Gabriel down, holding just his hands the little one started to kick his feet until he walked forward towards Ainslie giggling and bouncing the whole time.

“That is amazing!” Ainslie wrapped his arms around him and held him close. “You’re doin’ so good little man! We need to celebrate. Cake. Something...” He looked up at Michael and smiled as he held their son close. The little one toying with his ear.

“Cake? For walking?” Michael chuckled. “You are going to spoil this child rotten.”

“Maybe... I’ll spoil you both rotten...”

“How are you going to spoil me any more than I already am?” Michael smirked.

“I’ll show you... after Gabriel goes to bed.” He smirked and kissed Gabriel’s fingers as he tried to shove his hand into his mouth.

“You’re silly.” Michael said and tilted his head to the side.

“So... all of us going to eat or just the three of us?” Ainslie asked and peered into the living room where the three protectors of the house were lounging on the couches.

“Yeah, let’s go have a good time... all of us. It can be a pack thing.” Michael smiled.

Ainslie smiled wide and nodded, he went around and got the other three to come along. The car ride wasn’t very far, but where they were living nothing was very far.

***

Ben watched them carefully, wondering what it was like to find that one person that they’d throw everything away for. He couldn’t imagine it. The thought of it nearly made him sick... at least it had before. The pressure of the festival, the way his parents fawned over certain things. He couldn’t handle it. He had refused to look at anyone in the eye, he wouldn’t be polite to anyone, he wouldn’t even bother with dates. Even now he still refrained from looking, from enjoying that kind of luxury. But he watched Ainslie with Michael and wondered what it felt like to feel that way. Wondered if he could even sort of give it a go.

As the others went inside he pulled Ainslie back, the tiny squirming child in his arms looked up at him with such wide and happy eyes that he couldn't talk for a minute or two, he ended up cooing and smiling at the child before he looked up with a questioning gaze at Ainslie.

"What?" Ainslie arched his brow, the uncertain look in his eyes was almost frightening.

"Uh... rules... about... dating..." Ben finally said.

"What about them?"

"What are... they?" He couldn't help but speak slowly, he tried to talk normal but nothing wanted to form in his mouth.

"Oh, uhm... no one dangerous. Can't put the little one in danger. You know?" Ainslie said and tilted his head to the side.

"That's... that's it? Really?" Ben tilted his head and blinked.

"What are you looking for? I mated with an Omega, from a different pack that was always at odds with my own, that all of my pack advised me to stop looking at." Ainslie pointed out and tilted his head to the side.

"Well yeah... but..."

"Ben, if you find someone you like, date. You're free to explore that... but if they are dangerous, don't bring them around the pack. Don't get hurt yourself either. Sometimes you just have to do what's best for yourself before the pack. Which is what I did when I decided I was going to have Michael." Ainslie said softly as he smiled at their little one. "I wouldn't change it for the world. Look at this little guy, I won't have a pack like my fathers... so don't worry about that. If something needs to stop I'll tell you. If you don't like it, you can leave, but we'll still make sure you're okay."

"Really?" Ben couldn't believe it. Though he liked it. He looked at the others standing by the door of the restaurant waiting to be seated.

"Really. Don't worry about it."

Ben did worry though. He still didn't want to fall into that *trap*, but weirder things did happen, right? He pursed his lips and looked at the ground as Ainslie walked into the restaurant. After a moment or two he followed and put on a happy face. It wasn't time to worry about that, he had an awesome nephew-pup to look after and help to guide into trouble and various fun things.

Or so he thought until the guy walking up to take them to their seats accidentally caught his gaze with fierce blue eyes and a firm square jaw. Something inside stirred and he couldn't pull his eyes away. Ben felt his heart flutter and blinked profusely once the other seemed startled and turned quickly, leading the way as fast as he could it seemed to get away from him.

"My name is Eddie, I'll be your server today," The guy with the square jaw said in a calm voice. All Ben could do was focus on his name.

Acknowledgements

Thank you so much for helping me improve the book! If you would like to be credited, please leave your name, nickname or however you would like to be called under the Acknowledgments. This will be put at the end of the final version of the book and let everyone know that the book would not be the way it is without your help!

Danielle S. R.

Made in the USA
Middletown, DE
19 April 2018